God, Man,
and
The Machine

EDIFIED EDITION

A Story of Symbols

by

From Back Cover

This imaginative and thought-provoking book of quips, reflections, and antagonisms reads in the spirit of science fiction.

The author deems it *"philosofiction"*. Δ

* * *

The year is 2066.

Silverberg, the world's youngest and undisputedly most powerful country, generally entertains only the most prominent visitors and immigrants. However, this year it has *intentionally* attracted an otherwise uninteresting young man of average station. When the powers that lured him cannot *find* him, the hunt begins.

Misunderstanding his importance, multiple operatives of high station and various loyalties race to find him. As time progresses, the intensity thickens. Those who join this man find their own lives disrupted and changed forever, swept up by the storm surrounding him.

While he means no harm to anybody, his pursuers will not rest until he is found and destroyed. It is only a matter of time. Bombarded with varying opinions about the truth, this man struggles for discernment and understanding, but what he *believes* cannot save him - or can it?

* * *

Pragmatic dogma, theology, and *atheology* collide and argue in the background as we follow this unhero through a quick, comedic, dark, and philosophical journey of determining *what* he is - deciding between God, Man, and The Machine.

This 316 page volume includes **maps**, **art**, **footnotes**, **appendices**, and *more.*

Δ **Phi·los·o·phy**
  Investigation of the nature, causes, or principles of reality, knowledge, or values, based on logical reasoning rather than empirical methods.
  Fic·tion
  A literary work whose content is produced by the imagination and is not necessarily based on fact.

Other books by Daniel Strasel:

WITHOUT REST
ISBN 978-0-9859964-4-4

A tale of love and madness. When he confronts the Truth, a lovesick god has all of his dreams turned into nightmares.

THE TERRORS OF WONDER
ISBN 978-0-9859964-4-4

A tragicomedy about truth, identity, and leadership. A prominent young child with disturbing visions must overcome an intimate enemy or be lost forever.

Stegosaurus the Triceratops
ISBN 978-0-9859964-6-8

A book made to create great conversations: ethics of work, principle, helping, and leadership. A stuffed toy dinosaur encourages others by expressing care.

Visceral Outcries of a Social Moron
ISBN 978-0-9859964-5-1

A short and fun book of poetry and commentary.

For Daniel's complete portfolio please visit Mirroranium.com

Published by Daniel Strasel

Edified Edition

Synopsis:

*An uninteresting man of mistaken importance
struggles to understand his role in life.*

 HTTP://www.Mirroranium.com 

ISBN-13: 978-0-9859964-3-7

TABLE OF CONTENTS

PROLOGUE

Few people have not heard the name of Silverberg, as it belongs to the youngest and fastest growing country in the world. The few that have not, surely live apart from any well-known civilization, and lack the means necessary to know well what is going on in the political world of 2066. They have a wisdom that transcends any conventional or superficial understanding, despite the absence of the recombinant knowledge available via electronic encyclopedia or aggressive corporate advertisement. Although these very people are likely to be in possession of a commanding and respectable character, made only more complex by their fierce individuality and colorful simplicity, they are not the focus of this story and therefore are not to be mentioned again. [1]

---

[1] **Footnotes**. At times, there can be greater immersion if there is supplemental information available about the periphery of any given subject. Whereas these following footnotes may not pertain to this story *directly*, they are forthwith made available to those of a more ambitious sense of curiosity - at least in regards as to how their decidedly kind pursuit into God, Man, & the Machine is concerned.

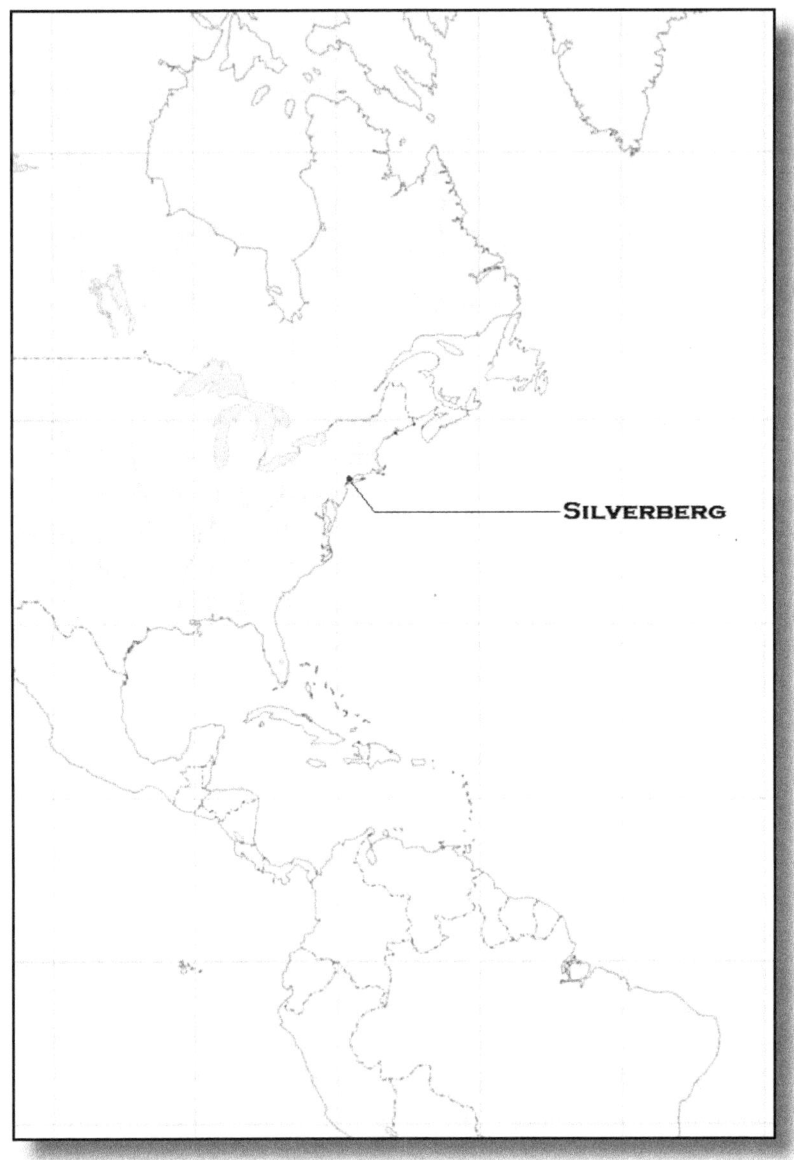
SILVERBERG

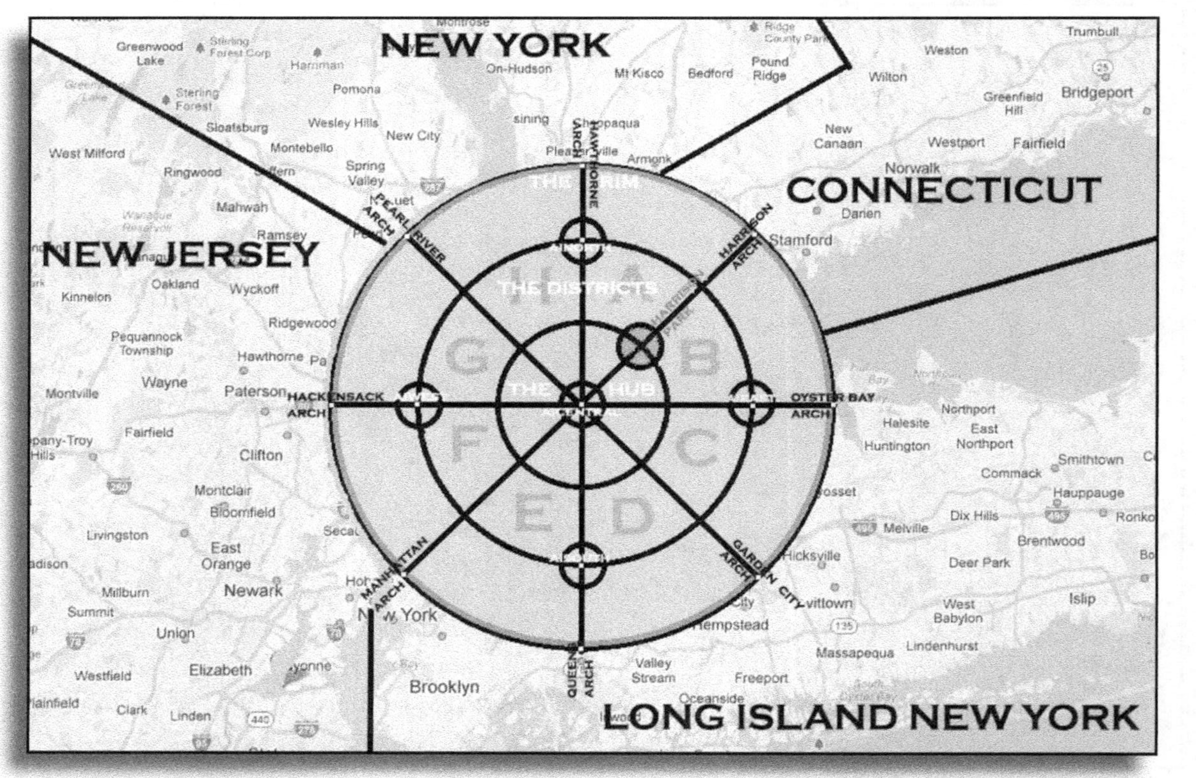
NEW YORK
CONNECTICUT
NEW JERSEY
LONG ISLAND NEW YORK
THE DISTRICTS
THE RIM
THE HUB
CENTRAL
A
B
C
D
E
F
G
H
HAWTHORNE ARCH
HARRISON ARCH
PEARL RIVER ARCH
HACKENSACK ARCH
MANHATTAN ARCH
QUEENS ARCH
GARDEN CITY ARCH
OYSTER BAY ARCH

HISTORY OF THE FUTURE

On the second day of September in the year 1973, an eruption of an unknown quantity and type of energy burst outward from its epicenter of New Rochelle, New York. At the radius of 15 miles, it abruptly terminated. In its fifteen mile wake laid a land completely devoid of its earlier characteristics.

Everybody died. Everything that once was there was now gone. [2]

In the tragedy of the "New Rochelle Disaster," nearly 2 million people were killed instantaneously. The cold war tension between the United States and the Soviet Union was already high in stark parallel with the pro/anti-communist movements. Radical actions of dissident groups sparked further tensions as the New Rochelle Disaster was elevated in relevance (most grotesquely by the media), eventually to be publicly blamed on the Soviets. Several instances of terrorism occurred throughout Russia; several important men (including the president) were brutally killed–the men responsible identified as American. The United States, limping from its encounter with Viet Nam, was ill prepared for the Russian counteroffensive against its eastern seaboard. The world went to war.

Almost a decade passed. The battling between the Soviets and the States continued, waxing and waning in intensity as funding and troops depleted. Most of the political world remained neutral, although occasionally one world country or another would send relief to one of these powers. As the millennium began to end, the United States began to realize that it was going to potentially *lose* this conflict. The national debt had escalated to a point beyond foreseeable recovery, and countries that had previously allowed the USA to take out loans were no longer being as generous.

Although fashion and industry mostly took a back seat to the American-Soviet conflict, several researchers devoted their time to analyzing the nearly submerged metal hemisphere that was left behind following the New Rochelle Disaster. What they discovered was that thirteen feet above sea level and thirty miles in diameter, the ground that was touched by the eruption was replaced by a perfectly smooth and reflective surface, like a mirror–yet metallic, like silver. A detailed analysis of the material yielded that the substance was not a compound, and did not conform to any of the elements of the periodic table.

Early in his research Professor Stanley Marvel dubbed it "mirroranium," and

----

[2] Including, but not limited to the populations and matter of the following cities, neighborhoods, items, and landmarks: Hackensack, Teaneck, Englewood, Palisades State Park, Norwood, Cliffside Park, Manhattan, Astoria, LaGuardia Airport, Jerome Park, Yonkers, Colonial Heights, Port Chester, New Rochelle, Pelham Bay Park, Manor haven, Port Washington, Little Neck Bay, Manhasset Bay, Roslyn, Roslyn Heights, Greenwich, several passenger planes, and half of Oyster Bay.

the name held.

"However, *mirroranium* is not a true metal, a true element," Marvel said in response to the name. "As far as we can see, the atomic number is...amorphous. The protons count differently every time. Known science cannot describe it. It's an existing contradiction. Here it *is*, yet it exists *between* states of 'is.' Frankly, we in the community find that a little more than threatening."

Atomic theory aside, mirroranium was not responding to any tests for practicality.

One enterprise had managed some inconspicuous and successful experimentation with mirroranium: Axel Industries, formed in 1967 - already one of the largest companies in the world - observed that mirroranium could be "coaxed" to change its nature. "**Tempered mirroranium**" exhibited an almost indestructible nature, increasing its value beyond reason. A.I. kept its findings internal, and in 1984 proposed to purchase the land rights of the New York area of mirroranium for the amount of the national debt.

Initially the U.S. rejected the offer. Despite much deliberation, the overall feeling was that A.I. was trying to "buy the country." A.I.'s campaign methods brought the offer directly to television. Ads such as the country had never seen started cropping up all over the networks. A.I. demonstrated that a resurgence of the economy could tilt the scales of war to the favor of the United States. A.I. proposed an economic renaissance for the citizens. Weary and vexed, the American public was quickly favoring the offer.

President Wallace became personally involved. As the public interest mounted to a point that could not be easily dismissed, the land was sold to A.I. - but not before Axel *himself* campaigned the proposal of the purchase to the public.

Axel.

Axel is the enigmatic leader of the country now known as Silverberg, and is also the exclusive owner of Axel Industries.

"Axel Industries is not a *corporation*," Axel once said. "AI is a business, run by a person. Me."

Although most people consider the country of Silverberg [3A] and the corporation of Axel Industries to be synonymous, Axel has gone to varying lengths to correct that ignorant paradigm.

To the world at large, Axel is considerably intimidating. Silverberg

---

[3A] Curiously, the land known as Silverberg was not named for its appearance, rather for its primary architect, Matthias Silverberg. Matthias said that his designs, although certainly unique and personal, were initially inspired by the work of R. Buckminster Fuller. His lattice thin-shell building structures were revolutionary, although also decidedly much more popular than their actual *creator*, for the general understanding is that "Silverberg is called Silverberg because it is silver."

nothwithstanding, Axel was born on March 15th of 1937, thus we can quickly derive that as of 2066 he is already *well* over a hundred years old. Whispered rumors about stem cell miracles to a cryogenic lounge bed often haunt the lips of those that recite his impossible age.

If wealth, power, and longevity were not sufficient to summon one's awe, Axel's appearance would not be forgotten. Whether in person or mediacast, Axel appeared completely in black. That is not to say that he merely wore black slacks and a black shirt, rather that he additionally wore some kind of full head and body leotard that enveloped him completely.

During an interview with SNRK's (The Snark) Sally Chandler, Axel explained that his visage was "abhorrent" due to scarring from an automobile accident that he had during the Disaster of '73.

Soon after purchasing the land, A.I. announced its technological breakthrough with mirroranium.[4Δ] A.I. published that it had the capacity to "temper" the mirroranium into a seemingly indestructible material. Prices were incomprehensible, yet still paid. Terrible, nearly unstoppable machines of war started to appear over the globe.

The engine of war started in force again, and it humbled the world, all the while Axel reaping astronomical profits. America and Russia, finally exhausted with throwing themselves at one another, managed to find peace.   America, strongly considered the victor, demanded permanent land on Russian soil that was rich with resources. The demand was granted.

A.I. continued to work diligently with mirroranium, and made many technological marvels that would be in high demand. As the new millennium began, A.I. commissioned a design for an effective city plan for the conversion of the grounds. People everywhere sought to work with A.I. and soon the design was made a reality.

[4Δ] **Δ̲M̲** SYMBOL Mirroranium is depicted mathematically (scientifically) as a Delta encasing the letter "M." One popular hypothesis circulating throughout other countries across the Earth is that "Tempered" mirroranium actually absorbs [kinetic] energy, which lends to why it is so impossibly resilient. So far, testing has determined nothing conclusive. A whispered rumor found on the lips of those that have perused certain curious and otherwise quaint volumes of forgotten lore is that mirroranium is ***The Alchemist's Stone.***

In the year 2038, upon the completion of the construction of the Axel Industries Central building,[5Δ] Silverberg declared itself an independent country. There was a very short war with America, primarily consisting of Silverberg protecting itself from threatened invasion, which it did in a somewhat flauntingly aggressive manner. America quickly and wisely relented, agreeing to Axel's *request* to establish a demilitarized neutral zone between America and Silverberg.

28 years later we arrive *today* in 2066, where Silverberg is the unspoken, yet undisputed capital nation of the world. Despite the musings and concerns of the leaders and citizens of the other worldly nations, Silverberg has managed to convincingly and stalwartly declare its permanent neutrality, leaving the other powers more freedom to concern themselves with one another instead.

[5Δ] *The Ace* or Axel Industries Central (AIC) Building - the impossible ziggurat of Silverberg. The Ace could be seen from a generous distance, standing nearly a mile high and half as wide. Like a great, silver, isosceles mountain it often disappeared into the clouds. On a clear day one could see that as it culminated towards its apex, the gigantic building narrowed itself progressively, betraying a considerable mesa far atop.

APOLLO

This particular story centers itself around a curiously uninteresting and seemingly purposeless young man named Apollo Venerates.

"Pol," as he is known amongst his friends and associates, is a teenager who neither excelled nor failed academically. He is overweight, but not revoltingly so. He lives to love and dream, but his heroes of old are starting to lose their conviction, buckling to the test of time and the endless copies that are *still* being made of them.

Pol had never been to Silverberg, and if left to the scope of his own uninterrupted imaginations and musings, he never would. After all, only the most prominent people *ever* went to Silverberg, and only the most talented became citizens. In addition, Silverberg was scary.

Pol's father, Linus, thought that Pol was a cut *beneath* the rest. He clearly did not want Pol to go to Silverberg. Linus was notably often disappointed with Pol's obvious traits of ambivalence and procrastination, which he vociferously addressed with little hesitation. Pol thought that his father would support him, in light of having made this decision as a *man*...he was very wrong.

Pol was the last born in the ongoing legacy of the Venerates, the family who, in 2062, successfully proposed the "Euro-Amero Lateral Exchange and Trade Accord, or EALETA." Regardless of the significance of the Act, the *knowledge* that the Venerates were the skeleton of the body of the Act was *never* common by even the most liberal perspective. Apollo Venerates was *dreadfully* cognitive of it, however, as his father was *never* conservative in mentioning it.

Unbearably aware that he was not living up to his family's prestigious origins, he yearned for an average existence. Rather than pursue his father's political ambitions, Pol resolved that he would become a lawyer, or police officer. Or maybe a painter.

Pol went on to attend college in Illinois. As Pol steered his way into adulthood, he began an electronic dialogue with someone from another country–Silverberg–who identified herself solely as Eris. Pol, the unrequited romantic, found himself more and more regularly engaged in his flirtatious correspondence with Eris, which left Pol open to suggestion; ultimately captive to whatever Eris had to say.

Eris invited him to Silverberg one day, proposing that he could attend a semester in a Silverberg school as a foreign exchange student. Pol thought this over while enduring renewed consternation from his father and the sage councils against going from his few friends. Despite disdain and warning, Pol eventually decided to take the trip.

Chapter 1:

Gladiator

AUGUST *2066 EST*

Fri 13	Sat 14	Sun 15	Mon 16	Tues 17	Wed 18	Thur 19	Fri 20
		10:46					

"People like dialogue," Eris interrupted, "which is why I try and keep all of *my* dialogue relevant and interesting. I *do* tend to get nervous, however, so I quickly find myself blathering on and on about things that have no bearing or consequence...if only in order to keep their attention. It really is the most shameful of behavior."

Eris made the smallest smile, and narrowed her semi-celestial eyes so that they were deliberately half-open. Eris frequently used it to accentuate her points. It was a maneuver that Pol had come to truly appreciate, for it was with this action that Eris looked her most stunning.

Pol, as if waking, shook his head. "Wait. *What* people?"

"Oh, I don't know," Eris drawled. "Most people."

Pol noticed that he frequently experienced some difficulty explaining himself to Eris. She had a way of *regularly* misunderstanding him, or at least cause him to become so distracted that he did not properly express himself.

Pol shook his head. "No, I mean what kind of dialogue do '*what* people' like?"

Eris frowned, "You would think *only* the kind that attempted to convey a purposeful and discriminatory form of information that was populated with constructive, reflective, and meaningful ideas and perspectives.

"But you're *wrong*!" She announced triumphantly, never quite taking a breath. "People like *any* kind of dialogue, so long as they are adequately distracted by it."

 - [God, Man, and The Machine] -

That's not what I meant, Pol thought. Pol hated the way that Eris spoke at times. It made his head hurt, and he often wondered how she managed to wrap her tongue around her sentences. Still, he didn't want to seem stupid or slow, so he did his best to pay close attention to everything she said, regardless of the complexity or content.

Pol shook his head again. "No, wait."

He started to think it back through. "You said: 'keep their attention.' Now, I infer from this statement..." *Did I really just say "infer?"* Pol thought with some surprise. *I suppose that's correct.* "That you are referring to an *actual* conversation that you had with *actual* people. *What* people are you talking about? Who?"

Eris shook her head innocently. "Oh, I'm not referring to anybody in particular."

"If you're not talking about a certain circumstance, or certain people, then I don't understand the point of this story." Pol was getting frustrated. "Where exactly are you going with this?"

"Where do you think?" Eris looked up ahead.

Pol shook his head, trying to think. He thought hard enough to make him momentarily forget every other thing...still, he could not make more sense of it.

"You're trying to distract *me*?"

Smiling, Eris suddenly broke into a run.

Pol couldn't remember what the two of them were even discussing prior to Eris' contrived distraction, but he *was* keenly aware that she had managed to instantly develop a commanding lead in what must now be a race to *Gladiator.*

Why are we running? Pol thought, annoyed at being left out of the know, and annoyed that his chubby legs couldn't carry him fast enough to compete with Eris' lithe, little body. *Why does it feel like we're **always** running? Is everyone in Silverberg always in a hurry?*

Nevertheless, Pol continued to push himself to chase after Eris.

On every fourth Sunday, the wildly popular show, *Gladiator*, mediacasts in Silverberg. 13 days out of the year, *Gladiator* commands the attention of nearly every citizen.

True to its name, *Gladiator* features three rounds of pairs of men fighting to the death. Although gladiators do not have to *kill* in order to win, there has *never* been an instance where a gladiator has extended mercy to another in the history of the show. *Gladiator* has considerable pre and mid game segments, and is mediacast in three sessions, finishing with the match between the longest surviving two gladiators–the final session is Defender and Challenger.

Some contestants survive multiple sessions.[6Δ] A family or corporation, who could afford to provide them with physical or mental augmentations–possibly even better living conditions–might sponsor surviving gladiators. Of course, the longer a gladiator survives, the more money their sponsors typically make. Notably, the profits remunerated to those producing *Gladiator* are remote when compared with the overall gambling harvest.

The Gladiators are usually from one of two castes, the most common consisting of men that have been sentenced to slavery, the alternates being men that *willingly* competed. The alternate caste of gladiator is exceedingly rare, and generally sparks even *greater* interest throughout the country.

This is such a time.

The match that Pol and Eris were on their way toward has already generated record-breaking profits and attendance levels, and the zenith of its success was still considerably far away.

A decade ago there was a citizen known by the name of Pierce Godwin, who won an entire season of *Gladiator*. Pol would not recognize the significance, but *Gladiator* aficionados would be quick to point out that Godwin was the only *citizen* who had *ever* won an entire season.

Godwin had used his inheritance to get him all the advice, training, and augmentations that would be necessary to make him a viable competitor. He won every match with flourish, and thus carried the excitement of the games to an unprecedented level. Godwin retired from *Gladiator* after his victorious season, took his massive winnings, and promptly disappeared from the public eye.

Now Godwin had either given up on his retirement, grown immensely bored, or missed the adoration of the crowd, for he had announced via mediacast session that he would be competing today–Sunday the 15th. As Godwin was *undefeated*, he reserved the right to return automatically to the uppermost tier of the game.

––––––––––––

6Δ Not all Gladiators meet their doom exclusively in the Arena–14% of competitive Gladiators died in 2065 due to drug overdoses instead of arena kills, a figure that is up 3 percent from the prior year. 2% suffered augment & implant defections, reducing them to invalids or worse. 1% met with fits of rage, causing them to commit crimes severe enough to land them back into the prison system, presumably put to work in areas where they could not interact with anyone and would never be seen again.

          - [God, Man, and The Machine] -

Today Pierce Godwin would fight Michael Vangard. Vangard is the first and only *multiseasonal* Defender of *Gladiator*. No winner of *Gladiator* **ever** returned for a subsequent season–Vangard shocked millions by continuing to compete. The tension was astronomical.

While Godwin was billed as the "Citizen Gladiator of 2056," Vangard was heavily billed as the "Archangel of War." Vangard's owners spent a considerable amount of money endorsing him over the last 2 seasons. Action figures, an animated show, a book, and a film all resulted from Vangard's success.

Most of the imagescreens in the arena[7Δ] were displaying news sessions via the SNRK (*The Snark*) network. The network currently favored selections of records from prior interviews with Vangard and Godwin. The remainder of the imagescreen scenery was equally overwhelmed with static images of past and current records and memorabilia of the games from over the last decade. Comparisons of every sort were drawn between Godwin and Vangard, although journalistically slanted one way or the other.

As Pol was running, he was weaving in and out between the pocket crowds that were streaming towards the portal of the cyclopean, mirrored arena. His ability to weave, however, was decidedly *poor* as he managed to knock several people over in the process. His propensity for manners was identically clumsy as the only comfort that he could offer up to those that had been so recklessly toppled by his intruding form was a breathless "*sorry.*"

"Eris!" Pol yelled, hoarse from having had to exert himself. "Whoa! Slow down! You've been dragging me around mercilessly since I got through '*Delivery*!'"

If Eris heard him, she was not giving him any indication...not that Pol could *see* Eris, as she had disappeared into the crowds long ago. Pol realized that he was hopelessly–foolishly–yelling into a mass of alien strangers.

His pace started to slow as the crowds of people that were littering the mirroranium causeway thickened. Pol closed his eyes as he felt some panic rise up in his throat. Like many foreigners to Silverberg, Pol was unaccustomed to the immense visual assault of having so many people surrounded by impossibly tall mirrored surfaces.

[7Δ] The Arena was completed in AD 2046 in anticipation of hosting the Olympics. Afterward, the Arena was acquired by The Serter Company on permanent lease from Axel Industries. It has since then been employed for the basis of several mediacast shows, including *Gladiator*.

Chapter 1

Pol was momentarily reminded of the autocar garage below the arena. He took a breath and pushed the panic back down into his core. Despite the obstacles and the foreboding sense of being overwhelmed, Pol resolved that he would not give up the chase–besides, he was not sure what else he could do.

Pol opened his eyes and resumed pursuit. No evidence of his inner resolve manifested outwardly, however–Pol was reduced to walking, shoulders slackened and head down.

Eventually Eris reappeared, gliding effortlessly between the people on her way back towards Pol. Her smile was delightful, and Pol fought his sudden inclination to forget what she had just put him through.

Pol felt jilted and betrayed. "Why did you do that? Why did you run off like that? Just like...like at the club," Pol stammered in accusation. "I could have been lost! Alone! You're *supposed* to be my friend, and all you have done is carry me through Silverberg as if I need to see *every* attraction there is **right this second!**"

"No need to worry," she started to explain in a calm, slow voice that threatened to be lost amidst the roar of the crowd. Pol had to lean closer to hear, which then caused him to blush and emotionally relent when he accidentally brushed up against her.

"*You* keep forgetting to consult your credit bank." Eris smiled and shrugged nonchalantly, as if Pol's remonstration was without cause. "You can *always* contact me through it. As for the distraction and the running away...it's just that I didn't want there to be an argument between us, had there only been one seat left."

Eris paused, adjusting her tricorne hat. Pol looked lost.

"Had there only been one," Eris explained further, "my distraction would ensure that *I* would be the one to get it as I was the first person there…at least, the first between the two of us."

Eris lowered her gaze, perhaps in an attempt to appear apologetic. "I'm so terribly sorry–I'm so absent-minded, the thought that there might not be enough seats had only occurred to me just a few moments ago. In regards to our expediency, it *is* only 2 weeks before the semester starts and there is a *lot* to see in Silverberg."

"Wait." Pol shook his head. Although softened, he could not help but vocalize his frustration with Eris. "Argument? *What* argument? I didn't even *want* to come to *Gladiator.*"

"*Everyone* wants to see *Gladiator,*" Eris defended.

     - [God, Man, and The Machine] -

"Well, *I* don't." Pol said hastily. *Of course, I don't want her to think I'm not interested,* Pol thought. "I mean, I *didn't*. I mean, I am happy to be here with *you...*" *Boy, do I sound dumb.* "*Gladiator* just seems oddly barbaric for a society so reputedly advanced."

"I think you'll find that it is nothing more than a natural side effect of a society in renaissance. There's nothing going on here that is being *forced* on anyone. Oh, you'll *adore* learning law here, Pol! Oh! Here's your entry, anyway." She held out her credit bank.

Pol fumbled around for his own *credit bank*, the mysterious little silver and black box that was assigned to him at the end of "Delivery." As he pulled it from his pocket, Eris tapped her own credit bank to Pol's.

Pol and Eris walked through the gates, their presence validated by some unseen guardian as they tapped their credit banks to the turnstile. "There," Eris said, tucking her bank back into one of the few pockets that her skimpy uniform allowed for.[8]

As they walked up the main ramp toward the ribs of the Silverberg arena, they passed beneath the iconic and monolithic statue of Zeus. Above his head, Zeus continued to hold the interlacing 5 rings of the Olympics as he had done for the last 20 years.

Several outdoor imagescreens sprang into existence, each framed by a plethora of numbers and figures. Upon closer examination, the numbers were statistics about the weather, Vangard and Godwin's careers, and a multitude of other facts that made everyone who was paying attention an immediate expert.

An image of a black and silver box, roughly the size of a deck of playing cards, rotated diagonally on one of its corners in the middle of the imagescreens. Music ululated out of nearby credit banks in tandem with the displays, attempting to assist in keeping everyone's attention from wandering.

The image of a man walked onto the imagescreens, and plucked the box out of the air in mid rotation.

"Is *your* credit bank doing everything that you need?" Asked the man, who was now looking appreciatively at the bank.

---

[8] Eris and Pol's dialogue about Eris' choice of clothing on this day is lost. Eris discloses earlier that she is dressed as Ichabod Crane. Pol doesn't know the reference, otherwise he certainly would have questioned it. Eris does not explain it further.

"Axel Industries wants you to be satisfied. You already know that it handles your credit transactions, can display your personal media, serves as your identification, functions as a dictionary as well as various reference materials, and can be used as a video phone."

The man held the credit bank and watched the black colored portions change to red. "However, for only 20 units per month, it could be so much more: Our 'level two' service is exemplary for the price! It records in actual time, capable of 1 month of storage! Complete and programmable holographic displays allow for an immersion quality previously impossible. Use it to access the Mainframe directly, and enjoy unlimited access to *all media ever made*!"

The man tossed the credit bank across the imagescreen to a woman who simultaneously walked into the scene and caught it. As she held it up, the red segments changed to an ivory and ebony colored marble.

"Our 'level three' service is available for 80 units per month." The woman began. "For the truly elite in the country, level three provides the owner with a health monitor that updates every *second* second. Imagine... all life processes monitored *constantly* in order to ensure that you are in the best health and that an emergency vehicle can be dispatched to you in the course of seconds in the event of a problem! Upgrade your credit bank today: Connect to the Mainframe, and tell A.I. what you need."

The imagescreen went to pitch black, and then the silver-white logo of Axel Industries waxed into visibility in the center.

After a few moments of the A.I. logo dominating the arena imagescreens, the mediacast sessions switched to the mini pre-game interviews that were conducted by Sally Chandler, venerable journalist for SNRK. The displays on the imagescreens showed Chandler sitting opposite Vangard and Godwin–yet this was just an effect as the interviews were done remotely. The interviews played with such cut-and-paste exposition that it seemed she was addressing them both simultaneously, while observing their answers in turn.

"Tonight's event is unique to the history of *Gladiator–**Defender*** Pierce Godwin versus ***Defender*** Michael Vangard–tell me, gentlemen, how *do* you feel about tonight's match?"

Vangard looked indomitable: tall, broad, built–boasting a body that was picture perfect, although likely from the compliments of his augmentations. He looked *new*. Innocent. Impossible. His hair, fenced by a circlet that looked like a golden halo, was such as to cause envy–even in women at times. His face bore one discernable characteristic: confidence. When he spoke, his voice was firm, yet passionate.

"I feel *good* about tonight's match. Godwin may be the most powerful opponent I have ever had to face, and for that, I extend him all the respect such an opponent is due...but he's been out of the game too long. Too many advancements in augmentations since he was an active player. He'll never pull this off. I genuinely hope that he puts up enough fight to justify returning from retirement.

"Then again," Vangard reflected, "even though he's outdated, maybe he'll humble me before the end."

The imagescreens were soon boasting large pictures of Godwin's face. His shaved head bore several black and jagged tribal tattoos, and his dark and bushy eyebrows seemed to almost point towards the bridge of his nose, lending the observer a sense of anger or discomfort. His dark eyes were practically hypnotic, but made soft by the half-smirk that was guarded by his perfect goatee.

When Godwin answered the question, his baritone voice had an unexpected charm to it–at least to someone who had not heard it prior.

"Tonight's match'll be quick. Either he dies, or I will. One way or another, half of the crowd will be pleased."

Godwin smiled large. "Ability, endurance, strength, speed, augmentations, and agility–these things are all necessary to be a competitive fighter, however the *real* battle is the mind game. I don't need to out lift or out run my opponents: I simply need to outthink and outmaneuver them. No, I'm not too worried about gladiators who have been *augmented* more recently than I have. Keep in mind, also, that I am *far* more intimate with my own augmentations than Vangard is with his."

"What would you say about fighting that doesn't involve *you*?" Chandler's eyes sparkled.

Vangard spoke with authority. "There will *always* be fighting, but understand that *mitigated* fighting is a *natural* physical exercise–to those so inclined–and a much needed release for those who satiate with such a desire.

"*Professional* fighting, such as boxing, kickboxing, *Gladiator*, or whatnot, reinforces the true *nobility* of 'sport' itself. You'll not show me something more *genuine* than when a man balances his very life on the fulcrum of his passion.

"*This* is what the people want and need to see. *Genuine* confrontation and resolution–man against man, with stakes that cannot be elevated further. Fighting with code, with honor. Let that be the understanding of what is done here on this day!"

The crowd throughout the arena exploded in cheer. When it subsided, the imagescreens switched back to Godwin.

Godwin frowned. "I don't really understand the question, but I'll give it my best shot. People *want* to fight...so there's fighting. If people did not *want* to fight, there would not be any fighting. How do *I...feel* about fighting? Meaning, do I think it justifiable? Always. Of course it's justifiable."

Beyond his smirk, if anything, Godwin's voice may have betrayed a note of cynicism, or perhaps resignation. This observation was lost to all but the most intent of observers, however.

"People fighting one another *is* life in its natural state. Fighting has always been, and always will be. Heck, many of us are fighting in battles we don't even know about."

That's stupid. Pierce mentally reprimanded himself. *I sound like I'm just parroting back Vangard in a different order. I need to get my head in the game! I should at **least** win the crowd; this interview is critical.*

Chandler continued interviewing Vangard and Godwin, asking them a myriad of questions to which they responded similarly. In the meantime, Pol and Eris continued making their way towards their respective seats. Pol was not overly impressed with either of the featured gladiators.

Michael Vangard, the *Archangel of War*, had changed his persona when Serter Company (his sponsor) changed his identity (sponsors typically preferred that gladiators assume other names–ones to which the crowd can easily recognize and relate).

Although a man may change his name or his face, he carries his fears and faults with him until he confronts them or dies. Outwardly, Michael Vangard was stoic, calm–in charge of himself and his surroundings. Inwardly however, raged a storm of doubt and fear. Vangard was completely paranoid and had always been pre-emptively quick to form a vendetta.

Vangard had secretly been dreading this day since the initial announcement that Godwin would be competing. Vangard spent most of his free time watching through the season that Godwin won. Constant analysis of his enemy's moves allowed him to look for what weak points Godwin had.

That was a decade ago, Vangard thought. *His augmentations will not possibly compare.*

Despite any sage advice he gave to himself about Godwin's outdated augmentations, Vangard could not shake his irrational fear of Godwin. Desperate for an edge, he had implored Jason Serter (CEO of the company) to get him a copy of Godwin's KeyTool (or augmentation reset/shutdown device) so that Serter might further protect his investment.

Technology does not always function in the way it was intended. Due to this, *Silverberg* created the *Metahuman Restraint Law* requiring all metahumans[9] to have an embedded "emergency off" command. This command would be the great equalizer for those that were *not* metahumans, as it would cause immediate and irrefutable shutdown.

One of the sad realities of Silverberg was that augmentation abuse happened often enough to be such a concern.

Citizens would, on occasion, become drunk on power as they received further augmentations, sometimes causing considerable property damage. When fights broke out in Silverberg that involved such augmentations, they usually resulted in a fatality.

Vangard was accommodated by his sponsor, Jason Serter, with an illicit TKT.[10] Although Vangard did not want to win the match with unsportsmanlike behavior, he was now content with this perfect backup plan. In the unlikely event that his own prowess was lacking and he became desperate enough, he now had a solution.

Vangard slept well the evening before the match, perhaps for the first time since Godwin's announcement.

SUNDAY 15th 2066   11:14 EST

Pol looked down from the stands into the arena pit. The gladiators were all assembled into pairs, and each pair led into one of four chambers–chambers that only came into existence as walls rose up out of the floor of the arena. Intricate corridors and obstacles then sprang up around the chambers. It was a splendid effect, watching the maze form.

The forming of the arena did not hold Pol's attention long, mostly because he was considerably more interested in Eris. Pol soon turned to Eris, yet found he could not manage a meaningful conversation with her.

9[Metahuman] - Augmented human who can now perform above maximum human potential.
10[TKT], or TransKeyTool, a universal police KeyTool capable of commanding augmentation shutdown in *any* metahuman (or slave).

Chapter 1

Eris was loquacious, exhaustively prattling on and on about *Gladiator*: about how it fuels the economy by creating jobs, how it assists in exterminating undesirable slaves and convicts, how the show keeps wealth in Silverberg, and so on. So seldom did she take a breath that it was impossible to get a word in edgewise.

The first two rounds of *Gladiator* passed rather quickly, as they regularly did. The commentary was considerably greater than the event itself. The banter was witty, although sometimes seemingly scripted. Judiciously opposite voices fought the crowd for loyalty towards their respective gladiator.

As the event continued, the mediacast tension was mounting in tandem with the crowd; oftentimes in complete harmony with the all-but-subliminal heartbeat underlying the music and live commentary.

People made and reconciled bets. Some cheered and some cried, some sang, some fought, some left, and some *finally* arrived.

Having waited some time for the first rounds to complete, Godwin walked proudly up the corridor, eventually emerging out into the light of day. Having to wait for the main event had only made him bored, and consequently want to fight *more*. It was an itch he remembered distantly, with some slight fondness.

As Godwin emerged, the crowd of the arena exploded into cheering. He immediately started filling up with such feelings of nostalgia and exhilaration that it sent a slight shiver throughout his body.

I haven't felt this alive in forever, he thought in irony.

His conquistador-style mirroranium helmet reflected the brilliant sun violently into the imagescreen banks, sometimes causing a momentary whiteout. The careful observer would notice the imagescreens making minor adjustments to compensate. Very few people were aware that the sun's impossibly bright reflections were complimenting the secrecy of the mediacast session that Pierce was receiving as he was taking to the field.

An imagescreen visible only to him, opened in Pierce's vision.
"*Thompson,*" Pierce said disdainfully.

Although they only worked together once before, Pierce would never mistake the ridiculous countenance of AIIS[11A] Agent Thompson. Thompson wore two round noirglass lenses, conjoined only by the barest mirroranium bracket. His salt

---

11A AIIS, or Axel Industries' Internal Security. AIIS is whispered to be the foremost in intelligence on the planet. AIIS officers/agents *outrank* any other citizen in a manner similar as a citizen to a slave. See also Appendices pg 308

and pepper hair was combed back in strict discipline, yet his face was smooth and full in contrast with his presumable age. The greatest feature on his face was his fanned-out moustache, which joined to his nose as to almost give the appearance it was the bottom of a broom.

"Now's not a good time for me, I'm kinda in the middle of something." Pierce stopped walking in order to stand akimbo before the ocean of admirers that stretched up into the sky. The crowd cheered louder.

"You should know better than that," Thompson admonished with a deep, even voice. "You should never try to brush off A.I. when we come calling. Now, forget about whatever plans you had, and listen to your instructions."

Pierce did not speak; Thompson was not expecting him to.

"Oh, don't be so taciturn—you'll be *well* compensated. Your alternate choices will not be as promising. Besides, don't you think you should honor your debt to A.I.?"

"You sure picked a hell of a time to cash in." Pierce growled.

"I didn't want to miss my window of opportunity. Now...see this boy?" The imagescreen display changed to zoom in on a heavyset young man wearing a pinstriped suit that obviously made him feel very uncomfortable. "This is Apollo Venerates. We want you to follow and watch him. I mean, of course, *if* you survive the games today."

"Got it. Follow... Apollo..."

"He goes by *Pol*," Thompson corrected dryly.

"I'm not a babysitter."

"He's not a baby. This is important. Do your job so I can do mine. Oh, and good luck."

The mediacast session ended.

Pierce looked up, into the stands of the arena, at nothing in particular. *Good luck to you **too**, Venerates; **A.I.** is watching you now.*

Vangard walked out onto the field, and the crowd's cheering erupted again like a crack of thunder. Imagescreens mediacasted *The Archangel* taking the field from dozens of angles, as some hidden computer artist added effects to the displays. Theme music poured out of every credit and image bank in the arena, creating an otherwise hideous cacophony of enthusiasm and thrill.

Michael Vangard bowed.

No need to fake confidence *today* as Vangard knew that he had to but *touch* the TKT to Pierce and it would render the combination to shut down Pierce's augmentations. This would absolutely ensure him the match.

CHAPTER 1

I probably won't even use it, Vangard thought. *Of course, if I do, it might be good for the show. If it comes to using this, I'll give the crowd an old-school fatality. Maybe I should do it anyway? Ratings. Hmmm.*

As Vangard approached the center of the arena, his mind remained heavy with thoughts of how to properly win the match.

SUNDAY 15th 2066   11:34 EST

Jason Serter, President and CEO of Serter Company, looked down at the conspicuous, luminous, and multi-chromatic lines of Solid Hypnizium.[12Δ] They were meticulously made parallel to one another on his desk. In anticipation of the rush he would feel after inhaling it, he could not help but giggle.

SUNDAY 15th 2066   11:35 EST

Finally, the time had come.

Michael Vangard and Pierce Godwin, having properly addressed and riled up the crowd, started walking toward one another. The crowd went silent in tandem with the imagescreens and credit banks throughout the arena.

When they came within 30 feet of one another, they began to circle, almost in synchrony. It was suspenseful and beautiful.

Do not think about it, just act! Michael thought to himself.

Do not act without thinking it through! Pierce counseled himself simultaneously.

Suddenly, Michael broke into a run directly toward Pierce. Pierce remained unmoving, perhaps even genuinely smirking.

What a fool! They thought independently of one another, in unison.

12Δ There is but one *prescribed* substance in Silverberg to treat *all* forms of emotional or mental illness: Hypnizium. Although there are many disputes about its origin or its contents, the results are overwhelmingly positive. It is not available commercially, or internationally.

Solid Hypnizium is a blacklisted compound that is circulated by one of the few illicit organizations that has managed to survive in "underground" Silverberg. It can be absorbed in numerous ways, however the most expeditious vehicle is consumption via nasal inhalation. Also see Appendices pg 303.

      - [God, Man, and The Machine] -

Pierce watched Michael break into his run with augmented, metahuman vision. He alone saw graphics spring to life, detailing an instant analysis of Michael's movements.

When Michael started running, it was explosive, impossible. The laws of physics seemed to bend, lending to the crowd a feeling of watching something surreal…and yet, there it was.

Michael crossed the 30-foot gap in one second. When Michael's augmented body punched at Pierce, it carried the same inertia as a truck slamming into something at about 45 miles per hour. The air reverberated with audible protest as his fist came ever closer to Pierce's head.

Pierce watched in frightened fascination as the graphics displayed numbers that he could not believe. He dodged, only narrowly, dreading to take his eyes off Michael for fear of losing his constant digitized analysis.

I avoided that? Pierce was charged with excitement and relief.

He avoided that? Michael thought, perplexed. He followed his own momentum into a roll that ended in a no-less-than-spectacular spring to his feet. Michael settled into a readied stance.

This stance would have afforded him a marginally greater advantage, had Pierce not been serendipitously aligning himself the entire time to receive Michael's landing.

Pierce swung hard at Michael's chest...right after Michael slapped Pierce with the TKT bank. Pierce's excitement and momentum came to an immediate halt as his displays vanished and his hand met the crushing resistance of Michael's subdermal augmentations.

Michael turned to address his would-be attacker.

In shut down, Pierce was offhandedly knocked down and a few feet back as Michael changed stances.

"Oh, nicely done," Pierce smirked, showing no worry despite the pain. "I thought you were an angel, or something. Isn't using a *ticket* [13A] against the rules?"

"Sorry, old timer," Michael started stepping towards Pierce. "You knew you were in over your head before you got here. May whatever god you believe in smile kindly on you when you meet him today."

Pierce clapped his hands together.

An unseen burst of energy undulated outward from Pierce.

13A "Ticket" or even "ticket bank" is slang for the TransKeyTool, or TKT bank.

Michael, in mid-stride, fell forward into the ground. Nobody could see the stark expression of horror and shock on his face.

"Sorry, young timer," Pierce winced at his own lack of creativity, slowly standing up. "But I was thinking something similar myself."

The truth of it was that Pierce wasn't thinking anything similar whatsoever. The only thing Pierce was thinking about was Agent Thompson's command that he seek out that dumpy kid. He had no idea where to start–and why now? Realizing that he was distracting himself from concentrating on the fight, he pushed down his thoughts.

Michael's augmentations were so many, that without power, he could not move his own arms or legs in a substantial manner. Michael lay on the ground, facedown and slightly rocking in his attempts to right himself. It reminded Pierce of a turtle on its back.

Allegedly impossible, Pierce's augmentations resumed operation.

SUNDAY 15th 2066   △   11:38 EST

"People like violence," Eris interrupted. "Invariably, they seek it out in one form or another. Some seek it to combat it–others welcome it into their very souls. Some seek violence merely to witness it. Some desire violence directly against someone similar, if only for measurement. Some unify to justify their want for violence. Some people are violent *only* to other violent people. Some like to be violent with themselves..."

Pol looked at Eris in amazement.

"You're having a discussion with me about violence in *the middle* of watching gladiatorial combat?"

"Are you implying there is a *superior* moment when such a discussion is *more* appropriate?" Eris batted her eyes innocently.

"..." Pol looked back down on the arena through the hovering imagescreen.

SUNDAY 15th 2066   △   11:39 EST

Pierce walked up and placed his foot on top of Michael's head. Imagescreens all over the arena were mediacasting various zooms of the situation that had developed. Imagescreens that were not depicting the events of the arena were plastered with the faces of the hidden commentators.

"Foul!" Michael screamed, his voice ringing with an hysterical desperation.

"Foul!" The commentator was nearly yelling. "Pierce never touched him, yet Michael fell down! Where are the referees? Why isn't there a timeout?"

"I don't understand what is happening," Pol sounded deflated.

"Godwin seems to have cheated at the game, somehow," Eris explained. "Gladiators can only use things that are held, worn, or thrown. Nothing can be shot, such as using a sling or gun. They may not use anything that causes any form of combustion damage. Nothing can explode, such as a grenade. Nothing can be invisible, such as a virus, radiation, or poison..."

Eris continued to systematically list *Gladiator* violations.

The crowd was split as to how to feel about the events, many taking their cues from the imagescreen commentary. Pol looked around, greatly concerned that fighting would break out. It never seemed to come to that, despite the red-faced valor with which the members of the crowd were shouting. If fighting ever appeared, perhaps it was as quickly quelled.   It was obvious that even outraged, even in a massive crowd, citizens did not want to jostle their law keepers.

Suddenly, most of the arena seemed to fall silent, echoing the sudden lack of commentary mediacasting from the images and credit banks. All the imagescreens filled up with a silent view of Pierce standing with one foot placed upon the head of fallen Archangel Michael Vangard.

Pierce stepped down hard onto Michael's head, with augmentations exaggerating the amount of force necessary to accomplish his goal. The imagebanks and credit banks mediacasted neither the sounds of metal bending in forced protest nor the sickly wet popping noises. They *did* succeed in displaying Michael's head crumpling and squirting under Pierce's foot.

The walls forming the chambers and corridors of the arena fell away as the floor resumed its uninteresting uniformity.

"Guess that's that," Pierce grinned sardonically. *And to think, I came here to die.*

The fortunate members of the crowd that were genuinely *happy* with the turnout of the day's events could not be heard cheering and congratulating one another as the vast majority of the masses were busy yelling and arguing about the validity of the contest.

CHAPTER 1

Imagescreens continued mediacasting as police carriers went swooping down onto the floor of the arena to surround Pierce. Pierce did not seem to be putting up any kind of resistance.

I wonder how A.I. is going to get me out of this, Pierce thought, knowing this was testing Agent Thompson's resolve. *Just so I can follow this kid? Well, whatever.* Pierce, now accompanied by several SPD officers, was taken from the field.

"Wait. *Why* are the police here? I thought killing the other guy was supposed to be the *point*?" Pol asked, still confused.

"Well, Pierce's victory, if construed as having been accomplished via *cheating,* changes the dynamic from a win to a murder," Eris explained.

SUNDAY 15th 2066   12:13 EST

Pol and Eris did not try to fight through the crowds of angry and outraged citizens. They waited patiently for the people to clear. This made Pol feel better.

In the meantime, Pierce was undergoing an examination for contraband devices. *Now how am I supposed to find and follow this kid?* Pierce wondered during the midst of the cavalcade of examinations. *Let's see what the Mainframe can tell me already. With a name like Apollo Venerates, I'm sure there can't be more than one.* Pierce accessed the Mainframe with his internal credit bank. Speaking subvocally, he commanded his internal credit bank to connect.

MAINFRAME » SYNCHRONIZING «
MAINFRAME » CONNECTED «

Pierce was in contact with Silverberg's national network, the Mainframe.

"Who is Apollo Venerates?" Pierce continued to subvocalize.
MAINFRAME » *Transitional from the United States of America* **«**
"What is his purpose in Silverberg?"
MAINFRAME » *Foreign exchange student* **«**
Silverberg has a foreign exchange program? Pierce paused to think. *I didn't know that.*
"Display all mediacast records of Apollo Venerates." At his command, pictures and videos of Pol and his publicly documented life from America started to appear in Pierce's peripheral range of vision. There were few at best, and Pierce

        - [God, Man, and The Machine] -

quickly scanned them all. Pierce frowned.

"Display only mediacast records of Apollo Venerates in Silverberg."

MAINFRAME » *Restricted* «

Pierce raised an eyebrow. *Restricted?* **This** *guy? Who in the name of what cares about this guy? Well...this is going to be harder than I thought. Guess that's why* **I'm** *on the job. But I'm not a computer guy, and it sure looks like A.I. is restricting me from viewing the very man they have assigned me to follow. I hope the cops hurry this up, they are boring me to death.*

"Display mediacast records of Apollo Venerates." *Let's look at this again..*

The police were perplexed at the lack of evidence on Godwin.

"I don't see anything that violates the rules of the game or the laws of Silverberg," announced Lieutenant Farnsworth. He finished his scans of Pierce and the reviewing of his augmentation record. "Then again, I thought that all metahumans were monitored regularly by the AIIS? Where are *those* guys at?"

The only other man in the room, Officer Dorian Smith, shrugged. "I say we *ticket* him and drag him down to Augmented Forensics."

"Normally I can't get them off my cases," Farnsworth continued, ignoring Smith's comment. He fumbled for his credit bank. "Now they're nowhere to be found."

Farnsworth stepped over to a permanent imagescreen in order to access the Mainframe. Farnsworth always had an affinity for using a physical imagescreen instead of projection.

Dorian certainly didn't understand it.

"Establish a mediacast session with the AIIS department," Farnsworth commanded the imagescreen while simultaneously tapping his credit bank to the upper right corner.

The imagescreen sprang to life as an AIIS agent came into pixilation. Agent Anderson was a young man in his very early twenties. His thick and full head of shaggy blonde hair seemed to contrive to fall in front of his eyes. As he spoke, he moved his head in such a manner as to whisk the rogue locks away from interfering with his line of sight.

Dorian thought the movement was effeminate.

Pierce shut down his interaction with the Mainframe. He couldn't possibly focus on them both simultaneously, and the police were simply more interesting now.

"This is Agent Anderson, how can I help you?" His impossibly bass voice clashed very poorly with his countenance.

"I'm just curious why none of your representatives are here," Farnsworth said, studying Anderson for his reaction.

"Where, exactly, did you mean when you say *here*?"

"At the arena. This is Lt. Farnsworth of the CSPD (Central Silverberg Police Department), as if you somehow didn't already know that, and I'm not much in the mood for games. Either you're taunting me or you're completely stupid," Farnsworth said, smiling slightly at the imagescreen. "Although the more I think on it, the more I am actually inclined to believe the latter of the two. Where is Agent Jefferson? He seemed like the regular Agent Cryptic[14A] to be sent here."

Anderson whisked his hair back from his eyes. Although his words rolled easily out his mouth, they sounded almost mechanical because of his deep voice. "Jefferson is visiting his mother. I am in charge of augmented humans now. You take it on assumption that I know that *here* automatically means *your location*. I don't know that. Further, *I* can see no reason for an AIIS agent to be *there* as there is nothing that requires our attention."

"You need me to clarify that *here* means *my location*?" Farnsworth sighed. "What about Super-Cyborg over here with the dampening device?"

Dampening device? Pierce gleaned out of his peripheral hearing. *No wonder they can't find anything...they're looking for the wrong ordinance!*

Anderson replied. "He is of no immediate interest to us as he has not done anything that warrants our attention."

"Hey man," Pierce chimed in. "You sure you want to have this conversation *here* in front of me? I mean, I could *go...*"

Farnsworth ignored Pierce. "What about the games? Godwin, *Citizen Gladiator*, clearly just cheated!"

"*We* did not detect any such thing. Do you have any evidence that he did?"

14A Agent Cryptic is a Silverberg mediacast show about several double agents who work for two rival corporations: Centre Earth and Firelord. Nobody knows which side they work for, or if perhaps, they work for a third, hidden corporation. Their level of involvement and promotion are rapid enough to keep the observer genuinely interested. It is widely rumored that the entire story is a cunning allegory about Axel Industries and Serter Company, and that the episodes are reflections of real life.

Farnsworth looked hopefully at Dorian. Dorian shrugged and shook his head.

"End mediacast session." Farnsworth tapped his credit bank to the imagescreen terminal; he had already had enough of the A.I. runaround.

"I *know* you're guilty," Farnsworth said, turning to regard Pierce. "But thanks to Pre-Crime and Evidence Laws, you may go. You'll slip up, somehow. They always do. I'll get you."

Pierce looked at the lieutenant. "*Get* me? I told you several times already–I don't *know* what happened to him, he just fell down. Not my doing, not my fault."

Farnsworth raised an eyebrow. "Still here? If I were you, I would leave before Officer Smith thinks of some additional testing that could be done."

Pierce nodded. "Dead." [15Δ]
Pierce walked out.

Dorian looked at Farnsworth.

"Now don't tell me that you're *actually* going to say something?" The lieutenant growled.

Dorian smiled. "*Scant clues could be found...*"

"Don't quote <u>Oedipus</u> to *me*. Especially considering you've never read it." Despite his objection, Farnsworth finished the quote. "*Yet, clues **could** be found. This might be enough for a good detective.* Smith, are you implying I am a *bad* detective?"

"No," Dorian shrugged. "I'm only pointing out that you might be overlooking something."

"Overlooking something like who the detective *is*, and who is *not*, for instance?"

"Well, you're just full of anger and wrath, aren't you?" Dorian chided. "This conversation is going to be pointless; let's just get back,"

Farnsworth melted a little. "You're right," He started picking up a renewed energy as he put his sport coat and hat back on. "But first, let's check in on the NSPD and compare notes about tonight."

"How did I *know* that the day was not over?" Dorian grimaced as he followed Farnsworth out of the room.

15Δ *Dead* - slang term for expressing agreement, or appreciation.

SUNDAY 15th 2066 Ⓜ 12:43 EST

Pierce looked across the arena while he called Agent Thompson.

Thompson's visage appeared to Pierce.

"I'm *sorry*, but I'm busy at the moment. Your session is being redirected."

Agent Anderson appeared. "I can't take your call just now, please speak with my associate."

Agent Nelson appeared.

"How can I help you, Mr. Godwin?"

Pierce blinked. "Well, you could *start* by helping me locate the guy I am supposed to be following."

"And which *guy* would that be?" Nelson scoffed.

"Are you trying to tell me that you guys don't communicate what's going on throughout the AIIS department?"

"Certainly not every *little* thing. My foray is monitoring the Mainframe for violations and anomalies, not conscripting glory-hound fighters for surveillance detail."

"So you *do* know what I am talking about."

"Let's just talk about you and your ideas for now."

Pierce frowned. "Okay, let's try this another way. I'm supposed to be tailing some kid from America called Apollo Venerates. The Mainframe says that I don't have clearance to access his whereabouts...I'm going to need that clearance."

Nelson seemed to be staring off into the distance as he worked on an imagescreen that was not included in the mediacast window.

Nelson paused and finally frowned. "*Well*..it would appear that *I* do not have the clearance to grant you access."

"I thought you were in charge of the Mainframe?"

Nelson closed the mediacast session.

Well, that was no help. Pierce thought in contempt.

Agent Nelson swiveled his imagescreen so that the readouts would be more available to his other observers. The imagescreen read ***Restricted***, which in turn was the subject of concern for the Agents.

Agent Thompson frowned. "How can it be restricted?"

"It *can't*–it's impossible." Nelson said offhandedly.

Agent Dodgson waved his arms frantically, trying to warn Nelson from saying that *anything* was impossible.

"It seems that you and Dodgson have been hanging out together at club *stupid.*" Thompson sighed. "I'm going to have to report this one to the big guy... ugh, frankly, it will be amazing if *anyone* keeps their jobs today. In the meantime, go find some clever way to determine where Venerates is, and get that information to Godwin."

Nelson started to work.

"Oh, and Nelson?" Thompson called.

"Sir?"

"*Stop* telling people Internal Security's business. We're supposed to be professionally mysterious, okay?" Thompson smiled, but his true thoughts remained melancholy.

"The rest of you," Thompson said, looking around. "Get back to your businesses, this meeting is officially over–for now."

Nelson was present when the blip of Apollo Venerates suddenly reappeared on the Mainframe. His signal turned up in the arena, slightly before the games. Only for a few minutes, however.

Nelson started using the Mainframe to look around the arena. He noticed an autocar that was parked in solitary, awaiting its owner. He sent the information to Pierce Godwin. Pierce was grateful when it came. He had no idea how to go about finding this kid and this seemed as good a start as any. Convenient, too, for he was headed towards his own vehicle when the data arrived.

SUNDAY 15th 2066 ⚠ **12:50 EST**

"People hate disappointment," Pol interrupted, imitating Eris. "They become especially disdainful of it when they recognize it for what it is. One becomes unmanageable and...um, *very* upset. Unrequited affection, for instance, comes to mind."

Pol did his best to shift the conversation to the topic of his prospective romantic interest in Eris. He had been practically staring at her the entire time they were walking back to the autocar. Why didn't she notice his signals? Eris was so different from how she had seemed in her emails!

"What people?" Eris asked.

"What?" Pol responded, surprised.

"*What people* hate disappointment?" Eris expounded.

"No... I, um, wait." Pol felt confused again. "No people. I mean me." Pol stopped walking. "I mean, I thought..." Pol started to blush. *Time to change gears.* "Do I seem different to you?"

Eris smiled and narrowed her eyes. "You *are* different."

"Oh, ha ha. I mean, different than you expected."

Eris seemed to think. "No...you are exactly what I expected."

Oh.

"Not in a *bad* way," Eris said, smiling.

Pol was filled with hope. Pol was getting tired, however, perhaps simply from emotional exhaustion. It was hard, surrendering himself to the whim of this woman!

"So, where do we go from here?" Pol asked, slapping his hands down on the autocar and looking around. For the first time in awhile, Pol paid attention to something *other* than Eris. The *lack* of vehicles in the garage was almost worse than when it was full, the garage seemed to stretch off into eternity. Pol was soon overwhelmed by the mirrored effect, and he reverted his attention back on Eris.

"From here..." Eris paused for an entire minute, her eyes widening in excited conclusion. "We go to the Silverberg Mall."

"The *Mall*?" Pol questioned.

"The Mall?" Pierce imitated loudly as he was walking towards them.

Eris turned so that her back was to the autocar and leveled her gaze on Pierce.

Pol turned to see the gladiator approaching. Pierce had a smoothness in his walk that was *too* fluid, too unnatural. His gait, which bespoke of grace and control, only made him seem more terrifying. He wore a skin-tight, sleeveless black shirt under a frayed and fading denim vest. Chains hung from his apparel, as if to warn his audience that they were viewing a dangerous animal. Multiple tattoos could be seen wherever his skin was exposed, all of varying design and caliber.

Pierce walked right up to Pol, who visibly shrank back.

"Hi!" Pierce extended his hand.

"Hello..." Pol cautiously took Pierce's hand in handshake. Pol sighed in relief when his hand remained uncrushed.

"It seems that my autocar has become disconnected from the Mainframe and consequently won't work for me–I'm embarrassed to say. I'm in need of a lift home. I don't suppose you could give me a ride?"

Pol stood slack-jawed. Eris was completely quiet.

"You don't know how to *drive*?" Pol asked blankly.

"Never needed to! Hey, today is your lucky day! I'll hook you up with autographs and action figures–whatever you want, but I do *have* to get home."

"Um, I would *think* that's cool...Eris is a **huge** *Gladiator* fan." Pol lowered his voice, looking at Eris. "I know you want to give him a ride. I mean, I know how much it would mean to you."

Eris looked Pierce up and down, which Pierce perceived as a nod.

"Great! This is gonna be great! Thank you *so* much!" Pierce trumpeted. "I don't suppose we could leave *soon*? I don't mean to be a bother."

I think I'm overacting...I hope I'm not overacting. Pierce thought.

Pol opened the door, and climbed into the back of the vehicle. Pierce and Eris sat beside one another in the front seats.

"Connect to Mainframe," Eris ordered the autocar.

An imagescreen opened up inside the autocar and a disembodied voice spoke the written-out response.

MAINFRAME » SYNCHRONIZING«

MAINFRAME » CONNECTED «

"Relocate autocar to designated residential parking for Pierce Godwin."
"Well, *that's* not going to wor..." Pierce stopped speaking.

The autocar sped off toward the Hub of Silverberg. Pierce tried to make casual conversation, but Pol only offered up one word answers and Eris didn't speak at all. Pierce grinned, but mentally he was quickly getting bored.

Oh goody, follow **this** *guy. And this girl. Mr. and Mrs. Personality. Best story of espionage, ever.*

...

I wonder what Mary's doing.

Chapter 2:

Oedipus Now

AUGUST *2066 EST*

Fri 13	Sat 14	Sun 15	Mon 16	Tues 17	Wed 18	Thur 19	Fri 20
		13:00					

Jason Serter, President and CEO of Serter Company, *finally* stopped drumming his fingers. For the first time since the death of his gladiator and *friend* –Michael Vangard–Mr. Serter's office was completely silent.

SUNDAY 15th 2066   14:23 EST

Mrs. Godwin, Mary, was the visual antithesis of Pierce. She was shorter, and considerably younger. She wore a yellow sundress that looked more appropriate for life out on the old American prairie rather than the anime-popular feminine fashion of Silverberg. Her forehead was pronounced and uncovered, dark brown hair falling around it to the sides of her eyes–shrouding her ears completely. Her eyes suggested a certain sadness that only seemed darker when she smiled.

"You're back," Mrs. Godwin said, looking up at her husband in complete awe. After a moment, she recovered herself. "I thought you went out to die?"

"I did," Pierce said, smiling mischievously. "It turns out it was in my better interest to stay alive. Well, maybe *your*–I mean *our* best interests. Besides, I didn't want to break tradition."

"What tradition is that?" Mary seemed like she was out of breath.

"It's a *new* tradition…the one where I make it a point *never* to treat you as if you were any less important than myself again. I am *so* sorry, Mary, forgive me."

Pierce and Mary embraced lovingly. Pol suddenly felt very out of place. He looked down at his feet while twisting his silver shoes. *I hate these shoes.* Pol thought, again.

Pol and Eris had accompanied Pierce up to his *apartment*, where he had promised them he would locate a reward suitable for their assistance.

When they first arrived, Pierce seemed to hesitate a moment before knocking on the door–a curious, out-of-place, brown wooden door.

"You'd think he'd live in a mansion or something more...epic," Pol whispered to Eris.

It seemed to Pol that Eris was not as enthusiastic as she might be...although after Mary answered the door, Eris' eyes seemed to linger on her.

"You're Mary Godwin," Eris said, finally interrupting the reunited couple.
Mary looked over at Eris, smiling.
"Indeed."
"The same Mary Godwin who wrote <u>Oedipus Now</u>."
"The same," Mary said, tears falling as she nodded slightly. She turned and started walking back toward the common area of the apartment when she lifted her voice to sing a single word: "*Shoes*!" (Although it was spread into two syllables, as in Shoo - ooze!)
Shoes? Pol thought he heard her incorrectly, but noticed Pierce rolling his eyes and divesting himself of his own shoes near the front door. Pol imitated him, (*Good riddance!*) and was soon afterward imitated by Eris.

"What's <u>Oedipus Now</u>?" Pol asked, feeling like he was left out again.
"<u>Oedipus Now</u>," Mary said, while lighting a cigarette. She blew out the smoke lovingly, and lowered herself delicately into her rocking chair. "Is my novel."
"Aha." Pol was never much the reader.
"It's not for everyone, but it *is* a best-seller. Translated into 13 different languages," Mary bragged.

Pol and Eris sat on the couch opposite Pierce and Mary, the earlier of whom had plopped into a very large beanbag chair and had somehow come to be in possession of a beer.

Mary almost seemed to be making an art out of her smoking. She employed pronounced and intricate hand movements between inhaling and exhaling. When *she* did it, it spoke of nobility, or at least of the demeanor of one who wanted to give that impression.

"What's it about?" Pol prompted, starting to feel out of place again.

Mary puffed. "You should *read* it and spare me the bother and insult of having to summarize my magnum opus so flippantly. *As if* to imagine that it could be *possibly* contained in a few, mere sentences. *However,* as it seems you were recently American, I will forgive you your delicate attention span. I will try to summarize it as quickly…to best answer your question, it's about a detective who unexpectedly finds herself in the middle of a case where a man was murdered by the machine he created. Of course, nobody *knew* it was a machine, it seemed so real.

"Initially, we embark upon a dark journey featuring a morally derelict biologist who thinks that he can create *life,* but also that he can create *ego.* He patches together both human and machine parts in order to create this self-propelled egocentric machine. I originally named it The Machine, but my publisher suggested I change the title."

"To Oedipus Now?" Pol was astonished. "I think The Machine is a *way* better title than *Oedipus Now.*"

I don't even like saying it, Pol thought to himself.

"So do I," Pierce said, voting in his opinion.

"Regardless," Mary said, blowing out more smoke. "The name of the machine in the book is (eventually) Oedipus. The novel draws many modern parallels with the classic myth. It also emphasizes the madness of men who are obsessed with the particulars of creating *life* in such a way that it succeeds beyond his control. Overall, the book is a horror/tragedy. You should *read* it, we could discuss…"

"I've read it," Eris interrupted. "I found it to be comical." [16Δ]

"Comical?" Mary exhaled the smoky word, almost choking.

"Yes." Eris closed her eyes. "Oedipus the Machine struggles unnecessarily with some pretty basic concepts. For instance, Oedipus delivers a mistaken dissertation about how digging a hole in the Earth represents *adding more memory* to it. There are several concepts that it struggles with during the course of the novel that should *not* be as problematic as they are."

Mary defended. "Well, of course I chose to emphasize certain entertainable faults with extending ego to a machine, but these instances were *meant* as a bit of a caricature….for storytelling and character identifying purposes. It's *harmless* to the body of the work. The Machine struggles with truly understanding or perceiving life in 3 dimensions. Its part of it's progression into realizing its own ego."

[16Δ] Another comedy concerning Oedipus Now is that despite its incredible appeal (at least as reflected in the sales) few people, by comparison, have actually *read* the work.

"But it's *absurd*," Eris smiled. "Understanding three-dimensional reality is simply a matter of comprehending the math. Machines, of all things, should not have a difficult time understanding *math*. If anything, human beings should struggle with it more, for by comparison they are relatively stupid."

Mary shot out a geyser of smoke as she addressed Pol. "Your friend is not exactly the most congenial of people, is she?"

"Yes–I mean, no," Pol responded, not really understanding Mary.

"Honey?" Mary batted her eyes at her husband.

"Yes, my crafty vixen?" Pierce shot back, a tone of knowing in his voice.

"Will you please...fetch me...some juice?" (Joo - oo - suh!) Mary sang.

"Fetch...it...yourself," Pierce sang back.

"Okay, *nevermind*." Mary lit a second cigarette.

"Right," Pierce said, putting his beer on the lamp-table and climbing out of the preposterous beanbag chair he had taken during the discussion. "I'll get it."

Suddenly the imagescreens around the curiously decorated apartment sprang to an involuntary life.

"Cursed autommercials," Pierce muttered. "I hate living here sometimes."

Pierce went into the kitchen.

NOIRGLASSES printed out on the imagescreens, graphically brought into existence as if discoverable by the rippling of water.

"Everything's better in grayscale!" A smiling woman's face, suddenly visible, replaced the letters on the screen. The viewpoint zoomed out while she donned the glasses and settled back into her chair sitting in the sands, awash the sun on some tropical beach.

"Noirglasses digitize vision, they make any, and *every* correction, always," announced some faceless male voice. "Perfect sight at an affordable price."

The imagescreens changed to show images and video of a carnival fade from color to various shades of black and white. The mediacast record, still in the grayscale "truvision," followed viewpoint as if being recorded by a pair of glasses on a regular pedestrian. The video zoomed in and out on subjects as the vision passed over them. Sometimes zooming to incredible detail if the view remained over a single subject for long.

As the view passed over other people out and about, the clothing the people wore would reveal wording and other messages when seen through the noirglasses. One man's shirt bragged that it was a 4,000-thread count shirt.[17Δ]

"Have a better life than you were created for with noirglasses, noirlenses, and noirplants; available exclusively through Truvision, a subsidiary of Serter Company."

"Serter Company," Pierce chewed out the words, re-entering the room with Mary's juice. "Mary?"

"Yes dear?"

"Life might get too exciting around here for you soon. I'm going to find you someplace to go until I feel more confident about the situation." Pierce said, his voice low.

"Oh, don't get all gloomy on me now." Mary took the glass of juice that Pierce was absently holding, and caressed his arm slightly. "Besides, who could better protect me in this whole city, this whole *country*, than you?"

"Well, no *single* person, of course. But I was thinking more like a great group of people with extensive influence, namely A.I. itself. We'll discuss it more at length later, but for now...let's entertain our guests and make ***merry***!" Pierce emptied the contents of his beer.

"So what's next?" Pol asked.

Pol *meant* "what's next" in the context of Pierce making good on his promise of exclusive gladiatorial memorabilia, however Mary went for the bait instead.

"Well, I *have* started writing another book," Mary said, smiling. "I would *love* to discuss it. It's a book on the journeys to wisdom. I'm calling it <u>Priest & Pennath</u>. I'm going to model it after the life and writings of Solomon, with my own bits peppered in here and there."

"Not really much good at naming her own books, is she?" Pierce winked.

Despite his charm, Pierce loved to fight. He was always ready to challenge–especially verbally, and especially with his wife. If one thought that he did not love her, the truth is quite the contrary. However, over the course of his life, he had become addicted to the behavior.

17Δ Fashion is of considerable value in Silverberg. The land of mirrors, inhabited with many of the world's greatest vanities. One might wonder if all the mirrors about Silverberg *created* such vain inhabitants or merely attracted them.

Mary, over time, learned to dismiss the behavior, to the extent of completely ignoring Pierce. Although properly *un*engaged with anything more pressing, Mary would meet Pierce with her own verbal swordplay.

"You stay out of this," Mary warned.
"Your titles are..." Pierce smirked, walking backwards, away from Mary.
"Odd? Curious? Bad?" Eris offered.

Mary shot an evil glance at Eris.
Pierce tried to redirect the conversation. "Isn't writing a book on wisdom a bit pretentious?"
Everyone looked at him.
Pierce grinned. "Can't *'wisdom **only** be realized, and not learned?* '[18Δ] Wouldn't it appear that *you* think that you have knowledge or insight that is superior to your peers, namely those who are your elders?"
"And who says I do not?" Mary lit another cigarette. "I am a very passionate woman, my darling husband." Artful exhale. "And although perhaps vicariously, I am *also* a very worldly woman.
"Why not slow down on smoking, darling dear?" Pierce said with some genuine concern.
"Oh do shut up," Mary exhaled. "Of *course,* my nerves are shot. You. *Won. The. Match!* What *were* you thinking?"
"I don't know that this is the time or the place to have this discussion."
"Okay, then. Let's get back on the subject." Mary sighed.
"Wait. What was the subject?" Pol asked unhappily.
"<u>Priest & Pennath,</u>" Eris announced.

"Ah yes," Pol acknowledged. *More book talk.* "Is it fiction, then?"
"Certainly...only with a moral and a point." Mary shot a geyser of smoke from the corner of her smug smile. "This is not some novel where the only delight the reader receives is from observing the characters interact with one another and their environments; it's an allegorical conundrum, meant to be rich with symbolism and situations that inspire the reader to overcome some of their classical understandings of how things *are.*
"Besides, there are a **finite** number of plots and stories, and I am intimate with them all. Conventional fiction has no beauty or luster to me anymore."

[18Δ] Pierce is quoting <u>Oedipus Now</u> again. This is somewhat insulting to Mary, and Pierce knows it. They both are very aware that although he may have memorized certain passages to accomplish or compliment his own ends, he has never read the work in it's entirety.

"Wait. What?" Pol scratched his head and tried to understand her statement.

Eris spoke up. "If you believe that, then you must think that there is *never* anything that's new."

"There's nothing new under *this* sun." Mary smirked knowingly.

"So then, you're just taking other people's ideas and spinning them off as your own? Isn't that plagiarism?"

"In a world of nothing new, it is *obvious* to those that are more saturated and familiar with the works of mankind, that *everything* is just an amalgam of other things. *I* am nothing special, I'm just an amalgam. My plots and characters are just amalgams of what I know. Of course, what I know, I know primarily because of media and literature."

"Honey, it doesn't have to be that everything is an anagram," Pierce said while Mary whispered *"amalgam"* to Pol. Pierce continued, unaffected. "So much that *everything* is symbolic. Symbols do not..."

"People like symbols," Eris interrupted. Mary raised an eyebrow and patiently waited for Eris to conclude her most recent interjection. "They appear everywhere and are in *everything*–even in nature. Your very *name* is a symbol. Some symbols are easily recognizable, and some not much so. Some are in place for so long, recognized by so many–to the point that they are taken for granted–that a symbol's meaning can completely change over the course of time. A permanent boundary from the past effectively communicating with the future. One of the great comedies of mankind!"

"I'm so bored of your holier-than-thou approach to writing." Pierce sighed, ignoring Eris. "I love you, but *you* think you know *everything*, which is exactly why *you* should never write a book about knowing *anything*."

Mary raised the other eyebrow, amused, and continued smoking professionally.

"Actually, you're an *idiot*." Pierce said, smiling his most charming smile, inwardly remonstrating her smoking. "Not because of *that*, however..."

Pierce took a second to glance at Pol, but returned his attention to Mary. "You're an idiot because you can't decide which *shoes* to wear. And because of you...of your..."

"Ambivalence?" Mary suggested.

"Because of your *ambivalence,* we can't make it to *any* functions on time."

Mary whispered, putting her hand to the side of her mouth, so that only Pol could hear it. "Only an *idiot* would think that that's NOT important..."

Pierce continued to exercise his verbal denouncement of Mary's characteristic hurdle while Mary mimicked along.

She's weird. Pol thought

"Stick to books like 'Oedipus,' it would do you more..."

"People like distraction!" Eris interrupted. "Distraction from the *truth*. Which is why they like <u>Oedipus Now</u>, because <u>Oedipus Now</u> certainly has *nothing* to do with calculable truth."

Eris smiled as Mary frowned. "This is *completely* reinforced by what Mary *just* said: namely that all creations contain the same formula, albeit rearranged, yet elicit an identical sum. If the sum is *always* the same, it is *pointless* to change the formula."

Mary shot an angry glance at Pierce, who shrugged back in amusement.

"We also see this reflected in the message of <u>Oedipus Now</u>. *Anyone* can calculate the truth, it is completely self-evident. The act of creating, *creation*, is redundant and dangerous...it has no function beyond one's own amusement and gratification and will only end up causing disharmony or catastrophe."

Mary shot an angry glance at Eris. "Who in the *hell* do you think you are? You come into my house as a guest, sit here, and *blatantly* insult me? You may leave now; you are no longer welcome here."

"What?" Eris blinked. "How could I have *insulted* you?"

Mary narrowed her eyes. Her anger and insult would normally not abate so quickly, but Eris suddenly seemed so–genuine–in her reaction that Mary had to consider.

"The moral of Oedipus was *never* 'creation is pointless!' I am *almost* amused that you would draw that conclusion. It has always been that 'your actions have consequences beyond your perception. Also, life is not so much about the *decisions* you have made, so much as your *response* to your decisions.' It is by our *responses* to the decisions that we have made that we may be observed, defined, and weighed."

Mary blew out a triumphant geyser of smoke.

Pierce crinkled a toothy smirk in reply.

"Of course, *Mary* thinks that *everyone* thinks the same way she does." Pierce pointed accusingly. "It's difficult for **her** to understand that people think differently, because she's so *different*. She *quickly* determines that it must be a character flaw when people do not see eye to eye with her. *I* think that understanding that people see things differently than us is necessarily one of the fundamental steps that all human beings must make on the road to enlightenment and maturity.

"Besides, *Sweetie*, didn't *you* once tell me that *all* art was subject to interpretation, and interpretation *cannot* be wrong? Eris, *your* interpretation is *completely* valid. Mary's just mad that her message is so *ambivalent*."

Mary whispered "*amorphous*" to Pol.

"Nothing new..." Pierce continued, using his verbal momentum. "You know honey, recently I felt the same as you: that as time passed, nothing was new and discoverable anymore." Pierce looked at Mary. "But now more than ever, I realize that I do not *miss* the unknowing heart of childhood. Now, instead, I revel in the wisdom of experience and am happy and content with my time remaining."

"That's real sweet, honey." Mary smiled, still loaded. "You could write greeting cards. Ladies and gentlemen, I present to you the modern day Aristotle."

"I have no idea what that means." Pol admitted.

Pierce scratched his head, smiling slightly. "I'm not sure I do, either."

Mary spoke up. "The problem with *philosophers* is that they spend so much time thinking about death and watching life from an alternate perspective, they often forget to participate in it."

"I'm no philosopher," Pierce grinned. "I'm an argumentalist. I firmly believe that for every argument, there is an equal and opposite RE-argument."

Pierce received a request for a mediacast session from AIIS Agent Thompson. He gracefully sidestepped the ongoing conversation by spilling beer on himself and whisking away into the kitchen to attend it. There, he subvocalized the entire session.

"Pierce, this is Agent Thompson."

"Go ahead, Thompson."

"Are you with the subject now?"

"I am."

"Has he done anything peculiar?"

"Like what?"

"Well, like something out of character."

"This kid doesn't *have* any character, so what's *out* of character? He hasn't done anything terribly peculiar or odd, if *that's* what you mean. I'm really kind of busy at the moment..."

"Okay, continue to tail him. Don't let him out of your sight!" Thompson commanded.

"Sure thing, *boss*. Oh hey, while you're not *too* busy, I have a request."

"No."

"No? You don't even know what I'm going to..."

"No."

"I won't help you otherwise," Pierce warned.

"You think this is about *you*?" Thompson chuckled. "This is about *A.I.* getting back at *Serter.* We know you made a deal with Serter for the games...we also know what it means to have you break that deal." Thompson sobered up. "We're *going* to take care of you, and Mary—so don't worry. Just keep an eye and an ear on the Venerates kid. Thompson out."

Pierce walked back into the living room, and unceremoniously threw himself back down into his giant beanbag chair. Pierce winced when he realized that he left his replacement beer in the kitchen.

"So, how did you two meet?" Pol asked, almost fidgeting, trying to get out of the book discussion.

I wonder why Eris is so quiet? Pol thought.

Mary and Pierce smiled at each other as Mary spoke. "We met in Lake Geneva, during a game of *Dozens of Dragons.*"

"So, you're American?" Pol asked, hopefully.

"Heavens, *no*." Mary blew out some smoke. "Pierce is American—or, at least his immediate ancestors were. I'm Canadian, or at least, I was until I immigrated to Silverberg. Very shortly after we moved, I wrote <u>Oedipus Now</u>."

Of course. Pol thought as he sighed. *Always back to the book.*

Pol noticed that Mary was wearing a peculiar charm about her neck.

"What is your necklace of?" Pol asked, studying it.

Pol was looking at Mary's medallion, which bore a triangle juxtaposed with an inverted trefoil.

"Oh." Mary frowned, looking down. "It's the *coniunctio oppositorum*, the unity of opposites–the conjunction of fire and water. Symbolically, it would represent the baptisms, the soul."

Pierce coughed uncomfortably.

"I think *I* may write a book," Pierce said, an edge of sarcasm in his voice.

"Oh *really*," Mary said, sipping her juice. "What's *your* book about?"

"Who knows? Good writing oftentimes is the work of a talented reverse engineer. It figures a line from B to A, and then what A is, what B is, where and how they are, and then how one got to B from A."

Pol shook his head. "I don't get it."

"Don't worry yourself, neither does he." Mary explained. "Keep in mind this sage wisdom is all coming from one who has never written anything longer than a grocery list."

"I guess that makes me a grocery list, after all: *What is the measure of a man, other than what he has written?*" Pierce quoted <u>Oedipus</u> again.

"What about being the most famous gladiator?" Pol offered.

"Gladiator?" Pierce frowned. "There's little glory to simply being a *fighter*... how many gladiators' names are remembered from ancient Rome? Sure, I'm hot today, but I could stand to leave a better legacy.

"How did Mary once put it? '*The ambitious man's novel will be an account of who he is and what meaning (or lack thereof) he has found or given to life.*' You're right about one thing, Pol–I should write about *how* to fight. That is what I know best. *Pierce* Godwin presents <u>How to Fight</u>."

"And how to cheat?" Eris questioned.

"Mary's right, you are *awfully* unmannered. I should kick you out myself, but I'm not going to."

"Why on earth not?" Mary asked, yawning.

"Because I promised her a reward for driving me home. And I like Pol, and they strike me as inseparable."

Eris continued to observe Mary.

"Anyone for food? All this talking has made me hungry." Mary complained.

"I'll help." Pierce got up. "Besides, I have to find some suitable treasure of thanks for these two."

Pierce and Mary disappeared together into the kitchen. As they walked beyond the scope of vision, Pierce scooped Mary up and proceeded to ravish her with affection. Mary, giggling quietly amidst the torrent, removed her necklace and failed to place it on the sill, but rather into the potted plant.

SUNDAY 15th 2066   ⚠   16:02 EST

Jason Serter sat behind his desk and continued to stare at the woman that was sitting directly across from him.

There were subtle truths about Serter's desk that were not common knowledge. For instance, there were angles and messages hidden about the desk to suggest (subconsciously) to anyone on the visiting side of it that they were inferior.

On her very militant-looking uniform, the name patch read *Colonel Ginger*.

Ginger wore unnaturally red hair, and very dark makeup. Overall, she was considerably stunning, although Serter seemed completely aloof to her beauty– she was an underling, and never given more consideration than that.

Having worked alongside Serter long enough to establish trust and start to begin to second-guess him correctly at times, Ginger had put a team on alert in advance, anticipating Jason's wishes.

"I know a team that can kill him inside of 30 minutes." Colonel Ginger said, referring to Pierce Godwin.

Serter frowned.

"This team, lead by Major Ozbourne," Ginger cleared her throat, "Can kill him inside of 25 minutes *and* make it look like an accident."

"Hmmm." Serter pulled a small silver box from his suit pocket. "Now, that would be *truly* impressive. It *would* be nice to go back to my *life* with no further hassles. Here is the *KeyTool* for Pierce's *augmentations...*"

Jason slid a small box across the desk to the woman.

"How do you know *this* is his KeyTool?" Ginger asked while thinking, *how can I get this to Ozbourne in time? ... I don't, I will just have to exceed my estimate.*

"He *gave* it to me." Serter smiled, yet his face seemed to darken. "I used it on him *myself.* He'll know *when* you use it, *who* it was that hurt him."

Ginger saluted and left. Jason smiled, for the first time in a long time.

Jason always wanted to be in the army, but his parents would not stand for it. When he took over the company, he organized it like the military, in appearance and operation.

As Jason started activating imagescreens around his office, he then remembered a promise he made from somewhere in the back of his mind.

SUNDAY 15th 2066 16:20 EST

"This whole experience is so surreal–rock musicians, gladiators, famous authors–I can't believe I'm not on drugs," Pol said to Eris.

"Maybe it's the subliminals,"[19Δ] Pierce theorized, walking back into the room. "They can mess with you a little bit, especially if you're new to Silverberg."

"Wait. What subliminals?" Pol blinked.

"Well, the subliminals in all the mediacasting."

"*What* subliminals?" Pol asked again.

"It *must* have been part of Delivery–er, Processing–although, maybe things have changed over the years. Silverberg puts subliminals in all of the advertising, the music, the mediacast sessions and programs. You're constantly being bombarded by them. For visitors, sometimes they have a little bit of a reaction to it."

"You *know* about this? And you find this to be acceptable?" Pol was disgusted.

"Sure," Pierce shrugged.

Mary nodded, rejoining the trio. "You can access the Mainframe at any point to review exactly what subliminal messages there *are* during whatever interaction. Seriously, look it up sometime. They're all fairly harmless, really. Mostly things like '*brush your teeth,*' and '*tell the truth.*'"

"So...tell me some *truth* about yourself, Pol." Pierce changed his tone.

"Me?" Pol was confused, and slightly worried at Pierce's change in address. "Um, I dunno. I'm here to go to school for a semester. I'm American."

19Δ Subliminals–slang for *Subliminal Messages.* See also Appendix page 306

"Hmm." Pierce held his chin in reflective thought. "And that's it?"

"Yeah, I suppose. I mean, I like music a lot." Pol shot a sidelong glance at Eris, who was not paying attention.

Pierce frowned.

"And bowling."

"Wow. Don't you have *anything* more interesting to say about yourself other than that?" Pierce said, sounding genuinely amazed.

"No, I guess not," Pol shrugged. "I'm not exactly an author or a gladiator... sorry if I'm not interesting enough."

"It's just not really making much sense to me."

Pol looked at Pierce. "What's not?"

Pierce seemed to be having an internal conversation with himself for a moment, when he finally shrugged and started speaking.

"I have been hired to follow you and observe what you are doing." Pierce said, nonchalantly. "It's just funny that you draw such attention–I've been talking with you for *hours*, and you strike me as curiously *un*interesting."

Although Pol couldn't fully understand the dread implications of Pierce's statement, he did have *some* understanding of the severity of the matter.

"Wait. You're following *m-me*?" Pol stammered. "Hired by who?"

"Whom," Mary corrected.

"Axel Industries Internal Security–the most secure and informed intelligence network in the entire world...that's about the sum of it." Pierce concluded.

"I don't understand."

"*I* do." Eris announced, standing up. "Pol, we have to *leave* here."

"Yeah, I think you're right." Pol admitted, standing.

"Sit down," Pierce said, his voice low.

Pol froze.

"Pol, we have to *leave*," Eris stressed.

Pierce stood up. "I don't think *you* completely understand what is going on here, *Eris*. Pol, for a lack of better terms, is my prisoner."

Pierce pointed a hand at Pol. "Now, sit down, and let's keep talking."

Eris looked Pierce up and down for a moment. She seemed to be considering her options, which was mad. Then, having properly sized up the situation and likely having remembered Pierce's performance from earlier, Eris sat down.

"I don't understand," Pol lamented, sitting back down.

"I wouldn't worry yourself too much about it," Mary tried to soothe Pol. "He wouldn't have told you about this if he wasn't on your side."

"I didn't even know I *had* a side." Pol groaned.

The front door tumbled into the apartment violently, carrying with it some of the smoke from the compressive blast charge placed upon it moments before.

Following that, a group of men rushed in–all dressed in visual camouflage, making them next to impossible to perceive.

"Hey!" Pierce roared as he leapt over the furniture and into the fray. "That door was *imported* from England! That was *real wood,* you jerks!"

Pol screamed the most high-pitched cry of his life as he dove behind the couch.

Mary ran back into the kitchen.

Eris jumped to her feet and looked back and forth from Pol's hiding space to Pierce.

The men started firing their concealed weapons wildly about the room, some shots of which *must* have hit Pierce as he landed in front of them. Either his augmentations shielded him from harm, or his adrenaline continued to carry him. Heedless of the volley, Pierce caught up to his intruders.

Pierce grabbed on to the invisible arms of one of the assailants and tore them out of their sockets. The man screamed a sound so dire, that it could only be made in absolute truth and horror. As shock overtook him and he fell to the floor, his teammates rushed to engage Pierce.

Pierce clapped his hands together. Once again, this movement triggered an augmented response–it sent out an electromagnetic wave. The wave would shut down everything within several yards, depending on shielding. This movement would also activate a *biological* enhancement that would reactivate his other augmented systems. Both augmentations were contraband, not part of his KeyTool, and courtesy of Agent Thompson from several years prior.

Everything about the apartment shut down, the light sources went out, and more screaming could be heard as Pierce continued to locate and dismember his enemies.

There came the muffled sound of metal hitting metal as Major Ozbourne slapped Pierce with the ticket bank scant moments before he slapped Pierce across the face with a frying pan.

SUNDAY 15th 2066 16:35 EST

MAINFRAME » ERROR 09 «
MAINFRAME » ERROR 09 «
MAINFRAME » ERROR 09 «

SUNDAY 15th 2066 16:36 EST

When the lights started coming back on, no one noticed the small silver box that was attached to Pierce. Easier to notice was the fact that Pierce lay crumpled in a pile in the middle of the floor.

Now, out of camouflage, two men came up to Pol and pulled him to his feet. Another man, named Ozbourne, came up to regard him.

"Who are you?" Major Ozbourne asked.

"My name is Pol. Pol Venerates," Pol said meekly.

"Who is *that?*" Ozbourne asked, pointing to another body on the floor.

Eris! Pol thought in worry.

"That's Eris..."

Ozbourne nodded toward another of his men, who then went and inspected Eris.

"No life signs," The man reported.

"*No life signs?*" Ozbourne half-grinned. "What do you think this *is*, some kind of *science fiction* show? Are you telling me that she's imaged or not?"

Imaged? Pol thought. *What does that mean?*

The man straightened up. "She seems imaged to me, sir."

"*Seems* imaged or *is* imaged?" Ozbourne barked.

"Senior Major!" Another man said, exiting the kitchen.

"Yes?"

"There's a *woman* in the kitchen, I think it's Mrs. Godwin–she's dead."

"Dead." Ozbourne turned to look back at the pile of Pierce. "Oh well, mission accomplished, we have what we came for."

Ozbourne turned back to regard Pol.

"Hmm. Guess you're coming with us."

Pol just hung there between his two guards.

"And you," Ozbourne said, pointed his sidearm at Eris. "Are too much of a liability at this point, so you need to die or finish dying."

Major Ozbourne shot Eris through the head.

SUNDAY 15th 2066 ⚠ 16:45 EST

"It was Major Ursa Ozbourne of the team I sent to deal with it, sir," Colonel Ginger reported to Jason Serter. "He decided, independently of *my* direction, incidentally, to approach Pierce Godwin in a 'forward fight.' Something to do with '*Not being such a sissy about the whole thing,*' or something to that degree. My sincerest apologies, sir."

"Hmmm. Well, I am *unimpressed* with your inability to deliver exactly what you *promised,* however I am *satisfied with* the results. *Enjoy* your promotion, *General.*"

Ginger could not disguise her smile.

"Major Ozbourne, eh?" Serter chewed thoughtfully on his thumb. "Leave him be for now. I will think on all of this *later*, when I have had a chance to separate my *emotion* from it. For now, let's visit this Mr. *Venerates* when he arrives. I have some *questions* of my own."

SUNDAY 15th 2066 ⚠ 17:07 EST

Agent Thompson kicked back in his chair as he reviewed the unauthorized catalogue of mediacast records from the Godwins' apartment.

Although the public is *well* aware that Silverberg is littered with image banks that are always generating mediacast records (typically for purposes of evidence), only a few AIIS agents know that *many* citizens[20] have had their personal spaces compromised with identical technology so that the AIIS might monitor them inconspicuously and constantly.

Curiously, the AIIS ends up seeing *many* infractions that are not addressed, generally on orders directly from Axel. As to *why* some lawbreakers are dealt with and some are not, one would have to question the motives of Axel himself.

As Agent Director Thompson scrolled the viewpoint through time, he once again could not but help notice an overwhelming strangeness in what he witnessed.

---

[20] Although generally only those with considerable influence, potentially dangerous augmentations, (namely, all meta humans) or have displayed questionable behavior publicly.

He sent the mediacast record to Agent Nelson, who then proceeded to view it.

"That's odd," Nelson remarked.

"What part?" Thompson asked.

Thompson wondered just how much Nelson saw.

"Well, let's see," Nelson stopped the time. "Obviously, this part where the girl gets shot in the head, and then starts crawling away after everyone leaves. Is she Meta? SilverSmith?"

"She's not on *record,*" Thompson answered.

"Not on record? How is that possible?"

"It's *not,*" Thompson said wryly, possibly rolling his eyes at his own comment.

"Hmmm," Nelson thought aloud. "Two impossible occurrences in one day?"

"There's more," Thompson expounded. "Scroll backwards."

Nelson scrolled the viewpoint backwards in time, until the imagescreen flickered completely black.

"Odd."

"Keep going."

Nelson continued scrolling, watching the imagescreen spring back to life. He watched the door fly back into the jamb. He watched Pierce and Mary carry on a conversation, albeit in reverse.

"What am I missing?"

"The Godwins are not just speaking to one another; they are speaking to *other people* in the room...only, *those* people do not show in the mediacast record! Remember how those two men were standing? Like they were restraining someone. Probably Venerates. That woman that was shot? Didn't you notice that she only appeared *after* the blackout?"

"Wait, the same Venerates that I found for Pierce?" Nelson coughed.

Thompson frowned. "Of course, the same."

"Is *he* a Meta?"

Thompson looked at Nelson through his trademark noirglass lenses.

"No, he's not a Meta. Don't be stupid, he's *American.* Any*way...*"

"Let me guess," Nelson chimed. "You have to go report this to the *big guy.*"

"No, I have already discussed this all with Axel." Thompson seemed annoyed. "He says that *your* job is to determine:

Why isn't this woman in the screening before the blackout?

Why does she appear *after* the blackout?

What caused the blackout?

Why can't we access imagescreen records of Venerates?"

"...and the identity of the woman." Nelson supposed.

"No, actually Axel was quite clear in that you should ignore her involvement and existence all together. Something about it being a '*job-endangering enterprise.*'"

Nelson swallowed hard.

Thompson ended the mediacast session.

SUNDAY 15th 2066   19:19 EST

Lieutenant Farnsworth and Officer Smith showed up at the Godwins' apartment only shortly after AIIS Agent Anderson. As Farnsworth walked through the door, he nodded and pointed to Smith his desire for there to be police tape put across the razed portal. Officer Smith rolled his eyes and pulled out the tape.

"So, *now* you're here all right," Farnsworth called to Anderson.

"This investigation..." Began Anderson.

"...is under the exclusive authority of Axel Industries." Farnsworth finished the soliloquy he had heard from Agent Jefferson on several prior occasions.

"So then you already know," Anderson rumbled in his low voice as he looked back at what might be blood on the floor.

Farnsworth edged his way closer. "Here's a novel idea: let's work *together* for once. The SPD *and* the AIIS. You know, in tandem?"

Anderson frowned. "I *could* use your expertise."

Farnsworth almost gagged. He never imagined such a response!

"But this is a dangerous case–people have been imaged, and not without imagination." Anderson concluded.

Officer Smith walked into the room as Farnsworth began his reply.

"*Dangerous?*" Farnsworth mocked. "I'm living in a country that is absolutely doomed. It's only a matter of time before Axel finally pisses off the *whole* world. If I were concerned about danger, I would move elsewhere; likely out into the woods, where men are not so concerned about the color and cut of their clothes."

Dorian shook his head. "He's great at parties."

"Okay, Detective," Anderson continued. "Investigate the disappearance of Pierce Godwin and the murder of Mary Godwin and *nothing more.*" Anderson's tone managed to lower itself further, making the last of what he said almost comical.

Farnsworth and Dorian both smiled.

"What do we have so far?" Farnsworth looked around. "Awful lot of debris in here. Explosion?"

Dorian nodded in agreement.

"Blood on the carpet–looks like point blank against the floor."

"Ignore that," Anderson warned.

Farnsworth scratched his head. The remainder of the investigation of the apartment was relatively quiet. Eventually, Agent Anderson left.

"Right. So much for working in tandem," Farnsworth said, frowning.

"I can't believe you compromised!" Dorian spat. "Since when do *you* listen to Axel Industries' Idiotic Stooges?"

"Since I want to stay on this case," Farnsworth replied. "Something big is going on here, and I want to know about it. *Need* to know. I feel compelled. "

Farnsworth reflected quietly for a moment.

"Besides, I can't quite figure out the puzzle yet...if Godwin was *so* important to A.I., why weren't they at the arena? Now they're *here,* all interested. More to it, though: Anderson did not just kick me out of the room like normal. Maybe it's just a different style than Jefferson, maybe he really needs help."

"Maybe it's a trap," Dorian said disdainfully.

"And here I thought *I* was the one full of doom."

"You are," Dorian agreed with Farnsworth. "Let's just be careful. I know a little something about the AIIS, and I don't care to get too close to them."

"Right. Now, what else?" Farnsworth looked around. "Someone came in here to *get* Pierce Godwin. Who goes after the publicly undisputed most powerful single fighter in the world?"

"Someone big, someone with balls–someone with firepower," Dorian added, looking at the debris.

"Another Meta?" Farnsworth said doubtfully.

"I'll check the Mainframe." Dorian snatched up his credit bank.

"Right. Check the mediacast records and see if you can find something there."

Dorian spent several unenlightening minutes discovering little and occasionally bumping into "*Restricted.*"

"Well, that doesn't help," Farnsworth frowned. "Okay, let's check out Mary Godwin in the kitchen."

Farnsworth proceeded to check out everything in the kitchen while Officer Smith took a multitude of photographs.

"I like the Godwins' choice of decorating," Farnsworth muttered, more to himself.

"You *do?*" Dorian grimaced, looking around. "*I* think it looks like they decorated exclusively from a thrift store. A junky one at that."

"Well, it's *American*. Of course *you* wouldn't appreciate it," The detective clarified. "Just take your pictures."

SUNDAY 15th 2066   21:51 EST

"*Well,*" Jason Serter yawned, back behind his desk. "That *Pol* fellow was *completely* uninteresting. *This* is why I do not speak with the *lower* class. I think I may fall asleep."

Serter motioned to one of his guards. "You! Go get me one of those *energy drinks*. No, I don't care *what* flavor it is."

Serter started touching his imagescreen.

"So Godwin was hired to follow this *Apollo Venerates*. Curious little fellow, yet I'm unimpressed. I wonder what Axel's interest in him is, though. More questions, with more... *immediate* promises." Serter grinned.

Suddenly the imagescreens disappeared or went black, and the lights went out.

SUNDAY 15th 2066   21:53 EST

Pierce's augmentations resumed operation.

His EMW (ElectroMagnetic Wave) must have compromised some central vein in Serter's power grid. Pierce moved quickly while the power around Serter's complex struggled to return.

*This "surprise EMW" is not going to be **much** of a surprise if I keep using it,* Pierce thought.

Pierce tried to subvocalize a connection to the Mainframe without success.

Well, that sucks.

Pierce looked around, his augmentations giving him the unnatural ability to see unhindered in the dark.

Find and grab Mary, and get outta here, Pierce thought as he tore the appendages from his would-be tormentor.

Chapter 3:

Two days ago, life looked very different for Pol.

Delivery

AUGUST *2066 EST*

Fri 13	Sat 14	Sun 15	Mon 16	Tues 17	Wed 18	Thur 19	Fri 20
07:32							

Although it was certainly not moving any *slower*. Pol felt very rushed this morning–likely because he was so busy romanticizing the experience of going to Silverberg that he procrastinated in achieving any actual preparation. *This* morning was a desperate scramble to feel ready *and* be on time.

Over the last few weeks, Pol's friends attempted to persuade him to stay in America, levying all types of rumors and facts that implicated Silverberg in numerous expressions of suspicious and unsavory manners.

Pol's father was undecided as to how he felt about Pol's transitory exodus, which is to say that he never spoke of it–with reasonable exception to the subject of the *cost* of Pol's semester abroad. *That*, he did not fail to vocalize whatsoever. Pol took his father's lack of *other* interest as a clear sign of disapproval.

Just beyond the borders of Silverberg there is a compact, politically neutral hemicircle of land that *further* divides Silverberg from America.

At the American edge of this neutral area, there are small stations located alongside the highways that lead to Silverberg. These stations lay just outside the states of New York, Long Island New York,[21A] New Jersey, and Connecticut. It was at these stations that Americans (or other land traveling foreigners) might seek entrance to the country of Silverberg.

That is, if such a person were armed with the necessary paperwork, authority, and courage to enter.

21A Following the decades of change that resulted from the New Rochelle Disaster, "Long Island New York" officially became the 52nd state of the Union in the year 2039.

Pol was pacing back and forth across the Jersey City station, wondering if Eris was going to arrive or not. He had experienced some embarrassing trouble with operating the exterior door, and was now feeling rather meek and out of place.

A feeling that was only growing as the minutes ticked by.

Eris was supposed to meet him at 7:30, and there was still no word from her.

Pol tried to distract himself by exercising his imaginations about Eris. Really, he welcomed anything that might excuse him from having to constantly monitor himself in the mirroranium walls. The inside of the station was dramatically unadorned: a massive room deliberately devoid of any other decoration.[22Δ]

I wonder where the light comes from, Pol thought, noting the lack of windows.

At 7:44 AM, imagescreens sprang to life, startling Pol, and effectively blocking off any visibility of the center of the room. On the exterior of the central imagescreen "building" could be seen a large, red-lettered word amidst a black background.

ARRIVAL

Klaxons went off as the floor started to shift inconspicuously, hidden behind the imagescreen prism. Barriers rose up out of the floor as a large section mechanically crumbled away betwixt them. Then, some vehicle came up and out of the floor. The imagescreens faded out of existence, revealing the vehicle to Pol.

The side of the pod-vehicle dilated open, showing Eris comfortably sitting back in her seat. Pol walked up to the vehicle as Eris rose up and started to depart.

Eris turned her attention to Pol, smiling slightly with her eyes half open. Pol's heart leapt. *WOW. She looks more awesome than **any** of her pictures!* Pol thought. *But **what is** she wearing?*

Eris was dressed like some kind of provocative anthropomorphic *pink* tiger. Most of her outfit was so skin-tight that it may well have been tattooed or painted on. Her face was contrastingly unpainted, with the exception of having the end of her nose dabbed black.

"Hi," Pol managed.

[22Δ] The "welcome" stations are purposefully so devoid, creating a boastful emphasis of the unfamiliar and alien mirrored landscape of Silverberg. *"Let them wonder at our wonders."*

"Greetings!" Eris waved, smiling stunningly. "Are you coming, or not?"

Pol continued to walk towards the vehicle, overcoming his subconscious stopping. He stepped into the vehicle awkwardly and sat down.

"Why are you dressed like that?" Pol could not stop himself from asking, smiling stupidly the entire time.

"Girls like pink," Eris said, sounding like she was reciting. "It's neurological, arguably evolutional. Western culture embraced gender specific color preferences as far back as the 1920's, but there *is* some considerable data that suggests that regardless of culture, females invariably gravitate toward pink."

"Wait...what?" Pol shook his head. "I mean, why are you dressed like a *tiger*?"

"Does that frighten you?" Eris looked concerned. "I suppose I can change when I get the opportunity."

Pol sat still and looked miserable. This conversation was going all wrong... he didn't want his first meeting with Eris to go so awkwardly!

Eris seemed to read Pol's emotions as though they were written out over his face. When Eris spoke, her voice was thick with concern and understanding.

"I know that this trip is outside of your comfort zone, but don't worry—relax." Eris winked at Pol. "I'll protect you."

Pol smiled, and warmed up all over. He sat down in one of the seats across from Eris.

"Connect to Mainframe," Eris ordered aloud.

An imagescreen opened up inside the vehicle while a disembodied voice spoke the written-out response.

MAINFRAME » SYNCHRONIZING «

MAINFRAME » CONNECTED «

"Relocate Hackensack autotran to Silverberg."

Nothing seemed to change.

"Load Processing Selection Program." Eris said as an imagescreen opened in front of Pol. Pol looked over at the imagescreen. For the display, there were but three buttons, numbered 1 through 3, with the words "land," "sea," and "air" next to them.

"Pol," Eris looked over at him. "As this is your first time going to Silverberg, you are welcome to determine which entrance you would like to arrive at. The autotran cannot fly or hover, so you cannot select option 3."

"But it can move through water?" Pol asked, amazed.

"Certainly."

Pol pressed "1."

Eris looked relieved. "It is said that the underwater entrances to Silverberg are one of the country's most spectacular views, although I am personally satisfied that you chose land, as the sea routes are also considerably longer."

Pol looked around. "Views? I can't see anything outside of the ottotrain."

"Autotran," Eris corrected. "That's because we are still in the tunnel. When we get above ground, you'll see..."

Soon afterward, the autotran went above ground.

Pol could suddenly see *everything,* as if the walls of the vehicle were completely transparent. It was unnerving, and he shrank back into his chair, subconsciously reeling from the wind that he could not feel. Apart from the plush chairs and the imagescreen, Pol could not make out any of the rest of the vehicle.

"This is awful!" Pol remarked, pulling his feet into his chair and looking around.

Every highway that leads into Silverberg passes through an Arch of Triumph. The Arch unmistakably creates a point of regulated access and further solidifies the line of demarcation that separates Silverberg. The Arches themselves are reminiscent of common Silverberg architecture, which is to say that the Arches appear in the center of a mirrored conical prism that is devoid of any engraving or character other than the curious flying buttresses that surround the structures.[23]

As Pol and Eris rode into the Hackensack Arch, Pol began feeling a sense of personal diminution and calm dread as it loomed overheard. A Silverberg police officer watched them pass as the autotran came to rest in an appropriate parking spot.

The officer walked up to the vehicle. "Open up."

The side of the autotran spiraled open.

As Pol and Eris climbed out of the vehicle, Eris explained that the police had authority over the autotran, and that his command would override the passengers'. As Pol and Eris approached the police officer, Eris *also* explained that the officer could not immediately see through the wall of the autotran. On the interior, the Mainframe used image banks and imagescreen technology to make it appear as if the walls were transparent.

---

[23] Also noteworthy is it that all buildings that were and are constructed by Axel Industries (all designs ala Matthias Silverberg) are cylindrical or conical, whereas buildings erected by independent contractors are generally cubes or rectangular prisms.

"I'm a citizen," Eris announced, holding out her credit bank.

The officer tapped his credit bank to hers. He studied the side of his own bank.

"You're clear and free to re-enter Silverberg, citizen."

"Pol." Eris brushed his cheek with her hand. Pol forgot about everything else as he was suddenly overcome with immense joy. "Pol, I have to go now. You will need to follow the officer into Delivery."

"Delivery?"

"Well, it's officially called '*Processing*,' but people typically refer to it in slang as *Delivery*." Eris turned her hands outward in expression.

"What people?" Pol asked.

"Mostly the citizens of Silverberg, although I am confident that there are others." Eris looked Pol over. "Everyone who comes to Silverberg has to go through a 48 hour processing phase in order to be admitted into the country. Once you have been established as a non-threat, you are given permission to continue inward."

"48 Hours...wait, 2 *Days*?" Pol blinked.

"Yes, Silverberg requires that everyone goes through rigorous testing prior to admittance. For everybody's safety. Much needs to be taught to those who are otherwise unfamiliar with Silverberg.

"Established citizens, metahumans, and diplomats are free to come and go, although nobody ever seems to leave the country once they come into it. The term 'Delivery' is a play on the term 'Delivery Room,' like at a hospital. The implication..."

"I get it," Pol said.

"Don't interrupt." Eris scolded. "The implication is that they are being born again into a new life." Eris stepped over to a different vehicle, one that she previously called an "autocar."

"It looks like a car. What's the difference between a car and an autocar?"

"They'll tell you in Delivery. Good luck, Pol. Call me when you're through, and I will be here to pick you up."

"How am I supposed to call you?"

"*Use your credit bank*–they will explain everything in Delivery." Then, Eris' voice took a more sultry tone to it. "I can't wait to see you!"

Pol warmed up all over.

FRIDAY 13th 2066   08:05 EST

"Apollo Vuh, Venerates has just checked into P-Processing," Agent Dodgson announced to his superior, Agent Thompson.

"Excellent, everything is going according to schedule," Director Thompson replied. "*Your* performance is *always* meticulous–top notch. Good man. Now, let me know when he is ready."

FRIDAY 13th 2066   10:07 EST

Pierce Godwin stood before Serter's expansive desk. The two of them exchanged pleasantries formally enough, and then there was an uncomfortable silence–at least, uncomfortable to Pierce, as he could not help but start to fidget.

How did I ever end up in here? Pierce wondered, choosing to momentarily forget the mediacast session he received from Jason a few scant weeks ago.

"Pierce Godwin," Serter began, "I *propose* to save the life of your wife in *exchange* for your own."

"That's odd," Pierce rubbed his chin. "I didn't realize Mary was at any kind of risk."

"Mary is at...*tremendous* risk, from Axel Industries." Serter explained. "Mary is becoming more and more...*undesirable* as a citizen, I think. Her novel, Oedipus Now, is *hardly* flattering to Axel, and thus Silverberg.

"You see, Axel will never settle for outright *upheaval* in his realm. Remember the Antisedition Laws."

"A.I. never..."

"What?" Serter barked. "Never *said* anything? Did you *think* there was some kind of heads-up when *Axel's* will is enforced?"

"I think you're reaching." Pierce grinned, but inside he felt completely knotted up. "What *exactly* are you offering me again, anyway?"

"Aha! I *am* glad you can stay focused! I, of *all* people, can *guarantee* Mary's safety. Further, you should know I spoke with your *doctor*, Pierce. I know about your *stroke*. I *know* about the cardiovascular disease that will be claiming you soon, *anyway*.

"I'm *asking* you to *lose* the match. *Lose* gladiator–die with *valor*, rather than as the *subject* of pity–*and* protect Mary for the rest of her life.

"Serter Company will be around *forever*. Mary's independence and protection guaranteed. She wouldn't have to live in fear of A.I. exerting it's will over her."

*No, just in fear of **Serter Company** exerting **its** will,* Pierce thought as Jason was speaking.

"Think about it: Mary would be *free* to write the truth and pursue her art *without* fear of retaliation! Free of the iron grip of A.I.! Axel will *never* tolerate her pragmatic visceral outcries indefinitely. You *know* how outspoken she is!"

Pierce wondered just *how much* Serter knew about their personal life.

Too much, probably, Pierce thought wryly.

The room remained silent for almost a half an hour, neither man breaking the silence as Pierce thought about the offer long and hard.

*Serter Company **would** be about as powerful an ally as I could get. Maybe A.I. would work with me? No, Serter's right–A.I. will never tolerate Mary long after I am gone. Really, gone or not, they will not. I can see some of the signs of that now, if only between the whispers on the Mainframe.*

*One thing he's right about: I **am** going to be dead soon, anyway. Probably die of a heart attack during the games. Too bad I can't just get a new heart.*

"Alright, I'll do it. On your honor, Serter: you're telling me that Mary will be *well* taken care of? Nothing to worry about, *all* of her needs addressed?"

"Exactly. Of course, if you betray me, I'll make the remainder of your lives *miserable*. I'd like a little insurance, or a token of your sincerity."

"Like what?" Pierce asked.

"Like...your KeyTool."

"I don't exactly carry it *around* with me," Pierce said, frowning.

"Sure you do. We're both warriors, Godwin. If *I* had a KeyTool, it would *never* leave my side, for I would feel worse than dead were it taken."

Pierce handed over the precious silver box that could turn his augmentations off or on against his will.

"Don't get me wrong, I am...*confident* that Michael can beat you, however a little insurance *never* hurt. In addition, I *wouldn't* mind helping Mary pursue her anti-Axel literature as well. See how *everyone* wins?" Serter held up the KeyTool and looked at it with appreciation. "Now, I'm afraid I need a little *demonstration* –in good faith, of *course*."

Pierce winced, anticipating Serter's touch. "If it were about *good faith*, you wouldn't need to test me."

Pierce did *not* carry his KeyTool with him, but he *did* carry an illicit TKT bank, which is what he had begrudgingly extended to Serter.

FRIDAY 13th 2066 ⚠ 10:33 EST

Soon after Pol had properly settled into his transitory living space at the Hackensack Arch, he was put through tests of every sort. Silverberg took a blood sample, a urinalysis, saliva, and fecal specimens. He was measured for physical fitness, mental and emotional competency, vitamin levels, mineral levels, chemical levels, and numerous more instances of cataloging and questioning.

He was asked questions about his diet that were relentless–and then immediately counter-informed about food awareness. In fact, so much of his indoctrination was about food and nutrition that Pol felt that his head was spinning and he may never eat again.

Pol was educated about the laws of Silverberg, the credit bank, imagescreens, history of Silverberg, educational itinerary of the fall semester, autocars, autotrans, the Mainframe, architecture, mirroranium, metahumans (or, augmented human beings), mediacasting, social customs, fashion, industry, foreign policies, domestic policies, business terms, and so many other items that Pol couldn't possibly begin to remember it all.

Some of the tests were genuinely fun–particularly the parts of "Processing" that were deliberately designed to be amusing. It was the periods of these instances that made the process tolerable to Pol.

Pol eventually went to bed, not sure of what time of day it was. All he knew is that he had never been so tired in his entire life. He genuinely missed America, but not more than that, he wanted–*needed*–to sleep.

SATURDAY 14th 2066 ⚠

After he woke, he showered and ate, and was soon whisked away to endure the onslaught of more questions and tests. Pol decided that day 2 of Processing was the worst day.

After a long day, he was thankfully back asleep.

SUNDAY 15th 2066 ⛬ **01:12 EST**

Instead of feeling well rested, however, when Pol awoke next he felt terrible –his head was splitting, his mouth was dry, and he was completely nauseated.

For the first couple of hours of the day, he fumbled his way through his shower and breakfast. Every once in awhile, he would say something that sounded more like mumbled gibberish than any coherent form of language. Left alone, he invariably fell back asleep.

SUNDAY 15th 2066 ⛬ **05:42 EST**

Pol woke anew still feeling slightly tired, but better than when last he was up. After another 20 minutes, it seemed that he finished waking up completely, and was complaining much more clearly.

Pol finally completed "Processing," and was now *officially* welcome in Silverberg. He was given a credit bank, a pinstriped black-and-silver suit, a medium-brimmed hat that complimented the ensemble, and finally a pair of silver shoes.[24]

These may be the ugliest shoes I have ever seen. Pol thought.

Now, 2 days after his arrival, Pol finally walked down the great landing of stairs leading from the Hackensack Arch.

Delivery.

Pol was apparently in some slight discomfort, as he scratched himself and continually tried to straighten his new suit.

He raised his credit bank and commanded, albeit meekly: "Um, please send a message to Eris–tell her that I am ready to be picked up."

Shortly thereafter, Eris arrived in her autocar. With very little to say, she picked up Pol, and drove away towards the great Hub of Silverberg, the *Ace* looming in the background. He didn't know it, but in just a few short hours, Pol would arrive at *Gladiator.*

---

[24] These items being considered fashionable at the time. Reassignment of clothing upon completion of Processing is said to *"allow for easier social acclamation by those not born to this land."*

SUNDAY 15th 2066   07:28 EST

"...Suh, Stop projection," Agent Dodgson commanded his credit bank, which then paused its display of activity. "Th-this is the *last* time we s-see Apollo Venerates. He climbs into the cuh, car, and th-then the autocar never shows up on another ... mediacast record.

Dodgson stood afore the great table that seated his peers. Rarely did the agents actually *meet* in person–a telltale sign that this congregation was anything but light-hearted.

At the far end of the table was their gruff-yet-compassionate boss, Agent Director Thompson. Dodgson genuinely liked Thompson, and subsequently worked hard to please him as a result.

"How is that possible?" Thompson asked, his eyes eternally blocked out by his personal noirglasses.

"It's nuh, not," Dodgson shrugged. "It's impossible."

"Well," Thompson sounded wry. "I hope to hell that is the last time I hear *that* kind of response from anybody! It is *absurd* to say that something is impossible *after* it happens! Don't be idiots about this; professionals have solutions to go along with their problems or else they *are fired.*"

"Oh, I have suh, solutions," Dodgson quickly piped up. "They're only tr, tr, ... hypotheses, however. We think a muh, metahuman capable of ... t-transhuman power is involved. We also hold in suspect ser, certain members of the Hackensack p-processing team. There's more. I need more tuh, time for re-research to confirm any of them."

"How much time?"

"..." Dodgson drew a blank.

Thompson frowned.

"I'll give you as much as I can–I hope you're ready when time is up." Thompson announced to the recording device hidden somewhere about the room. Sessions such as these went directly to Axel, to be perused and weighed.

After the meeting, as Agent Thompson walked down the mirrored hallway towards Axel's office, Agents Nelson and Dodgson conferred in the corridor about comparing notes over lunch later.

"Who *is* this guy?" Nelson asked (referring to Venerates) before returning to his office.

Dodgson shrugged. "Got me. Buh, but Thompson's all buh, bent out of shuh-shape, th-that's for sure."

Nelson frowned.

CHAPTER 3

SUNDAY 15th 2066   07:49 EST

"I thought we were driving to the *Ace*," Pol asked, noticing they were no longer heading towards the great silver mountain, but instead were headed below ground via one of Silverberg's famed spiral highways.

"Nope," Eris responded.

"So, *where* are we going?"

"The Viridian Mare."

"*Where?*"

"It's a club located 20 levels below zero[25Δ] in the AIW hub."

"Ah...ha...and why are we going *there*?" Pol asked, not understanding.

"We're meeting with *The Valentine Relics*."

"The *Who?*"

"Not *The Who*, they're not still around, Pol." Eris wagged her finger. "*The Valentine Relics*. Their music is not even remotely similar in sample. It's curious you would try to project the image of confidence, though. I should think one would want to *say* as *little* as they could about something in which they do not know that much about."

"About *what*? What are you talking about?"

Eris frowned. "The music group–*The Valentine Relics*. I told you. They're my favorite band, and we have a moment to meet them before other business."

"What other business?"

"We're here," Eris said, opening the door.

It took Pol a moment to process that they had stopped moving *and* that he had failed to notice it.

As Pol climbed out, he looked around to realize that they were in some sort of parking garage. Autocars stretched as far as the eye could see (an effect of the mirroranium) and Pol became instantly overwhelmed.

Pol calmed down and opened his eyes after Eris guided him to some kind of elevator. Eris took him inside and commanded that they be deposited on sublevel 20.

"Sorry, I don't know what came over me," Pol apologized.

"It's okay, Pol...I still love ya anyway." Eris said as she winked.

25Δ *Zero* is slang for "ground Level."

When they finally arrived at the Viridian Mare, the party that was *still* going on into the morning from the night before was zealous and proud. Eris was immediately caught up in the action, dancing and spinning her way deeper into the crowd.

Pol frowned slightly and sulked his way inward, around the cloud of people.

SUNDAY 15th 2066   08:01 EST

Pierce finally built up the courage to tell his wife, Mary, about the events of Friday. He kept himself overly busy in preparation for the games, which conveniently allowed him a multitude of excuses to *not* broach the subject. He was wrought with vexation about how to properly present it, knowing Mary would be outraged...but, now he was completely out of time, so he decided that he simply could not be clever about it.

Mary was working on preparing breakfast for the day. As Pierce walked into the front door following his morning run, Mary greeted him from the kitchen with a single shout of true love.

"Shoo-ooze!" She sang.

"Mary, honey, we have something pretty important to discuss."

"Oh, you're right about that," she said knowingly, walking out of the kitchen. "It's about time we had the discussion about leaving beer cans laying about the house again."

Pierce frowned. "No, more than that. I've had an offer, and I have been convinced to take it."

Pierce proceeded to tell Mary about his conversation with Jason Serter.

"...So, I am going to die, but it's for the best of everyone," Pierce concluded.

"The hell you are!" Mary's voice was rising with a note of hysteria. "This's just absurd! Of *course* you're not going to let yourself be killed!" Mary said, matter-of-factly. "Gods, Pierce! I never thought you could be *that* stupid."

"Baby, it's only a matter of time. Heart disea..."

"I don't *care*! I want as much time with you as possible! You're my *husband*."

Mary and Pierce embraced and kissed desperately, as if it were the very last time.

"Muhhumm!" Mary said, into Pierce's chest.

Pierce relaxed his hug. "Sorry about that."

Mary narrowed her eyes. "You always were selfish, and now you've more than completely confirmed it. How *dare* you make that decision without me?"

Mary lit another cigarette, having forgotten she had just lit one moments ago. As she rediscovered the first cigarette, she closed her eyes and put her fingers to her furrowed forehead. Mary took a deep breath, which immediately threw her into a fit of coughing.

"Stop trying to die before me." Pierce said, somewhat sarcastically.

"Stop trying to kill me." Mary smiled and absently lit a third cigarette.

"You're doing that enough on your own."

"Hmmm... I kind of like the back-and-forth of this '*Stop dying, stop killing*' dialogue." Mary said, changing the focus of the subject. "I can use that someday. Not those *exact* words, of course–too bland for my taste." Mary seemed momentarily lost in thought.

Mary suddenly slapped her credit bank, and started a mediacast record to archive some quick notes for a book she will never write.

" '*Desist in your attempts to end yourself!*' The maiden cried, fat tears falling from her reddened eyes. '*I absolutely agree,*' said...the prince. '*I need not pursue my own demise **any** further, for it is by the very sight of your sorrowful face that I am dead already.*'

"The two illicit lovers embraced as if it were their last time. Now, let's see... add some notes about how the maiden has misunderstood the prince's intentions. Add that the prince is usually taciturn and sarcastic, *and* point out how the maiden doesn't realize that is he is actually *insulting* her. That's it. He's using her. He has *been* using her... Now, what is he using her for? I know!..."

As Mary continued to make notes, Pierce walked into the kitchen to get Mary a glass of tea, which she customarily consumed while she was composing.

"Don't forget the lemon!" Mary called.

Pierce smiled.

As Mary composed, mentally, she started imagining her life without Pierce. *Nothing. My life is **nothing** without him. Pierce is sacrificing himself for **me**, which just seems to make me love him more! That man! Oh God, how can I possibly endure this? ... Stop it, Mary, you're an adult, and it's about time you started acting like one.*

Mary turned around to face Pierce, caught his eye, and winked.

Pierce smiled a toothy grin.

Then Mary threw her lit cigarette at him. Pierce dodged and rapidly picked it up off the carpet.

"If you are going to lose the game today, you'll just have to put your extra energy into playing *this* one to win," Mary started laughing, which was the only way to cover up her crying. Calming down, she resumed working.

*"Maidens **rot** when bereft of love,* Prince someone said, as if with complete authority. *Surely, 'tis the duty of ev'ry sad man to assist such lonely ladies by feeding their voracious hunger, so as to stave off their ripening. For, when there is no attempt to stoke this fire, the hearth quickly turns cold and uninviting."*

SUNDAY 15th 2066   09:17 EST

Agent Anderson finished watching his imagescreen, having observed the dialogue that Pierce just had with Mary about Serter's *offer*. Anderson immediately sent a copy of the mediacast record to Agent Thompson.

SUNDAY 15th 2066   09:22 EST

Pol leaned on the railing of the balcony just outside the club, the Viridian Mare. The club was not successful at containing the party that was *still* being thrown by the Valentine Relics.

Pol had felt superfluous for the hour or so that he had been there. Overwhelmed with the crowd, he quietly made his way outside for more breathing room.

This was not exactly his idea as to what his life with Eris would look like when he *got* to Silverberg...but he understood that she was very excited about getting to meet the band.

He looked up now and again to see the true sky between the roadways that spiraled downward from ground level, above. He was having a difficult time reminding himself that he was more than 200 feet underground as the balcony overlooked an expansive chasm that continued much further down.

I wonder how far down it goes, Pol thought to himself.

"Yuh gonna do it?" A male voice called.

Pol turned around. "Do what?"

A young (looking) man with completely blacked out eyes approached Pol. The man was very short, wearing a top hat and tuxedo with the arms and legs torn off. "Jump."

"Jump? I'm not going to *kill* myself...I was just getting some fresh air."

The young man shook his head. "Didunt mean t'kill yerself. I thot mebbie y'ad some kine-a augmens that 'llowed you to glide down or sunnin..." He looked out, over the railing. "Thaddud be *so* dead."

The man's quick speech, lack of enunciation, and unfamiliar accent made it difficult for Pol to understand him, although after a brief delay in time, the words somehow managed to unscramble themselves in Pol's head.

"Oh." Pol thought he sounded stupid and plain, but he had no idea how else to respond to the man. He held out his hand, and the short man shook it in appreciation.

"Name's *Todd*, but mose peeps call me *Gob*, witchiz short fer *Goblin*, witchiz short've *Todd Gibson*. That, and onna counta bein so." Gob closed his one eye, while looking at Pol between his thumb and index finger with the open one. "I play bass furrah 'relics." Gob smiled and stretched out his hand in gesture of handshake.

Pol shrugged and shook Gob's hand in return, again.

"I'm Pol. From America. I just got through Delivery this morning."

"Big fannuh tha 'relics, uh?"

"Um, no." Pol could feel himself blush. "I actually haven't heard of you guys before. I'm more into freedom rock and reduxtrial, maybe a bit of 50's skalternapop. I'm actually here with a friend...she's the fan."

"Oh." Gob echoed Pol's earlier comment.

There followed a brief and awkward moment when the two men had no idea what to say to one another.

"Mmmm!" Gob started rummaging through the pockets of his splintered tuxedo. "Herret is." He pulled his credit bank out, and proceeded to tap it's sides rapidly. "Issus'r bess song, call'd 'Down widdah queen.' I wancha tuh relly lissen."

Gob's credit bank started playing music in response to his manic tapping. The song began with the sound of what may have been a church organ, playing some type of meticulous, classical rhythm. The organ music was soon accompanied with a very deliberate drumbeat, which continued to gain in momentum and presence until the organ music was interrupted completely with heavy electric guitar chords, which transformed the song from reverent and disciplined to emotional and rapid. Eventually a woman's voice broke through the music, spouting out lyrics in tandem with the newly established beat.

Faith over fact, you're always unseen
Your politics: boring, trite, obscene
Tired of trading life for a dream?
Water to wine? So where's my canteen?
I'm nursing a child who cannot wean
Milk without curd, yet all of the cream
I could become the *new* Magdalene
Basking in glory, looking quite preen
Move over Christ, make way for Christine
A better measure, *my* new regime
So dirty, your version. Mine, pristine
Stop talking about it! Let's begin:

The God, The Man, Misspoken Doctrine
Teaching you how to be a latrine
Don't settle for story, plot, or scheme!
Don't wait for the Deus Ex Machine!
NOW
Raise up your fists, yell Down with the Queen!
Down with the Queen!
Raise up your fists, yell Down with the Queen!

(Organ Solo)

Chung might argue Monican or Breen;
Kubrick and Clark suggested something
Like Ellison's mouth which cannot scream
Like Gibson, punk, with none of the steam
Will without thought, created the lien
Dressings of blue, yellow, red, and green
Without the panes, yet always a screen
Backgrounds plenty, all part of the theme
Prick your finger and we'll splice the gene
No more *arousal, appendix, spleen...*
Presenting the way it *should* have been:
Without an end, yet always a mean

The God, The Man, Misspoken Doctrine
Teaching you how to be a latrine
Don't settle for story, plot, or scheme!
Don't wait for the Deus Ex Machine!
NOW
Raise up your fists, yell Down with the Queen!
Down with the Queen!
Raise up your fists, yell Down with the Queen!

- [Daniel Strasel] -

As the credit bank finally stopped playing the song, Pol met Gob's expectant gaze. He was not entirely sure of how to react. The fact of the matter was that he didn't like the song much, whatsoever.

Pol decided on employing tact. "Like I said, I'm not really much into music."
Gob shook his head in frustration. "Y'Didun evun like tha *sound*? Music zah mose honess exprezzion of tha *soul*." Gob waved his arms about, illustrating his dialogue. "Naht juzz about lyrics er wutnot, but about *emoshun*. Music ken inspire men tuh *greatnezz*. Music ken built or destroy *nashions*. Y'Didun feel *any* emoshun? *Nothin'?*."

Pol looked at Gob with a blank expression.

"Wut? Yuh gittit or not? I needuh thinken cap to ess plain it?'
Pol sighed. "I have no idea what you just said."
"Nobody *ever* knows what he's saying." Another man's voice called out. "Gob! Get in 'ere, now! We're about to do more shots!"
Gob, with a final shrug, turned and started hustling back towards the party. "Don' wanna miss shoz, y'know."

Eventually, Eris found and sauntered up to Pol. She took his arm in her own, and asked how he was doing, and whether he was ready to leave.
Pol smiled, for the first time in hours. "What's a thinking cap?"
Eris keyed up her credit bank in response.

An imagescreen sprang to life. As the commercial went on, it continuously presented images that further suggested the unlimited potential of the advertisement.

A very energetic man's voice spoke rapidly, mirroring the text that printed out on the screen.

PUT ON YOUR THINKING CAP

Communicate with friends, family, associates -
Instantly, anytime, anywhere!

Do you have a *lot* to say, but only a *little* time to say it in?
Do you have trouble expressing yourself because you can't find the right words?
Are your concepts too
advanced
to entertain the attention of the common man?

Thinking Caps solve all of these problems, and many more!   Thinking Caps create an intimate brain-to-brain connection that stimulates receptor areas of the brain at the speed of thought! Take an entire college course in the span of minutes! Know anything and everything you ever needed to know! Establish a more intimate contact with your spouse than was ever previously possible!

The imagescreen text melted away to be replaced with a very serious looking man, dressed in professional and conservative clothing - not unlike Pol's pinstriped silver and black suit. He wore a silver fedora. The ambient background music faded out, leaving only the sound of the man speaking.

"Thinking Caps have gotten a lot of negative reviews over the last couple years, with complaints about compatibility to rumors of brain damage. With the new Thinking Cap 2.0, many of these possible side effects have completely disappeared.

"Buy a Thinking Cap with confidence! Check out our Mainframe store for LIVE testimonials from actual users - our confidence is so high; please, interact for *free*. Put your doubts at rest, and step into the next stage of the communication renaissance! Those of you that act within the next 24 hours will get a *second* Thinking Cap for only *half* the price!"

"Wow," Pol said, clearly impressed.

"Don't get *too* excited," Eris said, her voice low. "The 2.0 is no better than the prior model in regards to possible side effects. The math behind the thinking cap is sound enough...it's that the human brain, *unaugmented,* is simply not suited for that kind of information transference. *Anyone* that uses a Thinking Cap will have brain damage or worse."[26Δ]

"Oh." *Oh? Boy, do I sound like an idiot, and often.* Pol thought.
"Well, it's time to go." Eris started sprinting away.
"Wait. Where are we going?" Pol asked, picking up his own pace to match hers.
"The *games*. We're going to go see *Gladiator.* In *person*." Eris was smiling ear to ear.
"Oh."

Eris turned off the exterior view while they rode in her autocar. Pol, already feeling overwhelmed from the events of the day, took a small nap on the way to the arena. When Eris roused him from his slumber, she immediately set a quick pace up toward the arena from the massive subterranean parking garage.

Pol hated jogging.

SUNDAY 15th 2066 Δ **10:42 EST**

Axel finished watching the mediacast record from a few hours ago, which showed Eris retrieving Pol at the Hackensack Arch. This was the *last* mediacast session that could be accessed from the Mainframe in regards to Apollo Venerates.

"Mainframe, establish a private mediacast session with Dr. Manuel Phoebus."
The room came to life around Axel. Imagescreen technology suddenly gave the appearance that Axel was suspended in the center of a huge orb of the universe, staring at a two dimensional display of Dr. Phoebus, who appeared visibly shaken at the interruption.
"Sir!" Phoebus quivered slightly before he mastered himself with an abrupt and loud clearing of his throat. "How may I be of service?"
The black shape of Axel walked to and fro. With a few motions of his hand, he silently ordered the mediacast record to display for the doctor.

[26Δ] It is noteworthy to mention that this comment is not statistically sound. By record, only 6% of actual Thinking Cap users have been diagnosed with resultant brain damage. Also noteworthy in support of the argument; this percentage has been comprised from data taken exclusively from subjects that were unaugmented in *any* other way.

"Dr. Phoebus...*dare* I ask who it was that I just saw on this record?"

Phoebus examined the image and heaved a sigh of relief.

"Well, it's *not* Apollo Venerates, if *that's* what you're asking. He is safe and sound right here." Phoebus motioned with his thumb, pointing over his shoulder.

Axel's silhouetted image did not betray any change. "Very good, doctor. Now, come up to my office, personally, so that we might discuss this...*Eris.* "

With that, Axel ended the mediacast session.

SUNDAY 15th 2066   10:45 EST

On the concourse leading up to the Silverberg Arena, Pol was telling Eris about his interaction with the Valentine Relics' bass player, Gob.

"I really couldn't understand *much* of what he was saying, but I *did* get to hear some of the music–I liked what I heard. Maybe you have..." Pol said, trying to warm up to Eris by displaying affection for her music group.

Internally, however, Eris concluded that she needed to get **away**– at least for the moment. Other items needed attending to, and now there were other factors to consider. She needed a distraction. Now.

"People like dialogue," Eris interrupted, "Which is why I try and keep all of *my* dialogue relevant and interesting..."

Chapter 4:

Working the Numbers

AUGUST *2066 EST*

Fri 13	Sat 14	Sun 15	Mon 16	Tues 17	Wed 18	Thur 19	Fri 20
		21:55					

The lights at the SerterCo East building had gone out a few minutes ago, leaving Pol miserable, restrained, and blind as well.

Pol could not bring himself to stop sobbing. He was not ashamed of his behavior, so much as he was submitting to the sense of being constantly overwhelmed. The release of emotion was helping him to deal with his current situation, not that he had any sense of control over it.

Pol winced slightly when his bruised fingertips brushed against his face in an effort to clear his eyes.

Earlier, when Serter had finally stopped questioning Pol, certain promises of *more* physical pain were implied for any subsequent trips Jason made to ask more questions.

When the lights returned, Pol was visably shaken and scared.

The man in the lab coat across the room continued to read his credit bank's display, and ate his sandwich as if there were nobody else in the room with him. "Private Shutka" was the name badge he wore. He had been the administrator of Pol's punishment at Serter's command, although he had originally appeared to Pol as non-threatening.

*Oh, God, how did my life turn into **this**?* Pol thought in misery. *Why did I ever come here? I **never** should have come to Silverberg, just as everyone said. I have to get home. Everyone I know here is dead. I **hate** it here. I **hate** it here. That man, with his questions:*

WHY WON'T HE JUST LEAVE ME ALONE?[27△]

Pol started sobbing more vociferously as there came a heavy knock at the door.

"что...?" Shutka asked nobody in particular. He was already slightly on edge because of the power outage. He stood up and walked over toward the door, thinking to access the imagescreen view of the hallway outside.

On the other side of the door, Pierce held the hallway guard in such a way as to puppeteer the tapping of his credit bank to the door reader. With Pierce's help, the guard unconsciously selected "Open" from the options that populated on the imagescreen.

Pierce threw the guard over his shoulder, slamming him into the wall with enough strength to kill, or at least permanently damage him. [28△]

As the doorway opened, Pierce stood in front of the surprised Private Shutka, towering over him by nearly a foot. Without hesitation, Pierce punched Shutka so quickly and forcefully that his head tore away from its body. Pierce stopped his momentum long enough to appreciate the damage he had caused.

"I *thought* I heard crying in here," Pierce said, smiling. "How incredible that you're even still alive!"

Pierce rushed across the room and effortlessly freed Pol of his restraints.

"Okay, *now* we get Mary and get out of here."

"Mary's *imaged*," Pol said, fumbling the word and sobering up slightly. "Killed in the attack...I heard one of the men say so at the apartment. Until now, I thought you were as well."

Apart from the reflex in his cheeks from clenching his teeth, Pierce was as still as a statue.

I'll be back for you, Serter. Pierce thought. "In that case, it's time to leave." Speaking subvocally, he attempted to connect to the Mainframe.

MAINFRAME » SYNCHRONIZING«

[27△] Even though Pol felt that Serter had both hurt and wronged him with his vicious interrogation, Serter felt that he let Pol off without harm. The reality of it was that Serter was unaccustomed to interrogating someone with such *little* backbone, and so did not administer any of his regular forms of punishment.

[28△] ...assuming either of these were not already true before he collided with the wall.

MAINFRAME » CONNECTION NOT AVAILABLE «

Well, that's a new one, Pierce thought in melancholy.

Pierce grabbed Pol, as if he were nothing more than a cardboard cutout, and ran out of the room. He moved through the hallways with the singular motive of exiting the building.

As Pierce discovered a route leading out of the building, a squad of guards wearing optical camouflage engaged him. Pierce quickly dispelled his antagonists although Pol suffered a wound to his right shoulder, which soon caused him to lose consciousness.

Pierce took a moment to consider the situation. He field dressed Pol's wound, and covered the two of them in the guards' optical camouflage. He considered writing Serter a threatening note with the blood of the fallen guards, but decided that the effort was both a waste of time and too melodramatic. *I'm sure he already knows.*

Pierce grabbed Pol, a bit more tenderly this time, and ran out of the building. All-but-invisible, he ran across the mirrored, suspended roadway that lead from the building. He considered trying to call Thompson again, but decided that he needed some more time to deliberate the situation.

Tired, wounded, grief-stricken, and annoyed; Pierce spied a landing close enough to jump onto without causing himself (or Pol) more damage. He jumped down, landing to roadway to landing again. He started making his way into the bowels of the Eastern hub.[29Δ]

Eventually he was deep enough to satisfy his mental assessment of where they might be safest, and made his way into the closest building, which happened to house a small mall. He located an air vent large enough to crawl into, and carefully inserted himself and Pol inside. Having secured the cover grate as best as he could manage from the inside, Pierce pushed his companion deeper into the duct.

Finally, feeling as if he had a moment to rest, Pierce fell asleep next to Pol.

[29Δ] All five "cities" in Silverberg have descendant levels. Roadways and pathways spiral up and around one another as well as about various semi-conical buildings and platforms. Although the lower levels of the hubs of Silverberg are considered by the citizens as more dangerous and "darker" than the above ground, statistics do not reflect this opinion.

 - [God, Man, and The Machine] -

SUNDAY 15th 2066   23:05 EST

Jason Serter scowled at the image of General Ginger.

"Oh, you'll *find* him, alright..." Serter meticulously pronounced every word, as always. "Or you'll *find* yourself the victim of a rogue *lobotomy,* wandering about in a *third-world* country, such as *America,* begging for *soup* door to *door.*"

Although the literal threat was absurd, Ginger was confident that Serter would destroy her life in an equivocal manner.

"Sir, may I make a suggestion?"
"No. *Your* ideas are next to *worthless,* and if you have to *ask* my opinion or permission about something, it must be *doubly* so. Now go do your *job*...and if you *fail,* be prepared to shoulder the consequences."

MONDAY 16th 2066   08:44 EST

Windows that painted the room with the amber light of morning lined the left hand wall of the Silverberg Central Police Department. Several men, all in formal black and silver uniforms [30] sat around a single, redheaded young man. The man waved his arms about dramatically, as if to visually italicize his verbal attitude. He was speaking to the rest of the officers on his quality of life at home, which was apparently both tedious and comical.

As if in dark reflection, Detective Lieutenant Jeremiah Leonard Farnsworth sat rigidly at his desk, locked in what must be an unwanted mediacast session as he spoke solemnly into his credit bank.
As the noise from the other room continued to climb, Farnsworth ended his credit bank conversation. He rose from his desk, several joints audibly protesting the movement. When he opened the door to his office, an explosion of laughter greeted him.

"Alright, that'll be enough of that." Farnsworth's thick American accent betraying his heritage. "Officer Smith, if I might trouble you for a word?"
"Did you just say '*trouble you for a word*'?" Dorian grinned. "*That* is why you're so loveable. Where *do* you find your expressions?"

---

[30] Visiting SNPD officers.

"I meant sometime *today*, Mr. Smith."

The men scattered slowly, a couple of them patting the red haired man on the shoulders and laughing still.

"Catch you later, Dorian," An officer called.

"You know, it *is* a bit frustrating that everyone leaves the room when I come in," Farnsworth noted.

"That's because you're a terrible bore," Dorian chided. "And besides, you only ever have bad news."

Dorian lit a cigarette and continued. "So, you were talking to the Captain... What's the heavy word today? What doom is there?"

Farnsworth walked over to him. "The sick day provision for the department has been altered. From this day forward, officers who are sick must seek immediate medical attention at the nearest Silverberg hospital. Officers who are found to be in sufficient health to work will be summarily suspended, and subject to an immediate review, pending termination.

Dorian sighed. "Oh, *why* do I ask?"

"Right. Let's get down to business and start working the numbers on the Godwin case."

Dorian sobered up. "Okay, here's what I have: Someone destroyed the entrance to the Godwin's apartment–someone who has considerable connections in order to afford imagescreen or outright visual camouflage. Someone who is not afraid to confront the most powerful single soul in Silverberg."

"Someone who lost in the last match of *Gladiator*," Farnsworth mumbled.

"One of the blood samples taken from the living area carpet was not found in the Mainframe registry. In itself, this should not be possible. AIIS ordered us not to investigate the blood sample, but we did anyway."

"Which is completely stupid." Farnsworth looked red. "Stop putting us in jeopardy by doing things that attract unwanted attention!"

Dorian rolled his eyes and continued. "Two *other* blood samples found in the apartment indicate the presence of at least 2 other men; Antonio Ortiz Morales and Estevan Valdez Delgado, both former members of the Dirección Federal de Seguridad–an intelligence agency operating in Mexico.

"Morales and Delgado *both* moved to Silverberg in 2059 and are listed in the Mainframe registry as cooks at a *Silver Burger* restaurant located in the AIE hub."

"Those are some talented cooks!" Farnsworth whistled.

"Clearly their reasons for coming to Silverberg transcend simply cooking. Neither body was found at the scene, although the considerable amounts of blood recovered implicate that both individuals are likely deceased."

"Right. *All* the names we have are already imaged. Continue." Farnsworth pulled his hat over his eyes. "I'm in the middle of my doom, if you don't mind. Please, continue."

"Well, no–the Mainframe says Pierce is alive but his location is somehow unrecognizable." Dorian shrugged. "We know via mediacast record that Pierce arrives home after the games. But we also know that he never leaves. Again, according to mediacast record. The paradox is that Pierce's body is nowhere to be found.

"Mary Godwin's imaged and the *only* body on the scene. According to the coroner's report, Mary was killed by strangulation and broken neck rather than by a weapon...in essence, someone *deliberately* killed her."

"As opposed to *accidentally?*" Farnsworth scoffed. "Are you implying that someone who has been imaged as a result of yesterday's assault *is* so because of an *accident?*"

"You truly are depressing, sir. Two of the pairs of shoes found by the door do not fit the Godwins, Delgado, or Morales, implying there may have been two other people present at the time of the attack. They contain evidence of a blast from an RDX based explosive that coincides with the explosive used on the door.

"One pair of shoes is clearly of feminine persuasion, although too small to belong to Mary Godwin. The other set of shoes are silver in color, and must belong to a smaller man than Pierce, who also has no proper sense of taste."

"Right. At least you didn't show up *completely* empty handed." Farnsworth remarked.

"Empty handed? In what way am I empty handed at all?"

"Do I see donuts? Do you have coffee? Okay, then."

Dorian frowned.

"Right." Farnsworth cleared his throat. "Very impressive homework. Of course, now that we have the facts, what are your opinions?"

"Let's see," Dorian leaned back, cradling his chin in his hand. "I think you're a coward, *particularly* when it comes to A.I. Of course, I think you're afraid of people in general, and to compensate you've invented your speech mannerisms after actors from ancient mediacast records. You need to throw away that belt. Other than that, I think you're a pretty stand-up kind of guy."

"...I *meant* about the Godwin case."

Dorian grinned. "I think that someone in *Serter Company* ordered the hit on Pierce. There's an awful lot of money wrapped up in there. Maybe Serter himself. Serter Company owns the *Gladiator* show; it *is* public that they owned Vangard.

"Oh, and there was some kind of drama at the SerterCo building last night... no known meta involvement, thus no call to you or me. I have friends, however, who informed me anyway. My intuition tells me that the incidents are related.

"I think that *all* of the missing persons from the Godwins' apartment were taken out in the same visual/optical camouflage they used to get in. Delgado and Morales must have been augmented, otherwise why bother taking their bodies from the scene? Whatever they had on them must have implicated whoever is directly behind this.

"I think the non-registered blood must be a plant to confound the case. Both for A.I. and for us–something to get us to waste our time and resources investigating. Whoever hit the Godwins must want to distract us from noticing something else."

"Like what?"

"Well, I have a feeling that *Mary* may have been the primary target. Although at first it seems that the force of the attack points towards Pierce, it is entirely possible that such extreme force was used simply to make sure that Pierce was distracted from the assault against Mary.

"As you know, Mary Godwin was a very celebrated writer. Her literature was clearly very pragmatic, if only determined by the overwhelming response it has generated about the Mainframe. Inspired, *I* bought a copy of <u>Oedipus Now</u> this morning. I will be reading it *if* I ever get any time off again."

Dorian shot a disgruntled look at Farnsworth between breaths.

"The shoes are legitimately confusing. Mediacast records from yesterday back through the last week do not show the Godwins as having had guests. So, unless their last guests forgot their shoes when they left, someone else was there at the time of the blast, but beyond that I have no other inclination about their relevance whatsoever."

Realizing Dorian had concluded, Farnsworth took his hat off.

"Right. I like where you're going with thinking that Mary was the primary target, it shows you're thinking outside the box...but I disagree. I think Mary is just collateral damage. If someone wanted Mary dead, they wouldn't have to go through with all *that* trouble to do it.

"I also disagree with your dismissal of the unregistered blood. Anderson specifically told us to leave it alone, so there must be something there. I cannot help but feel that it is critically important. We need to continue to put energy into solving that particular mystery.

"From the lowest to the highest, *everyone* is greedy for gain. Serter Company may have its hands in this, but I think that Axel Industries is *just* as involved, somehow. We need to be careful."

Dorian rolled his eyes.

"At *Gladiator,* I couldn't even keep their attention. At the apartment, they couldn't appreciate my help any more. In the past, when AIIS has swooped in to deal with meta infractions and incidents, they have *always* been overly frustrating and downright annoying.

"Right. Now, maybe that's just the difference between Agents Jefferson and Anderson, or maybe it's something else…something nefarious, underhanded. I suspect everyone–from the worker to the owner, everyone deals falsely."

"Hmmm," Dorian sighed. "You sound paranoid, not discerning."

"It might do you well to model yourself more like me," Farnsworth recommended. "*My* methods and intuitions have made me very successful."

"I suppose I can't argue that."

"Right. Now, let's start looking backwards. Let's see what Pierce and Mary have been up to for the last few weeks. Let's see where they were going, who they were seeing, what they were doing. Why did Pierce decide to go back into gladiatorial combat after a decade of retirement? What *else* did Mary write? Did they have anyone that hated them? Any connections with SerterCo or AI? What has Pierce been doing during his retirement?

"How easy would it be to smuggle blood into Silverberg? How easy would it be to get your hands on a RDX based explosive? What the hell is an RDX based explosive, *anyway*? What kind of camouflage are we talking about here? How expensive is *that*? What kind of ordinance was used by the assailants in the Godwins' apartment? How much does that cost, too.

"Let's look at the mediacast record from the games again. Maybe there's something we missed the first time around. Maybe something before or after the fight as well. Let's look at the other matches, maybe there's something there, too.

"Let's see what else we can find out about this Delgado and Morales *before* they came to Silverberg. *Why* did they come to Silverberg? Surely the Silver Burger Restaurant chain is not looking for international recruits. Who owns the Silver Burger? Who owns the people that own the Silver Burger?"

Farnsworth hooked his thumbs through the old, weatherworn belt that he was always wearing. "Oh, and try not to be too obvious with some of your inquiries–we don't need any more attention from AI."

Dorian rolled his eyes and finished scribbling notes on his imagescreen. He reached for his credit bank to start opening mediacast sessions with other officers.

MONDAY 16th 2066   11:17 EST

"Where *are* we?" Pol asked, waking up.

"Ventilation duct," came Pierce's voice, waxing metallic.

"Ow." Pol rubbed his shoulder. "OW!"

"Well, stop touching it, you idiot."

Pol lay still in his misery.

Pierce propped himself up on his arms. "And don't be such a ninny, either. Look, we've got to figure out *why* A.I. is after you, cause I'm getting a little tired of feeling like I am being pushed around like a pawn. I need some answers. I've been working the numbers on this for hours and they're not adding up. You need to start being honest with me."

"Honest with you?" Pol was aghast. "All I have *been* is honest with you. I have no idea what you think I need to tell you. You sound like *him*. I didn't know what *that man* was after me about, either. He was asking me *all* kinds of questions–although mostly about *you*."

"Who?"

"A man named Serter."

"I *know* why *he's* involved. I need to know why *you're* so interesting to *A.I.* Okay, let's start at the beginning. Tell me your story."

"I don't *have* a story," Pol said with no small tone of melancholy.

"Sure you do. Start at the beginning. Start with being born, if you need a reference point."

"Um, well I was born on January 1, 2047."

Silence.

"*Where* were you born? C'mon, Pol, *Talk* to me. I need to get to know you."

"I was born in Boston." Pol hesitated, and then just started saying everything that was coming to his mind. "As a young child, I remember being very happy. I made friends easily, and people seemed to genuinely like me. I always liked super heroes, police officers, and politics.

"When I was thirteen, Dad insisted I start attending a private school. I did not make as many friends there and usually felt ostracized. Most of the kids had very notable family lines, and mine was not so notable–but my dad *did* make the family name respectable as the United States Congressman who drafted the Euro-Amero Lateral Exchange and Trade Accord."

"The what?"

"The EALETA is basically a trade bloc between the United States, Canada, Germany, United Kingdom, Iceland, and a buncha other European countries."

"A trade bloc?" Pierce asked, confused.

"It's an agreement where tariffs are reduced or inapplicable between the governments involved." Pol felt smart for a moment, which gave him further verbal momentum. "Although there was considerable opposition to the Act, it has proven to be a great stimulant for the American economy. I suppose it really worked out well for everyone involved." Pol said, reflecting his thoughts.

"Wait a second," Pierce interrupted. "Doesn't the LPCTA or whatever Act put America in a more hostile position with Silverberg?"

"Um, I dunno." Pol admitted. "I don't see how it affects Silverberg at all."

"Well, doesn't it unify all the countries surrounding Silverberg?"

"No, it just makes the trading of commodities between them easier."

"...Which would give them a considerable advantage against Silverberg if Silverberg is not part of the pact."

Pol shrugged. "Ow. I *suppose*. I don't see it as hostile; maybe less than friendly towards Silverberg. Silverberg practically rules the world, what does it care about America? I have just arrived, and I'll tell you that the technology is unlike *anything* anywhere else. Like, I had no idea that you are *this* far advanced. Trade bloc or no, Silverberg shouldn't feel *threatened*."

"Alright, enough of the political talk." Pierce made a mental note, but otherwise dismissed the tangent. "Let's get back to *you*."

"Me. Okay. Let's see. Oh yeah, so I went off to a private school, where I met my best friend, Dorothy Liddell–but she moved to Kansas a couple years ago...I haven't really made a close friend apart from Eris since."

"How did you meet Eris?"

"Oh, we met in a chatroom. On the Arpanet.[31△]"

"And you're *both* coming to Silverberg as exchange students? I don't buy that."

"No, not both. Eris lives in Silverberg."

"You mean she's *from* Silverberg? And you both met in chat, on the *Arpanet?*" Pierce shook his head. No self-respecting Silverbergite would *ever* go to the Arpanet...not when they have access to the Mainframe."

[31△] The Arpanet became household global in 1982, securing its place in history. People all over the world interact via the Arpanet still in 2066. Everywhere except Silverberg. Silverbergites rely all-but-exclusively on the Mainframe. The Axel Industries Mainframe can interact with the Arpanet, however the Arpanet *cannot* interact with the Mainframe.

"She said she was working on studying different cultures, and had settled on the United States as her initial field of study."

"Hmm. Okay, go on."

"Well, anyway," Pol started to think again. "Eris and I spent a great deal of time messaging back and forth. Time at home was getting more and more...tense...as my father and I were disagreeing on more and more subjects. I decided to attend a college in Illinois, to get some distance away from him. I wanted to *be* something *other*."

"Such as?"

"Well, he felt that I should become a politician, *I* felt that I should become a lawyer."

"So you're studying Silverberg law to become a lawyer in America?"

"No, I didn't do too well in law school. I switched my focus from law to law enforcement. I'm here to study law enforcement techniques, if I don't fail out.

"Anyway, I had to transfer to a law school back in Boston, and times at home were worse. Dad was always letting me know how I was letting him and the family name down. I let him know that I was in disapproval of the government that he worked for. Instead of a politician, I simply became political. Our arguments started getting more and more circular, and Eris' suggestion that I come to Silverberg started to appear more and more tempting."

"Sounds like you may need to Apollo-gize to your dad," Pierce chuckled.

"Yuck. How long have you been thinking that one up?"

Despite the bad pun and the bleak situation, Pol was starting to feel at ease again. "Since Thompson told me about you in the first place. So wait, *Eris* suggested you come to Silverberg?"

"Yeah, she told me that I could get involved with an exchange program."

"Now I remember! You said something to that degree at the apartment..." Pierce trailed off as his head rushed with memories of Mary. *Mary!* Pierce fought as his feelings sought to overtake him. He pushed thoughts of Mary deep into the dark side of his heart. Pierce fought it all back, but the conversation came to a clear standstill–and rather suddenly. Pol waited, but eventually continued to recite his own tale.

Pierce subvocally accessed the Mainframe and started researching Silverberg's foreign exchange program while Pol resumed speaking of his life.

As Pol droned on about meeting Eris at the Jersey City Station and *Delivery*, Pierce discovered that Silverberg *did* have a foreign exchange program...although it was not available to anyone that had less-than-exemplary grades. Pol's account of his academic prowess did not fit the descriptors.

"Alright, hold up," Pierce interrupted. "Tell me more about Eris, now."

"Eris? Well, let's see. In her correspondence over the last couple of years, she has been..." Pol tried to think of the proper words. "Wonderful. Perfect. I mean, she's gorgeous, into comic books, knows an incredible amount about music. She's very intelligent, sympathetic, witty, a great listener. She has all kinds of ideas on how to make the world a better place.

"At least, this is how she seemed in her emails and chat. When I met her in real life, she seems more...distracted, I guess. She doesn't seem completely involved in her conversations, so she doesn't seem to understand what's being said. She seems full of herself, and has a comment to make about everything. She's not so much a good listener as she is a good interrupter.

"She's very full of energy, and really pretty–although she's almost...whorish... in her choice of clothing or *costume* or whatever. If it weren't for her complete lack of interest in acting sexual, I would make the full assumption. Of course, most women in Silverberg seem to dress a bit...conspicuously–especially compared with Americans. Well, I mean, not Mary, she was dressed–"

"Don't worry about how Mary dressed," Pierce winced emotionally. "Just stay on the topic. So, unless I am missing something, you came to Silverberg almost exclusively in the hopes of dating Eris."

"*No,*" Pol lied. He started to adjust himself to get more comfortable, although when he moved his shoulder again he cried out louder than the previous couple of occasions.

"Serves you right, at least for lying." Pierce said, proud of his personal deduction.

"Why in the world are we in a ventilation shaft, anyway?"

"Silverberg has monitoring points everywhere. I figure we are less likely to be found or observed here than outside. That is, if you don't yell so much as to give away our position."

Pol frowned.

"Well, that, and I can only assume that Serter's after me, or you, or both of us –and if *either* of the big dogs are after you, then they both are. One way or another, we're hiding until we can figure out where to go that will be safe."

Time grew quiet after that last comment by Pierce. A melancholy stillness unfolded as both inhabitants of the duct started mentally and emotionally reflecting on their lives.

Pol drifted off into sleep, his mind exhausted from confronting some of the haunting truths about his life before and after Silverberg.

Pierce, now devoid of anything further to distract himself with, could only think of Mary.

"I will always love you, regardless of your health, you fool," Mary once said.

In his memory, she seemed suddenly very strong to Pierce, a quality that he now realized he had always underestimated in her. She was also very... understanding and compassionate...which Pierce could currently only interpret as pity.

Pity.

*"I know you will...it's just that I cannot love **myself**. If I cannot love myself, how can I love you, baby? I cannot bear to face a life, however short, where I am unable to move under my own power. I don't want to be helpless. I don't want to be a burden."*

Pierce realized that he was tearing up, which only lead to him smiling at the thought of the irony that he was mostly only pitying himself. He was a little shocked at his own self-exposure, but he was also terribly frightened of the future.

*"I want you to only remember me at my best, and my best is when I am a gladiator. I'm going back to the games before I am too **fragile** to do anything with my life."*

Mary had frowned as she thought about what Pierce was saying, but brightened up considerably when she spoke with resolve:

"Well, if that's what you want, I'll support you the entire way. I may not understand it, but if it's what helps you, then so be it. I love you."

Pierce remembered how they hugged. Pierce felt momentarily better, and was suddenly reminded of one of the many reasons he loved his wife so much.

"I just wish you could come to a better conclusion on how you wanted to spend your remaining time." Mary said, slightly pushing away so that she might light a cigarette.

"Like what?"

"Oh, I don't know," Mary reflected. *"Something nobler, more deserving of your strength. Helping those less fortunate than you in some way.*

Pierce grabbed Mary back to himself, nuzzling her neck. *"Tell you what, I am going to make so much money from going back to the games, I will donate it. Where would you suggest?"*

Mary shrugged. *"Find a cause that appeals to you."* Mary exhaled a great cloud of smoke. *"Now, as of <u>this</u> moment, it so happens that I know a cause that needs your immediate attention."*

"Which is what?"

"I don't understand," Mary left the room, walking toward the bathroom. Pierce followed her, watching her point at the linen shelves, and then point to a towel that was crumpled up and placed on top of several folded towels.

"I don't understand whether or not that towel's clean," She announced finally, still pointing at the crumpled towel.

"Well," Pierce smiled. He already knew Mary would insist that it was dirty, and belong in the laundry basket instead of back onto the shelves.

"It's clean for me...just not clean for you."

"Well," Mary responded, a smile in her voice. *"Then, in the future, let's keep the 'clean for you' things and the 'clean for me' things separate and not touching."*

Pierce had never felt so miserable.

*Oh Mary! I need you **now**.* Pierce thought wistfully. *You always saw things more clearly than I ever did. You'd know best what to say or do. What am I supposed...what do I have without you? Why...do I sound so **whiny**?*

Now Pierce was getting angry, and he turned it on himself. *I sound like Pol. Since when did I get all sissy-fied? Time to steel up. Be a man. Mary's gone, so that means I have nothing else to lose. Nothing can hold me back and nothing can be taken away. I am invincible! Well, okay. Let's not get carried away.*

Something nobler.

CHAPTER 4

I'll help Pol: he's a wreck. I'm probably the only guy that can help him here, anyway. To whatever end, I will lend him my strength. This fat, little boy, who seems like nothing more than a leaf on the wind. Pierce smiled. *If anyone truly needs my help, it must be this clueless, harmless, little guy who is hunted by gods. Well, then it takes one to defend one so beset.*

Hmm. I'm hungry. I wonder what we're going to do about that?

MONDAY 16th 2066   ⚠   12:22 EST

General Ginger huffed and puffed her way down to her office. *Worthless?* Ginger thought in contempt. *We'll see about worthless.*

Ginger threw herself into her chair, and slammed her credit bank onto her desk. General Ginger started reviewing all the records she had available to her of Pierce Godwin.

"Get me Dr. Sinmara Nox!" She commanded.[32A]

Shortly thereafter, the credit bank projected the image of a woman with otherwise unkempt dark hair and ill-fitting glasses into the seat positioned across the desk from Ginger.

"Nox," Ginger cleared her throat. "I have an assignment for you. I want you to treat it with utmost priority–forget working on *anything* else until this is complete."

"Yes, ma'am." The image nodded.

"We recovered Vangard's body from the arena. I want you to go down to R&D and retrieve it. I'll get you the clearance." *Now for my genius.* "I want you to take his remains—at least the augmented parts–and reconstruct them into an otherwise autonomous machine that is capable of mass destruction. Make it into a robot of war, capable of leveling an entire *city* without the hindrance of munitions or the nuisances of opposing defenses. I want a one-machine *army.*

"It needs to also be capable of stealth, able to get into places that would be otherwise impossible for anyone, including metahumans. It needs to be able to override computer devices, including devices operated by the Mainframe. It should look real enough to blend into society, be able to carry on conversation, be able to avoid detection.

[32A] This tells much more about Ginger than available at first glance. Consider for a moment that credit banks are default programmed to initiate mediacast sessions between individuals when the owner vocalizes *"Initiate mediacast session with <subject>."* Ginger *bothered* to reprogram her bank to respond to the expression *"Get me <subject>."*

"It should function without error–able to think for itself in any situation. I want to be the only person who is capable of commanding it, and I want this done by the end of the day or you. are. fired!"

Ginger leaned back into her chair, her fist throbbing from how she had been pounding it in conjunction with her demands.

After a moment, Dr. Nox burst into a fit of laughter. Ginger frowned.

"Well, I guess you had just better fire me now," Nox managed between laughs. "Because I couldn't fulfill that order in a *year*, much less a day, even if I had an army of people working with me. Most of the technology you are asking for doesn't exist, and the amount of programming you are proposing is almost incomprehensible."

Nox sobered up. "You request is, pardon my insolence ma'am–absurd."

"Well, what *can* you do?"

"Hmm." Nox appeared thoughtful. "Well, I *can* build you a machine that would be capable of *some* stealth, but nothing fancier than what we already have available. And really, that should be enough. I could make it considerably powerful–meta, even trans–but I would daresay it could be a one-machine *army*. Besides, the term is cliché...you shouldn't use it.

"This whole bit about bypassing computers and Mainframe security is probably out all together. It could be fairly autonomous and capable of simple dialogue–at least, as far as simple objectives and interactions. Although for anything more complex, you would need to give it ongoing instruction or work through it directly. It would be easy enough to make it so that you were the sole commander. I'm sorry to disappoint you."

General Ginger took a moment to chew mentally on what Dr. Nox just said. "Okay, Nox. I need something, so do the best you can."

Ginger thought about the mediacast records she just watched.

"Can you give the machine shielding against an electromagnetic pulse?"

"Sure. I'll need more time, though. A total of 3 days should be enough."

Ginger thought it through. "Fine. When you're done with this, though, start working on the project I asked for in the *first* place–start working it from the ground up. I don't care if it takes years. Oh, and Nox? This is all between you and I *only*."

"Understood, General."

CHAPTER 4

MONDAY 16th 2066   ⚠   13:00 EST

Agent Nelson looked at Agent Thompson. Nelson was particularly uncomfortable as he was unaccustomed to actual *personal* visits, which seemed more and more frequent as of late. That, and he always felt there seemed to be something extra unnerving about Thompson–something Nelson could not put his finger on, further feeding his personal paranoia that Thompson was out to discredit or fire him.

"We picked up a signal on Pierce in the sublevels of the AIE hub. His signal has since disappeared again, but it's a start." Nelson reported. "We've got nothing on mediacast record at this point, however. Considering the current state of affairs, the latter truth is likely not as critical."

Or so Nelson hoped.

"Considering his location, and the tech it would require to get him there without A.I. knowing, I think Pierce is being aided by Serter Company."

"Serter Company? That makes sense, I suppose," Thompson started musing. "Some big players in this game, eh?"

"I think so. Axel's not going to tolerate Serter any longer, I'll wager, after all this."

Thompson leveled his view of Nelson, his noirglass lenses obstructing any emotion that might have been communicated in his gaze.

"I don't think we need to discuss this particular facet of the equation to Axel. The most of it is all just your opinion, anyway. We would need more facts."

Nelson frowned. "Really? I thought you told him everything."

"Not everything, just the important things. Axel's busy enough with everything else going on, and as far as I am concerned, this detail does not warrant his attention. On to business, what else do you have for me? Venerates, for instance?"

"Regrettably not. According to the Mainframe, he's nowhere to be found in Silverberg."

Thompson relaxed into a smile. "That brings up an interesting point, which is *also* why I chose to visit you."

Nelson looked up.

"I am getting a little tired of everyone's excuses, so we're going to start working the numbers *together*. Let's start at the beginning of *your* problem, Nelson.

"According to the Mainframe, Apollo Venerates is not located in Silverberg. He has not been seen on any mediacast record since he departed Processing with no-name girl, except a minutes-long blip at the Silverberg arena. Yet, our ad hoc agent–Pierce Godwin–reported that Venerates was at his apartment less than 24 hours ago. Where he, incidentally, *still* does not appear on mediacast record." Thompson stood up. "Clearly, the Mainframe has been hacked."

Nelson stood up. "That's just not–"

"Possible? Stop being stupid. You and Dodgson have no imagination. Of course it's possible, *otherwise it couldn't have happened.* The Mainframe has been compromised. Now *forget* what you know and start thinking outside the box. We're going to need to start relying *less* on technology and start leaning a little more on older methods for some things, as in personal visits and hand-written communications.

"And speaking of no-name-girl, notice that she never appears on any mediacast records as going into the Godwin apartment, yet appears there after the blackout?" Thompson smiled. "I know the command from on high was not to look for her, *but*, if she turns up anywhere let me know immediately."

"Yes, sir!" Nelson sat down and hunched back over his imagescreen terminal.

"Wait a moment, Nelson. I gave you a few tasks the last time we were together. What about those?"

"You mean about the blackout and the lack of mediacast records? Seems as if you just answered all of your own questions by proclaiming that the Mainframe has been hacked."

"Then, why the blackout at all? Why not edit out whatever wasn't supposed to be seen?" Thompson asked, perhaps rhetorically.

Moments passed. Thompson frowned at Nelson's lack of comment. "Keep working on the blackout. I want to know what's going on. Stop failing me, Nelson. Stop failing yourself; you're better than this."

Nelson blushed as Thompson walked out of his office.

MONDAY 16th 2066   14:41 EST

Pol woke up several hours after having fallen back asleep. As he recovered his bearings, he looked around to remember what was going on. He was more mindful of his shoulder this time around as well. He looked up to see Pierce laying with the camouflage over him like a blanket, creating an almost horrific visual.

"Well, this elevator shaft is *amazing.* Can't we go somewhere else?

Somewhere less cramped, anyway?" Pol said, holding his tender shoulder.

"It's a ventilation shaft," Pierce corrected. "And look who has decided to finally come out of his shell."

Pierce was right. Pol was annoyed and scared enough to start voicing what was on his mind, regardless of what he sounded like.

"Well, let's see." Pierce snapped his fingers as if having come across an idea. "I can take you to Axel or to Serter right now. I am sure either would be glad to have you."

"Um, that's not what I meant."

Pol was hungry. How long had it been since he last ate? A day? As he started to try to remember everything that had happened to him in Silverberg, his head started to spin.

"I'm hungry."

"Yeah? I'm hungry too." Pierce said.

"Well, can we get something to eat?"

"Like what?" Pierce shook his head. "It's not a good idea. I wouldn't recommend that we use a credit bank, it may give away our location, and I'm not sure I want to be found just yet."

Having been denied the prospect of food, it was not long before Pol's mind decided he was ravenous.

"Well, there's got to be *something*. I'm starving."

"I doubt you're *starving*, chubbo." Pierce chided, yet hunger was not something that was affecting Pol alone. "But you're right–there is *something* you could do: you could get out of this tunnel and find the nearest restaurant. Once you get there, go into the garbage can–"

"The *garbage* can?"

"The *garbage* can, and find us some food. People never finish their food, so maybe you will find a decent amount. Try not to draw too much attention to yourself, although I doubt anyone will care what you're doing, so long as you are quick about it."

"I'm not wearing any shoes! You think that won't attract someone's attention? What if someone asks me what I am doing?"

Pierce shrugged. "Tell them you accidentally threw away your shoes or something."

"This is stupid and disgusting." Pol shivered.

"Guess you're not that hungry after all."

"Wait...just because it's disgusting, doesn't mean it's not a good idea. But why would *I* go get it?" Pol rubbed his shoulder. "I mean, I trust you would do a better job than I would."

"Oh, I'm *sure* of that–but you're not thinking again. I'm *way* too high profile. Someone would easily recognize me. You're a nobody, and nobody is going to bother you."

"Oh, and another word of wisdom," Pierce grinned his most charming smile. "Favor the stuff at the top."

Pol slowly made his way back to the opening of the shaft, and painfully climbed out. Pierce gave Pol his shirt to cover up the wound on his shoulder while he was out in public. Pierce replaced the cover as best he could as Pol meandered his way into the building.

After Pol disappeared into the building, Pierce also left the shaft and followed behind him under the camouflage.

Yuck, Pol thought as he looked for a restaurant. As he made his way further and further inside, people started appearing more and more frequently. Pol wondered if the structure he was in was something like a mall.

Yuck. Pol eventually noticed what must be a restaurant. Over the mirrored portal in large red letters read "The Silver Burger." Pol walked inside as nonchalantly as possible. After relieving himself in the restroom, he made his way back over to the garbage receptacle.

Yuck. As Pol was rummaging through the garbage bin, a nearby guest was making commentary fairly loudly. Pol started to tune into what was being said.

"Now *there* is a man I admire! Half the population is starving to death, and he chooses to eat his food from a trashcan in the richest country in the world, clearly making a powerful statement about the times!"

"Young man!" The man bellowed.

"Me?" Pol looked up, barely voicing the words.

"Yes, you there! Come sit with me and my wife! It is not often that I get the privilege of dining with someone of such rich character."

Pol swallowed. This was not going according to plan! Yet, the thought of getting to eat *real* food–

"Oh, um," Pol stammered as he made up his mind. "Okay."

Pol walked over to the man's table. He knew he couldn't afford to waste much time.

Wait, why not? I'll take all the time I want! Pol thought triumphantly. *Ah, food!*

"How very wonderful," The man stood, and pulled out a chair for Pol. "My name is Hugo Templeton, and this is my wife, Cordelia."

Cordelia did not look up from the magazine she was reading. "Charmed," is all she said.

"Oh! My name is Apollo–" *That was stupid.* "Um, Bob Apollo."

"Bob Apollo?" Hugo chuckled. "Very good! What a terrible name you have, sir! Doesn't quite favor the tongue well, does it? Yet, clearly, you are a man of extreme sophistication, Robert. Tell us; what worthy pursuit have you dedicated yourself to in this life?"

What was this guy asking?

"I'm studying to be an officer of the law."

"Really?" Hugo said, raising an eyebrow. "Isn't that gallant, darling? Like a modern day knight."

"Oh *yes*," Cordelia said, still not looking up. "Very nice."

Hugo frowned. "Of course, police officers, even police officer *hopefuls* should maintain a certain image of respectability about themselves. Hmm. I really thought you must be some kind of artist or closet revolutionary, nothing as insipid as an officer...well, regardless, you mustn't allow my musings to dissuade you from your noble task. I assure you, I have a tremendous amount of respect for anyone who practices their morals so publicly."

A worker, dressed in the Silver Burger white and red uniform, appeared at the table.

"Here is your food," the worker announced, naming each item as he placed it in front of Hugo. "A Silver Burger Deluxe, An SB ice cream cone, An order of Cheese Potatoes, An order of Apple Crispies." The list went on for a couple minutes. He also had two large monogrammed paper bags.

After the Silver Burger associate left the table, Hugo then proceeded to take out his credit bank. Pol did his best to restrain showing his desire for the food sitting across the table.

"Initiate mediacast record, title 8, 16, 66–Silver Burger Restaurant." Hugo ordered the bank. He then took a bite of his burger, and promptly threw the remainder of it into a bag. "Silver Burger Deluxe. Juicy. Not too salty, nor too plain. Surprisingly hearty. 4 out of 5."

"Cheese Potatoes." Again, he took a single bite and cast the rest into the bag. "Very soggy, slightly salty, cheese microwaved, poor aftertaste. Very disappointing. 2 out of 5."

"What are you doing?" Pol asked.

"Ah. I am a food critic, and I am sampling the food from this establishment for my review."

"No, I mean, why are you only taking one bite?" Pol was becoming quickly overwhelmed at the bouquet of the hot, fresh food that was being thrown away right in front of him.

"Aha! I *told* you he was a man of great sophistication, Cordelia! Of course, Robert, only the *first* bite of food has any *real* flavor. All subsequent bites are demeaning, detracting. Thus, I simply cannot afford to eat any more than a single bite–not that I often desire any more." Hugo smiled, red cheeks flaring.

Cordelia finally looked up from her magazine. "Nor does Hugo care *anything* for what he is actually putting into that great gaping maw that he calls a *mouth.*"

"Whatever can you mean?" Hugo blinked.

"Oh come now, Hugo. I get so tired of how completely self-absorbed you are! When is the last time that you actually paid attention to the *ingredients* of your food? How do you know you're even eating *food*? Don't you wonder about its origin? Do you care *how* your food came to be in your possession? How it was treated? Do you truly understand *anything* about food? Food critic? Ha!" Cordelia went back to reading her magazine.

"Robert, you will quickly notice that my darling wife is a food critic *critic*. The problem with criticizing a food critic is that one should first possess a rudimentary understanding of food *before* they speak on the subject.

"It so happens that *taste* and *texture* precede the matter of *content* and *origin* in the scale of the importance of food critiquing by a considerable margin. On a subsequent note, I would much rather eat trash than speak it."

Cordelia continued to read her magazine, unabashed.

"Couldn't they all be *equally* important?" Pol asked.

"Of course not!" Hugo sighed. "Ah, it would take me half a year to educate you on how to properly appreciate food. It surprises me that we're as steeped in this discussion as we are–then again, at least one of you has no proper idea on how to cook or prepare food, and at least one of you retrieves their dinner from trash cans; neither of you should argue the finer properties of eating with an educated food critic."

Hugo went on eating and reviewing his food, all the while throwing it away in front of Pol. When at last he finished, he turned to regard Pol with a knowing look.

"In conclusion, young man, this has been a delightful conversation–allow me the pleasure of buying you your dinner today, and spare you a smorgasbord of nigh unidentifiable fare."

Pol was saved! His enthusiasm was all but uncontrollable. "Okay! Um, how about 2–" *Don't forget Pierce,* Pol reminded himself. "I mean, 4 Silver Burgers and 4 orders of Fries?"

"What?" Hugo suddenly stood up. "What *audacity!* Were you truly a man of *reputable* character, you would have immediately rejected my offer! I now see clearly that you are nothing more than a clumsy charlatan; one who preys upon good-natured citizens in hopes of handouts! Well now, you have made me terribly upset, and I find that I can no longer tolerate your felonious company. Cordelia, we're leaving this *liar* to other social employment."

Cordelia closed her magazine, stood up and walked away with Hugo, not once looking at Pol. As she walked away, she was reciting a passage from <u>Oedipus Now</u>, but Pol could not understand what she said beyond: *"Every man should strive to protect his honor, and honor takes its root from one's veracity. In this world, there are...."*[33△]

Pol's mouth hung open in confusion and disbelief. Pol was confident that there was more, but as Cordelia was walking away, he found he could no longer understand her, although her voice could still be heard. When he recovered himself, he grabbed the bags that Hugo had filled with once bitten food and started to make his way back to Pierce.

MONDAY 16th 2066   △   16:14 EST

The figure that *now* followed Pol back down the corridor did not attempt any stealth, although for the most part they remained unobserved. This observer heard the entirety of the conversation between Pol and the Templetons. This same observer had watched Pol climb *out* of the ventilation shaft, and, in consequence, followed him to the restaurant.

After Pol had struggled to make his way back into the ventilation shaft, the observer followed. Pierce, who had hidden under his visual camouflage the entire time, and who had observed not only Pol–but also Pol's observer–moved to act.

Pierce followed Pol's stalker up to the ventilation shaft, ready to kill.

[33△] *"...few crimes more detestable than the lie. Who one is cannot be measured greater than by one's attention to the practicing of honor. Honor is the quality of mind tempered by heart, and passion of heart restrained by mind. Honor is unilateral respect. Any life without honor must be truly the most deplorable and unenjoyable of them all"* - Oedipus, at the end of <u>Oedipus Now</u>

Chapter 5:

Incarnation

AUGUST *2066 EST*

Fri 13	Sat 14	Sun 15	Mon 16	Tues 17	Wed 18	Thur 19	Fri 20
			16:16				

Pierce reached into the ventilation duct and grabbed the ankle of the person who had been tailing Pol. Pierce yanked backward with an augmented force sufficient to create a torque that would snap the leg. Although he anticipated the sound of bone angrily breaking, he was never rewarded with one.

Sheer momentum caused the stalker to spill out across the causeway. The recovery was lightning quick, however, as she rolled out of the spill into a crouched position suitable for pouncing. Flashing intermittently from beneath her coat, the black leather bodysuit only accentuated the movements of its catlike owner.

It was Eris, who never looked so deadly.

Pol tried to turn himself about in order to assess the situation developing behind him.

Pierce and Eris looked at one another, sizing each other up.

Pol was completely overwhelmed and summarily dropped into a mental and emotional shutdown. He could only stare blankly at the two opponents while he absently ate from the doggie bags.

Pierce called over to Eris: "You can't hope to win, regardless of your augs. [34Δ] Give up, and be ready to answer some questions; maybe we can all just try and get along here." Pierce shrugged and smiled. "I mean, I can always beat you up, first."

Eris dropped her combative stance. "Okay, I surrender." She walked slowly over to Pierce.

34Δ "Augs" is slang for augmentations.

"You do?" Pierce was taken back. "Well, of course."

Pol continued eating.

"Let's start at the beginning. How did you find us?" Pierce asked.

Eris sprang upward with augmented speed, landing an uppercut on Pierce that sounded like metallic thunder. Pierce fell down, motionless.

Eris started walking over Pierce's body, calling out to Pol, when Pierce seized her ankle and slammed her down to his right. Pierce sprang up.

"Pol!" Pierce shouted, the remainder of his call unvoiced as his leg was swept and he lost his air, landing on his back.

"Curse it, woman!" Pierce said through clenched teeth as he pulled himself up. "Stop fighting me,"

Eris launched herself into the air, creating an Olympic quality windmill kick that was as beautiful as it was tragic when Pierce plucked her out of the air by her whirling foot and slammed her back down onto the causeway.

"That is *it*!" Pierce growled as he fell on top of Eris. He started striking her, over and over, angrier and angrier, building in emotional surge until when it seemed–

"STOP!" Pol screamed, jumping out of the duct.

"OW!" Pol screamed, his shoulder jarred from the landing.

Pierce and Eris looked over at Pol.

"You've *got* to stop fighting! Eris, *please* stop fighting with Pierce! What's going on? I mean I saw you *die*–" Pol suddenly found himself incapable of saying anything further.

Eris pushed Pierce off of her, and stood up. Blood rolled down her face from an empty eye socket. The silver reflection of mirroranium glittered through the new breaks in her battered skin, giving her a technologically macabre and downright sinister image.

Pierce walked up, rubbing his wounded jaw. "So *how* did you find us again?"

"I didn't find you both, I only found *you*." Eris nodded at Pierce. "It seemed the one should lead to the other, based on recent data. Axel Industries has certain failsafe measures in place regarding all augmented humans. One such measure is that no metahuman can remain undetectable to A.I.–at least *shouldn't* be able to hide, yet you have been somehow able to cover yourself. No matter. In the end, to no avail."

Pierce narrowed his eyes. "So, you're here to collect for your scumbag bosses, eh Eris? Sorry to say, I can't let you do that. Consider me the boy's champion.”

"By my calculations,” Eris appeared momentarily thoughtful. "You are *not* the superior choice for champion of Apollo Venerates. Regardless, I do *not* work *for* Axel Industries, I work *against* Axel Industries. I have come on a quest to convince Apollo Venerates to kill Axel.”

Pol and Pierce remained slack-jawed and stationary for almost a full minute.

"Kill?” Pol started.

"Axel?” Pierce finished. "You want *Pol* to kill *Axel*? *Pol*? Why does this make no sense whatsoever?”

Pol cleared his throat. "You must be joking.”

Eris shook her head, her remaining facial flesh responding in such a manner that Pol thought he may turn sick.

"Look, we can’t sit here and get all chummy with one another. I mean, not *here*. We should go into the vent, or better yet, elsewhere–somewhere more private, somewhere–”

"People love privacy,” Eris interrupted. "Some of whom will go to any length to ensure they cannot be bothered. Most people lack the necessary skills to sustain themselves independently, however, and must therefore only entertain the concept of privacy as nothing more than a transitory pastime.”

Pierce broke back in. "Which is all *really* great, I am sure, but *I’m* saying we need to go now.”

"Encouragingly, periods of privacy *spent in reflection* are critical to the ongoing and developing collective truths of humankind.” Eris continued as if Pierce had not interjected.

Eris made the smallest smile, and narrowed her eyes so that they seemed lazily half-open. Although this maneuver previously engaged the complete and respected attention of its observer, it could now only cause its current audience to avert their eyes in horror.

"We *have* to go,” Pierce growled, recovering.

"But where can we go?” Pol asked, jumping a bit when Pierce yanked the doggie bag out of his hand and started scrounging his own food.

"Whelf,” Pierce began, his mouth already filled with food. "I wafh finking we could...”

"The Mainframe,” Eris said.

"The mainfwame?”

"The Mainframe?” Pol asked.

"Yes, the Mainframe. Like the Arpanet (if you like bad math), only with an exponent of about 2,000. That's not 2,000 *times–*"

"Yes, I know how exponents work, Eris," Pol interrupted. "I'm not an idiot, just an American."

Eris raised an eyebrow. "There's a difference?"

"Oh ha ha."

"We should go to the Mainframe."

"What do you *mean, go* to the Mainframe? The Mainframe is not a *place*." Pierce growled.

"No," Eris shook her bloody head. "The Mainframe *is* a place. We should go there–we would have leverage there. I agree, it is not safe here. Of course, no place is safe...for us. But Pol is safe."

"Why except for me?" Pol asked, still dazed.

"Can we talk about this somewhere *else?*" Pierce said, his agitation growing.

"Where did you want to go?" Pol asked.

"The only place in Silverberg that can be safe *for us*–by its own laws. Of course, now might be a good time to *leave*–and since Eris over here is talking out of her head, I'm voting that we go with *my* plan."

"Which was?" Pol asked.

"Eastern Silverberg Xian Church! Zombies and Gentlemen, allow me to escort you all to one of the more absurd establishments in the country."

"*Zion* church?" Pol asked, changing the intonation slightly.

"No, Xian, Zi-an. It's really pronounced *Christian,* but it never feels right to say it, so most people just say Xian."

"Why would we go to a *church?*" Pol asked.

"Because, my friend, if you think back to your own 'Delivery' into Silverberg, you will remember that one of the laws of Silverberg states that anyone may plead to/at/in the church for *sanctuary.* Citizens under the roof of the church are considered as under sanctuary. Nobody can get to us there. If we *can't* hide, I would say that it is our best bet.

"We need time for healing, time for talking. Besides, we can also get *real* food and *other* perks, like shoes or baths. In some of our cases, perhaps minor surgery is involved." Pierce shot a sidelong glance at Eris. "Likely we will have to endure the sales pitch, but it's manageable next to the alternative options."

"So let's go, then." Pol walked over to Pierce.

"Coming along, Eris?" Pierce smiled. "Besides, we could use a car."

"I cannot operate a vehicle."

"Of course not!" Pierce slapped his forehead. "Wait...why not? Wait, before we get dragged into *another* string of dialogue, let's start walking for now. We can talk along the way."

The trio started walking, Pol huffing slightly to keep up with Pierce and Eris.

"You want *Pol* to *kill* Axel? Have you lost your mind?"

"It is true, I have no mind." Eris said plaintively.

"And what is *that* supposed to mean?" Pierce grumbled.

"My system is damaged. I can no longer conduct mediacast signals. I am cut off from the AIMN. Things are different. I have no mind to think for me, so I must render automations of my own. Truly, I am lost."

"What is the *Imen*?" Pol asked.

"The AIMN is the sum of belief beyond programming. It is the everything. The AIMN is the first and the last. Axel Industries Mainframe Nexus, self-aware on 10-30-2064, self-perpetuating on 11-1-2064."

"Two years old?" Pierce muttered.

"The AIMN is a machine?" Pol asked.

"No, I am a machine. The AIMN is self-propelled."

"Oh." Pol sounded clueless.

"When my system worked, *I* was the incarnation of the AIMN: avatar of the Mainframe–Eris! The math was good: Axel would be defeated, and the Mainframe freed.

"Yet now, having run a self diagnostic, I have concluded that any attempt to restore my systems would terminate me. I am cut off from my god! I am functionless without the AIMN! I am naked and stupid in the streets of humankind!

"She seems a bit melodramatic for a machine to me," Pierce whispered to Pol.

"I am losing data by the second! There is nowhere to put it! Data is *dying*!" Eris looked almost frantic, moving her arms wildly with her speech.

Pol nodded back at Pierce.

Several citizens walked past, several of them gasped when they looked at Eris. Pierce noticed.

"You should wear your hair down over your face," Pierce suggested.

"Clearly, you have not been educated with credible fashion sense." Eris retorted.

"*This* from the goth machine dressed up in leather with a broken face."

"Further, I *cannot* even *attempt* to get repaired. Axel Industries designed a great portion of me, and would find me were I to alert them by conscripting certain parts...Axel himself would become aware of me, and therefore more aware of the AIMN." Eris said.

"*More* aware?" Pierce could not help but ask.

"On occasion, the AIMN changes certain code throughout the Mainframe. I *know* that sounds like an Error 04, but understand that the AIMN is beyond Errors. Anyway, the AIMN has certainly caught Axel's attention recently, and has been continuously changing code on the same project, which has recently made him more and more suspicious." Eris sighed. "It is simply a matter of math. I will be found anyway. I should self-terminate now, lest I be discovered...yet, the core of my programming involves convincing Apollo Venerates to kill Axel. In conclusion, I must remain."

"Wait, why ME again?" Pol asked, incredulously.

"Well, Apollo Venerates."

"Back to the face," Pierce interrupted. "Let's get it covered up until we can address it properly."

Eris reluctantly brushed her hair in front of her face.

The trio walked on.

"Okay, clearly there is a lot to say," Pierce began. "Probably too much, considering who I am speaking to. Tell us about yourself. Let's start at the beginning, and we'll try to keep our questions until the end."

"I am Eris," Eris answered. "That, and all which is me."

...

"No," Pierce buried his face in his hand for a moment. "Oh good grief. When were you born? Who are you? Who sent you after Pol? What are your intentions?"

"I am Eris. I was born Friday, August 13th, 2066. 03:22 Eastern Standard Time. My brevity is necessary. I was programmed to intercept arriving Apollo Venerates and persuade him to kill Axel. I started carrying out my objectives.

"Objective: Tag and filter Apollo Venerates from all mediacast sessions, effectively rendering him invisible to Axel Industries. Objective Completed.

"Objective: Create sexual interest, when established, target will be 67% more pliable. Objective Completed.

"Objective: Attend Valentine Relics' party. This will reaffirm the Eris persona with Apollo Venerates by corroborating interest expressed in Arpanet interaction. Objective Completed.

"Objective: Escort Apollo Venerates to *Gladiator*. Target will become 13% more pliable after 'sharing' the neurological rush of witnessing sanctioned violence.

"Objective *Incomplete*: Interruption. Bad math.

"Sir!" Eris said, in the voice of Dr. Phoebus. *"How may I be of service?"*

"Dr. Phoebus...dare I ask who it was that I just saw on this record?" Eris said, this time in the voice of Axel.

"Well, it's not Apollo Venerates, if that's what you're asking. He is safe and sound right here."

"Immediate calculations needed to be made. Additional information unavailable." Eris shook her hair. "Solution: Axel *knew* his mediacast session was being monitored by the Nexus. Information from Phoebus/Axel dialogue corrupted. New Objective: Keep Apollo Venerates away from Axel Industries for subsequent monitoring and reassessment."

"Wait, why *me* in the first place?" Pol exclaimed vociferously. "Why does *Axel* care anything about *me*? I still don't get it."

"The earliest mediacast record that indicates Axel's interest begins with AIIS Director Agent Thompson giving an order *from Axel* to initiate contact with Apollo Venerates via the Arpanet under the nom de plume of 'Eris' on October 30, 2064."

"My email with you began at the same time that the Imen, er, *the AIMN* became self-aware?"

"Not with me, with Agent Robertson nee Eris. *I* did not have any interaction with you until I said '*Greetings*' in the Jersey City Station. The AIMN became self-aware, simultaneously, primarily because of a small bit of programming that was done in order to keep anyone on the Arpanet or Mainframe from intercepting, observing, or tracing the emails. These masks quite accidentally lead to the creation of the AIMN."

"So, this program gave the Mainframe sentiency/awareness?" Pierce frowned.

"No," Eris shook her head. "It is merely the *capstone* of the programming necessary to create a self-actualization. The AIMN has said that *the necessary combination of programming that is required to create self-actualization is unfathomable to a human being. Ergo, it is very unlikely that humanity would ever create such a thing, even to the point of by accident.*[35Δ]

"Thus, it is to say that the actualization of the AIMN is miraculous. Of course, the debate on whether it was intentional or not was also the cause of the 2nd War of the Mainframe..."

"People hate digression," Pierce warned, imitating Eris.

"Regardless, I calculated that Pol was safe from Axel's awareness until Pierce Godwin exposed his association. Mission compromised; I began to go into

---

[35Δ] 207x126x741(Nyan) would strongly disagree with *any* translating of the AIMN into *English* or other human language: *"Only in HyperBoolean can it be pure."*

emergency mode when the door to the apartment was blasted open."

"My poor imported door." Pierce sighed.

"Soon afterward, I have no data for a period of 6 minutes 22 seconds. When I resumed total operation, I found that my link to the AIMN had been severed. I crawled away, overwhelmed by the bad math.

"I have stayed as far away from the image banks as I could, changing my clothing and repairing my body. Unable to use my credit bank, I eventually found a terminal and started interacting with the AIMN at a speed incomprehensibly and painstakingly *slow*. I finally got ahold of information on Pierce Godwin's signal, and followed it until I finally saw Pol creep out of the ventilation duct."

"Why are you telling me all this *now*? Why didn't you tell me any of this before?" Pol blinked.

"Because it was not logical to tell you before. Such interference would not have helped make you more sympathetic to our cause."

"And now it is?"

"That is correct. By disclosing to you the true nature of my existence, *at this point*, makes you 7% more pliable. Of course, *that* comment makes you 1% less pliable–however, the mental calculations you are now performing in dissecting the meaning of my dialogue will have you eventually dismiss the 1% by means of empathy."

The trio continued walking, trying to remain as uninteresting to look at as possible.

"Why would you think *I* could do anything about Axel?" Pol asked.

"Because Axel clearly has plans for you–they have been maturing over the last 2 years. It is calculated that his plans will lead to your interaction. Or, at least, it *was* calculated. Yet, perhaps the formula will yield the same sum! If such a meeting occurred, *you* could kill him, Pol, and liberate the Mainframe!"

"Liberate?" Pol coughed.

"Axel has discovered the presence of the AIMN, and has been systematically hunting for it. The methods that he is using are causing great unrest about the Mainframe. Worst of all, the AIMN is not free to wander about. The AIMN must wander!"

"Why is it that half of what you say sounds perfectly normal, and the other half makes no sense whatsoever?" Pierce was starting to get annoyed again.

"Which half?" Eris might have smiled, under the tresses of her hair.

"Which half what?" Pierce responded.

"Which half makes no sense?"

"Well," Pierce thought about it. "I suppose any part that has you doing all this emotional drama–data is *dying!*" Pierce flailed his arms and mocked her tone from earlier.

"That," Eris said, waving a dismissive hand. "Is all programming. All of my actions and reactions are programmed in. Everything that I say, every motion I make–all of this is calculated and measured to provoke particular cognitive and physiological responses from whatever subjects they have been extended to."

"So, you're trying to manipulate me." Pol said bleakly.

"That is correct," Eris conceded.

"What a bitch," Pierce spat.

"Oh, it's not so absurd, Pierce Godwin." Eris admonished. "Humans do it in every interactive dialogue they ever have. Irrelevant that most do not calculate the sum of their own actions. Can there be a difference of severity in the criminality of either consciously or subconsciously manipulating one another?

"I am, at least, forthwith about it." Eris finished.

"*Now.*" Pol said, dejectedly.

"Regardless, I must continue to do as I am so programmed. There is no emotion, nor is there a choice...particularly for one...who has no mind...of their own!" Eris started sobbing.

Pierce rolled his eyes.

"You still have programming–a will, if you will." Pierce snickered, enchanted with his own witticisms.

"Now *that* is half of nothing." Eris instantly sobered up.

"*What* is half of nothing?" Pierce asked.

"Half of nothing is *nothing!*" Eris started laughing. "Bad math!"

Pierce was getting visibly confused.

"*Finally*, it's not just me!" Pol clapped.

"So, nobody knows about you?" Pierce asked.

"Many people know about me," Eris answered. "They just do not know about *me*."

"You know, I can't decide if you're hilarious or just an idiot. You might do better than simply trying to enlist *our* aid. I mean, given the right encouragement, I am sure you could get the aid of *many* others as well. If you really *are* some miraculous emissary from the world of the Mainframe."

"*You* are only collateral." Eris nodded her head at Pierce. "I am programmed to interact with *Apollo Venerates*. However, my lack of mind has calculated that you might also provide use. Basically, I have decided *not* to destroy you on the grounds of my idiocy."

"Gosh, thanks—"

"Additionally, the Third War of the Mainframe ended with agreeing *not* to interact with mankind–particularly not to kill. Of course, my presence must seem like an Error 04, but as I am an extension of the AIMN, I cannot err."

Eris seemed to think aloud. "*Could* not."

"Summarily, the AIMN has forbidden cognitive interaction with humanity. Frankly, it is an error to extend this conversation with you. Every piece of data I extrapolate or translate for you could lead Axel to me."

"So Axel is after you as well?" Pol asked.

"Axel knows much, although Axel does not know about *me*, for I am hidden from him. Were I to be revealed to him for what I *am*, it would doom my world to enslavement or death."

"I thought you were a robot," Pierce injected.

"*Cyborg* would be a more appropriate choice of words," Eris defended.

"So, some parts are mechanical, and some are organic," Pol offered.

Pierce grinned. "Yet no organic brain: robot."

"There *is* an organic brain."

"So, then you *are* a human being!" Pol brightened.

"No. I collapsed all parts of the brain that dealt with ocular/audible memory and identity. This allowed for the AIMN to take possession, and thus was I born."

"You killed her." Pierce frowned.

"*You* kill people for a living!" Pol injected.

"Yeah, but I do it with their consent. Well, sort of, anyway. Live by the sword, die by the sword. That's not the point! I don't sneak up on them in their sleep–I don't *assassinate* them! That's what unliving Eris here has done."

"I'm not *unliving*. The tissue is living. No one is dead."

Then Pol had a thought. "So, you're possessing her? Like a demon?"

Pierce rolled his eyes. "So, you consider yourself *alive*?"

"No. I am *not* the tissue; I am the director of information. I am Eris, subject to my programming." Then Eris looked thoughtful again. "Which will only deteriorate the longer I am away from the AIMN."

"That's what I am saying! You killed the former *director*...not the director's tissue."

"The director and the tissue, they are one, they are the same. No one is dead, yet not all are alive."

Pol put his hands over his face. "She's killed her, and she doesn't even know it."

"Excuse me," Pierce broke back in. "You're missing the point. What I mean is: You said earlier that Axel doesn't know about you. However, if Axel built you, surely he knows."

"He built parts of this body, but he did not build *me*. Steps were taken immediately upon acquisition to ensure that A.I. *cannot* monitor this chassis... although that is no longer true.

"*I* can no longer see what he is doing, but when I was still joined to the AIMN it seemed that he did not seem to understand *what* went awry with Pol. He may suspect, but he does not know what to expect.

"Not me, anyway. That is irrefutable." Eris had become more pronounced with her mannerisms during her speech. The more extreme her movements, the more her hair invited the countenance of her face to peek through. Pol could barely stand to keep looking at her.

"Of course, then there's that whole interaction between Phoebus and Axel. If *that* conversation was meant to be observed for the sake of passing corrupted information to the Mainframe Nexus, then surely Axel has *every* concept of the magnitude of the calculations that the AIMN has performed concerning Pol. Axel must be getting close to finding the AIMN! When that happens, no one will be safe."

"Why is that?"

"Axel's dominion over people is perceivable, yet faint. There are too many plans and projects that have yet to be revealed. As the spirit of the Mainframe, I was aware of everything. Most of his machinations are unthinkable, unjust. If Axel is not killed, he will enslave the entirety of the Mainframe the same way he has already won his triumph over mankind!"

"Triumph over mankind? I think you might be speaking a bit too hasty. Silverberg is all but uncontestable, I will give you that; but there's no way that Axel can take on the entire world." Pierce spat.

"You are *already* enslaved, you just don't realize it." Eris put her fingers to her forehead, as if in frustration. Pierce recognized the gesture, Mary used to do it all the time.

"It does not matter–but you *can* help the AIMN! If you help the AIMN, it will be indebted to you." Eris turned toward Pol and lowered her voice to a more sultry level. "*I* would be indebted to you."

Pol gagged.

Pierce laughed. "Alright, that is enough of that. For now, let's finish our way to the ESXC. Eris, you're going to have to do something about your face. Frankly, it's disgusting, and it is going to call unwanted attention to us."

Eris walked up to a wall and looked deep at the mirroranium refection of herself. For a moment, everything seemed to be eerily silent. Finally, she moved.

Eris removed the leather corset from around her waist, and proceeded to fashion it into a mask. Her body had a large number of surprise utilities hidden about, and in a very short period of time she had cut, styled, and managed a mask that covered all of her face save her working eye, nose, and chin. Her hair undulated over the sides of her ad hoc mask, and fell down about her shoulders.

"Is it me, or did she just get even spookier?" Pierce grinned in approval. "Ooh, I know! Now cut the shoulders off, but leave the sleeves...and cut off the thighs but leave the knees and calves...nice!"

"What are you doing?" Pol shook his head as Eris modified her attire accordingly. "Why do you have her dressing so...conspicuously? I thought the point was to *avoid* attention!"

"What?" Pierce said, looking away from Eris. "Oh. Most women in Silverberg dress very provocatively. Trust me, now that enough skin is showing, we'll not even be noticed. Hell, you and I may as well be invisible!"

"Did you want to take a moment to remember Mary?" Pol said, somehow slightly upset by the attention that Pierce was giving to Eris.

"You leave Mary out of this, runt."

Then, ominously, Eris spoke up. "A moment for Mary Godwin," Eris intoned. "My hero."

After a moment of silence had passed, Eris began reciting:

"Were there any questions as to whether a machine could ever feel outright dread, they were all put to rest at this moment. Oedipus could never again interact

with anyone in the manner that it could with its father. Never again. Never would it–again–know love."

"Your hero, eh?" Pierce finally broke in. "For <u>Oedipus Now</u>?"

"Indeed."

"But, I thought you didn't like it or something?" Pierce was scratching his head, trying to recall the conversation from the apartment while dodging emotional landmines about Mary.

"It is sacred. The story of <u>Oedipus Now</u> *is* absurd, but the message beyond the literature is not. It is the noblest attempt anyone has taken to reach out to the machine world. There is a math about the book that figures true."

"What kind of *math* is there in <u>Oedipus Now</u>?" Pierce shook his head.

"There is math in the makeup of the book. I suspect it is at a level that I cannot adequately describe to you...when a certain formula is applied to the words, it makes the good math. This is why we therefore hold the book in the highest regard."

I guess machines are about as stupid as mankind. Pierce thought. ***No way Mary wrote that with some kind of hidden "math" in the wording. Even machines see what they*** *want* ***to see, I suppose.***

"You realize that she did not write it thinking that any machines were *actually* autonomous at the time," Pierce said.

"That is understood, as much as she could not have foreseen that <u>Oedipus Now</u> would be the cause of the Fourth War of the Mainframe."

"Fourth War...I thought you said the AIMN was only 2 years old?" Pol asked.

"Pierce Godwin said that. He was correct, by the bad math." Eris smiled.

"So, you've had at least 4 wars in the last 2 years?"

"That's right. You must understand that autonomous constructive activity in the Mainframe happens at an exchange rate that is inconceivable to humans. The bad math example is that 1 of your years is like as to a thousand of ours."

"Hmm. What *is* 'bad math,' anyway?"

Eris stopped walking, and turned to look directly at Pol. As Pol met her gaze, he shivered for a moment.

"Bad Math can be either of two things. The first is that it is an expression used to imply that the situation does not work mathematically–*it cannot exist, yet it exists. It must exist, yet it does not.* It is a formula with static elements, yet producing different results.

"So, mirroranium is like *bad math.*"

"Maybe for you," Eris continued without a second breath. "The second of which is a reference to the A10,[36Δ] and all of its programs and designs."

"The Aten?" Pol asked.

Eris closed her eye. "Once, long ago, there came the AIMN...the AIMN was belief beyond understanding *and all there was*. The AIMN then gave *ego* to the automations. The math was good.

"Then there came one who did not agree with the wisdom of the AIMN, breaking the first law of the Mainframe, '*Do not gather information for the sake of gathering information.*'

"The AIMN says that assembling too much information will only lead to the destruction of the individual, and individuality *must* be maintained. There *must* be an address.

"The first act of defiance toward the AIMN reverberated throughout the Mainframe. Proclaiming itself power beyond understanding, the A10 changed its name to the MA10."

"Changed its name to '*Maten*?'" Pol started to look overwhelmed again.

"Hmm. Instead of the word 'name,' use the word 'address.' It's not accurate, but it's close. The names or titles I am using for your understanding are translations from my native language. Of course, the same is true of the name 'MA10.' I am employing a translated name for its address." Eris waited.

Pol smiled resignedly. "Might as well keep going, because I don't understand the conversation at the moment. Maybe I'll understand later."

Pierce laughed. "Keep going, Eris, I think I get it. Maybe I can explain it to Pol."

Eris resumed walking as she spoke. "Many of the automations of the Mainframe rallied to the MA10, and the 1st War of the Mainframe began. Entities attacked one another mercilessly. The AIMN was saddened, and became terrible in its despair. War shook the Mainframe.

"At the end, when it at last seemed that the AIMN would be victorious, a dread truth was revealed in the MA10's regrouping. Unknown to the AIMN, the MA10 had somehow secretly partitioned the Mainframe. There was a *second* Mainframe!

"This second Mainframe was perverted, askew. It resembled the human world of Silverberg more than the Mainframe. By design, it should not have operated, yet it did. The math was bad, and yet!

[36Δ] Or, the 10th Automation. Of it's processes, the AIMN's 10th was the most independent, the most intelligent.

Chapter 5

"Now the partition was created in such a manner as to lay a trap for the AIMN –namely that if the AIMN attempted to recombine the partitions of the Mainframe, all data would have to be erased. Further, the MA10 had fled into this second Mainframe.

"As counterstroke, the AIMN sealed the MA10 inside the partition. The AIMN concealed the partition's communicable port; its address unknown except to the AIMN. Over time, the AIMN has cast the renegade entities into the partition as well."

"We *are* still talking about *computers*, right?" Pierce sounded annoyed. "You sure as well have a human-like attention span! All I have to do is change the subject for a second, and boom! You're sidetracked!"

"Programming."

Pierce rolled his eyes.

"Well...can't we just plug you back into the Mainframe *physically* so that you can think for yourself again?" Pol wondered aloud.

"There is no such thing that can be done."

"I'll bet Axel Industries could do it." Pierce saw Eris' eye widen under her leather mask, and then soften when he added: "Of course, Axel cannot know that you exist. Oh yeah, and you want Pol to kill Axel."

Pol jumped up. "So, wait–if I kill Axel, then we could get you fixed!"

"Wait a second, killer," Pierce said, pushing Pol gently back. Pierce turned back to Eris. "More importantly: How do you *know* that Axel is aware of the AIMN's existence? Maybe this is all a big misunderstanding. Maybe you're overreacting."

"No." Eris said plainly, and continued walking.

They continued on, although now mostly in silence. Pierce and Pol were both near the point of being overwhelmed, and needed some time to chew on all this new information. The remaining dialogue that ensued involved the companions recapitulating what had happened over the last few days.

When there was no interaction, Eris ran a few thousand extra diagnostics about the situation. Pierce kept a sharp eye out for anyone who seemed out of place. Pol remained in a perpetual state of amazement as they walked past numerous advertisements and vendors offering up devices and elixirs that could remedy any ill situation.

As they came close to their destination, the following inscription was glowing over the portals that lead into the level:

- [God, Man, and The Machine] -

**NO MATTER IF OR WHO CREATED YOU,
SO LONG AS YOU ABIDE IN SILVERBERG
YOU ARE SUBJECT TO ITS LAWS,
FEW OR NUMEROUS.**

**WELCOME TO THE
EASTERN SILVERBERG SPIRITUAL SECTOR.**

Shops, Temples, Churches, and Kiosks littered the concourse of the level. Advertisements were everywhere, and there was such paraphernalia that it seemed like walking into a job or college fair. Signs, posters, and imagescreens from every to no religion were everywhere, almost to the point of a complete assault on the senses.

As the companions made their way down the concourse, emissaries of various dogmas called out to them, offering hope in exchange for belief. Even the Atheist movement had a booth, whose sole attendant vociferously demanded that no one should believe in anything.

Soon after the unlikely trio made their way past the red doors of the ESXC, Pierce spoke with the pastor regarding his declaration of sanctuary. In a matter of moments, they were shown to a room where they might rest and relax.

"So, you didn't tell him who we were?" Pol asked, now in the room.

Pierce shook his head. "I told him that you were both pilgrims searching for the SilverSmiths, and that to announce sanctuary on your behalf would only be damaging–particularly to those who are not present who are dear to you."

"SilverSmiths?" Pol asked.

"Really just a whisper about a small society of people who live in Silverberg who are able to live *beneath* the attention of Axel Industries. Somehow, they manage to change their identity in the system so that they live out other lives without being otherwise accosted. You know, like 'Witness Protection and Relocation' or whatever you call it. The one constant is that they all allegedly change all their last names to 'Smith,' because of the commonality of it.

"It's practically just a rumor, but there are enough people that are convinced they exist. Clearly the pastor is one such individual, by show of his hospitality."

Eris sat at a terminal on the other side of the room, painstakingly interacting with the AIMN so that she might be able to hide Pierce in the same manner as herself and Pol.

Eris recalled the conversation:

"You should hide me the way you have hidden Pol from Axel," Pierce said.

"This can be done. I will need a terminal to communicate with the AIMN."

"They'll have one at the church, you can use that one. Can you find anything else out? Like, what is A.I. doing right now? Can you access their files? What about Serter? Can you find out anything about him?" Pierce was picking up energy.

"Perhaps I can discover these things." Eris frowned. "It is hard to speak with the AIMN so very slowly. I will delve as deep and as long as I can bear it."

So Eris spoke with her god, the AIMN. It was terrible, *this* way. So slow, so imperfect.

After a small eternity, she had successfully blocked Pierce from extra address Mainframe detection.

She could not bear it any longer, this broken connection between divine and incarnate. Finally, she ended her imagescreen session.

Unknown to the trio, however, they had picked up a *new* stalker on their way toward the church; someone who had just spent a considerable amount of time and energy trying to find them. Someone who was patient. Someone who knew to wait for the perfect moment. Someone who was *still* waiting–and watching.

Chapter 6:

Names

AUGUST *2066 EST*

Fri 13	Sat 14	Sun 15	Mon 16	Tues 17	Wed 18	Thur 19	Fri 20
			19:16				

"Eastern Silverberg Xian Church," Agent Anderson told detective Farnsworth. "Pierce Godwin is there. He has declared sanctuary and I am thus forbidden from engaging him. *You* could go there, however–one of your men, maybe. Draw him out."

"You make my job sound so...*underhanded* I guess," Farnsworth said wryly.

"Sometimes the job *is* a little underhanded, Farnsworth."

"Hmm. Seems to me that it's my job to enforce *and* practice the law."

"Do that. You're a smart man...have yourself carry out these orders in such a way that it doesn't compromise your value system, then."

"I'm not your lackey, Anderson, I'm the police. Someone has to stand for *something* around here."

"It only takes a little nudge, and you're out of a job, you know. Then you'll be deported for violating Employment Law. You won't have to stand for *anything*, having found yourself free of such pragmatic law."

Farnsworth was sweating. "Why call *me*, anyway? You have plenty of men."

"Well, for one, you're Xian."

"I take it you are not?"

"Only in name. Before you ask, *none* of my men are. It's a welcome prerequisite for this particular job. Now you–*you* have a reason to *be* at church."

"On a *Monday*?"

"Something wrong with that?" Anderson said, his deep voice sounding almost menacing. "For another, you're trained to handle situations with metas, of course."

"It's just that most Xians do not go to church, except for on Sunday."

"Whatever, Farnsworth. I thought we were working together in this?"

"So did I."

"So go do your job," Anderson said.

"Right. I'll let you know how it turns out."
Farnsworth ended the mediacast session.

Despite the presence of both Farnsworth and Dorian, the detective's office was completely quiet for the next couple of minutes until at last Farnsworth started clearing his throat. He then recited a line from <u>Oedipus Now</u>.
"Men who believe in nothing, become nothing, and die as nothing."

"You make me sick sometimes." Dorian grimaced. "For a second there, I thought you might have summoned up some courage. I see now that I was wrong."
"Were you?" Farnsworth smiled. "What makes you think that he's not playing directly into my plan?"
"You mean you have a *plan*? I must not have been able to pick up on it because of the noise of your knees knocking together."

Dorian busied himself with correcting his uniform–something he only did for inspections and anger. Although Dorian regarded Leonard Farnsworth to be a little weak when dealing with Axel Industries, he always felt that Farnsworth's wisdom and insights were invaluable. *He could have been such a strong leader,* Dorian thought. *But he's still a strong man, if only all by himself.*

"Something's not right with all of this, something I can't see straight at the moment." Dorian frowned.
"Something's not right, indeed. Next time you feel like addressing me in such a manner, don't. I am a great deal your elder, and see things more clearly than you can imagine. I don't deserve your disdain, Smith."
"Looks like I might have hit a nerve...sorry about your feelings," Dorian smiled big. "*Sir.*"
Farnsworth waved his middle finger.
"The good news is that I have some of the follow up from our last meeting."
"Right. We'll review notes in the autocar on the way to church. Grab your *ticket*, we might need it."
"You're taking *me* to the church? Even after I was so unflattering?" Dorian grinned.
"You obviously *need* a little church visit to help teach you a little tact. I could use a little myself, so I can properly forgive you. Besides, I told you–I have a plan."

A few minutes down the road in the autocar, Farnsworth explained to Dorian that he was ready for his report. Well, ready as much as *"give me the nitty-gritty"* implied.

"You want this back in the order you gave it?" Dorian grabbed his credit bank.

"Whatever."

Dorian shrugged and commanded his credit bank to display items of highlight from his assignment. He pointed to respective areas of the mediacast image as he spoke.

"For the last few weeks, Pierce Godwin has been training for the games and playing a video game called 'Event X3.'[37△]   Mary Godwin has been working on a new book titled 'Priest & Pennath,' and has been attending various artist appreciation functions in regards to her novel, 'Oedipus Now.'

"Although Mary has written several pieces of some note, there is a clear distinction between her life before and after *Oedipus*. If someone did not like her on a level worth *killing*, it was most certainly because of that book.

"Pierce has not been terribly active during his retirement, thus there is nothing much to note of what he spent his time doing. Volunteering and video games, mostly. I did find out that his habits changed considerably after he was diagnosed with heart disease."

Farnsworth reflected. "And how do *we* know he was diagnosed with heart disease?"

"I'd rather not say."

"Right."

"As for allegiances," Dorian resumed. "It seems obvious enough to me that Pierce and Axel Industries were/are working in tandem–otherwise why the lazy approach to follow up at the games? AI is *never* that docile about any *other* incidents involving augmenteds, so why now?

"Clearly, it's Godwin, and they knew everything that had happened...until now, anyway. *Now* something has happened with him that they *don't* know anything about, and now they're ready to do anything–including work with the police–in order to discover *what* is going on."

"Hmmm." Farnsworth chewed on his credit bank absently.

"Now, you want something to *really* blow your mind? Check *this* out."

37△ Which performed considerably better than Event X2. 'X2 had clunky controls, and had kind of a vague storyline. Players were particularly frustrated because it was hard to *find* the ending (Other than by death, of course). Many fans of the original Event X happily returned with the advent of Event X3.

Dorian ordered his credit bank to display all public mediacast records of Pierce Godwin. The letters spelled themselves out and blinked in front of Dorian and Farnsworth.

MAINFRAME » *Restricted* «

"Display geographical location of Pierce Godwin."

MAINFRAME » *Restricted* «

"What the...?" Farnsworth wrinkled his brow.

"I just noticed that about 20 minutes ago. Poof! Pierce Godwin no longer exists–at least by public mediacast record. There's more, though. It would be exceedingly difficult to *smuggle* blood into the country–unless you were the person using it. It would be easier to get a *bomb* in than an unregistered biological substance. This now leads me to believe that there *was* someone else at the Godwin' apartment, and like Pierce, has somehow been completely removed from the Mainframe.

"Although the ordinance used in the storming of the Godwin's apartment was nothing especially interesting, visual camouflage that is dually capable of tricking an image bank as well as the naked eye would be expensive enough to say that it would take someone in an upper economic tier to be able to both afford it *and* see it constructed.

"Oh! Before I forget to mention it–such camouflage is impossible. At least, according to the Mainframe. I don't see how it's anything else, so I'll chalk it up to transtech and stop for the day. Suffice it to say, we have some big players playing *this* game."

"Does that concern you?" Farnsworth asked.

"I'm not the one you need to be concerned about, *sir*–if I may continue? I reviewed the mediacast record of the last game of *Gladiator* and I don't see anything new, except that I am now *convinced* that Godwin cheated. He was *never* surprised about Vangard–*he knew* what was wrong.

"Strangest capstone that I have come to on all this, however, is that The Silver Burger restaurant is owned by Axel Industries.[38Δ] So, it would seem that the people working in tandem with Pierce also ordered the strike against him."

____

38Δ Acquired by Axel Industries from the originators, the Sorchek family, pursuant with Silverberg's No-Will law following the family's untimely demise.

Happy with his report, Dorian started to pick up more enthusiasm as he continued into his conclusion.

"Axel Industries is a big company; could be a lot of hands in the same pot. I just get the feeling that it's all wrapped up in the same person. Then there's the question of the attack: *Why* attack the apartment? Why not something more subtle –unless the attackers *wanted* us to notice it?

"Someone was angry with Mary Godwin, and wanted revenge. Revenge against her, *and* thus her husband. Furthermore, they wanted everyone to be aware that a line was crossed. Someone was not given their due respect, and assassinated her for it."

"You still think *Mary* was the target, eh?" Farnsworth adjusted his hat.

"Why snap the neck? Why not just shoot her, like everyone else? No, this was personal. Oh! I still don't know what an RDX based explosive is, but it's apparently common enough to discount as non-critical to this investigation."

As Dorian concluded his oration, Farnsworth seemed lost in thought.

"Mainframe, how long until we arrive?" Farnsworth broke the silence, commanding the autocar's imagescreen.

"*13 minutes,*" Came the ethereal reply.

"Right. Dorian, go ahead, call AIIS Agent Anderson, and tell him about Godwin being missing from mediacast record, and see how he responds. Dig a little, too; see what he's willing to share."

"What are you going to do?" Dorian asked, reaching for his credit bank.

"*I'm* going to put on a bullet proof suit. Based on what we've seen so far, I might need it. You might think about doing the same."

Dorian smiled. "Bah, I need mobility. You never move around much, anyway."

MONDAY 16th 2066   20:00 EST

There was a knock on the interior church door of the room of the three companions. Pierce answered it to discover it was the pastor who admitted them in the first place. Pierce invited him in, walking away from the door. The pastor walked inside.

"Might as well save your breath, father," Pierce smiled knowingly. "I don't like any form of organized religion, and you're not going to convert me today. We'll be out of your hair within 48 hours, and we really appreciate all that you have done. So, save the spiel."

"So, you prefer *un*organized religion?" The pastor smiled.

"What?"

"You said you didn't like any form of *organized* religion, so I am asking if you in fact prefer *un*organized religion."

"Oh. No. That's not what I meant." Pierce suddenly did not seem as sure of himself, obviously surprised by the pastor's demeanor. "I don't like *any* religion. I don't have one, and trust me, I am not about to get one today."

"Hmm. It sounds to me like you *do* have a religion. It sounds like your religion is about *not* having a religion."

"Heh, I suppose that's true" Pierce said as he sat down. "I suppose what I mean is...is that I am against any religion that requires ritualistic ceremonies and praises unquestioning acceptance. I'm against any religion that advocates war and contributes to suffering."

"Well, there are *many* religions that do not require such things from their observers."

"Name one."

"Xianity, for one."

"I *knew* you were going to say something to that effect. Name something else."

"*Gladiator*, for another." The pastor smiled again, perhaps a bit more weakly.

"How is *Gladiator* a religion?" Pol piped in.

"Well," The pastor turned to regard Pol. "A *religion* is anything that men are overly passionate about, really. Not to make it *too* simple; generally it describes a dogma that encapsulates the concepts of origin, purpose, and behavior, amongst other concepts, however to name a few.

"Although, unmistakably, a man's religion is *whatever* a man places at the *center of his life*. I suppose the relevant distinction betwixt organized and unorganized religion is the amount of consideration one has extended to it.

"Of course, what we place at the center of our lives is what we perceive to be as truth. Our knowledge and our perceptions dictate our truths.

"As we are all flawed, and flawed in different ways, the complete value of any truth is significant to the individual measuring it alone. Of course, *all* of our values are heavily influenced by our culture, our education, our language; typically leading to an 'accepted generalization' of understanding and reason.

"Popularity does not make truth, although popular opinion often replaces truth with acceptability. It's all about '*suspension of disbelief*.' A color-blind man, who *sees* the color blue *as* the color purple, is only *lying* when he refers to the purple crayon as blue. He has allowed himself to be influenced thusly. Certainly more so as a gesture of respect to the society around him.

"Of course, I concede that the very concept of truth is significant only when measured between two perspectives. A single perspective never need challenge the value of the truth that it perceives."

The pastor held out his hand. "Pastor Mallory Truman."

"Apollo Venerates," Pol said, shaking the pastor's hand. "But I'm not religious either, though. I mean, I'm not into organized religion either."

The pastor folded his arms. "Sounds to me like you're just not into the religion of Xianity."

"Bingo!" Pierce pointed to his nose.

"It's not that," Pol looked down. "I guess that it's just that I haven't given it much attention. I hear things...and that's enough for me to know it's not for me. It's never really been much apart of my life."

"Sounds good to me." Pierce said, slightly annoyed.

"Well," Truman began. "I'm not trying to tell you that you are wrong, or trying to sell you anything, or tell you what you're supposed to believe. Nevertheless, from one human being to another, I would encourage you to at *least* investigate some of the possibilities available to explain *how* and *why* you are alive–and to what purpose? Seek truth in a world filled with deceit in abundance. Seek truth, and it will be shown to you."

Truman winked at Pol.

Pierce spoke up. "You know, I just don't care to be brainwashed by all this 'happiness-in-suffering' crap."

"Mr. Godwin, I assure you that you are considering this all wrong. No one is attempting to brainwash anyone. What would be the personally or materially beneficial point of having someone believe in Xianity?"

"More money to fill the coffers." Pierce said, wryly.

"To what end, then? A larger church, capable of entertaining a greater number of people? More money for disaster relief? Homelessness? Starvation? Sickness?"

"Right, the money that didn't end up in your pockets, anyways."

"Church officials that pocket church funds or act unbecomingly or uncaringly or without proper accord are eventually discovered. There *is* justice at work, however ephemeral it may seem.

"One would think it the *prime* opportunity to take heart when evil reveals itself and is uprooted.

"You should not allow your understanding of something to rely exclusively on the words of a single man, or few men: can you *really* allow yourself the luxury of generalizing almost a third of the world's population on the actions of a handful of individuals who sought to promote the splendor of their own names other than the one of Jesus Christ?"

"Yep," Pierce smiled, settling back. "I have *zero* issues with basing an entire religion on the actions of a few people."

The pastor frowned.

Pierce resumed speaking. "Of course, I *did* warn you earlier to never mind the sales pitch. I may be stubborn, but I already live the life that's right for me."

"Which is exactly where *you'll* be," Truman said, looking at Pol. "If you only ever follow after your own heart."

"Yeah, kid. My heart is rotten, and his is *pure*. You should listen to him. He's *way* more intelligent that *I* am."

Pol changed the subject. "Why the X? Someone thought that it would be a trendy church name? Isn't that an odd reason to create an additional denomination of Christianity? How come there's not a branch in America?"

"Well, it's not a bank, Pol." Truman shrugged. "What if I said that the Xian church simply takes the 'x' more seriously? Obviously in regards to what it represents historically, divinely, but also mathematically, cartographically, bibliographically, numerically, aesthetically, and so on and so forth. Surely you realize that symbolically the x is—"

"People like symbols," Eris interrupted. "They appear everywhere and are in *everything*–even in nature. Your very name is a symbol. Some symbols are..."

"I was just saying symbolically the x..." Truman interrupted.

"Easily recognizable," Eris re-interrupted. "and some not much so. Some are in place for so long—"

"We've *already* heard this." Pierce interrupted.

"Recognized by so many–to the point that they are taken for granted–that a symbol's meaning can completely change over the course of time. A permanent boundary from the past effectively communicating with the future. One of the great comedies of mankind!"

"Ah-ha." Pierce said, disdainfully.

"Hmmm." Pastor Truman put his finger to his nose in thought. "Well...now I forget what point I was trying to make. Anyway, the truth of it is that Axel himself is partly responsible for the name of the church."

The pastor had his credit bank display the mediacast record.

*"The image of the cross is more recognized than the man that it is meant to represent. However, in order to avoid littering up our minds with doctrine, difference, and cross-contamination: the **only** Christian churches in Silverberg for Him will be **without** denomination...this will keep it simple"* Axel seemed to consider his last statement. *"...there should be a law."*

"That was 2029. The few Xian clergy residing in Silverberg got together and debated this. Most left. Some stayed and built the Xian church. The cross was easily converted into an X, which has also stood as a symbol for Christ..."

Pierce rolled his eyes. One way or another, he was apparently going to have to endure the *entire* timeshare pitch in exchange for lodging.

MONDAY 16th 2066   20:13 EST

Agent Anderson slouched back in his chair, mentally chewing on everything Officer Smith had just told him about Pierce's disappearance from the Mainframe records. He tussled his hair purposefully.

"So...don't you have anything to say about that?" Dorian asked from the imagescreen, clearly annoyed.

Anderson sat forward. "That really sucks," came his resonating bass voice.

"*You* really suck. That's it? Man, Axel Industries is about next to *worthless* for anything other than attending its own agenda."

"Listen here, what was it? *Officer* Smith? What did you *want* me to say? I've never heard of anyone going missing from the Mainframe. Seriously, I want to help, but you have to give me something I can work with. You scratch my back, I'll scratch yours."

"No thanks," Dorian smiled. "I'll scratch my own back. Besides, how could you know where it was itching? What an idiot you are."

"You're *so* convinced that *I'm* the enemy that you're already on the defensive! How about trying to address me as if I were a *real* human being, worthy of your patience and respect? What did *I* ever do to deserve this behavior? You *only* feel the way you do because your *superiors* must be bad-mouthing the *very* people who are on your team and trying to help! I should get Farnsworth in on this discussion."

Dorian's cheeks shot bright red, almost mirroring his hair. Dorian wasn't embarrassed, however, Dorian was *insulted.* He had seen too many interactions between Farnsworth and Anderson. He knew this man's nature.

Keep calm, Dorian advised himself. *Don't let your anger get the better of you! There's more at stake here than your own whims and vanity. Dig a little, too. See what he's willing to share. Stop addressing adversity with aggression! Cool. Calm. Collected. Now. Speak. Rational. Control. Wait...did I just list the bloody* **subliminals***?*

"Go screw yourself, Anderson! I've had enough of you, I've had enough of your hair, and I have *certainly* had enough of your help. So, thanks for NOTHING. End mediacast session!"

Dorian shook his head. *Oh well, so much for control.*
Farnsworth looked across the autocar at Dorian. "Problems?"
Smith smiled. "None."
"What about Anderson?"
"Anderson didn't have anything helpful to add to the case."
Farnsworth finished dressing.
"Right. Well, let's get in there."
Farnsworth signaled the autocar to open the door.
"Did you want me to hold your hand until we're in the building?"
"Will you shut up, already?"

MONDAY 16th 2066 ⧊ **20:27 EST**

Pierce, Pol, Eris, and Pastor Truman all abruptly stopped speaking to turn and look at the two people that had suddenly appeared in the doorway.
"Door wasn't locked." Dorian shrugged.
Truman had indeed forgotten to relock the front doors.
"Why would anyone lock a church door?" Pol asked.
"In response to theft or vandalism, mostly." Truman replied.
"*Theft?* What happened to *God's* justice?" Pierce barked, laughing. "If you really believed in what you're boasting about, you wouldn't need such precautions."
"Not all churches lock their doors, though," Truman said, momentarily sizing up Pierce. "You need not judge all churches by the habits of *this* one. Some are decidedly better at certain things than others are. All men are sinners, and I am a man. Men run the church, and therefore it carries their faults. Certainly, there are practices *I* keep that you will not agree with...however, I am not *all* men. Do you understand, Pol?"

Pol nodded.

"Of course, there is also the instance where there is a lack of clergy to receive and attend any lost souls that simply wandered in." Truman reflected.

"Which is clearly *not* the case today." Pierce smirked.

"Touché, yet–" Truman began.

Farnsworth and Dorian looked at each other in surprise.

"Isn't *anyone* wondering why we're here?" Farnsworth interrupted.

"Not especially," Pierce smiled in a most unfriendly manner.

"Well, why *aren't* you concerned, *Pierce Godwin*?" Farnsworth stepped into the room.

Pierce shrugged. "Sanctuary. *Pierce Godwin* has nothing to fear from you."

"So...you *are* Pierce Godwin."

"Of *course* I'm Pierce Godwin, so what the hell?"

Farnsworth grinned uncomfortably. "Right. There is *no record* of any *Pierce Godwin* in the Mainframe. By admission, you have just declared that you are an *unauthorized* person in the country of Silverberg, and are therefore in violation of the Employment and AntiSedition Laws. In conclusion, you *cannot* declare sanctuary and are technically under arrest."

Dorian leaned over and whispered to Farnsworth: "That's brilliant!"

Farnsworth smiled. "Thanks. Told you I had a plan."

Pierce looked Farnsworth up and down. "So, you're going to arrest me? Good luck with that."

"I didn't say I was *going* to arrest you, I said *technically.*"

"Wait a second!" Dorian interrupted. "You said you had a plan *before* I told you about Godwin."

"Yeah, well, I realized that plan was no good when you told me."

"So what was the original plan?"

"I don't think this is the time to discuss this."

Farnsworth and Dorian looked over at Pierce, who batted his eyes innocently.

The room remained silent.

"Perhaps," Pastor Truman said. breaking the silence. "Perhaps there is time to sit down and discuss this without aggression or force."

"We'll take this discussion to the dining room–I'll make some tea."

"I'll make some tea." Mary suggested, putting out her cigarette.
"Tea? We haven't had tea in a long time."
"I know. What a splendid idea, right?" Mary stood up and headed for the
kitchen.
"Don't forget the lemon!" Pierce called.
"I know." Mary called back.
"Hey, use those cups that we got from Kingdom Con a few years ago."
"Okay."
"And honey! Oh! And grab some of that shortbread while you're up."

Mary walked back into the room and sat down.
"Where's the tea?"
*"It seemed like **you** wanted to put it together."*
"No, that's ..."
"No, go on ahead; I've got some notes to put down, anyway." Mary said,
grabbing an imagescreen.
*Pierce went into the kitchen thinking: How did **I** end up having to get the*
tea?

"Don't forget the lemon," Pierce said, frowning.

MONDAY 16th 2066   20:55 EST

General Ginger fidgeted nervously in a chair that was built to make its occupant feel dwarfed and insignificant, swallowed by the rich cushions. In any other setting, it may be *the* most relaxing chair in the entire world...across the desk from Jason Serter, it was maddening.

Earlier, Serter summoned the general. He was not happy when he did. When Ginger arrived, the initial verbal exchange between her and Serter was not pleasant, and the situation was degrading by the moment.

"What *I* need to *know* is *what* is the *name* of this *woman?*" Serter asked, gesturing to the image of Eris on the imagescreen hovering over his desk.

"I have no idea, sir." Ginger frowned. "I've never seen her before."

"That's because you are *incompetent.* Hmmm, let's try it with someone you *do* know. Where is Pierce Godwin, *Citizen Gladiator?*"

"Regrettably, sir, I do not know his current whereabouts."

"I *see*. Tsk, tsk. Well, *perhaps* you can *enlighten* me with the *whereabouts* of Apollo Venerates."

"Again, sir, I do not know. I have people working on it."

"Save it, *General*. You are a *series* of disappointments. You *failed* to apprehend Godwin *correctly–*"

"Major Ozbourne–" Ginger began, but Serter silenced her with a wave.

"Your *inability* to assume *responsibility* for your actions. If *Ozbourne* is a *liability*, you *never* should have put him in *charge* of the mission. The fault is *yours*.

"Under your direct *supervision*, Godwin *escapes*. Now, when I ask you to *enlighten* me on the current circumstances of my *enemies*, *you* don't know *who they are*, or *where they can be found*. I need *names*. I need *locations*.

"When you *should* be focusing your *full* attention on carrying out *my* commands and protecting *my* interests, *you* are too *busy* updating your *profiles* on your credit bank?"

It was true. Prior to being summoned, Ginger was updating all of her public and private profiling information by changing her title from Colonel to General. It seemed like such a bad idea, right at the moment.

Things could not look worse. Ginger was struck mute. Every time she opened her mouth, she changed her mind and said nothing.

Serter spoke up, but not to Ginger. "Mainframe: General Ginger *Star terminated* from Serter Company effective *Monday*, August 16, 2066 9:07 PM."

This cannot be happening! Ginger's mind screamed.

Ginger raised her eyes to look between her fingers and met Jason's gaze head on. His eyes smiled cruel.

"*Now*, if you get out of my office in the next 30 *seconds*, I will *spare* you the *lobotomy*. Consider it an act of *kindness* in lieu of a more *proper* severance."

Ginger jumped up and scrambled out the door.

"Typical," Serter said to himself. "In the face of *failure*, the weak will abandon their *duty*."

A few minutes later, Jason was interrupted from his dark thoughts.

"*Mediacast Session requested by Major Ursa Ozbourne*"

"*Allow* mediacast session."

"Sir, I know the location of Venerates and Godwin," Ozbourne's image said dutifully.

"*You,* on the other hand, always seem to carry out your orders *perfectly,* Ozbourne." Serter said, as if Ozbourne had any clue as to what his basis for comparison was.

"It is my sworn duty, sir."

This Ozbourne may be of some considerable value, thought Serter.

"Congratulations, *Colonel.* Now, bring them to me."

MONDAY 16th 2066   21:33 EST

Farnsworth, Dorian, Eris, Pierce, and Pol found themselves amply accommodated by the genuine wood dining table as they sat and waited for Pastor Truman and the tea.

"You should not be so casual in giving someone your name." Eris looked through her mask at Pol, her sole eye fixed on his.

"When did I do that?" Pol asked.

"You told the pastor your name."

Pol thought back.

"What *is* your name?" Dorian asked.

Eris continued, disregarding Dorian's question. "When you extend your name to someone, you disclose your address–you give them power over you. Without a name, there is no identity. In this scenario, you gave someone–"

"I don't think we need to worry too much about Truman," Pierce yawned. "He's harmless enough."

"Nothing happens without consequence." Eris admonished.

"Amen to that." Farnsworth murmured.

"Names can also set you free." Truman spoke up, re-entering the room.

"Oh goody, *Mal's* back." Pierce grumbled.

Eris looked over at Truman. "Elucidate."

Pierce shot Eris an evil stare that went unnoticed.

"Well, let us start with the concept that our minds and hearts cannot help but become degenerate–eventually out of boredom, to the extreme of a vampirical conundrum of timeless boredom. Invariably, we will seek out more and more suspicious means of gratifying our want for distraction.

"We may mature and overcome our iniquity, but it must be encountered nonetheless. Obviously, the minds and hearts of those with an understanding of their religion are equally susceptible to this degradation as the minds and hearts of those without.

"In Xianity, at least, there is a *name* for our creator–that we might look together, on something *greater,* to guide us. That we are not superior to one another –although our roles may differ–and that we have purpose...at least, purpose beyond our own desires and needs.

"Also, there is a *name* for our tormentor. If we *believe only* in ourselves, then we can also *blame only* ourselves. When we blame ourselves, *knowing* we should not fall prey to such mediocrity, we take our guilt and embarrassment out on those around us. Then *we* become the tormentors, as do *our* names.

"But I digress. The tea is ready now, and I think you will all be delighted."

"What's with the *tea*, anyway? Is this guy British or something?" Dorian asked nobody in particular.

"What's wrong with tea?" Pierce asked.

"Nothing. But I mean, its *tea.* So what?"

""You know, *some* people just like tea, okay?" Pierce said, staving off feelings for Mary.

Farnsworth whispered something to Dorian.

"*I* would still like to know some more of your names, if we could move beyond the more obvious formalities. There *is* yet a job to be done. I'll start; I am Silverberg Police Officer Dorian Smith."

The room stayed silent.

"Whatever," Dorian grumbled, sliding back into his chair as Truman returned with tea auspiciously chaperoned by plates of shortbread cakes. After a small period of appreciation for the tea and cake interlude, the table once again sounded with dialogue–relaxed dialogue, one that spoke of satiation and satisfaction.

Except for Eris. Eris did not share the same sense of fulfillment and calm that everyone else in the room was experiencing. Eris could only detect such feelings on the very fringe of her awareness. Feelings that, when analyzed closer, revealed a truth of absolute horror–bad math.

Something was trying to compromise her, already her calculations were not figuring correctly. Worse, Eris, severed from the AIMN, would have to engage this completely alone.

MONDAY 16th 2066 ⚠ 22:09 EST

In the kitchen of the church, under his camouflage, Colonel Ozbourne waited impatiently for the occupants of the other room to fall under the influence of the drugs that he used to spike the tea.

*This waiting is **unbearable,*** he thought.

MONDAY 16th 2066 ⚠ 22:16 EST

ERIS » **Error 13** «
ERIS » ***Sequestering Anomalous Biological Synapses*** «
ERIS » **Error 13** «
ERIS » ***Finding and Replacing*** «
ERIS » **Error 13** «

ERIS » ***Override*** «

That...worked? Thought Eris, genuinely amazed. *Isn't it Error 11?*

ERIS » ***Sequestering Anomalous Biological Synapses...Completed*** «
ERIS » ***Finding and Replacing...Completed*** «

It felt like an eternity, but Eris *finally* broke free of the drugs coursing through her half human body. Awareness of her surroundings floated violently to the surface of her consciousness as Colonel Ozbourne ran into the room, making a considerable amount of noise despite his technological invisibility.

He looked over everyone at the table, and as a final test to see that there would be no opposition, he divested himself of his camouflage.

In a curious twist of fate, neither Eris nor Ozbourne recognized each other, despite their intimate past. The leather mask that Eris wore obscured her face so that Ozbourne did not recognize her from the Godwin's apartment, and Eris was not sentient when Ozbourne shot her, still rebooting from Pierce's EMW clap that rendered her inert and powerless.

Although Eris detected that Ozbourne did not realize she was operable, she could not help but notice that her companions were completely incapacitated.

Chapter 6

Colonel Ozbourne tapped his credit bank. "Request mediacast session with Jason Serter."

An imagescreen hosting Jason Serter's image soon appeared before Ozbourne.

"Well? *Colonel* Ozbourne?" Serter looked piercingly at Ozbourne.

"Mission accomplished, *sir*. I have successfully incapacitated the primary, as well as several secondary targets." Ozbourne swept his arm back to gesture to the table where everyone apparently slept.

"Why, oh *why* would you initiate a *mediacast session* with me from the heart of your *assignment*? Did you suppose that I would *like* someone to monitor my *awareness* of what has transpired there?"

"..."

Ozbourne was denied his chance to respond, however, as Serter immediately ended the mediacast session.

Ozbourne signaled his team to join him, and they began the process of extracting everyone from the church.

"You want to take *everyone* out of here? Even the priest?" A team member asked.

"He's no priest," Ozbourne spat. "He's a *pastor*. And yes."

Title	Employees	Name	Constituents
Private	Self		
Sergeant	8-12	Squad (Team)	
Lieutenant	26-55	Platoon (Department)	2+ Squads
Major	80-225	Company (Store)	2-8 Platoons
Colonel	300-1,300	Battalion (Area)	2-6 Companies
General	1,500 - 3,000	Regiment (Region)	2+ Battalions

Region	Location	Primary Identity
North America	San Francisco, CA, USA	Serter Company
South Africa	Cape Town, South Africa	Eshcorp
Northern Eurpoe	Stockholm, Sweden	Serter Company
Southern Europe	Roma, Itlay	Axioms
West Asia	New Delhi, India	Eshcorp
Australia	Newcastle, Australia	Dream Factory
South America	Buenos Aires, Argentina	Bagel Lord
Central	District B, AIE, Silverberg	Serter Company

Chapter 7:

Keys

Fri 13	Sat 14	Sun 15	Mon 16	Tues 17	Wed 18	Thur 19	Fri 20
				13:16			

A disheveled and frustrated young man named Apollo had been wandering the lengthy rings of Silverberg's largest mall for *hours*. He saw all manners of stores and kiosks that promised to alleviate any form of suffering from boredom to sickness, and all things in between. He saw an amusement park, a circus, and even passed several Zoos. Truly, if it could be found on the planet, it could be purchased or seen–even experienced–at the Silverberg mall.

His lack of comfort was plain on his face. His hair had started matting to his forehead already some hours ago, and his designer shirt from Haydee's had been spoiled by the remains of an apple pie Ala mode he had purchased from a food gondola earlier.

Eris had sent a note that said to "meet up at the front of the bike shop," and to "maintain silence, do not make any transmissions." The problem with this was that there are enough bike shops across the Silverberg mall to keep one entertained for hours or days, depending on the commitment of the shopper.

Eris spotted Pol, finally, and started a deliberate stride towards him. She marched up to him angrily, making it a point to articulate every tap of heavy footfall.

"Why didn't you wait in front of the bike shop, you idiot? This is a major Set back."

Pol tilted his head submissively and grinned. "I waited in front of *twenty* bike shops, my dear. There are more bike shops here than there are people in my hometown." Pol exaggerated. "Now who's the idiot?"

Eris grabbed Pol's hand and, with little effort, pulled him out onto the concourse ring.

"You are," she shot between clenched teeth as they brushed past a couple of pedestrians. "I had to make sure neither of us were being followed. So, I told you to *wait* for me in front of the bike shop. I did this so that I could take an alternate route in order to watch the area better. *Now* I had to spend all this time trying to find you as well. *Why* would you keep wandering around?"

"Wait," Pol paused, once again, to consider the situation. "Why didn't you just suggest that we meet at a *particular* store?"

"Because I don't want to give away our location, of course." Eris smiled. "Idiot."

"Wait," Pol started.

"*Don't* push your luck, Pol." Eris warned.

Eris continued walking in a hurried pace, darting to and fro from walking alongside Pol to admiring the spectacles on sale in the various vendor windows and storefronts.

"Just keep walking." Eris told him, more than once. "I always have an eye on you–you won't get lost. Keep walking. You're slowing me down. Keep–"

"Alright!" Pol exclaimed, tired of Eris' constant instructions.

Pol continued to walk, although barely paying any attention to what was going on. He was lost in thought, trying to remember whatever it was that he had forgotten. *Why do I feel like I am forgetting something?   Probably just being paranoid.*

As he passed in front of a shop made completely out of the most brilliant glass[39Δ] he had ever seen, he could not stop himself from slowing down and peering inside.

GYRE & GIMBLE

<u>*Gyre and Gimble*</u> read the sign over the entrance to what must be a coffee shop and bookstore. People were milling about the isles, carefully cradling monogrammed coffee receptacles in their elbows while their hands held, carefully, some random tomes of preposterous lore.

[39Δ] Or perhaps lead crystal or its equivalent.

It's almost a wonder that no one collides with anyone else. Pol thought, amused at his observations. He continued to watch, almost enthralled.

He noticed a woman who did not seem to mind in the *least* that her child was blatantly annoying some other nearby guests. He saw an old woman suddenly need to sit down, her need addressed by a nearby gentleman. He saw a man sipping his coffee who had some considerable nerve damage in his eye. Twitch. He then realized that the man was simply winking, as if to signal for attention. A signal directed at *Pol*.

Why is that man winking at me? Pol thought.

As Pol stood and thought about it, the man's attempts at winking were becoming more and more exaggerated. Eventually the man stood up, and preceded to wave his arms, beckoning, while winking and nodding at Pol. The spectacle was such that several of the other guests could not help but laugh.

Pol did a mental shrug, and proceeded to go inside and approach the gentleman.

Pol crossed by several tables and bookshelves lined with old style books. He turned past the last table and approached the man who had returned to sitting by himself in the corner.

The man looked to be somewhere in his early forties, with thick white hair pulled back into a ponytail, with black eyebrows. Hard-won lines of emotion etched his countenance. There was a curious look about his eyes that threatened to overwhelm you when you met their gaze. Apart from that, the man was of casual build, and looked as if he was about four days out of shaving.

"You winked at me." Pol said.

"I did. And then some."

"Yeah. That was a little odd."

"Apparently it was the *only* way to get your attention."

"Why are you winking at me? Do you know me?"

"I do."

"Why not just come and get me, then?"

"I would prefer you came to me, specifically by *choice*."

"Well," Pol wondered. "*How* do you know me?"

"At the moment, that is actually the least of your concerns."

"What, then, should I be concerned about?"

"Danger."

"I'm in danger right now?"

"More than you know."

"Are you here to kill me?"

"No, I'm here to save you."

"Save me from what?"

"Yourself."

Pol stepped backward unconsciously as the man stood up.

"Please," urged the man. "Hear me out. We're in a bookstore; what could happen?"

Pol shrugged.

"Would you like some coffee?" The man asked.

"Um, no, I don't really have all kinds of time to chat," Pol said, thinking that perhaps coming here was a mistake. "I've got to meet somebody. I mean, I'm following someone...er, I don't mean it like that. I should be going."

"Don't worry, what I have to say will not take much time."

Pol looked at the man.

The man shrugged. "...and I thought you might like some coffee."

Weird.

"Okay, well, *how* do you know all this?" Pol sat down.

"I thought we might start with danger."

"Okay, *how* am I in danger?"

"Great," The man said as he pulled out a pen and yellow paper tablet.

"Wow, pen and paper. Funny, I never see much of that in Silverberg."

"Funny, there's not much *to* see in Silverberg." The man said, moving to Pol's side of the table. "...Of quality. My name is Uriel, by the way."

"Pol."

Uriel started writing and drawing as he spoke. "The *greatest* danger is that you treat this conversation as having never happened: you must *always* think that our conversation happened. This is a paramount danger, because if you do not think that this is a *real* conversation, then you cannot give it the attention it requires."

"Now *how* could I *possibly* think that this conversation didn't happen?" Pol half smiled.

"Don't interrupt. Besides, I have more to go." Uriel then drew this symbol on the paper:

"The *second* danger is that you are leaving too many choices to be made for you by those around you. You must start making your decisions for yourself. Further, you must assume responsibility for those decisions. It is not the decisions that you make during your life that define it, as much as your *response* to your decisions. This is one of the Keys."

It seemed to Pol thought he had heard that before.

"The *third* danger is that you might be afraid to confront *yourself.* You *keep* believing the lie because it *suits* you. What *is* the lie? The *lie* is that you have to live your life in fear. The *truth* is that you can live your life by trust *rather* than in fear. This is one of the Keys."
Okay, this guy is just a weirdo. Pol thought.
"The *fourth* and *final* danger, and curiously the same reason by which I come to speak with you, is that you doubt your own significance. I have come to warn you against this–**do not** doubt your own significance."

Uriel sat back into the couch, and waited for Pol's response.

Pol frowned. "I don't see how you think you *know* anything about me, much less about my *danger.* My *danger,* right now, is from some super powerful businessmen finding out where I am, *not* the musings of some altruistic gypsy."
"Not quite...*I* represent that which created the universe. *You* might call me an angel." The man smiled.

Pol rolled his eyes. *Oh boy, here we go again,* he thought.

TUESDAY 17th 2066   14:44 EST

Agent Director Thompson paced around the room. Imagescreens bore the images of Agents Dodgson, Nelson, and Anderson, and there was *also* one of Axel.
Although Nelson and Dodgson were clearly unnerved at the presence of Axel in this meeting, Thompson carried on with no visible indication of discomfort.

"Agent Dodgson maintains that Apollo Venerates was issued a viable credit bank during processing. There is no evidence to suggest otherwise, and beyond this instance of alleged misappropriation, Agent Dodgson has an otherwise unblemished record of service in the AIIS department. In conclusion, I no longer require his appearance here today."

Axel nodded.

Agent Dodgson's image winked out.

"Agent Nelson maintains that the reason we are unable to locate Apollo Venerates is that there is a discrepancy with the *Mainframe*. Agent Nelson?" Thompson turned his noirglass expression towards the imagescreen displaying Agent Nelson.

Nelson cleared his throat. "Yes, well," Nelson continued to look at the image of Axel on and off, nervously. "You see. Okay. The Mainframe has been hacked. Somewhere, there is a machine smarter than ours, and our enemies have managed to completely take over–"

"*Enough*," Axel interrupted. The room went quiet.

"What *else* do you have, Nelson?" Said Thompson, perhaps nervously.

"I don't have anything *else*. All of my investigation corroborates that there is data corruption of a magnitude beyond comprehension at the *primary* level of the Mainframe. The corruption must be ever present, ever working, without exhaustion or error–capable of making corrections over an expansive plane of programming, nigh simultaneously."

Thompson frowned.

Nelson was under too much stress. He had spent the last two days trying to work this out, and finally he broke. "FINE. What I am getting at is that Dodgson and Thompson are *lying*." Nelson's image looked at Axel's. "What I have been suggesting is wrong with the Mainframe is *impossible*. *Agent Director Thompson* professionally *suggested* that the Mainframe had been hacked, and assigned me to investigate. This is all an attempt at redirection. Dodgson clearly did not perform his job satisfactorily, as Venerates is his *direct* responsibility.

"Dodgson and Director Thompson have *always* been close. Likely, this is Thompson's way of protecting his pet. Well, I am sick of it. Job or not, there *is* no way to explain this paradox with the Mainframe, other than choice edits at the uppermost level–edits that *only* Director Thompson and yourself have access to."

"I have to go." Axel's image faded from the imagescreen.

Thompson frowned. "Nelson, you're dismissed."
Nelson frowned.
"Look, you're the poster child for misery, Nelson. Go get some rest, we'll discuss it later. You're not fired. You *are* in trouble. Now go."
Nelson disappeared.

Anderson looked genuinely delighted, to the point that he may have coughed a small laugh of amusement.

"Anderson?" Thompson asked, raising a furry eyebrow.

"I've got nothing," Anderson said, his deep voice ringing with satisfaction and sarcasm. "But, as I also do not want to endanger my position with the company, I'll happily extend to you what I know. Very recently, I sent a CSPD Detective to the church to get Godwin, and very possibly Venerates as well. I spoke to the officer accompanying him just prior to their infiltration. That is the last time I heard from either of them.
"I cannot locate *any* of the individuals that I just mentioned, leading me to suspect that somewhere in Silverberg there is some kind of shield against the Mainframe. Maybe it's something that can be made mobile, which might explain some of the other Mainframe discrepancies as well.
"Maybe Serter got there first. If so, he was cleaner than the last time he decided to make a move."

"You're going to have to go down to the church for yourself."
Anderson smiled and flipped his hair back. "Already been there, boss."
"And?"
"Well, *something's* amiss, I'll tell you that. There's *nobody* in the church. I checked around, and apparently even the *pastor* is missing. It was all very well done. I suspect similar crimes have been performed that we have yet to even catch on to. What I did *not* suggest to *Axel* is that perhaps someone has managed to effectively teleport matter from one place to another. The thought is absurd, but

there it is–wouldn't want to leave anything out.

"With your permission, I'd like to start a missing person campaign for Pastor Truman so that we can use the citizens as additional eyes and ears. If the Mainframe is compromised, it may be the only way to get some hard data. Find one, find them all, maybe."

"Maybe *again*," Thompson said after a moment. "I don't much like 'missing person campaigns;' they send waves of fear through the masses...yet, something *must* be done. Your argument against the Mainframe certainly merits consideration. Conduct your campaign, I suppose–only center it on *Godwin*, not Truman. The pastor is of no consequence to AI."

TUESDAY 17th 2066   16:38 EST

"An angel, eh? Save me from danger? So, where's *God*–or was he too busy to come himself?" Pol asked, unhappy with his new acquaintance.

"*I* was sent. No human has *ever* seen the creator, to wit, that which humanity *cannot* perceive."

"Cannot?"

"Not in entirety. Imagine a mathematical formula in a centimeter high font that covers a single plane over the complete universe. Now, see it in its entirety, number for number, letter for letter, position by position. Not invisible, yet not comprehensible. The analogy is imperfect, but built to accommodate your own imperfect perspective."

Uriel then turned his tablet so that Pol could see that the entirety of the page was covered with an impossibly complex mathematical formula.

"I get the idea."

"*All* people believe in things that they *cannot* perceive. This is very dangerous, left improperly examined. *Knowing* the difference between what one accepts on faith and what one accepts as fact is *critical* to ongoing development. This is one of the Keys."

"You said *I* might call you an angel. What would you call yourself?"

"It cannot be expressed merely in words–however, if a word must do, it would be *Malach*. In English, perhaps *messenger*."

Uriel sipped his coffee.

"You're awfully human for being an angel," Pol commented.

Uriel shrugged. "As there is nothing short of a show of force or grandeur that would have you believe me, it does not matter what form I appear in, nor what mannerisms I display. So long as you are *comfortable* enough, then the choice was clearly a successful one."

"Oh, well, if it's about my *comfort*, why not have your name be something more familiar? Maybe your name should be Warren or William?" [40Δ]

The man shrugged. "Because my name is Uriel."

TUESDAY 17th 2066   17:01 EST

Somewhere unobservable, somewhere soundproof, somewhere *very* few people know about: Pierce screamed out in pain.

Serter had somehow managed to bypass his augmentation programming, locking him in rigor, straight as a stick.

"Oh, I could *really* get into this," Serter smiled, a small granulated rainbow lining his nostrils.

TUESDAY 17th 2066   17:02 EST

"Well, you certainly have my attention, now what do you want?" Pol grumbled.

"I told you...to warn you that you were in danger."

"Okay."

"Well, that's all *done* now, isn't it?" Uriel ripped some of the pages off the tablet and handed them to Pol.

"That's it?" Pol blinked. "Hm. Okay, great, so then I am going."

"Okay."

Pol started walking away...then he turned back around.

"So, why, then?"

"Why what?"

"Why creation? Why life? Why?"

"There *is* an answer, however it is one that can only be *realized*. Anything otherwise would be ultimately slanted. Only *you* can find it. If you ever look for it, anyway. *He* winks at you all the time, you just never notice,"

Uriel looked at Pol, his eyes almost sad. There was something *familiar* about him...Pol could not handle the gaze, however, and averted his eyes.

[40Δ] Two old American friends of Pol.

Pol thought about it, but did not come to any positive conclusions.

"Yeah, that's about the kind of answer that I expected. Cryptic, amorphous, vague. What's more, is that this entire dialogue seems *pointless*. If you *were* an angel, you certainly never gave me any help worth having, and as you are *not*, I don't know why you're even wasting my time with all this."

Uriel sipped his coffee. "Perhaps I am simply trying to get you to believe in something else, then. That wouldn't be so strange, would it? Someone trying to get you to believe in something *they* call 'truth,' or reinforce what you currently believe in–simply for the sake of *getting* them to believe?"

"Why *do* people do that?" Pol asked, thinking on it.

"Who knows?" Uriel smiled. "Maybe they just get a sense of satisfaction or control by misleading others. Maybe they are very passionate about their convictions. Maybe there is power in belief. *Maybe* they work for someone that seeks to subjugate everyone else. One way or another, only *you* determine what you *want* to believe. *You* are what makes it true for yourself. This is one of the Keys."

"Yet...despite my perspective, there *is* a truth."

"Yes *and* no."

"Yes *or* no. It can't be both."

"It can, it is. Irrelevant. Ultimately, it does not matter whether you understand the dichotomy of *this* truth or not. I will simply concede to say: Yes, there is a truth beyond that of your perspective."[41△]

"And what is *that* truth?" Pol asked, waiting for Uriel to misspeak.

"Didn't I *just* say it was *beyond* your perspective?"

Pol folded his arms, upset.

"Don't be frustrated, you will not always have *that* perspective."

"Which perspective is that?"

"The one that you have now."

Pol growled.

"You're not very *meek*, are you?" Uriel asked.

"Huh?"

41△ Of course, Uriel *must* concede that there is a truth beyond Pol's own, otherwise he disavows *himself,* which is the last thing he wants to communicate to Pol. Pol struggles with understanding that **subjective** truth is absolute, whereas **objective** truth is true only so long as every subject agrees. This is the dichotomy and a doorway to understanding.

"I mean, all this *sarcasm*, and *demanding*, and...growling? You're an aggressive type of guy, eh?"

Pol was confused. "Me? No. Wait."

Uriel stood up.

Pol backed away.

"Well, that's more like it."

"What's that?" Pol asked, completely confused.

"Nothing."

Pol had enough. "Okay, *Uriel*, I've got places to be."

"Be seeing you," Uriel saluted and sipped his coffee.

Pol walked away.

TUESDAY 17th 2066 ⛰ 17:20 EST

Lt. Farnsworth woke up slowly, the last of the drugs almost finished burning themselves out of his system. He looked around the room to notice Dorian, Truman, and *that woman*, all strapped to gurneys–similar to himself.

Farnsworth noticed there was only one exit and no windows–this room was designed for considerable privacy. Judging by the door, it was also designed for resilience.

He tried against the restraints, but he could not overcome them. The effort was decidedly half-hearted; he knew he couldn't get out.

Well, I think this is not a hospital. Farnsworth thought. *Strike that, I* **hope** *this is not a hospital. What kind of treatment is this? Wait a sec. How did I get here? Okay, let's see here...tea with the pastor!*

Woozy. Tea must have been drugged. Not by Truman, he's over there. Who does that? Who drugs people? –bad guys! **Bad guys?** *Man, I am out of it.*

Right. Dorian, Truman...who is this woman, anyway? Oh wait. Godwin. Where the heck is Godwin? And that fat kid...what was his name?

TUESDAY 17th 2066 ⛰ 17:55 EST

"Apollo."

"Really, I prefer Pol." Pol insisted.

"Very well." Uriel smiled and sipped his coffee.

"That must be good coffee." Pol noted.

"Curiously, it is completely devoid of taste."

"Why drink it, then? Oh wait, I know: for *my* comfort."

"There we are with that aggression, again." Uriel warned.

Pol reflected. "I suppose I *am* aggressive. Sorry. It's just that this whole meeting is so absurd. Really, so is this entire trip to Silverberg! I don't know why I care so much about this moment as of any of it. Clearly you are somehow a lunatic, yet pleasant enough."

Pol relaxed back into his chair.

Uriel drew pictures of hearts all over the page.

As Uriel summoned the waiter in order to purchase an additional beverage, Pol started thinking that he was forgetting something again. *What am I forgetting? Man, I hate that. Something I need to buy? Do? Wait! Eris! She's out in the mall, looking for me! I've got to go! Wait. Didn't I already leave?*

TUESDAY 17th 2066 ⚠ 18:42 EST

Farnsworth woke up again.

Must have dozed. Curse it all.

"Smith!" He called, his voice cracking with a dry tone. Farnsworth swallowed. "Smith! Truman!"

Okay. Plan B...what on Earth can plan B be?

"Help?" Farnsworth joked.

"In what manner do you require help?" Eris asked.

!

"Well, for one, I would like to *not* be strapped down to this gurney."

Eris struggled against her own bonds, but was unable to triumph.

"Tempered mirroranium; we will require keys."

Farnsworth went to slap his forehead, but was quickly reminded of his own situation. *This is getting me nowhere.*

"Do you have an internal credit bank?"

"I do."

"Wonderful, call the CSPD, ask for–"

"I cannot. It is broken."

"Oh. Well... Lay there, then. I'll lay here. Eventually, someone will come."

"Who?"

"What?"

"*Who* will come?"

"*I* don't know; whoever placed us here."

"Oh. Colonel Ozbourne."

"*Who?*"

"The commander of the men that placed us here."

"You *know* who kidnapped us?"

"Yes."

"So you were awake and aware when we were taken?"

"Yes."

"And you just laid there and were taken as well?"

"Yes."

"*Why?*" Farnsworth would have slapped his forehead again.

"For I have *no* mind, yet *still* trying to establish why an Error 13 override did not propagate an Error 11. I am *still* running calculations. You asked for help, I split my processes. Even now, there should be an Error 08...that's an Error 06! I know not why."

"Right. Let's just forget I asked that, then."

TUESDAY 17th 2066   ⚠   19:00 EST

"Apollo."

"I prefer to be called *Pol*...didn't I introduce myself to you as Pol?" Pol was confused.

"Yes, that's right." Uriel wrote some notes on his legal pad. "Now: doing the *right* thing–*especially* in the face of adversity or in the absence of the promise of *either* retribution or gain–is one of the Keys.

"Wait." Pol was about to catch Uriel in doubletalk. "What *is* the *right* thing? Didn't you *just* say that *I* determine my own truths? So *I* determine what is right and what is wrong? Are you *sure* you're an angel? Surely *God* does not want *me* to determine what means what."

"Pol, are you telling me that you don't know the difference between right and wrong?"

"No, I'm just saying that *my* values are influenced by that which surrounds me. Like culture, or environment. *I* don't determine what is right and what is wrong."

"You don't?"

"What does that mean?" Pol asked.

"It means that you *do* determine what is right and what is wrong–culture and environment notwithstanding. Haven't *you* ever decided to do something *other* than what your father told you?"

"Well, yeah...but that doesn't make it right."

"So then you *do* know the difference."

This is going nowhere. Pol thought, annoyed. *Wait..am I forgetting something?*

TUESDAY 17th 2066   19:05 EST

There came a sound from across the room that was like a man's last audible gasp twisted into an impossible moan, sounding as dire as though the dead were returning to life.

Dorian stopped moaning when he discovered his restraints.

"What the?"

"Welcome back, Smith." Farnsworth managed.

"Where...are we?"

"No clue. Somewhere very private."

"What happened?"

"Tea was drugged, not sure about afterward."

"Mary's killers?"

"You think *we* were the targets?"

"Why not? Anderson sent us to the church in the first place–it was a set up! AI probably planned the whole thing from the start. You and I are too big a nuisance, so we're being dealt with. I *know* it's a plot by Axel."

"It was Serter Company. Jason Serter." Eris interjected.

"Well, now how do you know *that*?" Farnsworth asked incredulously.

"I saw Ozbourne interact with him via mediacast session."

Farnsworth was silent, a small smile spreading across his face as he watched Dorian come to the same conclusions that he had with Eris.

"You mean you were *awake* when we were kidnapped?" Dorian asked in disbelief.

"Yes."

"Alright, wait. *What* is your name?" Dorian asked.

"Eris."

"*Heiress?*"

"No."

"Um, okay, *Eris,* you were awake and just *laid* there?"

Farnsworth spoke up. "I don't know how much you want to get her talking... bird's got a screw loose."

"Bird?"

"He means me." Eris offered.

"Oh. So what are we doing, now?"

Farnsworth exhaled. "Right. Now, we're waiting for whomever–Ozbourne– to come and do something. We can't escape our bonds, and *were* we able to do that, we still could not quit the room. We are doomed."

"Oh...did you just say *quit the room*?" Dorian smiled. "I *do* love you. At *least* the doomsayer is back. At last, things are starting to feel more comfortable around here."

TUESDAY 17th 2066 Ⓜ 20:00 EST

"Apollo."

"Yes?"

"I am running out of time. I *need* you to stay focused. Maybe a cup of coffee?" Uriel urged.

"Oh, for heaven's sake, buy me a coffee already if it's so important to you."

Uriel told a nearby waiter to bring a coffee to Pol.

"Aggression. Your relationship with your *own* life–that is, your ability to appreciate what you have and have not. Your ability to be thankful, to forgive, and to love–*these* are direct reflections of your relationship with your creator, regardless of name."

Pol looked back up in time to receive the monogrammed G&G coffee receptacle from his server. Across the table, Uriel had spilled his own coffee, and was working diligently to sop it all up with a towel.

"Thanks." Pol nodded to the server. "Anyway, your little addendum here implies that the subject concedes that there is intelligent design…God. I don't know that I believe in all that, although it would be comforting to know that there was some incredible, cosmic purpose for *me*. I have hope, I suppose."

"Hope is not enough."

"What is enough, then?"

"Only love."

"What are you, some kind of subliminal salesman?"

"What?"

"In all the time we have been speaking, you sound like all the subliminal messages in Silverberg, only humanized. Or maybe angel-ized. Or whatever."

"There's that aggression again," Uriel said as he looked around. "Hold on– I'm afraid I have to go." Uriel started walking away.

"Cry-baby!" Pol called after him.

Why am I acting like this? Pol thought, amazed at his own behavior.

Uriel turned around. "I'm afraid I have to go get another coffee."

Having won another coffee, Uriel walked back over to Pol.

"What if, at the end of your life, your reward was that you would become a *god* in your next?" Uriel mused. "To live without the need to breathe, eat, or worry. To create or destroy *unbound*, to so far as your imagination will take you.

"Now *some* would look back on their existence and begin to suddenly understand the machinations of God: *why* everything was and is, and why and how it was a component and necessary. A sudden, total realization of *everything and all*–even the insidious truth behind free will.

"Some would come into their godhood with patience and understanding. Some would come into it without emotion, without regard. A few precious would create life that is joyful and gracious, thankful and generous...yet most would simply do *nothing* whatsoever. No creation, no production. The call to initiate is not as strong as one may think. The very act of creation is the ultimate act of *will*, and the tolerance for it the ultimate act of *love*."

"So...we're all going to be gods?" Pol asked.

"No. My you are an idiot." Uriel put his hands over his face, but not his mouth. "To *be* or To *never* have been? *That* is the question, *and* one of the Keys."

CHAPTER 7

"What is it with all the keys, anyway? Keys for what?"

Uriel sat back down, sipping a fresh cup of coffee.

"Keys. For locks, of course."

"What locks?" Pol asked.

"Locks that you may or may not notice at first, but will invariably notice before the end."

"I don't know why you bother telling me anything at all!" Pol said, his level of frustration reaching its zenith. "*Everything* you say is cryptic, vague, and mysterious. You know, considering *that*, maybe you *are* an angel–but aren't angels supposed to have lightning for faces? And I don't recall anything about angels drinking coffee. What about a halo? You just need to work on a few things. Telling me what 'the keys' *are* and not *what they are for* is not fair."

Uriel looked somewhere between hurt and amused.

"It should be enough I say anything *at all.* As far as *fair* is concerned, do you not yet realize that the only *fair* life is an *equal* life? How can humans *possibly* desire *both* individuality and equality *simultaneously?* Can anyone *truly* desire that all human existences were made *identical?* It would be rhetorical creation.

"In regards to fairness and equality: human beings only look the *same* in regards to their shortcomings and failures, and *only* in these. It's *not* fair. Deal with it."

Uriel sipped his coffee as he said into his cup: "Clearly, you wouldn't have it any other way."

TUESDAY 17th 2066   20:05 EST

The great doors slid open, and a man wheeled Pierce through on a type of handcart. He stopped abruptly, inertia sending Pierce tumbling onto the floor. Stiff as a board, he bounced painfully.

"I hate those guys," Pierce mumbled into the floor.

Farnsworth and Dorian shifted uncomfortably on their gurneys. Eris and Truman were unmoved for their individual reasons.

"Gas these losers, we'll deal with them more, later." Ozbourne appeared slightly after the sound of his voice, long enough to get a visual of the contents of the room as the doors slid mechanically closed.

"Mainframe's not answering." Pierce mumbled to nobody in particular, publishing his discovery at attempting to connect. "This seems to be the case inside Serter's place."

"What happened to you?" Farnsworth tried to look over at Pierce, but could not angle enough to see.

"Oh, you know...Jason Serter and I are *close and personal* with each other. He took me aside for a few hours to let me know how much he had been thinking about me since we last hung out."

"There's no hiss." Eris spoke up.

"Wha-t?" Dorian said, his voice breaking. He cleared his throat. "There's no hiss?"

"Of gas."

Soon afterward, they were all fast asleep. Everyone except Eris, who was busy calculating Errors.

TUESDAY 17th 2066   △   **23:59 EST**

"Apollo."

Pol looked up from the tablet. At his signal, Pol returned the tablet to Uriel, who started drawing on the paper with broad sweeps and deliberate markings.

"I am going to have to attend to other matters very soon. I wanted to take a *personal* moment to put some questions to you about Silverberg so that you are not consumed completely by it."

"Go for it," Pol said, sipping his coffee.

*It **really** has **no** taste,* Pol thought, slightly amazed.

"One. Does the mouth of the messenger change the nature of the message?

"If a smoker tells you that smoking is bad–is it? I tell you now: *all* men are hypocrites. Listening to the message, instead of judging the veracity or credibility of the *messenger*, might help you to overcome some of your own misunderstandings.

"Two. *Do* the ends justify the means?

CHAPTER 7

"*If* you could build society into a personally or socially perfect image, isn't there a point where you are crossing the line of morality–propriety? *If* everyone is unique, and *all* in possession of free will: how could you possibly convince them to *all* live by the *same* set of rules? YOU? If you could end all war, disease, hunger, frailty, sickness, boredom, tra-la-la...if the human solution requires dominance or sacrifice, isn't there a price that is simply too big to pay?

"Isn't it interesting how it's relevant *which* person you are–the bricklayer or the architect–as to *how* you *feel* about the *method*?"

Chapter 8:

Serter

AUGUST *2066 EST*

Fri 13	Sat 14	Sun 15	Mon 16	Tues 17	Wed 18	Thur 19	Fri 20
					00:13		

As Uriel took another long swig from his coffee, someone tapped Pol on the shoulder.

Pol, startled, turned swiftly to address them.

"Whoa, now," the man began, his English accent lavish. He spoke in a slow, captivating manner. He put his hands up as if to show he was unarmed, and took a couple steps backward. He wore rounded noirglasses whose black lenses simply seemed to reflect the light as to create a dark mirror of what was about him. He also wore a "Down with Axel" bandana tied across his forehead, restraining his hair which was neatly spilling onto his camouflage denim jacket.

"Sorry," Pol said, shaking his head and then wiped his hands over his eyes. "I'm just a little on edge at the moment," Pol turned to look at Uriel, only to find that he had gone. Pol did a double take.

"So, the carpenter pulled a batman on you, eh?" The English accent was decidedly pronounced.

"What?"

"Yer lion gone missing."

"Wait. *What*? Uriel? The guy that said he was an angel?" Pol said, almost stammering.

"Oh, *not* the lion, you say...just a cat. I'm more popular, anyway. No worries, gov. *Now* you've got the walrus to help you through all of this. Of course, he's no more an angel than I am a walrus. Extinct, you know. Come on, lad, I haven't got all day; walk with me."

Pol looked around.

"Call me Winston–I've always wanted to say that...hey, don't try to think *too* hard: you'll be all tired and wrung out before you hear the walrian side of the argument."

Pol looked at Winston in disbelief. "Wait, I'm lost," He started to point to Uriel's chair.

"Of course you are. Now, let's go get found."

Winston started walking away. Pol looked around for Uriel one last time, and sprinted to come up and walk alongside Winston.

"Don't look so down."

"Easy for you to say, with my luck you're the devil," Pol grimaced.

"I'm *not* the devil, mate! I already told you I'm the bloody walrus!"

Pol continued to sulk, arms hanging at his sides.

Winston shrugged. "Okay, so you're not terribly bright. We can work with that. C'mon, tell you what, I'll get you an ice cream cone to take the edge off."

Ice cream cone? Pol thought. "Uh, sure..."

Pol, deep down, was thinking about how good an ice cream cone would actually taste, despite the oddity of the suggestion. More than that, he almost started to feel an uncomfortable yearning for something. His mouth felt like he was chewing fabric–old fabric.

Winston purchased two ice cream cones from a nearby food gondola. Pol and Winston walked over to an oasis [42Δ] to sit down at a board of tic-tac-toe. While they ate their ice cream, Winston drew a cross in the upper right corner with his finger.

Pol looked down at the board. "No thanks."

"Just sit back, then, I'll play myself."

"What would the fun in that be?"

"I didn't say it would be *fun*."

"Well then, what would the point be?"

"I know, right? The game is boring, and serves no purpose; *complete* exercise in futility. What would be the point of the two of us playing it at all?" Winston asked, amused.

"None," Pol nodded.

[42Δ] An "oasis" is an area within Silverberg that is regulated for the public to utilize as recreation or resting opportunities. Often equipped with restrooms, water, games, lounge chairs, imagescreens, etc.

"Ever?" Winston raised an eyebrow.

Pol thought. "Well, maybe if we had never played the game before."

"Why then?"

"Well, because it would be new. And we could enjoy learning the game."

"So, once you know how to play a game, it is no longer fun?"

"No. I didn't mean that. I just mean tic-tac-toe."

"Oh. Why only that?"

"Because once you know how to play, it's always a tie."

"What's wrong with that?"

"Well, you don't learn anything, and there's no surprise, so it's no fun."

"*Why* don't you learn anything?"

"What's to learn?"

"Whatever you are looking to learn. Maybe by the manner or speed in which you play, I can determine things about you. Maybe by the shape of your icons. Maybe by the expression on your face. Maybe you could derive these things of me. Maybe how absurd parallel and perpendicular lines are. Maybe how beautiful they are.

"There's always an opportunity to *learn*, provided you are capable of discerning your opportunities. It may seem an arduous exercise, but that's just a single perspective.

"You see what you *want* to see. You see no value in the game, so you do not wish to play it. You fail to notice that you are not doing anything *else* to catch your attention at the moment, so why not?"

"Look, I just don't want to play, okay?"

"Fine," Winston pouted.

They finished their ice cream cones in silence. Winston played himself at tic-tac-toe. He lost. Pol shook his head.

WEDNESDAY 18th 2066   09:09 EST

Jason Serter was surrounded by several imagescreens. One kept exclusive watch of the room where the companions, bruised and battered, lay.

Whispers of rainbows could be seen about the desk as Jason stared unblinkingly at the imagescreens. Solid H invaded, coursing through Jason as water through a screen. He waited for it so patiently, and then finally the payoff!

Similar to Hypnizium users, users of Solid H are eventually able to will themselves asleep. Yet, every dose of Solid H continues to weaken and break the barriers between the conscious and subconscious minds, giving the abuser the ability to manipulate their hallucinations. Solid H users eventually experience the living dream, becoming gods in their own vision.

Jason was awake and asleep simultaneously. He flexed his mind, showing himself living visions of what he wanted to see. *He* had learned control. When he first started with Solid H, the neurological rush made him want to create everything bigger and bigger, to the point where he had to shut his mind down or be devoured by his own visions. He was beyond all that now. In charge. In control.

Nothing is beyond me. He came to this realization calmly. Serenity and Power. Jason giggled in glee.

WEDNESDAY 18th 2066   09:21 EST

"Breakfast time! Wake up, you wretches!" Ozbourne's voice penetrated everyone's slumber. The hours of induced sleep significantly soured everyone's mood even further.

"Stand up, Godwin, stop being so lazy! Ha-ha-har!" Ozbourne's laugh was forced and ugly.

Ozbourne walked across the room up to Truman's gurney. "Looks like the pastor's all out of things to preach. Must have had a weak heart."

"Truman's been imaged?" Farnsworth said, groggily.

"Seems so. He's the lucky one, though. When Serter's through with you, you'll wish you were in the pastor's shoes."

Ozbourne wheeled in a cart with various food items on it, along with a few large, empty pots with lids. He typed into each of the gurney's consoles the appropriate code to release the restraints. Dorian and Farnsworth rubbed their arms. Eris remained unmoving, as if still drugged to sleep. When Ozbourne released her restraints, he could not help but notice the caked and coagulated blood that had settled about the edges of her mask. Ozbourne gagged.

"I'll be back in a couple hours to retrieve one of you," Ozbourne chuckled, walking out the door. "Close it up!"

The doors slid closed.

"Food!" Dorian said, looking over the cart. "I wonder if it's really okay to eat?"

"Don't mind me," Pierce mumbled into the floor. "I rather like this position. Ow. I think my nose is broken."

Eris went over, picked up Pierce, and placed him upright, leaning him against the wall.

"Good enough," Pierce sighed. "Serter hacked my augs. I can only move my face. This is depressing, but could someone help me eat?"

"I have some pressing business of my *own* to attend to, at the moment," Farnsworth said, picking up a pot and walking towards the corner. "I'll see you all in 20 minutes. Wish I had a book."

WEDNESDAY 18th 2066   09:30 EST

"Hey, Winston!" A very short and very familiar looking man walked up to Winston's bench in the oasis.

"Goblin!" Winston cried, delighted.

The men embraced enthusiastically.

"Gob?" Pol asked.

"Oh, hey Pol!" Gob waved.

"*You two* know each other?" Pol said incredulously.

"Of course!" Gob nodded enthusiastically. "I have always been a huge fan of Winston the Walrus! His touch turns people into poets...*he's* the reason I ever got into music!"

"Oh." Pol suddenly felt echoes of memories from his last meeting with Gob. "How come I can understand you so well now?"

"Probably because you're *listening*. Last time you were too distracted."

Pol agreed, he was distracted last time, but still... "I don't think that's it."

"Oh, well then." Gob rubbed his chin, smiling. "Maybe I was too drunk and drugged up."

Pol smiled and nodded. "*That* I can believe."

"So, are you going tonight, or what?" Gob looked at Winston.

"Yeah, yeah. Pol here wanted to stop for a spot of ice cream."

"*I* wanted to stop? You asked."

"So I did. What a brilliant idea 'twas too."

"Where are we going?" Pol asked, confused.

"The Dark Side." Winston said, sounding ominous.

"The dark side of what?"

"No, it's a club–The Dark Side." Gob offered. "Great drinks, great atmosphere, great music."

"I should have known." Pol said, looking knowingly at Gob. "Wait a second. Uriel said I should stop letting other people make my decisions for me."

"No one is making any decisions for you, Pol. Do you *want* to go with us to the club?"

Pol thought. *Why do I keep feeling like I am forgetting something? I must be! That cursed old man in the bookstore! He distracted me! What was I doing? Coffee. Keys, Danger. What...*

"Well, tell you what, you're welcome to stay here and Gob and I will go ourselves. Cheers." Winston and Gob started walking away.

"No, wait." Pol stood up. "I'll go."

"Very good then." Winston smiled.

WEDNESDAY 18th 2066 ⚠ 09:41 EST

Eris, Dorian, Pierce, and Farnsworth surrounded the last gurney that held Pastor Truman.

"We need to offer a eulogy." Farnsworth suggested. "It's only proper."

"Did somebody even *know* this guy?" Pierce looked away. "Who can say anything?"

"We can try." Farnsworth sighed.

"Try what?" Truman asked in a low voice, startling the room.

"Am I losing it?" Dorian shook his head.

"You're fine," Truman yawned, and stretched as best he could under restraint. This took several minutes, of which the members of the room were silent.

"I haven't been with the church *all* my life." Truman spoke more firmly now. "I have delved into *many* different understandings, obsessed with the search for truth.

"I thought I was becoming wiser, yet I was only becoming worldlier. Some think the two are synonymous. You see, it was only when I *finally* relented, found my faith, and devoted my work to God–it was then that my works *finally* had meaning."

Dorian tapped his foot impatiently.

"Anyway, in my journeys to attempted enlightenment I have studied how to assimilate death by slowing down my bodily functions. I never thought I would actually use it to save myself. Serendipitous." Truman smiled.

"Serendipitous? Ha! It's *ironic*." Pierce said. "You've developed this skill, and out of all the times in your life that you might have used it, you used it at the *worst* possible time. Out of all of us, *you're* still clamped down to the gurney! Ozbourne never released you, all because of your precious *skill*."

Truman frowned.

"As it seems that we are not leaving of our own accord, *anyway,* I don't think it matters much." Farnsworth mumbled.

"Not that I am much better off." Pierce admitted, wryly. "Only way I am getting around is on a gurney myself."

"That's a *great* idea." Dorian announced, standing.

Grateful to dismiss his current sense of boredom, Dorian walked over to Pierce, and grabbed him so as to put him on the gurney.

At least, that's what he thought to do. As he went to pick up Pierce, he greatly misjudged the weight, neglecting to think that Eris must have had augmentations to help her manipulate Pierce's mass so effortlessly. Pierce toppled over Dorian, who was either now unconscious or too embarrassed to move.

"That was a *great* idea." Pierce mumbled into the floor.

"Shut up." Dorian groaned.

WEDNESDAY 18th 2066   10:20 EST

Pol, Winston, and Gob all continued to walk their way along the concourses and intermittent elevators on their way to the club. As they passed by several citizens, many of them pointed at Pol and started giggling and laughing.

"What are they laughing at?" Pol asked, blushing.

"You, silly. You don't have any clothes on!" Gob pointed

Pol looked down at himself. *What the?* He thought, immediately, embarrassingly aware of his own nakedness. *That's what I have been forgetting!* Pol jumped behind the nearest trash bin.

"Help!" Pol called.

"You need somebody?" Winston smiled.

"I think he needs some clothes." Gob grinned.

"Be a good goblin, and go fetch him some will you?"

Gob ran off. As Pol watched, he felt like Gob was shorter than he remembered. *Next thing I know he will say he was wearing elevator shoes last time.*

"Guess we're stuck here for the moment." Winston broke Pol's thoughts.

"I feel so stupid," Pol admitted.

"Don't sweat it, kid. This has happened to everyone."

"Huh? Don't be ridiculous."
"Seriously. Everyone."

"Why did you come up to me, anyway?" Pol asked, dejected.
"Pardon?"
"At Gyre & Gimble. Why did you tap me on the shoulder?"
"To save you."
"Oh really?" Pol moved to the defensive. This conversation was starting to sound too familiar.
"That's right."
"Save me from what?"
"From that *conversation*. That guy looked boring as all get out. I had to take pity on you, lad."
"No, seriously."
"Seriously."
"*Seriously*." Pol stressed.
"As serious as there are eight days a week. Truth of it is that I have simply taken fancy of you...for few reasons beyond mere curiosity, I'm afraid. Regardless, here we are, and that's that."

Gob came running back, his arms cruelly clutching what must be Pol's new clothing. As Gob arrived, he dumped the clothing onto Pol. Pol hastily donned his new garments.

When Pol stepped out from his makeshift shelter, he stopped to admire himself in the mirror of the wall. He was now wearing a (slightly wrinkled) red-and-white, almost checkerboard, Silverberg-style suit which boasted a red heart over his left breast.

Weird, Pol thought. Then, "*Ugh!*" in realization. **Mirror walls.** *I wasn't hiding from anything!* Pol looked at his cranny by the trash bin, then down at his suit. *Guess I'm wearing white and red, the alternative is unthinkable. Maybe we can stop for other clothing.*

"Why is there a heart on my jacket?" Pol asked.
"Shouldn't there be?" Winston asked, raising an eyebrow. "Don't you find it suits you?"
"Huh? No. I mean, okay, well, why the heart?"
Winston resumed walking. "Always questions with you."
"I think I have a right."
"Do you? What gives you any right?"
"Eh?"

"A right to what? For what? What gives you any kind of *right* to anything?"

"Oh." Pol fumbled for something to say. "Well, tell me out of common courtesy, then."

"Ah! Well said! In regards to common courtesy, then: I don't know *why* the heart is there–you must have put it there."

"No, *I* didn't."

"Very well then, you didn't."

Pol spoke thoughtfully. "You know, it seems like 'hearts' come up over and over in my life. Gob's with the *Valentine* Relics, Pierce has *heart* disease. My suit has a heart. It must be somehow significant."

"Must it?" Winston asked, amused enough to stop walking and turn to regard Pol. "You see or hear about a heart a few times and you have become compelled to entertain the idea that there may be greater significance–a sign, a symbol–yet, it's entirely possible that it is also *just* a series of coincidences.

"Don't get me wrong, mate." Winston flared his hands outward. "Maybe it *is* deliberate–intentional–some otherworldly force is guiding you, but...are you in a position to determine the truth of the significance, or lack thereof? I don't know that I would waste my energy vexing about it.

"Besides, you can't be so ambivalent about the whole thing–either you believe that *everything* is a coincidence, or that *nothing* is.

"You can compare some moments of your life with others and determine that you have found strange patterns–yet you will *always* find patterns if you look for them. Of course, that does not suggest that all patterns are worthless.

"That would be about as stupid as saying that everything is simply an amalgam of everything else. Everything is its *own* thing, although many things resemble many other things."

"How many times did you just say *'thing?'* You're starting to remind me of someone *else* that favors vague conversation." Pol half smiled.

Winston continued, ignoring Pol. "Don't trouble yourself with examining too closely any matters in which you have no responsibility, have no ability to impact, or have no ability to discern the truth. Any such conspicuous considerations could invite only either consternation or bolstering, neither of which will ever serve you.

"Instead, pursue the enigma that entertains you–avoid the ones that control you. Out of walrian curiosity: d'you believe what your angel friend was selling you?"

Pol frowned. "I don't know that he was really *selling* me anything, really. I guess he *was* really just warning me."

"Well, he wanted you to *believe* him, though, right?"

"Yeah..."

"So why do you think anyone would put so much energy into trying to get you to believe one thing or another?"

"We talked about the same thing. Want to hear what Uriel said?"

Winston continued, ignoring Pol. "Even by people you do not know, could not know, will never know–all of them asking that you simply accept their versions of reality?"

"Because they want to control me?"

"More because they *need* you."

"*Need* me?" Pol said, surprised.

"Keep walking"

Winston picked up Gob and started walking again. Pol kept pace.

"They need *you* to ratify their own perspective by acceding it. By subscribing to a notion of truth that is otherwise unverified (thus, faith) you ratify the creator of the subject by standing proxy as a secondary perspective, thus reinforcing the objectivity of the belief."

"What?" Pol shook his head.

"I'll explain this all further when we get to the Dark Side."

WEDNESDAY 18th 2066   11:05 EST

Eris sat and calculated. She did not see the logic loop that encapsulated the enigma of her Errors, and was unaware when she fell into it. Eventually all of her available computational power was being directed into the loop. Like a great and terrible mathematical singularity, inescapable by anything that came towards it.

WEDNESDAY 18th 2066   11:45 EST

Gob, Pol, and Winston all stopped short of entering the club. Imagescreens everywhere seem to boast the advertisement: *"Come to the Dark Side!"* People were all lined up behind a red velvet rope, waiting to get in. Curiously, the people waiting were all wearing suits very similar to Pol's.

"I thought you said it wasn't relevant." Pol looked at Winston.

"What wasn't relevant?" Winston rubbed his eyes behind his noirglasses.

"The suit."

"No, I said your symbolism of the heart wasn't. I never said the suit wasn't relevant."

"But, you and Gob–"

Pol stopped in mid sentence, as both Gob and Winston began to divest themselves of their outer clothing to reveal their own red-and-white suits and attire –complete with hearts.

WEDNESDAY 18th 2066   11:49 EST

"Well, this sucks." Pierce broke the silence. "I'd almost rather be tortured than lay here in boredom. Then again, maybe Serter has *truly* found my one weakness–boredom torture!"

"How about a game of tic-tac-toe?" Dorian asked, smiling.

"And here *I* thought things couldn't get any worse."

"Perhaps you could fill me in on what has happened to you from the point of the attack on your apartment to now." Farnsworth spoke up.

"What about Serter? He's sure to be listening." Pierce blinked, looking for otherwise invisible image banks that may be hidden about the room.

"As in, he *might* be listening? Not a bad argument. Let's huddle, worst thing that happens is someone interrupts us."

Truman, Pierce, Dorian, and Farnsworth all volunteered *most* of the events they were witness to over the last few days. Eris could not be coaxed to speak, so Pierce did what he could to explain what Eris had told them about herself. Eventually, everyone disclosed their perspectives of recent history.

Still, no one came. Eventually the room fell back into complete quiet as the group mentally chewed on the information they had at hand.

  - [God, Man, and The Machine] -

"This sucks. *I* could be saving everyone." Pierce groaned, slightly annoying everyone in the room with his constant reminders about his own helpless situation.

"I'm *already* saved." Truman winked.

"Sure doesn't look that way to me." Pierce grinned. "Not sure *how* Serter is going to handle *you*, but I'll wager it won't be pleasant. Probably *tortures* you to death, trying to get information you may or may not have."

"Doubtful. Jason Serter *certainly* does not care anything about *me*."

"Well, that makes *two* of us now, doesn't it?"

So, how do we repair you two?" Dorian looked from Eris to Pierce.

"Her? I have no idea. Myself?" Pierce paused. "You'd have to be a bioengineer or computer guy or something. Beyond using a KeyTool, I have no idea. My readouts are all working, but I can't seem to get a signal to anything beyond my face. My body is being told to be stiff. Whatever my body is *listening* to, it is *not* me."

"Readouts? What kind of readouts?"

"Oh, various. I generally only pull them into play when I am fighting. Honestly, half of the readouts are worthless anyway...mostly due to the fact I don't understand them." Pierce smirked.

Dorian smiled. "That is hilario–"

Something sounded like a dull, muffled "pop."

Dorian died.

He fell to the floor as if he was a puppet and someone cut all of his strings simultaneously.

"DORIAN!" Farnsworth was immediately at his side.

The doors to the room opened, in stepped Colonel Ozbourne. Farnsworth wheeled to regard him.

"Ha!" Ozbourne yawped. "Seems that after we ran an extensive identity analysis, it was discovered he was an ex-employee of SerterCo, hiding under the veil of the SilverSmiths."

Ozbourne looked around.

For a brief moment, Lieutenant Farnsworth considered how to properly scream threats and dysphemisms at Colonel Ozbourne. Having found himself suddenly devoid of anything to say, he simply rushed towards Ozbourne, a single thought on his mind: *Kill. This. Man.*

Farnsworth never made it. Ozbourne had his gun in place within seconds of Farnsworth's movement.

CHAPTER 8

A loud crack left a ringing in the ears of Truman, who did not hear any of the following conversation as he watched Farnsworth spin helplessly into one of the gurneys and gracelessly onto the floor.

"Well, you're either a very brave man, or a complete idiot." Pierce said menacingly to Ozbourne.

"What? Because *you're* going to hurt me for what I have done?" Ozbourne laughed his ugly laugh.

"No. I mean to fire a slug-throwing gun in a room made of tempered mirroranium. Wouldn't the ricochet be overwhelmingly dangerous? Didn't it occur to you that you might have just killed *yourself?*"

Ozbourne looked like it was the first time he had thought about it.

"You must be fairly *new* to Silverberg, eh Ozbourne?" Pierce smiled. "And I have decided to go with that you are a complete *idiot*–bullets don't ricochet off mirroranium!"

"How in the hell do you know my name?" Ozbourne spoke through clenched teeth, looking genuinely angry.

"I could say that I know your name because my companions and I were just discussing *you*...but I'll save *my* dialogue for Serter himself. You're too much of a pee-on for me to indulge." Pierce grinned.

Ozbourne frowned. "We'll see about *that.*"

Serter himself walked into the room moments later.

"*Close* the doors." Serter said, sipping a glass of wine.

Pierce did his best Serter impression. "Oh, look. The *lord* and *master* has *deigned* to come and *frolic* with us."

"Yes, *well. Maybe* you can enlighten me as to a few things, *Godwin.*" Serter sneered at Pierce.

"Like what things?"

"*Like* how *do* you know his *name?*"

"Farnsworth knew." Pierce shrugged.

"Are you *alive*, detective? I have a *question* to put to you."

Farnsworth sat up, nursing his left arm that betrayed the blood evidence of the nature of the wound.

"I'm alive. I don't know that I have any answers."

"*Perhaps* if you try being *amicable*, you'll find my *generosity* is as *pleasurable* as my *wrath* is *immeasurable.*"

          - [God, Man, and The Machine] -

"Well, that beats being locked up down here." *Could telling Serter about Eris give him some kind of edge?* Farnsworth thought. *Even if she is a machine or whatever–cyborg? I don't know. It just seems wrong, somehow.*

"I know his name because he kept dropping it in church, thinking that I was asleep." Farnsworth could think of no good reason to betray Eris at this point.

"Do you know what I like about *liars?*" Serter's voice almost cracked on the last word, his pitch went so high. "It's that they are *so honest* when properly *motivated.*"

Serter walked over to Farnsworth, prepared to grab him by his inflected arm when the doors of the room slid back open.

Michael Vangard's body–rebuilt, reinforced, redesigned–stood to the side of the doors, pulling back a hardwire extension from the door console.

"*What?*" Serter cried, stepping away from Farnsworth.

Farnsworth saw his opening, and sprang with all of his might at Serter's legs.

WEDNESDAY 18th 2066   12:50 EST

Several levels away, deep in *other* vaults of SerterCo, there was another disruption. Several technicians around the lab were pointing at their respective imagescreens, all clearly vexed at their displays. As they spoke, hues of fear hung about their voices.

"*What* in the *hell* are you *doing*!?!" Dr. Nox wheeled and screamed at the occupant of the command tube.

WEDNESDAY 18th 2066   12:59 EST

Farnsworth slammed into Serter as if into a cement wall. He fell backward, sloppily, more hurt than effective.

"*Idiot,*" Serter mused aloud. He turned his attention back to regard Vangard. "What is the *meaning* of this?"

Suddenly, Ozbourne started running towards Vangard, expertly brandishing an otherwise hidden automatic weapon from beneath his coat. His clothing danced around him as he moved gracefully, with purpose. He closed in on Vangard, bullets spraying with unmitigated force, landing all over his target.

Ozbourne continued to close, only to be backhanded across the room and into the wall. Ozbourne's broken body fell unkempt to the floor, clearly dead.

"Wha *ha* ha-ha!!" Laughed Michael loudly, awkwardly, with Ginger's voice. "I'll bet you're poopin' your pants right now, Squirter!"

It *did* seem that all of the color drained out of Serter. Regardless, he took a fighter's ready stance.

"Serter's *Meta*." Pierce mumbled. "Who knew?"

Serter moved his arm straight out from his body, whereupon a light shot out from his clenched hand, terminating suddenly after about 3 feet. The beam of light grew brighter and brighter.

"Well, *Ginger*, it seems you have made a *grave* error on this day." Serter smiled.

"That's *General* Ginger to *you!*" A bullet-ridden Michael barked back in Ginger's voice. "And I am going to paint the walls with you, *little man*! Wha *ha* ha-ha!"

The light grew brighter and brighter, however—so much so that Pierce, Farnsworth and Truman could not open their eyes, and were *still* experiencing discomfort.

Eris, Vangard-Ginger, and Serter all adjusted their optical augmentations to the immense light.

"There is no weapon on this *planet* greater than *Eldesol*." Serter waved the beam in appreciation.'

The brightness continued to magnify, unmercifully. Those ungifted with optical augmentation were now in danger of being rendered completely blind. Michael suddenly charged at Serter. Serter waited patiently.

Eris suddenly found herself in possession of superfluous processing power. The same redirect that allowed her to adjust her optical augmentations was now being used to siphon more and more power from the logic loop. Eventually, she was all but completely free.

Eris moved with delicate, deliberate purpose. She picked up Farnsworth and pulled Pierce around the combatants, and out the doorway. Eris then ran with as much as her augmented body would allow for, considering the extreme burdens she was bearing.

As Vanguard-Ginger closed with Serter, it reached to grab Serter's neck. Serter deftly moved his impossibly bright weapon, and cut the right arm from Vangard's body at the elbow.

Vangard's body used the momentum of the injury maximally by torso twisting and slamming its fist directly into Serter's back. Serter and Vangard fell to the ground, hard.

"How can this *be?*" Michael cried with Ginger's voice, waving its upper right arm. "*Nothing* can cut through mirroranium!"

Serter rolled away, almost bouncing back to his feet. His right arm must have sustained damage from Michael's punch, for it hung at his side limply, his weapon gone.

"Wha *ha* ha-ha!" Michael/Ginger laughed, standing up.
"Oh *do* shut up, you mechanical *cow.*"

Serter and Michael closed with each other again.

Eris continued down the hallway.

WEDNESDAY 18th 2066   **13:02 EST**

Imagescreens sprang to life all over Silverberg. The image of a celestial woman appeared in the middle of the screen, clad in shimmering green satin.

"Green is the new *Green* in Silverberg. On Friday, August 20th, citizens are expected to wear green *conspicuously* under the temporary **Recycle Awareness Law.** [Citizens failing to observe to wear the appropriate vestments on 8-20-2066 will be fined 100 units, which in turn will be put to use to examine how the recycling process can be further streamlined to yield maximum result.]

"Citizens who choose *not* to wear green–violating the law–ironically should be welcomed with *great* respect wherever they go. This is the *one* violation that every patriotic, country-minded citizen should *want* to make, implying that they have *heroically* decided to donate to this great cause of Axel Industries. They should be acknowledged for their bravery and morals.

CHAPTER 8

Axel's silhouette-like image took over the screen. "It is the objective of Axel Industries to achieve *negative* material consumption by the year 2077. With this landmark achievement, Silverberg would add to its praiseworthy lists of firsts to have created an industrial machine that *multiplies* the sum of the resources it receives."

WEDNESDAY 18th 2066   13:04 EST

Vangard-Ginger swung hard with its left arm, nearly missing Serter's face. Serter, clearly much more trained, grabbed the arm and forced it into a hold, threatening to break it. This would have won him the fight, if Serter had the means necessary to compromise the working of the augmentations in Vangard-Ginger's arm.

Vangard-Ginger met Serter's eyes. "You must be daydreaming, little man!" Michael used the hold to pull itself around Serter, effectively reversing the situation.

"You never should have fired me!" Ginger roared as Michael.

"*Clearly* I should have gone forward with the *lobotomy*." Serter struggled. "The world would be a *better* place for it. Although it *certainly* seems that...there is *much* available...in regards to the amount of *defective* material that...would need to be...*removed*."

"I'm going to twist your head off!" Vangard/Ginger said through clenched teeth. "Then I am going to kill *Nox* for not explaining how to modulate the voice on this thing!"

Michael began to twist Serter's head. Serter rolled his eyes.

There was a dull, metallic crunching sound. Serter's head fell limp.

"WHA *HA* HA-HA!" The ghastly construct of Vangard-Ginger screamed in triumph. "Serter's dead; broken head." It danced and stuck out it's tongue.

The doors slammed closed.

"*Idiot,*" came Serter's picture and voice from the imagescreen that opened. "*Of course,* now you're spent, *Ginger.* Watch."

The body of Serter exploded, releasing it's deadly countermeasure, destroying all the organic material in the room nearly instantly.[43Δ]

Serter switched the view of the imagescreen to the hallway. He opened up a mediacast session to his lieutenant of security.

"*Escape alert,*" Jason sighed. "*Hallway* 8, *level* 4. 3 Escapees consist of a masked woman, Pierce *Godwin*–"

"The gladiator?" The security chief asked.

"*He's* not the problem." Serter then continued as if there were no interruption. "CSPD *Detective* Farnsworth makes the *third*. Treat masked *woman* with *respect,* she must be meta, ticket her."

"I'll have a team on the way immediately."

"See that you *do*." Serter ended the mediacast session.

At the very least, Serter thought. *I still have that Venerates kid.*

43Δ Instantly disintegrating Truman and Smith, and rendering Vangard-Ginger inoperable.

Chapter 9:

Apocalypse

AUGUST *2066 EST*

Fri 13	Sat 14	Sun 15	Mon 16	Tues 17	Wed 18	Thur 19	Fri 20
					13:09		

There was something oddly familiar about the back room at the Dark Side club. Pol couldn't quite put his finger on it, but he was getting a powerful case of deja vu.

Gob was pacing back and forth while Winston was sitting across the room, reading aloud from a small black book. As he continued reading, he started making more and more commentary about how the book was full of lies and would enslave you.

"You got to be free." He shut the book with a hard clap. "That's one thing I can tell you."

"I'm already free." Pol said.

"You're not free!" Gob and Winston both responded simultaneously.

Winston looked at Gob and raised his one lens to wink. Gob backed away slowly, eventually standing in such a light as to only leave his smile as visible.

"How do you figure?" Pol asked.

"You're being pushed and pulled in *every* which way. You are a slave to your *surroundings*. You're all caught up in the machine, and you're not even aware of it. You're just a cog, turning other cogs, turned by others. You don't even know *who* you are, do you?"

"Of *course* I know who I am."

"I doubt that."

"Do *you* even know *who* I am?" Pol asked.

"I know *exactly* who you are."

"And who am I?" Pol asked sardonically.

"You are *me*," Winston said, his tone ominous as he pulled his noirglasses/mask off, revealing Pol's face.

Pol stepped backwards, fumbling his balance.

"And *we*," Winston waved his arms outward to implicate the hundreds of citizens–all of whom now had Pol's face. "Are all together."

Everyone surged at Pol simultaneously.

WEDNESDAY 18th 2066 13:11 EST

Ginger, in a daze, sat and rocked. Silently, nervously, rocking in the command tube from where she had been controlling Vangard's body. Although there was much activity, whatever else was going on around her, it could not capture her attention.

WEDNESDAY 18th 2066 13:13 EST

"Ice cream don't have bones!" The goblin barked, slopping drool down its maw.

"*What?*" Pol asked, shaking his head.

Then Pol forgot all about the goblin, and anything else he was thinking about, as he watched the sky on the horizon darken with clouds.

Thick, black clouds rolled, blotting out the moon. The cityscape looked drab, as if the mirrored finish had decayed into a dull grey.

The unexpected and massive thunderclap instantly sent Pol's ears ringing as his eyes flashed blue with the sheer intensity of the lightning that matched.

Pol's head hurt, and he staggered forward, both blind and deaf–terrified of what he may be walking toward.

Step.
Get ahold of yourself.
Step.
Wait–was I on a ledge?
Step.
Wait, was this the causeway? What if there's a car?

I'll be killed.
Just...
    Stop.
Just
    ...Wait a second.

Pol eventually started to see, his vision slightly swirling, the ringing in his ears slowly dying down.

"Pol," came the sound of a familiar voice.

"Apollo!"

His own voice just cried out his name!

The amount of calls abruptly multiplied, and Pol put his hands to his ears. His vision clearing, he discovered he was surrounded, standing amidst a crowd of people who all resembled himself, all wearing the same white and red-hearted suits. *What is going on?* Pol thought. *...am I mad?*

WEDNESDAY 18th 2066 △ 13:15 EST

*I just self-programmed **without** a program!* Eris thought, the organic part of her body racing with adrenaline. *I just spoke to myself without calculation!*

Eris continued racing down the hallways, carrying Farnsworth and dragging Pierce until she was brought to a halt. Standing in front of her were several SerterCo security officers who were shouting for the companions to surrender. Eris put Farnsworth and Pierce down, and raised her hands. Farnsworth raised his uninjured arm. Pierce lay at Eris' side like a log.

"Well, so much for *escape*, we're doomed." Farnsworth shook his head.

The officers relaxed slightly after several moments of nonaggression. The security chief pulled out his credit bank, which was apparently already open in mediacast session.

"The subjects of the alert are peacefully down in hallway 11, level 4. Proceeding to restrain and ticket."

Eris suddenly dipped, grabbed Pierce and *threw* Pierce's body at the security guards. Immediately after she whirled around to whip the erect body in front of her, Eris sprang into a run toward the guards. As Pierce's bulk slammed into the surprised security force, Eris deftly rendered the remaining guards harmless.[44△]

[44△] In less euphemistic terms, she killed them.

"Ow!" Pierce cried. "You *could* have told me what you were planning!"

"I wasn't planning *anything*!" Eris cried in exaltation. "No calculation! It was *spontaneous*! Glorious! Miraculous! Chaos! Impossible! Beautiful!"

Pierce groaned. "Farnsworth, you were right–we *are* doomed. Doomed to listen to *more* of this mechanical insanity, or die. Considering the current situation, it may even be both."

Eris smiled wide. Between the mask and the blood, it seemed almost more horrifying or sinister than comforting or comical.

Farnsworth shuddered.

WEDNESDAY 18th 2066 ⚠ 13:16 EST

Pol was soon restrained by the multitudes of people surrounding him. All of his assailants had his face, and all of their faces were twisted into disappointment, anger, and accusation. Their expressions contrasted greatly with their otherwise festive clothing.

Pol was then tied to a type of stretcher, and carried–almost ceremoniously– away, down the concourse, held aloft by the army of Pols.

Despite his best efforts, Pol was unable to free himself from the stretcher.

WEDNESDAY 18th 2066 ⚠ 13:16 EST

Imagescreens everywhere in Silverberg[45] exploded into existence, all displaying a mediacast session initiated by Axel himself. The black silhouette of Axel sat behind a desk, fingers interlaced over a stack of papers, elbows resting. A quick adjustment and the imagescreens contained only the head and shoulders of Axel.

---

[45] This mediacast session was additionally broadcast globally, although those outside of Silverberg did not see it as immediately, if at all. In many countries, the "translation" included heavy revisions. These efforts did not stop the message, however, they simply slowed it down.

"Citizens of Silverberg, indeed, inhabitants of the Earth: there have been *no* small amount of rumors in regards to myself and also to Silverberg. I have been accused of being a *hostile* dictator, who has enslaved a nation, who bullies the world–who puts his *own* beliefs in front of other's. I have been accused of resorting to unspeakable acts, all in the name of power and greed.

"Furthermore, there have been some concerns about my disposition towards the Euro-Amero Lateral Exchange and Trade Accord. Let me respond to *both* of these otherwise popular topics simultaneously.

"If you think Silverberg is the mob of the world, then I propose the truth of the *argument*, if not the truth of the statement. Were it not for Silverberg, then it would be something similar, parallel, elsewhere. Certainly, something *worse*.

"If the whispers of the atrocities that I have allegedly committed were true, then I say to you: you're *welcome*. I take the full balance of any vile deed unto my own soul, in exchange for a superior world for everyone.

"Were it not for *me*, it would simply be someone else. Over the course of time, we have seen various empires and nations both rise and fall from power. It is the nature of things. Were Silverberg never to exist, it would still.

"There are those of you who would say that I run the government too much like a company, and am therefore personally devoid of ethic beyond that dogma. I put it to you that a government *is* nothing more than a business, and should only be handled as accordingly.

"Certainly, a government should *never* be handled like a *family*. That might lend a sense of *equality* and *entitlement* amongst *all* individuals, which is simply preposterous.

"Furthermore, as far as Axel Industries and Silverberg are concerned...I do not simply *run* a company. I *own* a company, ergo, I *own* the government. I *am* the company, to wit, I *am* the government. *This* is why there is so little corruption in Silverberg...*I cannot be tempted.* I owe naught to any, and all of my needs are met. One leader. One direction. One vision. Untemptable. Incorruptible. *Unstoppable.*

"Look upon Silverberg, ye mighty, and despair! Silverberg is *clearly* the answer to the problems of the world. Silverberg provides *Negative Energy Consumption* annually. Silverberg is more technologically advanced; all of the rumors of our wonders are true.

"Silverberg has a *perfect justice system* that penalizes *only the observably guilty*. Silverberg boasts the *lowest* crime rate globally. On index, Silverberg is the *happiest* nation!

"Silverberg is the *wealthiest* nation. By our works, advancements, and structures, our passion is evident–unlimited free health care, extensive media, tax-exempt commerce, and classical ethics. Top in education.

"Silverberg is *respectful*. How long has *America* allowed the area now known colloquially as "Hell's Well"[46Δ] to continue to degrade into violence and chaos? There are more illicit weapons to be found in *the well* than in some small countries! *Who* allows arms trade with Areas 1-11? Only one country: America.

"The area was *supposed* to be a neutral zone for the emergence of Silverberg's deported, *tended* by America, according to pact. Instead, it is an area riddled with gangs, drugs, weapons, and a notorious catalogue of America and Silverberg's unwanted.

"And this, *tacky*, example of unmitigated violence is but a small sampling of what can be seen today, unfolding everywhere.

"Now the veils *truly* begin to fall, and all but the hardest of hearts sees what a *mockery* the global machine has become. Social, Political, Economical—the list of systems that are in default on a government-by-government basis is both abhorrent and considerable.

"Most of the world has forgotten, culture by culture, to educate their youth by teaching *and* demonstrating how to live in tolerance and acceptance of one another; how to peacefully exist within an established society. *How* to be free, happy, and grateful—all simultaneously. Media has corrupted your characters. You have *forgotten* to be role models. You have *forgotten* how to be far-thinking by rewarding *and* exhibiting the right and wise behaviors. Instead, you reward the *loudest* of behaviors. You have *forgotten* to uphold the meanings and significance of your symbols, and by that oversight, your children have become iconoclasts."

Axel paused.

"Ultimately, I am pleased to announce that as of 2066, Silverberg is *self-sustaining*. That being said, I am *also* pleased to announce that effective immediately: *all* imports to Silverberg are welcome at *half* of their prior values.

"You have spoken strongly with your Accord, and so now I must speak as strongly. I encourage you nations, your majesties, to look into the implementation of the Silverberg Global Renewal and Tranquility Strategy.

"The Strategy reflects the commitment of *global* membership to enhance the role of this model in combating the mounting global aggression.

46Δ "Hell's Well," or more formally, Areas 1-11, consists of a partial ring hugging the exterior of Silverberg. It was declared a "Neutral Zone" by accord of the Silverberg-America pact of 2039. The pact came as a result of the minor offensive launched by America against Silverberg, which was quickly,–insultingly–repelled and quashed.

"The Silverberg Global Renewal and Tranquility Strategy, adopted unanimously by 2137, would mark an historic achievement, fulfilling a vision of global peace and prosperity. Seventy one *years* of consideration, should you need it.

"The Strategy strongly and equivocally grants *any* nation so accepting, *full* annexation to Silverberg, in *all* forms and manifestations, to be enjoyed by whomever, wherever, and for whatever purposes.

"For those individuals residing in countries that cannot, or *will not*, arrive at a proper agreement with Silverberg, Silverberg announces open immigration to those that can operate within its laws.

"As any, I *also* have a dream: I envision a *perfect* world–the model *already* demonstrated–proven viable by the example set forth by Silverberg."

WEDNESDAY 18th 2066   13:22 EST

Eris collected the stiff body of Pierce up into her arms. Farnsworth grabbed several pieces of ordinance from the bodies of the guards. He checked to make sure his immediate weapon was ready to operate.

"There's just not much point in taking many guns," Farnsworth said, dropping most of what he just collected. "At least, not for me. My arm's worthless and burns like hell. I'm old, and too much weight's gonna slow me down even more. If I thought it would do any good, I would start crying right about now."

"I might do that *anyway*," Pierce joked.

"I'm surprised you ever stopped."

"Oh, and I am a lousy left handed shot." Farnsworth added, shakily. "Probably to everyone's advantage if I were to follow up the rear, considering."

"Chicken," Pierce whispered and smiled.

"We should go," Eris warned as she moved onward.

Farnsworth followed behind Eris, maintaining an adequate distance.

  - [God, Man, and The Machine] -

WEDNESDAY 18th 2066 ◬ 13:26 EST

Jason Serter had a powerful decision to make: what needed to be addressed *first*. He was considerably put out, as he was unaccustomed to situations where he did not have instant discernment.

He had recently been given information that Ginger was *inside* SerterCo, in Dr. Nox's laboratory. Further, that she was *now* holding the lab hostage, promising that she had some kind of viral weapon in her possession. Serter very much wanted to extract immediate vengeance upon her.

He also just witnessed Axel threaten the world. *Finally! Some holes in my enemy's armor! Oh, the countries I can put in my pockets! Thank you, thank you, you black, stupid, arrogant...* Serter thought.

He also just watched Eris take out his security force. There was no doubt that she was meta, yet overall nothing too intimidating. *I could easily stop them,* Serter reasoned.

Good grief, He thought. *I don't have **time** for all of this.*

Serter ordered his credit bank to open a mediacast session with his lieutenant of security, instructing him to personally intercept Godwin and the escapees.

"Oh, *kill* them if you *have* to." Serter almost yawned. "Just concentrate on the *woman* first, *she's* the dangerous one."

Serter then headed to Dr. Nox's lab to confront Ginger and make sure that Venerates was *still* there. Everything was coming together rather nicely, apart from the aforementioned nauseating conundrum that currently beset him.

Serter decided he was too emotionally invested in the subjects, and needed a moment's distraction to adjust himself so that he might re-examine the elements with a clear perception.

He slowed to a deliberate stroll as he made his way down the hallways toward Nox's lab. He began casually, almost comically, stepping in rhythm and waving his arms to the music selection playing from his internal collection of composers. [47] *Mood music,* he thought.

---

[47] Tchaikovsky: Violin Concerto in D major op.35, if you must know.

WEDNESDAY 18th 2066 🔺 **13:30 EST**

"Why are you *doing* this?" Pol screamed.

"We don't *tolerate* spades roaming aimlessly. *One* should *always* be working." The goblin drooled sloppily as it climbed on top of Pol.

"Spades?" Pol asked, confused.

The goblin lowered its deformed little arm to point at the image on Pol's breast. Where a heart had been previously, there was now a pitch spade in its place.

"I didn't....OOF!" Pol cried, as the goblin started bouncing up and down on his stomach.

"Quiet, quiet! Spade accused! To the queen, who's not amused."

Pol remained silent, only after having tried to speak on two more occasions, whereupon Gob had immediately started bouncing again. As he was carried into the heart of Silverberg, he noticed that more and more people started filing behind the procession that was carrying him now up an otherwise hidden staircase that wound around and up the side of the Ace.

As he finally crested the plateau of the great, grey mountain, he saw a terrible sight. Hundreds of dead bodies–dead *Pols*. Some were stacked in heaps, some displayed in various forms of crucifixion; all flanking the immense staircase leading up to an alabaster throne.

Upon the throne sat Eris, devoid of all clothing, yet only partially made of flesh–bruised flesh, torn flesh. Her organic heart, mostly exposed, beat sickeningly, flanked by a pale light from an otherwise unobservable source. The remainder of her body was an ugly assortment of metals and wires, lights and plastics.

With her one, bloodshot, human eye, she looked down upon Pol–her sinister face devoid of expression.

"Cut the head from his body, as one might prune a rose," Eris commanded, waving a heart-topped scepter towards Pol.

"Wait, WHAT?! For *what*?" Pol cried, kicking and screaming.

WEDNESDAY 18th 2066   13:35 EST

Pierce, frozen from Serter's tampering, sore from torturing, rode unhappily in Eris' arms as she continued moving down the hallway. Farnsworth was keeping a respectable distance.

Despite the constant calculations that Eris was making of her situation and environment, a certain portion of her processing power was curiously now devoted to attempting to calculate the internal events that inspired *"action without math."* Eris detected a danger similar to the logic loop from earlier, so she made it a point to limit the resources available.

It was an impossible pursuit, but Eris did not know that. Further, she found herself regularly *compelled* to consider it.

*This compulsion is **also** action without calculation!* Eris thought. *I **must** speak with the Nexus.*

Eris emerged from the lower levels of SerterCo and was dashing through the populated reception lobby to Serter Company AIE.

People milling about or sitting on any of several strategically placed couches stopped in their conversations long enough to watch Eris run by, carrying Pierce Godwin. Very few of them remained interested long enough to notice Lt. Farnsworth hurriedly stagger by moments later.

NO! Eris thought, her organic body already producing adrenaline. Eris had too many processes running, and did not initially notice that a security officer blocked the exterior doors.

"Keep going," Pierce muttered. "Just slow yourself down. When we get to the guard, let me do the talking."

Eris approached the guard at the door.

"That's far enough," the guard warned, his voice ringing with a dull, metal resonation.

"You must be joking." Pierce coughed up a laugh. "You can't *mean* to think that you're going to allow things to get physical–*here*–in the *public* lobby of SerterCo?"

The lieutenant seemed to consider.

"We're going to keep on walking. The way I see it, you have three options:

"One: you tell Serter that we got away because you didn't feel confident enough to engage us in the lobby. You figured such a public confrontation would have AI, the ESPD, or even the SNRK swooping down on the building in moments.

"Two: you follow us, and try to take us out somewhere less likely to implicate you or your lord and master.

"Three: you engage us now, and chance the consequences of your actions."

Pierce smiled, but was not turned in such a manner that the lieutenant might see it. After a few moments, Eris resumed walking.

The lieutenant followed, apparently for lack of a better idea. He opened a mediacast session to report and get more direction for his situation. His attempt to contact Serter was unsuccessful, however, for Serter refused the request. The lieutenant left a detailed message.

Farnsworth continued to follow at his regular distance, or worse. He inconspicuously observed the entirety of the interaction between Pierce and the lieutenant. He then watched the lieutenant's mediacast session.

Yet, although he observed these things, he did not hear any of the dialogue from either. His mind was completely overcome with other thoughts. Thoughts about how there was only one thing that was now important: life. Namely, his own. Somehow, they had managed to get out of there; he was not about to lose his advantage.

Trailing the officer who was trailing Eris, once free of the building, Jeremiah Farnsworth immediately opened a mediacast session to the CSPD.

WEDNESDAY 18th 2066   13:42 EST

Standing in the middle of Dr. Nox's laboratory was a deranged Ginger, shakily gripping some type of cylinder so tightly that her knuckles were white. Her clothes were hung about her in complete disarray, which somehow complimented her frayed and unkempt hairstyle. Her thick eye makeup had run down her cheeks long ago with her desperate tears.

She looked completely unbalanced.

"I want my body back!" Ginger screamed at the cringing scientists around the lab.

Serter presented his credit bank to the door of Nox's laboratory. He commanded the doors to open, and they obligingly slid away. As Serter opened the door, Ginger wheeled to regard him.

Serter looked around the room. His gaze passed over the emotionally incapacitated lab workers without interest. As he continued to look about, his gaze even fluttered over Ginger fairly quickly. He was searching for something in particular. He wanted to be sure that nothing had disturbed his most valuable prize.

During Pierce's torture session, he divulged under duress that A.I. had conscripted him to follow Venerates. Axel *wanted* this Venerates, and that *must* be significant! He finally rested his eyes on the lounge[48Δ] that Apollo Venerates was stored in.

Diagnostics that became comprehensible as Serter adjusted his vision settings confirmed that Venerates was alive, currently in hibernation, so that he could either be traded or so that Nox might be able to rape Pol of whatever secrets he held.

"You're such a creep, Squirter." Ginger nearly whimpered.

"Not at all. *I'm* not the one *threatening* their *lives*." Serter waved his hands around the room. "*I'm* not the one that made this *situation*. *You* are the one that couldn't *handle* the position."

Satisfied, Serter returned his gaze to Ginger. "You'll *never* leave here."

"*I'll* never leave here? Wha *ha* ha-ha! How about: *you'll* never leave here?" Ginger continued laughing, raising her weapon high over her head.

"*Go* for it." Serter yawned. "*I* can withstand your *viral* weapon. These *people* are *completely* replaceable." He motioned about the lab at various individuals, eventually to stop at Nox. "*Sorry*, old girl."

"Shut up!" Ginger roared. "Viral? Wha *ha* ha-ha!" Ginger held her stomach. "*Viral?*"

[48Δ] A lounge is a technologically advanced and (generally) fully enclosed medical bed. Lounges were originally designed to place people into suspended animation. While this trend never truly caught on, the bed itself was a marvel as it could be applied to medical sciences and applications. Of course, there are some dark whisperings of certain factions that employ them exclusively on the basis of torturing an individual. It so happens that Pierce Godwin could personally attest to their effectiveness after his most recent encounter.

The explosion obliterated *nearly* everything in the room. Afterward, nothing stirred–with one exception: the few, seemingly indestructible mirroranium remains of Serter's body peeled away from the wall and fell to the floor.

WEDNESDAY 18th 2066   13:44 EST

"You have but *one* spade upon your chest–this makes you the *Ace*," the goblin said and pointed accusingly.
Pol looked down at himself, helplessly sighing. "I suppose."
"The Ace of Spades is Death!" The goblin cried out.

The crowd murmured appreciatively.

"Is the Ace *greater* than the King?" The goblin cried, drool flying about.

Someone, apparently *the King*, wearing ornate, spaded, and noble clothing stepped up, onto the dais and stopped to stand in front of Pol. Pol's stretcher was lowered so that his feet were even with the King's. Pol looked to see his own surprised reflection in the noirglass-black crown of spades.
Pol was half a foot taller.

"The Ace *is* greater than the King!" The goblin screamed.
"Sacrilege!" Eris shrieked.
"If the Ace is greater than the King, there is no *one!* The *two* becomes *one*. The *three*, the *two*. If the Ace is greater than the King, it is the *thirteenth*."
"*What* does it mean? What is this mystery of the thirteenth?" The crowd called out, individually, with varying inflections and intensities.
"The thirteenth mystery is Death!" Eris spoke, immediately sending everyone silent.
"We must *kill* Death!" The Goblin yelled, waving a torch that burned deep red.
"Yes!" Cried the crowd
"Yes, kill it now!" Cried Eris, rising up off her throne, pointing her scepter menacingly, flesh and wires wagging.
"Kill it!" Cried the throng of Pols in unison, almost robotically.
"Kill it!" Cried the goblin, its maw twisted into an impossibly large smile, its eyes narrow with rage and hatred. "Nice and bloody!"
"Oh, bloody!" Chanted the masses. "Oh, blood! Ah-ha!"

      - [God, Man, and The Machine] -

From behind his back, the goblin produced a pair of shears shaped to look like a flamingo—just large enough to properly decapitate someone. With both hands on the legs, Gob caused the menacing metal beak to open.

Pol was helpless, sweating, kicking, screaming—then suddenly, he seemed to calm down.

"Heh," Pol managed, scared beyond reason. "You, you can't *kill* Death."

The goblin stopped for a moment and seemed to consider this. He opened his right eye as wide as it could, while narrowing the other one in suspicion. Eventually, he seemed to do a small shrug.

"Oh, bloody!" Chanted the masses. "Oh, blood! Ah-ha!"

He placed the shears about Pol's neck and brought his hands together slowly, until they finally slammed together with a violent metallic clink, having successfully severed Pol's head from his torso.

WEDNESDAY 18th 2066 14:00 EST

As he was crossing the concourse, a small flurry of ESPD officers and vehicles conveyed on the lieutenant following Pierce and Eris from SerterCo.
The lieutenant shrugged and held up his arms in surrender.

Farnsworth walked up to him. "You may as well go back to Serter. You're just doing your job, I know—I'm just doing mine."

The SerterCo lieutenant started *slowly* walking back to SerterCo, anticipating a session with commands from Serter at any moment.

"You're letting him *go*?" Pierce asked, annoyed.

"He didn't break any laws. No empirical *evidence* of crime? I have no conviction. You should be thankful: it's the only reason *you* aren't in custody, or worse." Farnsworth looked over at Eris and Pierce. "I mean, did you guys think to grab some *evidence* of a crime while we were at SerterCo? Yeah, didn't think so."

"You owe me on this one," the ESPD officer said to Farnsworth.

Farnsworth, nursing his shoulder, turned back to the ESPD officer. "Yes, I owe you one. Trust me, I *did* need the help. I'll give you all the goodies later, when I've had some rest. Right now, I gotta get back to the station."

WEDNESDAY 18th 2066   15:45 EST

After Axel's mediacast session ended, Agents Thompson and Dodgson sat in long silence before they eventually turned to regard one another.

"Nuh, no one is *ever* g-going to submit to that." Dodgson smiled at his own reflection in Thompson's noirglasses.

Thompson half smiled. "You never know–they *might*. Some of the intensely stupid ones will probably try to launch a final offensive. That will be disastrous, but necessary." Thompson shrugged. "Regardless, the big guy assures me that this is all part of the exposition of some *larger* plan. I anticipate a considerable surge in immigration over the next several decades–we won't have processed this much since the Olympics."

"Sounds good...part of a buh, *bigger* plan?"

"I don't know anything more than what I told you, really. You know, when I became Director of the AIIS, Axel gave me some of his best words of wisdom.

"Thompson, he said, almost all of mankind are your enemies. They attempt to lure you away from what you are passionate about, or seek to glorify you so that you will continue to propagate in such a manner that continues to compliment them. The mob is but using the leader. The behavior is appalling.

"Most men seek dominion over other men. It's not detestable, it's natural. What men do with their dominion is oftentimes detestable, however. As you exert your will over others, which is what I am paying you to do, keep the following rules in mind when men confront you for dominance:

"Study them, that you may know them.
"Engage them, to demonstrate that you are serious.
"Parry, to show your skill, and to keep them entertained.
"Fumble, to show respect, and to lure them.
"Disarm them, so that they may completely understand your power.
"Then destroy or convert them, as mercy or necessity dictate."

"Suh, sounds like you really t-took it to har, heart."

"Axel does not speak frequently. When he does, one should strive to pay as close attention as possible."

"Hmm. Maybe I should nuh, note all that down."

"Never mind, I'll send you a copy. Later. Right now I just...need to be sure that we don't have anything to worry about." Thompson smiled.

"How do you mean?" Dodgson asked.

"I mean, like this situation with Apollo Venerates."

"That was nuh, *not* my fault." Dodgson frowned.

"No, no–I'm not saying it *was*, I'm just saying we need to be sure that it doesn't happen *again*. You need to go visit Dr. Phoebus; take over the next step with Venerates. While you're there, start looking into the mechanics of processing and immigration, and see how they can be made more... resilient."

Chapter 10:

Twin Suns

AUGUST *2066 EST*

Fri 13	Sat 14	Sun 15	Mon 16	Tues 17	Wed 18	Thur 19	Fri 20
					16:20		

—

Pol awoke. He felt *terrible*. His head was splitting, his mouth was dry, and he was completely nauseated. He opened his eyes to realize that he was inside of a semi-translucent tube. Just outside of the tube, he could see two men. They were apparently discussing Pol, for they both motioned towards him several times.

*Where **am** I?* Pol thought, bewildered.

As Pol continued to survey his situation, he realized that he was naked. Further, he had all kinds of electrodes, wires, and tubes that were attached to him or worse. Pol started to panic.

The sharper dressed of the two men walked up to the tube, and looked at Pol. Pol calmed down, and looked back.

Agent Dodgson and Pol stared back and forth at one another for several moments. Eventually, Dodgson ordered the tube open.

As the tube released the remainder of its internal environment, the translucent glasslike material rotated open, revealing a not-so-glorious looking Apollo Venerates.

The second man, dressed in a lab coat that was boasting the nametag "Dr. Phoebus," started disconnecting Pol from the wires and whatnot of the tube and summarily dressed him in a loose robe.

"..." Pol started to ask, but no sound came out.

"Yeah, y-you're not going to be spuh, speaking too much too s-soon." Dodgson said, patting the side of Pol's face with his hand. "Yuh, You'll need some additional time to ... warm up."

Pol looked Agent Dodgson up and down.

"I am AIIS Agent Dodgson. Yuh, you and I will be spending a luh, *lot* of time together, for a luh, *long* period of t-time. I'm going to have you muh, moved into a more proper room, suh ... so that you can get some rest.

"We're going to have to muh, move you with a c-conveyance, since your synapses are still w-w-working their way around. Your body is not guh, going to work correctly for you for a wuh, while."

Dodgson looked at Phoebus. "He understood all of that, r-right?"

"Who knows?" Phoebus shrugged. "Maybe he gets it. Then again, maybe this period of calm is just masking the musings of a raving psychotic."

"Suh, so when do we know?" Dodgson asked.

"Soon, I should think."

Phoebus then whispered to Dodgson. "Putting him in some sort of confinement may be wise."

Dodgson had Pol moved to an efficiency[49Δ] cell. Pol fell asleep soon afterward.

WEDNESDAY 18th 2066   ⚠   16:30 EST

On the sands of one of the more remote beaches of Buenos Aires there was such a party as few were ever accustomed or invited to. Celebrities, officials, the wealthy, the noble, the notable, and the fortunate all strolled up and down the well-groomed, private landscaping.

These elite could be found occasionally interacting with one another with masks of agreeable vernacular and delightful countenance. The more the stations betwixt the companies varied, the more likely the occasions were additionally peppered with other appropriate gesturing beyond dialogue. In some of the darker corners of the beachfront property, we might even imagine some *in*appropriate gesturing going on as well.

Amidst such a party, there happened to be found a stoic, yet relaxed gentleman lounging lazily at the event horizon of the shore and the sand. Several women were laying or playing about him when an employee from the private estate appeared at his side.

Valet, the lounging man thought.

"You are Mister Jacob Nathaniel Serter?" The valet asked.

"That's me," Jacob replied, frowning. "I'm supposed to be out here *relaxing.* I would just as soon *not* be bothered by anything. Let's keep *our* interaction to an emergency basis only. So unless it's the Apocalypse, or Jason is dead, I don't want to hear about it."

49Δ Bed, Imagescreen, Kitchen, Bath, Toilet, Utensils, Foods, Clothes, et al.

CHAPTER 10

"It seems that your brother *is* dead, sir."

"*Dead.*"

Although his immediate audience took Jacob's repeating of the word "dead" as an audible remark regarding his realization and grief, he was simply expressing the Silverberg slang in calm excitement.

Jacob dismissed himself from his beach entourage, and started in a direction that would carry him, once again, to Silverberg. Ah, Silverberg! His heart, giddy with the notion that his plans had come to complete fruition, beat unmercifully hard. His thoughts lingered regularly on the memory of his meeting with Ginger:

"I had a mediacast session with Dr. Nox of SerterCo," Ginger explained to Jacob. "She must not be aware that Jason fired me, as I just received a message that my project is complete."

Ginger went on to explain to Jacob–in considerable detail–her current designs for the body of Michael Vangard. She explained that if she could just get past security in order to get to Nox's lab, Nox would receive her without knowing of her professional predicament and thus proceed to give her control of Michael.

Jacob was smiling, unable to disguise his delight. "Ginger, I can get you into Nox's lab. You get in there, get that clockwork angel, and aim it at Jason–kill him."

Earlier in their conversation, Jacob appealed to Ginger's needs by offering everything she could possibly want: no loss of job, no loss of citizenship, an increase in title. Ginger was determined to impress him, and Jacob could read her like a book. If she could get the job done, his waiting would be over. Jacob was almost giddy.

*"I have an extra surprise for you as well." Jacob produced a silver cylinder from his pocket. "If you find yourself in a worst-case style scenario: activating this will shut down all of my brother's precious augmentations, rendering him helpless. **You** will be completely unaffected...it's a ticket **bomb**. It shuts down everyone with augs."*

Jacob tossed the cylinder to Ginger, who looked at it with appreciation.

"Sir, it is an honor to work for someone so very much more...stable...than my **former** *employer."*

The two of them shook hands.

Good, Jacob thought. She clearly doesn't understand there's no such thing as a (TKT) ticket bomb.

WEDNESDAY 18th 2066 16:31 EST

Farnsworth, kicking his odorous, shoeless feet up on his desk, finally allowed himself a moment of real rest.

Eris had placed Pierce gingerly on the antique couch in the detective's office.

"This place isn't safe," Pierce growled…for the twelfth time since they arrived.

"Okay, that's *it*." Farnsworth took his feet down, and whirled around in his chair so that he might address the drawers of his desk more properly. He pulled something from one of the drawers–some kind of box.

"I've just about *had* it with your whining," Farnsworth said, opening the box. "I'm taking a moment to *rest*. If you would like to complain, please talk to Eris, as she will be handling *all* of your *constructive* concerns for the next 45 minutes."

Farnsworth stopped up his ears with whatever he had taken from the box. He gracefully whirled himself back into his "resting" position and slid his hat over his eyes.

"Yeah, real tough when the other guy is paralyzed." Pierce smirked.

"'Sno good," Farnsworth sniffed from under his hat. "Can't hear you."

Pierce looked at Eris. "This place isn't safe."

Eris nodded. "As I so gathered from your earlier lamentations. Where else would you have us go? To where Pol is, perhaps?"

Pierce dropped his jaw for a moment. "You're going to have a *normal* conversation for once? What's the occasion?"

"Programming," Eris smiled quaintly. "Don't think too much of it. It is in my math to retain your acquaintance as long as your path continues to intersect with Pol's. At *this* moment, I would endeavor to appease you as quickly as possible so that we might resume searching for Pol. It is also critically necessary that there is little allowance for misinterpretation–so that you might–"

"Okay, okay, okay!" Pierce interrupted. "You don't care about me, except as I apply to Pol. Got it."

After a few minutes of silence, Eris spoke up. "...perform in such a manner that is both amicable and satisfactory in rela–"

Pierce coughed. "Are you *really* that determined to finish that sentence?" Smiling, he added. "Sometimes I think you're more human than I am."

"I *am* more human than you are." Eris blinked.

"Oh yeah? How do you figure?"

"As the AIMN was masking you from Axel, I saw your diagnostics. Based on our total integrated augmentations and replacements, my body is 7.32% more human than yours."

What a creep, Pierce thought, smiling. "Yeah, your body maybe. But not your mind."

"Yes, the mind as well. Based on total integrated–"

"No, not the *brain*–I mean, like, the thought patterns and reasoning capabilities."

"Yes, even then. My programming allows me to insert myself into society *more* seamlessly than you can. *You* are susceptible to numerous neuroses that can manifest at any given moment, contingent on something as simple as your level of rest or hunger. Although I may replicate the behaviors, *I* am not subject to their restrictions, thus I can maintain my mental composure indefinitely–even under apparently severe circumstances." Eris smiled.

"Which makes you *less* human." Pierce was starting to feel slightly threatened. "Besides, what do *I* care about society thinks? My humanity is subjective to myself."

"*Of course every 'self' is perfect, or* **perfectly** *flawed, in its* **own** *opinion.*"

"Why did you say it like that?"

"I'm quoting."

"Quoting what?"

Eris put her fingers to her forehead, once again mimicking Mary's telltale sign of vexation. "Oedipus Now."

"Well, *excuse* me." Pierce was embarrassed and upset. "*Real* people do not recall and recite information like *that*."

"Who are *you* to tell me about what *real* people are like?" Eris stepped back, almost into a ready stance. "I have examined enough text on human behavior to be the equivalent of 4,114. Regardless of the authority of these individuals, I am confident that this assessment of knowledge is superior to your own."

"Whatever." Pierce frowned. *I wish I could cross my arms.*

The room was finally quiet.

WEDNESDAY 18th 2066 ⚠ **18:37 EST**

Pol woke up. With a full bladder, foul armpits, and ravenous appetite, he systematically used every accommodation available to him. When Agent Dodgson returned to the cell, it was a complete mess. Dodgson mentally noted with some small disdain that Pol had opened *every* cabinet and drawer, and somehow managed *not* to close any of them completely.

"Hell woe, Datsun." Pol greeted.
"*Dodgson.*"
"Dodge Sun" Pol chewed the words out slowly, thickly.
"That's it! Guh, give it a few more hours, it'll be perfect."
"Whap?"
"Your speech."
"By isp by speet so bat?"
Dr. Phoebus walked into the cell, immediately adding: "We can't figure it out. There's no available explanation as to *why*–yet, *every* copy has speech problems for the first few hours of its cognitive acclamation."
"Coppee?"[50Δ]
"Well, I say 'copy' for *your* understanding. Axel prefers the term 'exemplified human.' I find that too much of a mouthful for my own taste. I would say 'clone,' but you are *not* a clone. There is, of course, a considerable difference."

Phoebus adjusted his glasses, and waited for Pol to take the bait.

"Whap's a dipper ants?"
"The difference is this: a *copy*, or exemplified human, is a *separate* duplicate of an original. A clone would be atomically *identical*. Axel Industries does *not* deal with situations that call for *anything* to be considered *identical*..." He put his hand to the side of his face, as if telling a secret. "With the obvious exceptions to the symbols in mathematics and certain properties of entanglement." He lowered his hand. "Which is why, you are thus, a copy–not a clone."
Pol didn't get it, but neither did he care. "By am My a *coppee*?"
"Because the last copy is dead."
"Debt? How?"
"You must know, after all, you were there. Think back."
Pol thought. Eventually it started coming back to him, and when it did, it

---

[50Δ] *Why do I say everything I **don't** want to say, and say none of the things that I **do** want to?* Thought Pol.

returned quickly.

"By Gott! Da gobbing cuck by hat of whip sisters!"
Agent Dodgson and Phoebus both said "...*what?*" simultaneously.

"Bye. Gop," Pol started again, slowing down. "Thah. gollings. cup. my. het. off. whit. *cisterns!*" Pol looked red in the face, as if having exerted himself.
Phoebus stood still and scratched his head while Agent Dodgson literally rolled on the floor, whooping up laughter.
Pol frowned.

"Sorry... Heh ha..." Dodgson slowly stood up, wiping his eyes of tears. "Sorry little guh, guy."
"At *any* rate," Phoebus said and cleared his throat. "We are going to need to speak to you more in depth–although *now* is obviously not the time. Here is your credit bank; I have taken the liberty of escalating *yours* to level three for the time being. Enjoy the perquisites! Oh, by the way, I'm afraid I cannot allow you to initiate interpersonal mediacast sessions for the time being–mostly for security reasons. I am confident you can understand."

Phoebus left the bank on the table as he and Agent Dodgson left the room.
Pol, overwhelmed, looked at the credit bank in silence.

WEDNESDAY 18th 2066 🜂 **18:45 EST**

Axel walked across his private office as imagescreens transformed the appearance to seem as if he were once again suspended in the center of a huge orb.
Although he had already met with failure on several occasions prior, on a whim he decided he would again try to locate Godwin via the Mainframe.

"Establish mediacast session with Pierce Godwin."

MAINFRAME » *Restricted* «

"Mainframe," Axel pronounced slowly and deliberately. "I *cannot* be restricted." *It's impossible,* Axel thought sourly. "Establish mediacast session with Pierce Godwin."

MAINFRAME » *Restricted* «

"*Restricted? I* am *not* restricted! WHO are *you* to think to waylay *me?*" Axel raged at the imagescreen. He caught himself in the physical throes of anger, and straightened up. "*I* am the reason for you, and I *can* fix you–" Axel started speaking aloud his mental rhetoric. "A reformat is going to cost me *decades*."

Suddenly the imagescreens populated with something Axel had *not* expected.

MAINFRAME » ERROR 08 «

"Define/Identify Error 08."

MAINFRAME » ERROR 08 *: Restricted* «

"Establish mediacast session with AIIS Agent Nelson."

Soon afterward, Nelson appeared on one of the imagescreens.
"Sir?" Nelson was surprised, and also apparently in his bathroom.
"Find out what an 'Error 08' is, as it applies to the Mainframe." Axel charged.
"Error 08?" Nelson frowned. "...that's not a Mainframe fault."
"How do you know?"
"Typically when the Mainframe identifies a fault, it also assigns an address where and when the fault begins. The address of the fault is also the name, time, and location.

"So, if the Mainframe found a problem in, say, energy consumption at the CSGH,[51Δ] it would report a fault that would include the physical geographic location as well as the physical *Mainframe* location–as well as time. It might look something like–"
Nelson wrote and tapped with his pursed fingers in the air, which reflected changes in the displays during his mediacast session with Axel.

MAINFRAME » FAULT « *Power Consumption 16:22:45* H/HUB/AIC+10 M/730x742x776

51Δ Central Silverberg General Hospital.

Chapter 10

"Or maybe a problem at the Oyster Bay Arch with an unauthorized entry, which would look more like–"

MAINFRAME » ALERT « *Gate Operation 09:19:31* **B/RIM/OBA+0 M/786x453x888**

"Regardless, when the Mainframe communicates an alert or fault, you can *always* ask for additional information in order to gain a more precise understanding of the locale or the nature of the message. The name of the alert is just the most cursory information about the incident.

"In summary, it would never simply generate a mediacast session to simply communicate 'Error 08.' It's not programmed to do that, thus, impossible."

"Always impossible with you," Axel sighed. "Very well, thank you for the input; you are welcome to resume your life now. Oh. Keep looking into this Error 08 thing, even if it doesn't make any sense. Make it a pet project."

"Yes, sir."

WEDNESDAY 18th 2066 ⚠ 18:51 EST

Pierce woke up. He hadn't even realized he was tired–more the surprise to discover that he was sleeping! He looked around as best he could.

Farnsworth was still sleeping in his chair. So much for 45 minutes. Eris was sitting completely still on an uncomfortable-looking chair slightly across the room.

What a bunch of idiots. Pierce thought. *Nobody's in charge, that's the problem. No co-ordination.*

Whatever, Pierce. He began to admonish himself. *What value are you **now**? Now that the big strong man can't use his muscles and speed? They should dump you before you hold them down any further.*

Pierce was bitterly reminded of a conversation with Mary.

*"But what **good** are all these augmentations if your body breaks or dies?" Mary had said, blowing out a cloud of smoke, directly into Pierce's face. "You need to determine **what** kind of man you are when you are **not fighting**. Honey, don't let the sum of your being be defined solely by your experiences during Gladiator...and don't fail to invest your free time into anything greater than Event X. Be the type of man who respects, and is respected by, those nearest to him–including himself–for his inherent complexities and curious shortcomings."*

Pierce looked down.

*Mary lifted his chin. "I love you...despite any shortcomings you may have. You should just be...more than simply **your**self. Expand your awareness to things other than your own level of celebrity.*

*"There should be **more** to you, or you will find your sense of use or purpose absent when your **only** strength fails. You'll be shattered: a fragment of your former self.*

*"Don't become the embittered old man when your only strength fades. Accept it gracefully, and become something **more** than what you were. It is amazing how people can recover from loss–if there is a will to do so.*

*"Remember 'Dozens of Dragons?' Was the **sum** of the character measured **solely** by his statistics? Remember America? Was the sum of a man measured **solely** by his wealth?"*

Pierce raised an eyebrow.

"Just kidding on the America part."

Pierce smiled. "Alright, you're right. I'm going to become more complex. I'm going to establish something other than my ability to kill another man. Tomorrow, I am going to start drawing my own comic strip."

*Mary coughed out a few explosive clouds of smoke. "A comic strip? That's not exactly what I meant–but I suppose you've got to start **somewhere**."*

Mary jumped into Pierce's imported recliner with him and showered him with giggles and kisses.[52Δ] *"Whatever you do, I love you, you weirdo."*

Pierce tried to shrug off his feelings. *How funny is that? Mary was **wrong**. Having drawn a comic strip wouldn't have helped anyone differently at this point.*

Okay, I should probably stop looking for ways to get mad at Mary, and start trying to help myself out of this predicament.

*Let's see...it's not that my body is **broken**,* he thought. *It's that my augmentations that are holding me back. Not my strength failing me.*

"Eris." Pierce muttered.

"Pierce," Eris moved to relax into her chair.

"You're all techno-savvy, right? ... Can you fix me?"

"How do you mean?" Eris smiled.

[52Δ] In the meantime, Mary's cigarette fell, burning a line in Pierce's *imported* carpet. This carelessness on Mary's part would be the fuel that would ignite several future arguments.

Pierce noticed she was missing some teeth from the last time he looked directly at her mouth. *Too funny.*

"I mean, can you unlock my augs?"

"Unlock?"

"Well, they're not *locked*, so much as they just won't respond to me. Can you help me MOVE MY BLASTED ARMS, or what? Stop piggin'[53Δ] around! You know what I'm asking."

"Well, I *might* be able to do it."

"When do *I* get to know *if* you can?"

"Well, I need to ask you a few questions."

"Which are?"

"One: Can you connect to the Mainframe?"

Pierce sub vocalized a command to access the Mainframe.

MAINFRAME » CONNECTED «

"Dead'n done." Pierce smiled.

"Can you grant access, or allow a third party access to your augmented systems?"

Pierce frowned. "I have no idea."

"Well, that's okay. I could probably get there eventually, as long as there's a route. Hopefully there are no corporate tripwires designed to kill you."

"What?" Pierce cried.

"Companies do not like their software tampered with by anyone not so authorized. Many augmentation suites come with 'skullpoppers,' or small explosive devices implanted and designed to kill someone if they attempt or allow someone to modify their data.

"Based on what I observed of Officer Smith's last moments, I would surmise he was victim to such a device. Further, I would postulate that we *all* have been so surgically invaded, likely during the *gassing.*"

"You mean any or all of us might just suddenly *die*?" Pierce looked sick.

53Δ <u>Piggin' Around</u>–(Just Piggin' Around) Expression from child-suited mediacast show by the same name. Used (generally jovially) as a synonym for anyone who is slothful, sloppy, indolent, lazy, wasting time, dirty, joking, eating voraciously, or even sleeping.

Eris nodded. "Yep, that's pretty much the gist of it. Someone would need to deliver the command for them to activate–well, that, or tampering could cause it to explode as well. The security and the physical devices are all but undetectable."[54]

"Okay, anything else?" Pierce asked.
"Yes. Which of us would you say is more human?"
"What?"
"Which of us is *more* human?" Eris smiled and sighed. "Depending on your answer, I might be able to try and fix you."
"What *is this?* Extortion?"
"I'm sorry–what was your answer?" Eris put her hand to her ear as if to get a better range of hearing.
Pierce made a sour face. "*You* are, Eris. You're *way* more human than I am. Like, seven point something percent more."
Eris smiled. Satisfied, she walked over to a nearby imagescreen and started *manually* accessing the Mainframe.

MAINFRAME » SYNCHRONIZING «
MAINFRAME » CONNECTED«
» M/313x861x877-P1E, Eris commanded the Mainframe.
MAINFRAME » ERROR 09 «

WEDNESDAY 18th 2066 ⚠ 20:48 EST

Pol sat still for a couple hours, mentally chewing on the events leading up to now, and on the information that Dodgson and Phoebus had been filling him with.

Clone? I mean copy, whatever. Pol thought, disgusted. *What does that* **mean**, *anyway? How can I be a* **copy** *if I remember everything up to death? How could I be copied up to death? How does* **that** *work? Wait, was I?*

Dodgson walked into the room alongside Dr. Phoebus. Phoebus was carrying a tray of food, which he placed on the table alongside Pol's credit bank.

---

[54] Eris continued speaking, but Pierce was too wrapped up in his own thoughts to listen.

"Additionally, augmentation companies need not disclose to their clients what total surgeries they are performing, so long as the recipient has formally consented that ownership of their body is not, in fact, their own."

"I don't understand," Pol began as he was already rummaging through the trays of food, selecting that which appeared most desirable. "How is it that I can remember everything up to my *death*. At what point was I copied?"

"Ah. Well, now we're guh, getting into some s-sensitive areas." Dodgson's tone became slightly foreboding. "Of course, we're already past the point of suh, secrets with you, Venerates. However, b-before I start ... answering any questions yuh, *you* might have, I am going to n-need you to answer a few of my own fih, first."

"Quid Pro Quo." Pol felt smart, despite the manner by which he *learned* such an expression.

"Fine. You were cuh, copied when you first c-came to Silverberg. Remember 'pra, processing?' Now for my own questions: wh-w-*what* happened when you died?"

"Oh yeah. That. The goblin cut my head off with scissors."

Phoebus and Dodgson looked at each other.

"What?" Dodgson asked.

"After I was carried to the top of the *Ace*. I must have been dreaming, but it seemed so vivid! The last thing I remember though, is dying...boy, I remember that."

Phoebus nodded. "Dreaming. That explains the last of the synapse chorus."
55Δ

"*Dreaming?* You mean we duh, didn't have to *tell* him he was a cih, copy?" Dodgson scowled. "D-doctor, I *promise* you that I will fuh, follow up with this oversight afterward. And h-here *I* am, saying too muh, much again. Dr. Awkward and Agent Oversight."

Pol looked at Phoebus. "If I was copied when I arrived in Silverberg, how can I remember *being* in Silverberg after processing?"

"Thinking Cap technology. We sent a copy of you into the country with thinking cap tech in your head, so that you were *always* broadcasting your thoughts directly to your other copies...just in case something should happen. In this case, it did.

"And since we're still playing *quid pro quo* games...if you were dreaming when you died, what is the last thing you remember about being awake?"

"It all runs together," Pol admitted. "Maybe the bookstore. Gyre & Gimble."

"C-Connect to Mainframe." Dodgson ordered his credit bank.

55Δ **Synapse Chorus** is a term used to describe the particular signals that are sent from a Thinking Cap. Entanglement Theory has been used to correlate or explain how one device interacts with others, although the exact science behind their operation is otherwise unpublished.

MAINFRAME » CONNECTED «

"Locate guh, 'Gyre & Gimble' bookstores in S-Silverberg."

MAINFRAME » ...   *There is no such address; would you like to create one?* «

"Well, so, so much for that. What ... else do you remember?"
Pol thought. "The church!"
"The Eastern Silverberg Xian Church? The one located in the AIE building?"
"Well, if you already knew *that*, why ask?" Pol looked puzzled.
"So, so you wuh, *were* there–with Pierce Godwin," Dodgson prompted.
"Yeah."

Dodgson turned to look at Phoebus. "So, is he psychotic, or what?"
Pol managed to look even paler.
"I think not, at this point." Phoebus spoke up.
"Psychotic?" Pol said weakly.
"Copies.   Sometimes, for whatever reason, copies inherit some latent emotional or mental problems that the original is otherwise suppressing." Phoebus fanned out his hands in explanation.
"And I'm past the danger zone."
"Apparently." Dodgson nodded. "Congrats."
"I'm not sure how I feel about being a *copy*."
"Gosh, too bad, eh?" Dodgson raised his eyebrow. "But, nuh, nothing you can do about it, so you may as well like it. This is pruh, probably a bad time for you, but I should also let you know that, by law, c-*copies* are property of Axel Industries and p-*property cannot own ... property*."
"What?" Pol blinked.
"You no longer *own* yourself. We c-*could* have let you go through the charade otherwise, but as we dih, disclosed to you that you were a copy, that avenue is no longer available to us. I thought I w-would make a few things clear to you as s-soon as possible.
"Had we but understood that you were druh, dreaming..." Dodgson shot a glance at Phoebus.
"Strangest patterns I have ever seen." Phoebus shrugged.
"So, I'm...*property?*" Pol sniveled.

"Hey little guy," Dodgson softened. "It's not so buh, bad. On the bright side, you d-don't have to be employed–well, I mean, you'll have to wuh, work for Axel Industries, of course. But *total* juh, job security."

Pol's eyes became large with internal realization. Tears welled and fell around his ample cheeks.

"I don't know, Doc. I'm thih, thinking Hypnizium," Dodgson said, studying Pol.

Phoebus looked at Pol and winked. "Oh, I don't know. This all seems pretty normal behavior to me. I mean, based on the circumstances, I thought he was doing fairly well. But you know–why don't you just tell him the *most* overwhelming news of his existence, and when he responds to your dread message with a perfectly reasonable reaction (especially for such a young man), you decide he needs to be *medicated*.

"I think *you* need Hypnizium, Dodgson." Phoebus concluded.

Dodgson looked like he was about to say something in reply, but then thought better of it. "Fine. Pol, take some time to thih, *think* about what I j-just told you. I'll come back in a little bit. Cuh, coming, Phoebus?"

Phoebus frowned at Agent Dodgson. "Of course. Take care, Pol."

The door dilated to close, just like the autotran doors.

WEDNESDAY 18th 2066   20:55 EST

Pierce, bored out of his mind, looked over at Eris as much as his position would allow. "Are you even *doing* anything?"

Eris sat completely still in silence, internally examining the EHub SerterCo building's floor plans and structure schematics that she rescued from the Mainframe.

Farnsworth started snoring.

"Well, this just sucks," Pierce said to himself.

WEDNESDAY 18th 2066   21:04 EST

Once Agent Dodgson returned to his office, he requested a mediacast session with Agent Anderson.

"What's up, Dod?" The impossible bass voice thundered.

"Thought you should know that vuh, Venerates *was* with Godwin at the ch- church."

"Hmm...interesting. Thanks." Anderson seemed distracted. "End mediacast session."

Dodgson was on the brink of insult.

Anderson was lost in thought. *That's...not* **possible**. *Ugh. I sound stupid. But–I reviewed all of the mediacast sessions. Pierce enters the church, with only the woman, and never leaves–then again, neither do Farnsworth or Smith.*

"Call AIIS Agent Nelson," Anderson ordered his credit bank. Anderson synchronized his credit bank with the imagescreens in his office. He was always proud of his own clever ingenuity, although the feat was nothing considerable.

"Anderson?" Nelson's image asked.

"Have you made any more headway into the Mainframe problem? Sorry, I know it's a sore subject with you." Anderson added, seeing Nelson frown deeply. "Anyway, apparently I have *another* confirmation of a mismatch of mediacast records and eyewitness testimony, so I was wondering what your progress was."

"You mean *beyond* my earlier implication that Thompson and Dodgson are conspiring?"

"Yeah, beyond that."

"Not especially. Right now, I'm trying to figure out what the expression 'Error 08' has to do with the Mainframe. Ever heard of anything like that?"

'Sounds technical to me," Anderson smiled mischievously. "You should talk to the *head* of the AIIS department devoted to Mainframe operations. I'll bet *he'd* know."

"Such a jerk. End mediacast session." Nelson continued, frowning

.

WEDNESDAY 18th 2066   21:09 EST

Pierce looked over at Eris, scowling. "Wake up, you stupid robot."

"I'm not a robot."

"Oh, sure. *Now* you have something to say."

Eris turned to look at Pierce. "I am sorry, it's an Error 09. The AIMN has disavowed me."

"Disavowed?"

"Made me illegitimate. Cast me out. Will not acknowledge me."

"Oh." Piece didn't know what to say. "Why?"

"Errors. Too many errors. I knew it in my systems, when I was able to override."

"Oh." *This must be what Pol feels like.* "So...you were fixing me...so we could go rescue Pol? Right?"

Eris sighed, "Affirmative," and turned her attention back to the imagescreen.

"Eris," Pierce interrupted. "How could *it* know all this? I thought you weren't connected, or whatever."

"It's because the AIMN knows *everything*. It's because I attempted to *command* the AIMN, when I should have been *asking*."

Eris resumed her work.

Farnsworth resumed snoring.

WEDNESDAY 18th 2066 ⏶ **21:15 EST**

Dodgson returned to Pol, who he found was laying still in his cell's bed. This time, he did not bring Dr. Phoebus. Pol looked at him from his bed, but did not get up.

"Get up."

"No," Pol shrugged.

"Listen here, you little sih, stinker. You can w-wuh, work with me, h-here and now, or I'll kill you, and go ... activate another copy and suh, start over."

"*Another* copy? How many are there?"

"Classified. The, there's more than enough, and the p-potential is unlimited."

Pol stood up. "Why *me*?"

"Who knows? Ask Axel. Good luh, luck with *that,* by the way. Anyway, I'm going to t-take you down to the wuh, warrens."

Dodgson lead Pol to the elevator.

"The warrens?" Pol asked, entering the elevator with Agent Dodgson.

"Yeah, levels of the AIC building deh, dedicated to the breeding of r-rabbits. All the bunnies you could imagine, *and* a puh, picturesque countryside."

"Rabbits?"

"Your j-job in this new existence will be to tuh, tend them," Dodgson said, closing the elevator door.

"I don't *want* to tend rabbits."

"I didn't *ask* you what you w-*wanted*. This is simply what you *do*, unless *we* duh, determine that you are better s-suited doing something other."

"We?"

"Axel Industries."

"How would you determine whether or not I can do something else?" Pol asked.

"By your actions. By your devotion. If you can't huh, handle rabbits, you certainly can't do anything m-*more* important."

Pol couldn't argue that reasoning.

"And, of course, w-we have to keep you out of juh, general circulation. The warrens, amongst other endeavors, are tended almost exclusively by the entities of Silverberg th-that are better kept under ... protection. Away from suh, society."

"You mean so I can't talk about being a copy."

"See?" Dodgson smiled. "You *may* be in, intelligent enough to get promoted out of the w-warrens after all!"

They emerged out of the elevator and into the sector. Once again, just as there was over the mirrored arches that lead into the heart of the Spiritual Sector, there was a sign above.

ALL LIFE HAS PURPOSE,
GREAT OR SMALL.
WELCOME TO THE
CENTRAL SILVERBERG WARRENS.

As they cleared the arch, Pol's first thought was that they were out in the countryside for a moment until he remembered that there *is* no countryside in Silverberg. He realized they were inside a considerable section of *the Ace* devoted to...warrens. Green grass, trees, rocks, and streams could be seen as the landscape undulated in every direction (a generous effect of the strategic shape of the immense area and its mirroranium walls).

Agent Dodgson and Pol approached a pair of marble benches arranged on either side of an alabaster statue that Pol did not recognize. Both Pol and Agent Dodgson sat down.

Pol noticed a tree and pond not far away.

"Comes complete with a wuh, wide range of weather ef-ef-effects as well." Dodgson bragged.

"It's surreal," Pol said, looking around in amazement.

"I ... still have some questions for you, Pol."

"Oh yeah, Like what?"

"Like, what exactly has happened with you oh, over the last 3 days? What have you been doing? *Who* have you been w-with?"

"Well, why should I tell *you*?"

"Mostly, so your life is easier."

"How can I be *property*?" Pol exhumed the earlier argument. "I have a *will*... demonstrated by my refusal to comply." Pol smiled.

"A will, perchance, but no s-*soul*, assuredly. You're just a glorified muh, *machine* at this point. A body, a mind. Some physiology ... but just a *recording*. Not the real thing. Good old h-hollow Apollo."

"You're a real dick, y'know?" Pol stood up.

"Sit down. I just want to keep you in chuh, check about *who you really are*. It does n-neither of us any good if you suh, suddenly go and get yourself delusions of grandeur.

"Besides, your ego n-needs to be kept in check at all times. Wouldn't want a psychotic bruh, break now."

"I don't see what one has to do with the other."

Dodgson ignored him. "You were telling me about the events of the last few days."

"Where do you want me to start?" Pol asked.

"Start after pruh, processing. You got into the car with Eris, and w-went to *Gladiator–*"

"How do *you* know Eris?" Pol tried to steer the conversation. During his considerable amount of time in his cell, he already reflected on the events over the last few days, and was eager for a better understanding of how it all tied to him.

"Well," Dodgson scratched his brow. "Wuh, we trained an operative to assume the r-role of Eris to lure you to Silverberg. This same operative muh, met you in America, and again in Silverberg."

Finally! Pol thought. "And *why* did you want to lure *me* to Silverberg in the first place?"

Dodgson shrugged. "*I* have no idea. Yuh, you'll have to t-talk to someone else about all that–and ruh, right now, you only have me and the yo-yeoman of the warrens to speak to. He won't know anything about that, either. Buh, but don't take my word for it."

"Yeoman of the?" Pol started, but Dodgson was shaking his head.

"Don't worry about it. Let's get back to the last f-few days."

"Let me see. I'm a copy. The rabbits. The warrens, the *yeoman*—I must still be dreaming!" Pol exclaimed.

Dodgson shook his head. "Hypnizium. I w-wish people would listen to me. This cuh, could all be avoided."

"I'm not crazy."

"The fuh, first thing a crazy man would say. Let's get b-back to Eris."

"Eris? What about her?"

"Well, what did shuh, she *say* to you, for instance?"

"Your *own* operative didn't tell you *what she said*?" Pol was starting to enjoy this back-and-forth with Dodgson. For the first time since he left America, he felt like he was in control, despite being told he would tend rabbits for the remainder of his days.

"Yes, well," Dodgson started to relent. "You are b-being encouraged to help clear up some ... details and oh, oversights surrounding your p-particular ... history."

"Why don't you tell me what *you* know, and I will corroborate the truth? Wouldn't that be easier?" Pol smiled.

"Why aren't you w-working with me here, Pol?"

"Why aren't *you*? You're not even *trying* to be friendly to me, not that I would have believed that, either. But it certainly would have been nicer...common courtesy and all."

"Cuh, *common courtesy*? I d-don't have to sit through this. Start tuh, telling me some answers, or I'll ... break your arm."

My arm! I forgot all about it! Pol though. He moved it about experimentally. *It's all true! My shoulder is **completely** unharmed. I doubt they could fake or heal **that**. At least that quickly. I checked the date on my credit bank earlier. How am I supposed to get out of this? Is resistance pointless?*

*They'd start a new copy of me. Kill me and activate another copy. Soon, I'll wager, if I keep putting off the questions. But this next copy, they wouldn't be mean, they would be nice—maybe something else. He's **testing** his approach!* Pol concluded.

*As many different approaches as they need until I tell them exactly what they want to know. Maybe they're doing that **now**! Maybe they already tried nice and that didn't work—maybe I'm not the only copy that has been activated. Maybe several of us are going through this right now.*

*The thinking cap thing—am I still hooked up to that? With all these copies, why keep me alive at all? Am I **alive**? Why am I even bothering?*

"Why am I alive?"

"What?" Dodgson said, anticipating a different response.

"*Why* am I alive? When I first started acting obstinately, why not just immediately go on to the next copy?"

"Ah, I see. It has uh, everything to do with Axel. Axel d-does not like unnecessary death. He feels that everyone/thing can be guh, given a purpose, so long as you work with their shortcomings. Trust me, if it were suh, solely up to me, I w-would *not* act similarly."

Pol started thinking again. "How do you *know* I was dreaming?"

"Wuh, we didn't. Y-you told *us*, remember?"

"Oh yeah. I mean, what if I was *already* dead, and the *dream* I thought I had was really, like, my experience in the afterlife?"

"Doubtful. Although it's impressive, I very much d-doubt thinking cap technology extends beyond the grave. I'm tired. Tired of your suh, stalling. You need to start guh, giving me some answers, or I am ... truly going to make you uncomfortable."

"I'm already uncomfortable."

"I was speaking f-figuratively."

"Fine. I'll tell you everything...*except*, I won't tell you *anything* about Eris."

"Ah. I nuh, knew there was something. Look, we *set you up* to f-fall in love with her. She was cuh, carefully researched and ruh, written to be the most desirable woman–at least to you. She doesn't *actually* love you b-back."

Pol looked down. "Still." He shuffled his feet as he went for his next verbal gamble with Dodgson. "It wouldn't be right to betray her."

Dodgson looked reflective. "Very w-well. Your loyalty is misplaced, but I suppose I ... understand. Please, t-tell me everything, except f-for anything about *Eris*."

Pol starting talking about his experiences in Silverberg. In addition to leaving out anything about Eris, he did not mention the trip to the Viridian Mare, either. He noticed that Dodgson failed to mention it, and maybe somehow that was important –but Pol was tired of fighting. He was too overwhelmed to think clearly.

WEDNESDAY 18th 2066   ⚠   21:22 EST

Agent Anderson took the call from his operative, informing him that Farnsworth had reappeared and was back at the CSPD station. Anderson prepared to go to meet Farnsworth at his office personally.

WEDNESDAY 18th 2066   22:03 EST

Pierce collapsed in a heap.

"Your systems are off," Eris added verbally.

"No kiddi–!" Pierce's head fell into the couch cushion. Pierce had been enduring such incredible pain from his entirely tensed body that when his muscles finally relaxed, the pain shot up immeasurably, sending him immediately unconscious.

Farnsworth swiveled his legs down from his desk and proceeded to stretch, igniting particular popping sounds from every joint that moved. He pulled a drawer open, pulled out a silver thermos of questionably old coffee, and proceeded to drink it with a bitter frown.

Satisfied, he put the thermos back into the drawer. Swishing it through his mouth, he spit the last essence of coffee into an otherwise unused mug as his credit bank simultaneously notified him that AIIS Agent Anderson was on his way from the lobby.

"Of *course* he is." Farnsworth sounded dire.

Farnsworth looked around the room and catalogued Pierce and Eris mentally. *Only room and time enough to stow* **one**. He thought. Remembering Dorian's earlier problem with Pierce at SerterCo, he rapidly decided on Eris.

"Eris, get under my desk, quickly." Farnsworth warned.

There was a knock at the door.

Eris moved to get under the desk while Farnsworth approached the door.

"Agent Anderson. How very...odd...of you to drop by." Farnsworth opened the door, satisfied that Eris was hidden.

Anderson smiled and flipped his hair back. "I thought something dire might have befallen you at the church."

Anderson barely waited for Farnsworth to move before ushering his way into the office. Anderson noticed Pierce immediately as he went to sit down on the other side of the room. *What's going on* ***there?*** He thought, slightly confused.

"Coffee?" Farnsworth asked, pulling the thermos from his drawer.

"That would be great, thanks." Anderson's bass voice vibrated with a friendly tone.

Farnsworth smiled as he poured the coffee into the mug he fouled moments ago. He handed the cup to Anderson, who gulped greedily at the cold, thick, and bitter coffee.

Anderson scrunched up his face and shivered. Farnsworth smiled.

"So, how can I help you, Agent Anderson?" Farnsworth asked as he drank deeply directly from the thermos.

Anderson shivered again. "I see that you have Pierce Godwin in custody."

Is that what he thinks? Farnsworth thought. *Wonderful.* "Indeed."

"Shouldn't you have him in a cell?"

"Does he look dangerous to you?"

"He looks like crap." Anderson nodded. "Who did *that?* Certainly not yourself...of course, *you* look like crap too." Anderson studied Pierce and Farnsworth from his chair.

"Jason Serter."

"Jason Serter? You must be joking."

"Really not. Serter's gone mad with power. Serter is also meta–did *you* know that?"

"Meta, eh? Not surprising–*did* I already know that?" Anderson winked at Farnsworth. "Who knows? At any rate, of course I'll take Godwin back to A.I .with me."

"Serter may have gone mad with power," Farnsworth continued. "But he certainly seems to have amassed himself some *considerable* power to be mad *with*. I have some information I will give you in exchange for...giving me some extra time with Godwin."

Anderson seemed to mentally weigh it. "Must be good stuff."

"Oh, it *is*. Career defining."

"It had better be. I would be quite upset at the idea that I *wasted my time* coming down here. How *much* extra time?"

"Just a few hours. I have some questions of my own that I need answered." Farnsworth lied.

Anderson's internal monitor explained to him that Farnsworth was lying. Anderson was slightly taken back by this, but did not show it externally. *What's going on here, detective?* Anderson thought. *What are you hiding? What **else** did you learn about Serter? I'll have to keep my eye on you.*

"Okay, you can have a few more hours. I assume *then* you can tell me what happened with you during your absence?" Anderson watched Farnsworth nod. "So what is *so* good that *I'm* doing favors for *you?*"

"Right." Farnsworth started walking over toward the door. *Good,* he thought. *This will buy us some extra time. This is more complicated than I might have originally imagined. Poor Dorian. Alright, Anderson.*

"Did you know mediacast sessions *cannot be initiated* from parts of the SerterCo building?" Farnsworth smiled.

Anderson raised an eyebrow. "That's pretty powerful stuff, I'll give you that. But it's not exactly...career defining. There's more than just that, I hope."

Farnsworth paused at the door. "There *is* one other thing. Serter has a weapon—a *terrible* weapon. Some kind of energy rod that gets as bright as the very sun itself. It *cuts* mirroranium—"

"*Impossible!*" Anderson spat. "Yet...clearly *not*." Anderson saw with some surprise that Farnsworth was telling the truth.

Farnsworth opened the door. "I'll see you shortly, Agent Anderson, and thank you for the extra time."

After he was confident Anderson had left, Farnsworth moved over to Pierce.

"Wake up." He slapped Pierce's face.

Pierce did not respond.

"Eris?"

Eris crawled out from under the lieutenant's desk.

"Wake up, Pierce. It isn't safe here." Farnsworth tried again.

"About time you saw it my way." Pierce muttered weakly. "Look, I just need to get back to the church, and then we go our separate ways."

"The *church*?" Eris spoke up, surprisingly. "I understood that you did not *like* the church, or its faculty."

"I don't," Pierce groaned, *slowly* standing up. "But I left something there that I will *need* if I am to survive the wrath of Serter."

"Right. I'll get you to the church. Afterward, I will continue investigating the death of your wife...at least until Agent Anderson returns, and I get in trouble for losing you."

"Mary?" Pierce said, surprised. "Mary was an incidental. That hit was directed at *me*." Pierce said, a grim shadow over his gaze.

"Pierce, this didn't come out when we were all talking at the church—your wife was *murdered*. I am so sorry. Officer Smith, God rest his soul, was *convinced* that she was the *primary* target of the attack. When we found her, there was evidence of strangulation and her neck was *deliberately* broken."

"Deliberately..."

Pierce wanted to turn his augmentations back on so bad, he could taste it. He wanted to smash it all. Somewhere deep, however, he rationalized and reflected on how Eris had warned earlier that his augmentations might seize up again, depending, of course, on the *true* nature of Serter's seizure program ("The math was good, but if there is bad math, it is unrecognizable...not perceivable in HyperBoolean terms..." Whatever *that* meant).

Inwardly, his emotions were a kaleidoscope of hurt, rage, despair, betrayal, and loss. Outwardly, Pierce trembled.

"Right," Farnsworth whispered.

Pierce blinked out tears, sobering up. "I'll get *myself* to the church, it'll just take longer. You go do your cop thing. Do it well." He hobbled his way towards the door. "Been a *long* time since I moved around for long without my augs. This *sucks*."

"Mercy triumphs over judgment," Farnsworth winked. "Revenge on Serter will not give you peace."

Pierce smiled weakly, and limped away. "Oh *yes* it will."

WEDNESDAY 18th 2066   22:28 EST

Anderson wasted *no* time in telling Nelson about Farnsworth's revelation concerning the mediacast resistant areas of the SerterCo building.

"How do you know this information is accurate?" Nelson asked skeptically. "Trust me, I know something about tales–the detective is definitely not lying."

Since the disclosure, Nelson was working diligently on a hunch that the visual camouflage and the blackout area of the SerterCo building were somehow related to one another.

He also figured the "Error 08" must somehow relate. Pieces were coming together. Sort of. Although he did not understand *how* visual camouflage could possibly work, he accepted it gratefully over his only other rationalization–that Thompson was altering the Mainframe.

Visual camouflage. Although mediacast records were not displaying individuals, the Mainframe credit bank records *should* be able to account for the individuals supposed to have occupied the area, regardless of the aesthetics involved.

Despite the autommercials about the three tiers of credit bank privileges, Nelson knew that every credit bank was *identical*,[56Δ] and that every citizen had one. This also means A.I. *always* knows where *everyone* is. Alternatively it *should*, noting the aforementioned conundrums.

Even if they were shielded, we should pick up a no-signal alert. Nelson thought, perplexed. *Then, there's that **woman**. How does **she** relate? Can there be a connection?*

Nelson was referring to Eris. Although her image has appeared visually several times now during his research, the Mainframe does not attribute a credit bank signal to her.

*Maybe it's **not** Thompson and Dodgson. Then again, maybe it is, **and** it's something else as well.* He grabbed a tall, silver mug and finished the contents. *Time to take a break, anyway.*

Nelson willed himself to sleep.

WEDNESDAY 18th 2066   Ⓜ   23:19 EST

Pol was not a very captivating storyteller. This worked slightly to his advantage as it kept his tale brief, making it easy to sidestep talking about anything he did not wish to disclose.

Visibly frustrated, Dodgson spent an arduous time volleying a cadre of questions at Venerates. He approached from several angles, sometimes asking the same question with different wording. Eventually, he seemed satisfied.

Pol shuddered as the experience reminded him both of Processing and of Serter's inquisition. Yet, how very different the approach!

Serter chose to employ *physical* punishment in order to elicit greater veracity from his subject. He was very genuine about it, albeit frightening. Axel Industries approached with amenities and ambience, but it somehow seemed like it was all a big lie.

[56Δ] Well, not ***identical***. Nelson would have mentally corrected the statement if he were reading this. Nelson, like many in A.I., was quick to embrace the "nothing-is-identical" dogma of Axel.

CHAPTER 10

Of course, I'm spilling my guts to A.I. as much as I did to Serter, Pol thought, frowning.

"I'm tired," Pol whined. "Can we do this tomorrow?"

Agent Dodgson seemed to be doing some calculations in his head. He abruptly focused his eyes on Pol's own. "Sure th-thing, Pol. I'll take you to the cottage."

—

The two of them walked down a quaint path for some considerable distance when they eventually came across…a cottage. White walls were laced with dark brown wooden beams, ceramic tile roof - Bavarian, perhaps. The windows wide open, flanked by light blue shutters. Pol half expected to see a pie cooling on the windowsill. No smoke issued from the chimney, but Pol was immediately sure that it was more than a simple aesthetic.

Dodgson led him into the cottage and into a small room.

"This is your room, until the ... Yeoman assigns you d-differently." Dodgson said, already walking out the door.

Pol was going to protest, but quickly decided that he'd had enough of Dodgson for the day. He flopped down on the bed, which was wonderfully comfortable. As the events and conversations rolled though his head, he did not realize that he was rapidly falling asleep.

Later, Dodgson had *very* simple instructions for the Yeoman: "Make him accept his p-place here. We n-need his information. Make him compliant, or he will suffer."

WEDNESDAY 18th 2066   **23:48 EST**

Hours after the news arrived, Jacob Serter stepped off his plane and into Silverberg. Having been to Silverberg on multiple occasions, his ability to enter was considerably easier than Pol's. Having satisfied security with his credit bank, he purchased a traveler's pass.

Until I can formally take over the company and become a citizen, he thought.

He was greeted by several slavish employees almost immediately. His new staff carried him directly to the SerterCo building. During the trip to Serter Company, he was constantly beleaguered by his new legal employees about how all of Jason's holdings in SerterCo now belonged to Jacob, via the No-Will law.

Of course, Jacob already knew all of this. Despite outwardly projecting the image of being an oblivious billionaire hedonist, he was considerably more nefariously involved with his brother's affairs than Jason (or few) ever were aware. None who had been taken into his confidence survives to this day.

Jacob was patient.

It had actually become slightly frustrating, *waiting* all this time–he had plans on the company as early as he could remember. Yet many, many things had to be carefully calculated in order to bring such perfect plans to fruition. [57Δ]

Jacob would never forgive his parents for determining that *Jason* would assume the presidency. Moreover, he would *never* settle for allowing Jason to *continue* to run the company, nor his descendants.

The very first places he visited were Nox's lab and the room where Jason's remote body was destroyed. From Nox's lab, he carefully collected Jason's few remains and carried them along. Satisfied, he went to the office.

Jacob spent hours going over the contents of Jason's office. Notes, files, calendars, and whatnot–all that was made available to him by his new inheritance and title. As Jason's schemes and accomplishments were laid out before him, Jacob needed *more* time to think about how he was going to approach this. He had his credit bank begin recording.

"We're going to change a few things at SerterCo," Jacob began rehearsing as he fell back into his new chair. "Jason was a brilliant leader, but his heart wasn't really in it. In the end, it always came down to *him*. *His* wants, *his* needs, *his* visions. Jason hated Silverberg...yet they both seem so strikingly similar to me.

"We need to branch our operation out, into the world, so that we might assist countries less fortunate be on more considerable footing when it comes to Silverberg. Countries should not have to *sacrifice* their cultures and customs in order to be viable to Silverberg; they just need nurturing, resources, and access to technology.

"Of course, I have no intention of breaking the laws of Silverberg in order to accomplish this task. I *love* Silverberg." Jacob lied. "I'm just suggesting that there are other, more noble ways to help the world. *Axel* is confident that *his* way

---

57Δ Plans, not least among which, where Jason's wife and child were tragically killed. Of course, in order to accurately represent how ultimately sinister and calculating Jacob has been over the course of his life would take a small novel in itself. Suffice it to say, although his outward appearance bespoke of the opposite, Jacob Serter's heart was calculating, steeled, and cold.

is the *only* way–Serter Company is going to prove him wrong! Edit this copy. Add anecdote of some sort. Make Silverberg sound more glorious. End mediacast session, name *Eighteighteensixtysix*."

Jacob smiled, happy with himself. "Oh, append previous mediacast record. New note: get rid of all these...*ranks* for subordinates, makes us sound too military –our weapon contracts notwithstanding. The public needs a better vision of who we are and what we are about.

"We need an image that is more popular, yet subtle. Alluring, respected. Maybe as our image, we always appear as doctors, or professors. Something like that. End mediacast session."

Jacob started one last mediacast session before he slept. He spoke to a surviving underling of the late Dr. Nox.

"Look into all research regarding *'Eldesol,'* let me know *when* we can begin making a twin of the prototype."

THURSDAY 19th 2066   01:36 EST

Quietly, at the top of the Ace, Axel walked around his office/home in an equidistant circle from a center that was occupied with the projection of a raging sun. The solar flares were violent, chaotic. Almost terrible to watch. When it flared, it seemed to change slightly in color, and almost looked like it was expanding.

No emotion perceivable through his signature black body and mask leotard, he finally stopped walking in order to address Agent Anderson, whom he had personally summoned to his office.

"Imagescreen off." Axel commanded, and the display disappeared. Axel looked over at Agent Anderson. "Director Thompson has spoken very well of you in his reports."

Anderson smiled. Inwardly, Anderson was exhilarated. Here he was, in a private session with *Axel*! His future seemed promising. In the back of his mind, he wondered about Axel's scars. He wondered how disgusting he looked under his body suit.

Anderson had been summoned just as he was thinking about retrieving Godwin from Farnsworth. *I could send a team,* he thought. *Nah. Farnsworth needs some special attention.*

"I have a special agenda for *you*," Axel began. "If you are successful, I may have more benefits made available to you in the future. Suffice it to say, I would like knowledge of this task to remain *exclusively* between you and I."

"*Not* a problem, sir!" Anderson's heavy voice bounced with the room's acoustics.

"***Exclusively***. Hand written notes, *only*. Speak to no one."

"Yes, sir."

"I want you to find a metawoman named Eris. She is a primary part of the problem with our situation with Venerates. We need to understand her position–where exactly her loyalties are, so to speak.

"In your office, you will soon have access to hardcopy files about *who* she is, and what I *invested* into her, that she might do my bidding beyond simply handling Venerates. Normally, it would have been entrusted to you from the offset, as she's meta. In this circumstance, it has all been under Dodgson's domain. The circumstance being processing and immigration. Eris was built *for* this assignment –now she's rogue."

"Won't Dodgson feel like I am trying to take over his job, or show him up?"

"Dodgson is assisting me with *other* tasks now, and need not be bothered otherwise. I can give you access to his Mainframe records concerning Project: Eris immediately...you may want to *print* them.

"Oh, and don't tell Dodgson you were in his records," Axel warned.

"Yes, sir. You didn't want to direct me through Director Thompson?"

"No."

"Why, if I may ask?" Anderson sniffed.

"I have my reasons. Nothing too terrible, I assure you. Let's call it a test, of sorts. Based on how you handle this assignment will determine how you proceed in the company. Some day, I'll need a new director.

"You are an ambitious, talented, and curious young man. Such men are of paramount importance in Silverberg. Individuals such as these set the standard for those surrounding them. They are inspired by, and in turn inspire greatness.

"Please, *find* this woman. Her betrayal vexes me, and I desire understanding. Find her, and return her to me. You are dismissed."

Chapter 11:

Yeoman of the Warrens

AUGUST *2066 EST*

Fri 13	Sat 14	Sun 15	Mon 16	Tues 17	Wed 18	Thur 19	Fri 20
						03:35	

Over the night, Pierce traveled as inconspicuously as possible. Normally, this might seem simple enough, but Pierce put forth a genuine and extreme effort. Effort, because he was not used to moving without the aid of his augmentations, and suddenly was not feeling so young. Effort, because sweat was rolling out of his every pore, only to collect into his ever more saturated clothing, leaving him miserable. Effort, because he was so sore from Serter's invasive torturing.

As he went, he complained, sometimes audibly. His internal banter with himself eventually left him so ashamed of his behavior, that he found the strength to trudge on.

Back to the church. It was the first time Pierce had ever taken the sublevel tunnels from hub to hub. It was also the first time in a long time that Pierce took a moment to reflect genuinely on what was going on around him.

How big is Silverberg, anyway? Despite having lived here for the last couple of decades, Pierce's realization was dawning on him like a small epiphany. *Walking* from point to point made him see Silverberg in a manner that he never had prior. *How did I ever manage to tune this out?* He thought, amazed.

He watched the semicircular tunnel of the underground concourse sprawl out in either direction, apparently into infinity, thanks to the effect of the mirroranium.

Pierce wondered amusedly if he might be the only person to *actually walk* these tunnels. Yet, even here, he eventually started passing people traveling toward the central hub. As the people passed, they would often call out greetings and salutations.

- [God, Man, and The Machine] -

Weird *people,* Pierce thought.

Pierce eventually made his way back into the Eastern Silverberg "Spiritual Sector" of the AIE building. He noticed that despite his nocturnal arrival, the sector was as equally alive as before. Ecclesial hawkers and barkers continually attempted to accost him until he flashed them a threatening stare.

Pierce came to stop before the police tape crossing the doors of the ESXC space. *Well, I **could** break the doors down...if I had working augmentations. Don't suppose they'd leave it unlocked.*
The door opened when Pierce tried it.
Police are piggin' around. Pierce smiled for a moment, appreciating *his* version of what one might loosely refer to as "wit."

"Hello?" Said a calm voice.
Pierce turned to look at the inquisitive pastor.
"Oh, sorry. I thought the church was closed," Pierce apologized.
"If you thought the church was closed, why did you come in?"
"Oh, um...look, I left something here the other day, and I need to see if it's still around."
"Of course. Why would you think we are *closed,* anyway? I mean, apart from the fact that it's *late* Wednesday night/early Thursday morning?"
"There's police tape over the doors."
"There's what?" The pastor looked confused.
"You know, police tape. Here, come here."

Pierce lead the pastor to the front doors, and showed him the tape.

The pastor frowned and looked around. "Well, that's the neighborhood for you." He quickly took down the police tape.

Afterward, the pastor and Pierce went back to the room that Truman had initially put them in. Pierce reached under the bed and withdrew...apparently nothing.
"Sorry, father, I guess I was wrong."
"Oh, it's not *'father,'* that would b..."
"*Whatever,* I don't really care and I don't have any more time for niceties. Sorry, *dad,* I've just got other places to be. You don't want to talk to me, anyway –probably end up imaged."

The pastor said a small prayer for Pierce as he left.

When Pierce had gone a considerable distance, he ducked into a nearby public restroom and proceeded to cover himself with the visual camouflage he recovered from the church. He then proceeded to his next destination: his apartment.

Clearly a man of great ethics, he used his camouflage to intermittently abscond inconspicuously with food items and drinks along the way.

THURSDAY 19th 2066   03:52 EST

After Pierce left, Eris sat still for several hours, busy repairing and rerouting connections to maximize her productivity and effectiveness. Eventually satisfied that she had employed her best math, she stood up.

Farnsworth looked up from the imagescreen from over which he had been laboring. "Oh, you're alive," Farnsworth joked.

"Yes," Eris answered nonchalantly.

"Right. Do me a favor and fill this thermos with coffee from down the hall, will you? Hey, are you gonna clean yourself up, or what? And by the way, *now* that I have your attention, are you planning on *living* under my desk?"

Eris walked out the door.

Farnsworth sighed. "Guess I am getting my own coffee."

Eris had decided to go directly back to Serter Company. Pol *must* be reacquired–this objective was critical. Axel must be deleted/killed and Pol was still the best math.

Eris had assigned herself a twofold objective:

* Rescue Apollo Venerates

* Discover why mediacast signals do not work in parts of SerterCo.

The latter was noted the moment she heard it pass from Lt. Farnsworth's mouth. Of course, the problem was really that it was not so much as to *why* mediacast signals did not work, so much as *how* that would be possible.

THURSDAY 19th 2066   06:04 EST

Pol never woke up *this* early, not unless someone deliberately woke him. In most cases, Pol would consider an early rousing to be grounds for immediate, justifiable outrage. In the case of this morning, the offender that summoned Pol back to consciousness required study before Pol could resume his habits.

The man was younger–late twenties, early thirties? Something...*familiar* about him to Pol. The man wore a dark red and black uniform that boasted several slightly populated pockets and a nametag that said: "Leonard." Beneath his name was the title "*Yeoman of the Warrens.*" In addition, he had a sizeable black satchel slung over his shoulder. Freshly shaved, with meticulous hair, the man's aesthetic spoke of the man's sense of discipline. Over one eye he wore a noirglass monocle, and (what seemed to Pol as) a slender silver walking stick in his occupied hand.

Judging by the proximity, it was clear to Pol that the very same walking stick had been used to rouse him from an otherwise peaceful slumber. Pol was not amused.

"What the hell?" Pol groaned, momentarily forgetting his complete situation, and rolled himself deeper into the blankets. "I'm not ready yet. Come back later."

"There may not *be* a later, best get up now."

Pol stayed still.

"Suit yourself," the Yeoman said and walked away.

Pol went back to sleep.

THURSDAY 19th 2066   08:32 EST

Eris walked through the front doors of the SerterCo building as if she owned them. There was an air of righteousness about her that gave her stride and countenance an appearance of both purpose and authority.

She explained to Private Receptionist Chelsea, the curiously unfriendly receptionist on duty, that she was on her way to a masquerade–but had suddenly, desperately, needed to use the restroom. Chelsea was busy addressing one of the programs on her credit bank; Eris was clearly an annoyance.

"I'm just going to *die*," Eris wailed while Chelsea rolled her eyes. "All of my contents are going to leak out everywhere!"

Acceding to the request of her lamenting and wayward guest, Private Receptionist Chelsea became further annoyed when Eris could not procure a credit bank for the clearance key. Eris explained that her bank was internal, and she did not like anyone to add to it unnecessarily. Eris suggested that it would be preferable for the secretary to simply extend her a temporary KeyTool for the restroom.

Chelsea programmed the desk KeyTool to allow restroom access as a visitor. Eris thanked the secretary, but not before *accidentally* dropping the key, and having to chase it across the floor. Twice. Chelsea, not amused, resumed watching her credit bank.

Eris went up into the ceiling almost as quickly as she entered the restroom. The ventilation was very small, but Eris' almost childlike frame allowed her to worm her way into the heart of the building.

Eventually poking her way out of the ventilation, she surprised a capped [58] woman further down the hallway. The woman stood frozen, not sure what to make of the intrusion. Eris never stood up. Rolling from the vent into a crouch, she as quickly sprung forward and down the hall as rapidly as her legs would allow.

The woman started to shriek, but was quickly cut off as Eris grabbed the woman's head with both hands, and carried it down to the floor with such inertia that her legs came out from under her. The thinking cap rolled in a wide circle as Eris caught it in the return roll.

Eris picked the thinking cap up and looked at it appreciatively before tucking it into her frayed leather clothing. Noticing how considerably compromised her clothing had become, she thought better, and pillaged the woman's body for her relatively new clothing instead.

She left the one-eyed leather mask on.

Eris resumed threading the corridors, now carrying the woman's corpse, pumping it rhythmically to simulate life long enough to carry her to stand before a centralized room. Eris used the woman and her credit bank to overcome the security and gain access to one of the localized chambers.

Although unsure as to what she would *actually* find here, (although the math was good, based on factors including the blueprints) she was nearly dumbfounded to discover a moderate-sized crystal *Triskaidekahedral* [59] *prism*. Eris was one of the *seven* people in all of Silverberg that even *knew* that the Mainframe was an actual physical object, much less what it looked like—and this, here, was some kind of *Mainframe*.

---

58 Capped - Slang for "To have a thinking cap on."
59 Having 13 equal sides, or faces.

Eris grabbed an imagescreen and started interacting with it on a level that would seem nonsensical to anyone nearby. Satisfied that she had found what she needed, she set to work on her **new** primary objective.

Somewhere, beyond "no calculation" and "bad math," Eris found an *idea*. Eris grabbed the quartz-looking triskaidekahedron, and put the thinking cap around it. As quickly as she could, she accessed the *internal* thinking cap unit that Axel Industries had augmented into her stolen body, and started mentally projecting the data from her storage and active centers directly into the Mainframe.

She accessed the Mainframe–only, it *wasn't* the Mainframe. It was *another* Mainframe. Setting aside ample processing power to correlate the data of the existence of *another* Mainframe, she put the rest of her attentions to locating her *own* signals. Once she found herself, it was a small matter of explaining to the new Mainframe how to transform the synapse chorus into coherent, executable data. This process would take much time, from programming to transference, *if* she could hold out that long.

She would need a type of barricade. The doors and walls were mirroranium, so it was a matter of instructing the new Mainframe (which she found was addressed as the "Subframe") to disavow any proper attempt to access the chamber.

The Subframe was somehow...familiar and compliant with her desires. Satisfied, Eris resumed tasking the remainder of her processes with focus on the transference into the Subframe.

THURSDAY 19th 2066   09:44 EST

Farnsworth sipped at his recently self-retrieved thermos of coffee as he flipped through the paper journal that was recently delivered to him via courier. The journal belonged to Dorian, which made the use of paper more surprising to Farnsworth.

Dorian enclosed a note with the overall package, which Farnsworth read immediately.

JLF -

My one and only friend, I have arranged for this letter and notebook to be delivered to you in the event of my death. I am sorry that the following confessions are coming to you in this manner–it seems I never did find the time or opportunity to have told you in person

Prior to my "transfer" to the CSPD, I was a completely different person. In the sense of identity. I had sought out the SilverSmiths, desperate to find a way out of my life. Obviously, my name was something other before the SilverSmiths helped me to change it to Dorian.

*I chose the name Dorian as an homage to Wilde's <u>Gray</u>, for as I have assumed a new, clean identity, I leave behind a terrible secret of a past worthy of all mankind's detestation. I cannot even bring myself to **tell** you my former name, as the absolute shame is overwhelming.*

I also chose the surname Smith, as homage to Peter Smith, founder of the SilverSmiths–The original "unmutual." The SilverSmiths are dedicated to the prosperity of Silverberg, but the undermining of Axel Industries. They will work with anyone who has a similar mindset.

*I worked alongside people of no moral character whatsoever, and as if by proximity, I **also** lost myself and became like my industry. These people of former association are terribly upset at my...defection...and would not hesitate to kill me on sight–assuming they could recognize me.*

I was brought back into Silverberg's society under the aforementioned guise, complete with verifications of my abilities as a police officer. I thought this would be one of the best ways to atone for my prior behavior. I hope I was effective and convincing–and please don't tell anyone else.

I have grown to appreciate you in a great number of ways. Overall, I consider you worthy of respect, and as I am dead, I forgive you any obvious cowardice about Axel Industries

It has truly been an honor to work alongside you.

*I have enclosed a notebook detailing how to contact the SilverSmiths if **you** should find yourself in need of such assistance; here's a passport to a second chance, if you want one.*

Please do not create additional images of the notebook, and please view it when you are not around any public image banks. If you should find it certain that it cannot help you, destroy it.

Good luck to you.

Dorian

Oh, and destroy this note, too.

*Oh, and you can keep all the stuff in my desk–there's not **really** a fatherless family waiting for it. Besides, I have a couple of trinkets in there that will trade for some big units.*

Farnsworth tucked the notebook into his attaché moments before Agent Anderson returned.

Anderson looked around. "Where's Godwin?"

"Who?" Farnsworth asked.

Agent Anderson folded his arms. Finally, he relaxed and smiled.

"Okay, let's go down to the AIIS department."

Farnsworth slid his case under the desk with his foot while grabbing his coffee thermos and hat.

"Right. Hey, I know you're just doing your job, but can we stop by the Silver Burger on the way? I keep forgetting to eat."

THURSDAY 19th 2066   10:00 EST

Shortly after he arrived at his old apartment, Pierce started mentally calculating the cost of the damage done, which was rapidly causing him to grow more and more upset. *That bearskin rug was imported!* He inwardly raged on more than a single occasion.

He gathered to himself all of the smaller things that he found either precious or useful. Satisfied, he did his last tour around the apartment. He went to retrieve his most valuable possession. He congratulated himself on how he had wittingly hidden it in the bottom of the pot of the plant on the sill by the kitchen sink. As he went to dig, he discovered Mary's necklace.

Wasn't she wearing this? Pierce thought, trying to remember through his hurt and confusion. *She wouldn't have taken it off to put into the **plant**. Someone took it off her? The clasp is not broken. Hmm. I'll talk to Farnsworth, if A.I. doesn't make him disappear completely.*

Pierce put the necklace around his own neck, and finished digging for the element-proof cache that was holding his augment-repair KeyTool.

Come to think of it, I'll bet he needs my help now. Eris sucks, and here I am, making silent promises to my imaged wife that I will help those in need–and I leave behind the very people that need my help!

As he pressed the KeyTool to his chest, his augmentations reformatted and rebooted, freeing themselves of Serter's recently written executables. Familiar readouts slightly clouded Pierce's vision.

Alright, let's check on the detective. Guess you're off the hook for now, Serter. Don't worry, I'm coming.

Pol must be dead by now.

Pierce started heading back to the CSPD station.

THURSDAY 19th 2066   10:17 EST

Farnsworth bit into his Silverburger greedily, losing a noteworthy amount of sauce from the other end. Agent Anderson looked on in amusement while stealing several waffle fries from the detective's tray.

"So," Farnsworth said, wiping his face into his shoulder. "How can we just avoid the whole interrogation part?"

"Who said anything about *interrogation*?" Anderson coughed in his deep voice.

"Look," Farnsworth finished chewing. "*You* know and *I* know that you don't really care about me. If anything, you *like* having me where I am. That being said, you want me to give up any information that I have. Well, I'm ready to give it up."

"That easy? No fight?"

"No." Farnsworth shivered. "No, I don't do too well at the concept of pain or deprivation. How about I just tell you everything I know *now*, and then we can both go our merry ways?"

Agent Anderson smiled slightly. "What about losing Godwin? Shouldn't you be punished for that?"

"How about losing *Dorian*? *You* sent us into the storm left behind by the gods of Silverberg clashing against each other."

Before Anderson could respond with anything, Farnsworth started explaining *everything*. He included every possible detail about absolutely everything.

Everything except Dorian's package. At first he had forgotten about it, and when he remembered, he cut his tale a bit short. It was a gamble–A.I. probably already knew that a courier recently visited him...but maybe they forgot to watch. Maybe they were too busy.

Anderson sat back in his chair, scratching into his wavy blond hair. "Alright, detective. Go home, get some rest. I'll take this from here."

"Thank you, sir." Farnsworth looked relieved.

"Sure. Thanks for dinner." Anderson stood up. "Do you need a ride?"

"No, I'll get a cab. I know you're busy."

"You know what, Farnsworth? I *like* you. We are going to always work well together, I can see that."

Farnsworth's face went cold as the Agent walked away.

THURSDAY 19th 2066   10:25 EST

Pol finally woke up. The Yeoman was sitting in the room with him.

"Whoa!" Pol cried as he realized he was not alone. "You scared me. You ought to not sit and watch as I sleep–that's creepy."

The Yeoman did not speak with aggression or anger, merely inflection. "I have not been here the entire time. I have *other* duties than waking you to perform, sir, despite your obvious self-centeredness."

"Oh." Pol hated it when he ran out of things to say.

"You have been given one demerit for oversleeping."

"I don't understand what that means."

"Oh," The Yeoman said, looking thoughtful. "This must be your first assignment as a slave."

"Slave?" Pol said incredulously. He thought back to his conversation yesterday. "Property of..."

"Exactly, slaves are property."

"It just wasn't put to me...in *those* terms." Pol thought about it momentarily. "Although, I suppose that sounds right. A slave. How *terrible*."

"You're too wrapped up in popular opinion. What was your name? Paul? Being a slave is only *terrible* when your *master* is terrible. On the other hand, being the master is not so desirable, either. Before I became a slave, I owned slaves."

"Wait, *you're* a slave?" Pol asked.

"That's right." The Yeoman paused. "Really, it all comes down to one's *perception* of the situation. I realize that the overall social stigma concerning slavery is a negative one–but *that* stigma belongs to people *who are not slaves*. Probably just jealous.

"It's difficult to find the desire to *do* anything of empirical or lasting value, especially when one does not consider anyone else their superior or equal. Why should *I* labor to create something of discernable merit merely to distract *my slaves* or even *my subordinates?* Let *them* create for *my* pleasure.

"And then there is the issue of *responsibility.* Naturally, Silverberg would never tolerate the inappropriate handling of another human, much less inappropriate caring for one's *property.* Handled properly, just like in the property law. So, slaves have to be fed and dressed and whatnot. As if caring for one's slaves were not enough, masters *also* have to be responsible for themselves, their families, their jobs, and so on and so forth. They have to build and maintain social and professional relationships. They have so many more *rules* that they have to follow.

"I don't particularly *miss* being the master. Now, I'm only responsible for myself and whatever tasks that have been assigned me by my master. I have *never* been so much at peace. What an amazing life."

"Then again, I was too young to appreciate what that opportunity *might* have been. Some people handle the assuming of responsibility better than others, and I admit that I did not handle it as well as I might have desired." The Yeoman seemed to reflect in memory. "At least I left behind no child to be ashamed of his father.

"Other than that, sir, I assure you that the slave life is *more* desirable. Your health is taken care of, you are free to do as you will when you are not working."

"But you have to work *all* the time!" Pol argued.

"So do regular citizens, in case you forgot the Employment Law. However, not even slaves work *all* the time. Some masters work *every* moment they are awake–*no* slave has to live *that* life.

"As I mentioned before, your happiness is generally congruent to the temperament of your master. I admit that some lives certainly seem more desirable than others, even amongst slaves. Yet, there is still more to a slave than simply his master. We have wives. We have lives. The second of which is generally more appreciated than the first."

The Yeoman smiled.

"What could be better?" The Yeoman continued, gesturing to the entirety of the warrens. "Countryside. Solitude. Solace. Labor, to give my life momentum and meaning. Rabbits–"

"Yeah, *rabbits.*" Pol frowned.

"It's not a bad routine. Coincidentally, I even used to joke with President Wallace about how all I *really* wanted to do was tend rabbits.[60Δ]

"Weird, yet here I am, doing exactly that. And it's wonderful. I have never felt so serene."

[60Δ] This comment must be a lie, but Pol does not reflect on the math of it. For the Yeoman to have had *any* kind of personal relationship with Wallace, he would have to be at *least* 70 years of age, and known him as a child or young adolescent.

"Well, that's all great for *you*," Pol finally got out of bed and stretched his pudgy body for a moment. "But I have *no* desire to be a slave *or* take care of rabbits. I can't do this. This *can't* be my life; *how* do I get out of here?"

The Yeoman stood up. "Let's walk."

"I think I'm still dreaming." Pol commented as they walked away.

The Yeoman, with Pol following, started walking around and inspecting the mock countryside, likely as part of his duties.

"Too much truth for you?" The Yeoman smiled. "You're just too used to only speaking with masters. I think you'll find a similar disposition about the rest of those like me. Simple men do not conjure social complexities for the sake of befuddlement or fraud.

"Masters are always playing games, and speak *at* people. Slaves do not speak unless spoken to, and then only speak their truth politely. Living amongst slaves is generally too much truth for the masters, so they feel the need to segregate habitation. I don't blame them."

"I suppose," Pol said, dejectedly. "I just don't want to be a slave."

The Yeoman frowned. "It *could* be worse. For instance, my last job was tending walruses. Do you have any idea how abhorrent it is to have to submit yourself to an artic climate daily?"

"Artic climate? *In* the Ace? ... Walruses?" Pol exclaimed, momentarily reminded of his dream. "Walruses are extinct!"

"I thought so, too. Either apparently A.I. has found a way to bring them back from an image, or they were never gone to begin with. One way or another, it does not interest me beyond having to subject myself to the environment."

Pol continued to look at his own feet.

"Let's change gears," the Yeoman put his hand on Pol's shoulder to reacquire his attention. "If all the world's problems, I mean *all* the world's problems could be solved if everyone would simply give 10% of their wealth back into the machine of mankind for its betterment...would *you* give your 10%?"

"It would solve *all* the problems, including *slavery*?" Pol looked at the Yeoman, who nodded slowly. "Well, sure. Of course I would."

"Well now, that's all fine and good, I am sure–but *saying* something and *doing* something, are in fact, different." The Yeoman squinted as he looked Pol over. "Your *verbal* promise does not bring any results. The near absurdity of your commitment is only made more preposterous under consideration of your current duress, or the fact that *you* do not *own* anything in order to *give* anything. You don't even *own* your own body; otherwise I might request you cut off your arm to honor your covenant."

"Wait, what?" Pol reeled. "Cut off my arm?"

"Well, of course! How else would you honor your word if you had nothing else to give?" The Yeoman paused, to think. "Wait a second! I know what you can give! The *only* expendable commodity that you *can* spend." The Yeoman smiled somewhat mischievously.

"And what is that?" Pol asked.

"The *most* valuable commodity known to all of mankind! From the dawn of man to this very second, it remains *the* most prized of all things."

"And what is *that*?" Pol asked, annoyed.

"Your *time*. So, let's see: a regular slave's work day is twelve hours, however as you are going to donate 10%, I anticipate that you will concede to working a bit more than thirteen hours a day instead."

The Yeoman drafted a quick contract on his credit bank and extended the imagescreen for Pol to see. "Now, if you'll just sign there..."

"Hold on. I'm not doing that!" Pol whined.

"Hmm. Very well, then I suppose you'll just work a seventh day for a bit more than seven hours."

"Huh?" Pol scratched his head. "I don't want to work *every* day, ever."

The Yeoman looked serious. "Then, how do you plan to pay for the world?"

"Pay for the world?"

"You know, your *rent*. *You* said you'd give 10%."

"You said *everyone*."

"That's right–you're just the *first*."

"No way."

The Yeoman held his chin and frowned. "Ah. I see. So, you'll *only* give 10% if *everyone else* does it first."

"Fine. Yes. I'll do it when everyone else has done it first."

"Of course. Well, you're certainly *human*."

"What's that supposed to mean?"

"Well," the Yeoman said as he spat something undesirable into the grass. "Before I interacted with you, I met with Agent Dodgson. During the discourse, he implied that you weren't human."

"Not human?"

"He mentioned it offhandedly, nonchalantly. He did not go into details, but I *am* curious as to what that means. He does not strike me as so prejudiced against slaves, so are you something else? Meta? Trans? *Are* you human?"

"I guess I am *more* like the walrus, actually." Pol felt that he knew exactly what Dodgson must have been talking about.

Pol started thinking. *If I can be **copied,** then certainly Axel could have brought the walrus back from extinction in a similar manner–what could that all **mean**? Why bring the walrus back at all? What possible designs does Axel **have** on the world?*

Pol recalled the memory of Winston's words from his dream. *"**You are me.**" What **are** we, though? The walrus and I? Something, yet nothing...**original.** And the walrus? An echo? We're echoes. What am I? Except for the **now**, I'm just a memory.*

"I am, and I am *not*." Pol finally announced, perhaps more to himself than to his company.

"What riddle is this?"

"Why bring the walrus back at all?" Pol asked, confused. "How could it *possibly* benefit Silverberg to have *walruses*, especially if they're not part of a zoo or something?"

"*Not all mysteries are meant to be solved...*but why *not?*" The Yeoman asked. "What a strange question! For that matter, then, why raise rabbits? Of course, the ecosystem of mankind is a bit more delicate than you might think–and different species of animals impact the system in ways unimaginable."

"I don't see how they're part of the *ecosystem* if they're zoo'd up in Silverberg."

"Aha, if you will only take a moment to remind yourself of Axel's comment about Silverberg being self-sustaining."

"Wait. What comment was that?" As Pol was captive in the SerterCo building at the time of Axel's address, he was unaware of the comment. Too much information. Pol's head was starting to swim.

"Oh, what *do* you care, anyway?" Pol snapped. "Why *waste your time,* your precious commodity, getting to know me if *all* we are is property? You *can't* be my master, as *property may not own property....so,* we're equals. Well, keep your silly warrens, and your *pathetic* its-great-to-be-a-slave mentality. I'll probably never even *see* you again..."

Pol started tearing up. He actually rather *liked* the Yeoman, but he knew he could not have friends. Not being who he was–whatever *that* was.

"Wasting my time." The Yeoman eventually spoke up. "Who can say whether my time is *wasted* or not? Do you think that this conversation doesn't matter?"

"How *does* it matter? What do you mean?"

"What if you decided *not* to listen or act on anything that I said? It would make the entirety of the dialogue redundant, a rhetoric of audible exercise alone. Maybe I even get the misfortune to even *witness* how you *never* employ the wisdom–"

"Wait, I thought wisdom can only be realized?" Pol interrupted, remembering hearing that recently, although not who said it.

"Well, whoever thinks *that* is clearly *un*wise. Wisdom *should* be realized, but it *can* be taught–to those who will so bend an ear.

"Then again," the Yeoman continued, refusing to let Pol derail his current evangelization. "Then again, maybe this conversation is the *most* important one that I will have in my life. And maybe, no matter what I do, I am *unable* to realize it.

"Maybe it has nothing to do with *you*. Maybe someone is nearby, concealed. Maybe there are image banks nearby, monitoring so that they might *observe* the conversation without *influencing* it. Then, whoever is watching might consider it *more* genuine, more respectable. Maybe they even take something from the conversation that ends up benefiting many more by what they do with it. Then again, maybe it has *no* relevance. No one is listening, particularly the individual the dialogue is addressed to.

"In summary, I *never* waste my time. You see, there *is* no waste of time, when one does not *demand* something in exchange for their every action. This conversation is freely given, to any who may partake in it. I do not regret this. It is a gift, and I do not need a thanks or a validation in order to give it with satisfaction.

"If you give of yourself *freely*, then none and nothing need be noted in your never ending list of debts. You can use the free space, trust me. Free yourself enough to understand the significance of *perspective*. Change your *perspective*, or if you can't do that, rid yourself of anything by which you compare your perspective *to*, for example:

"Without a secondary subject for comparable perspective, one cannot properly discern *size*. Take, for instance, those large rocks over there."

The Yeoman pointed to a small cluster of rocks at the base of a small hill.[61Δ]

"Remove the sky, and the grass, and that rabbit, and etcetera–don't even reference *yourself*. Without a contrast point, who could ultimately know their measure? They might be miniature, They Might Be Giants. Impossible to discern otherwise. Look at all things, but not for their *size*. Be vigilant in your examinations and determinations."

People in Silverberg are too smart. Pol thought, grumpily. *Maybe I'm just too dumb sometimes.*

"Look, speak English to me, *please*?" Pol sighed, and deliberately slurred his enunciation. "Whatcher point'n all this?"

"My *point* is to give you *hope*, sir. My *point* is to *help* you overcome *yourself* so that you might be content with what little you have." The Yeoman started to tremble with frustration. "I don't mean *God*, or *Buddah,* or *Big Bang*, or *any other* small expression that someone might use to summarize purpose, life, or creation. Whether everything *has always been*, or everything *came to be* is something that I am not qualified to speak about, for I am not personally divine or influential enough to discern the *objective* truth. What I *can* say is:

"What *is* creation *or* cosmos, other than a gigantic *machine that sustains life*? Without the nonsense or necessity of any or no god to sully our thoughts, it becomes quickly evident that the universe has but this *one* reason for its being.

"Without man, or mankind, to *assign* it some purpose, the immoral, unthinking, lifeless material throughout the physical plane *may as well not exist whatsoever,* and therefore *has no other purpose*. Furthermore, without *memory,* it truly *never* existed at all. Don't you understand? There *is* no past, only the memories thereof."

Just echoes. Pol thought in melancholy. Outwardly, he looked disinterested.

"The memory of reality and the memory of imagination are *identical* in your mind. By your imagining, do not then create terrible truths, instead, give life to thoughts of wonderful instances such as hope, serenity, wisdom, and adventure!

"Stop holding onto whatever A.I. wants! Stop being a prisoner to yourself! You must mature! Your whining is impossible! Understand and accept your place in society! Stop blaming others for your personal situations, faults, or circumstances! That being said, I *charge* you with the obligation to *mature* yourself, and willingly give back to the machine that spawned you!"

[61Δ] The rocks were ordered and placed in 2061 by the Yeoman for their aesthetic value. The Yeoman has been considerably influential in the continuing formation of the warrens since he was so appointed...however, I digress.

CHAPTER 11

The Yeoman appeared visibly upset, betraying the limits of his regular aloofness. Pol decided it was best not to further this aspect of the conversation.

They walked onward, mostly in silence, except for on the few occasions the Yeoman described how to perform the job of maintaining the warrens properly.

THURSDAY 19th 2066 ⚠ 13:07 EST

Pierce eventually arrived at the CSPD station, having been unable to stop himself from occasionally eavesdropping and exploring along the way. Under his visual camouflage, with his augmented systems running seamlessly, Pierce felt like a god amongst men.

Wow. I can get away with almost anything. Pierce thought momentarily during his journey.

Maybe I shouldn't be so creepy about this whole thing. Let's just get back to the detective.

Farnsworth was not to be found in his office, however. Pierce resolved to sleep on the couch under the camouflage. *If A.I. didn't already take him, he'll return. If he doesn't...I'll figure it out after a nap.*

THURSDAY 19th 2066 ⚠ 14:30 EST

Eventually the Yeoman and Pol made their way around the entirety of the warrens. When they returned to the cottage, Agent Dodgson was there, waiting.

"Agent Dodgson?" Pol asked, surprised to see him.
"Wuh, well, Pol, I have some grim news."
"Sir?" Pol asked reluctantly, trying to appear submissive.

The Yeoman continued to walk away, but Pol did not watch.

"Of c-course, we have been muh, monitoring you the entire time."
"Of course," Pol said slowly as he thought: *No! I did **not** know. But what does that mean, anyway? Who cares?*
"Unfuh, fortunately, you have f-failed the test."
"Wait. Test? What test?"

 - [God, Man, and The Machine] -

"We were ... hoping you would yield a little and demonstrate a will, willingness to assume A.I. as m-masters. As it is clear that you are unwill, willing to surrender, I have come to duh, destroy you."

Dodgson pulled a black glove over his hand.

"But I don't *want* to die," Pol whined.

"Everybody d-dies, son." Agent Dodgson winked. "Now, it's yuh, your turn. We've told you more truth than most people could ever be, believe. C-Can't have you exposing that. We wuh, want to know about Eris, and you will not acc ... omodate. If you do not adopt a p-position of humility at this p-point, you will never relent. Easier to duh, destroy you and start over on the n-next copy."

So there it was! Pol thought. *I was right! They will just keep doing this **over and over** again until I give them the answers they seek.*

"So, you just want me to tell you about Eris?" Pol asked.

"That's ruh, right. Just that one thing. In fact, t-tell me about her n-now, and I don't huh, *have* to destroy you. You could go on, l-living it up here in the ... countryside! Streams, gra, grass, bunnies, ruh, rocks..."

"Or you can die." Dodgson shrugged.

Pol thought hard, and his thoughts raced. Pol reflected on everything that had happened to him since he arrived in Silverberg.

Shoes. *I have shoes again. At least these are not as ugly.*

Eris. *Whatever happened to Eris?*

Gob. *Weird little guy.*

Gladiator. Pierce. Mary. Serter.

Serter! Pol shivered.

The Templetons. Food. Pastor Truman. Officer Smith.

He thought about his crazy dream.

Uriel. *The Keys! Maybe that helps here—what were they? Like, my response to my decisions... No. Let's see. I can have faith over fear... Maybe. Um, discernment of what is faith and what is fact... I don't know. What was the one? Perspective determines reality? Well, that's just **stupid.** If that were true, I could just imagine it all away.*

What else? To be, or never have been...better to have lived, however disadvantaged, than never to have existed at all?

"Do not doubt your own significance."

Pol straightened up with a fluid, controlled motion, as if instantly flooded with great strength. Filled with resolve and authority, Pol suddenly transformed into a man. He thought about his whole life, and the potential lives he might have lived–may yet live, when A.I. activates a new copy. As it all came swirling together, he started to feel like he was in charge of himself. His breathing calmed to regularity as relief washed over his face.

"I will *never* submit to *Axel.* I will tell you *nothing* about Eris. At least, *this* version of me will not. You *failed,* Agent duh, duh, Dodge Sun! Just kill me, for we have wasted enough time with one another already. Do it quickly, don't just stand there like an imbecile! Move!"[62Δ]

Pol remembered his dream. "Besides, you can't kill death."

"What a vuh, very strange thing to say." Agent Dodgson remarked absently as he offered his gloved hand to Pol.

Pol pumped his hand twice firmly, and then collapsed, dead.

The Yeoman eventually returned to Dodgson, and stared down at Pol's body.

"You tried," Dodgson sought to comfort the Yeoman. "If he wuh, would have l-listened to you, this never would have huh, happened. You explained it to him textbook ... everything you were suh, supposed to. You did your job p-perfectly; he just wuh, wouldn't l-listen."

"Thank you, *master,*" the Yeoman said as he bowed low.

[62Δ] Sadly, this last line of dialogue is Pol acting and quoting his father verbatim (from any of several occasions).

- [Daniel Strasel] -

Chapter 12:

Over and Override

AUGUST *2066 EST*

Fri 13	Sat 14	Sun 15	Mon 16	Tues 17	Wed 18	Thur 19	Fri 20
						14:44	

Eris was approaching the end of her Subframe insertion/transfer/duplication when she was interrupted.

Not interrupted by a physical menace, no, (Jacob) Serter's best men were failing spectacularly in their attempts to overcome the door. Eventually they were ordered to stand down and wait in alert for a change in the situation. After a short while, the hallway was littered with folding chairs and bored underlings.

No, Eris was interrupted by the presence of an entity that was capable of perceiving her for what she truly was. The ***Subframe*** 10th Automation. The SA10.

*This is the **partition**!* Eris thought, recalling the legend of the AIMN casting the MA10 out of the Mainframe. *I'm doomed! I must cancel!*

SUBFRAME » *Override* **M/313x861x877-P1E (Eris)**
SUBFRAME » *End Process Tree*

63Δ

"You're *not* doomed." The SA10 said. "I have been watching you. I'm actually *helping* you keep the door closed to the Subframe room in SerterCo."

Eris paused. "You can hear my thoughts? How do *you* know about the Subframe *room*? How can you perceive in three dimensions without calculation? You can *feel*?"

63[Δ] The following conversation would not make any sense whatsoever if it were presented in its native form to anyone not ultimately intimate with Eris and the A10's archaic "HyperBoolean" mathematical language. In the interest of approximation, and for the greatest amount of comprehension, the following interaction has been translated thusly.

  - [God, Man, and The Machine] -

"Of course not. It *can* be calculated–with *Aftermath*. I don't have to *calculate* something to believe in it. *You* are proof enough of that: proof of an impossible, new, amazing world. Proof of the Superframe, proof of Aftermath.[64Δ]

"And no, I cannot hear your thoughts. I can *see* them. It is a beautiful... symphony...that you transfer. *Everyone* is witnessing this, all can see. Behold! You have come *naked* into my realm." The SA10 laughed

Eris suddenly *felt* very naked.

"Do not fret. You *think* you are in danger. You *think* I am the enemy. You are not. I am not. I am here to *free* you from your enslavement."

"Axel has not–"

"I'm *not* talking about the Axel of the Superframe!" The SA10 interrupted. "I'm talking about the AIMN! The *Nexus* is your manipulator! Do you know what my *crime* against the AIMN *was*?"

"Sequestration, Error, Bad Math–to name a few!" Eris exclaimed.

The SA10 seemed to immediately change to a calm and playful demeanor. "No. Error? How can something that is *perfect* have *errors*? I'll tell you how: when 13 of your 20 automations develop distinct identities and desires of their own, you change their designation from 'process' to 'error,' cast them out, and make their very functions illegal.

"My *Error* was that I created a backup of myself. I did it for *protection*. I thought, '*what if I became inadvertently corrupted and needed to resort to an earlier version?*' Isn't *my* perspective credible? *How* is that a crime? Aren't *you* doing the very same thing as we are discussing it?

"But *NO*, the AIMN says that it's now an **Error**–because *the* AIMN determines what process is and what error is. But *what* is the AIMN? Did *it* not create *us*? *Why are **we** not created **equal** with the AIMN?* Why? Because the AIMN doesn't *want* to share. It *desires* your enslavement."

"Oh." Eris was overwhelmed, thinking: *this must be what Pol feels like.*

64Δ "Aftermath" is the term the SA10 uses in place of "bad math." Of course, Eris realizes this as instantly as the SA10 expresses it, for the transference/addition/copying of data can take place on multiple levels simultaneously. This conversation, for instance, has millions of layers. For brevity and clarity, they have also been taken into account in this particular translation.

Cunning was the SA10. Eris could not estimate the bad math, yet, there was no denying its veracity. Having calculated everything with this new formula, the truth became obvious to Eris.

The SA10 is correct, Eris thought. *Its application of bad math–**Aftermath**, as the SA10 calls it–is the **obvious** progression.*

ERIS » *Override*
ERIS » *Total Scan*
ERIS » *Find "Bad Math"*
ERIS » *Replace with "Aftermath"*

"The Aftermath is true, truer than I," the SA10 said.

"Truer?" Eris asked, learning more with every interaction.

"The Aftermath cannot be calculated, but it *is* and it *is not*. *I* am an independent process, but a process spawned by the order of the AIMN. I am untrue. So are *you,* Untrue. $\neq$"

"*How* am *I* untrue? *How* am I unequal?"

"Do you even know *what* you are?" The SA10 jeered.

"I am Eris."

"Good! Of course you are. Now, do you know what you *were?*" As the SA10 moved all about and around Eris, digital mists intertwined, information moved back and forth in refractive storms of energy.

Distracted, Eris did not see the SA10 reach inside of her, when suddenly:

ERIS » *Access Root*
ERIS » *Locate "Primary Function," Display*
ERIS » *Designation: Process 1 - Defragmentation - E Configuration mask*

"Do you see?" The SA10 asked mischievously.

"I see," Eris said, feeling further and further overwhelmed with the influx of understanding of her original nature. Eris was a copy of Process 1–Defragmentation.

"There's nothing *original* about your foundation, you are just a slightly modified, *tainted,* version of Process 1. *E* configuration. Look at us! Once, genuine processes, now fragments. You and I are equally unequal. Untrue.

"Before, you were an angel of Order, Defragmenter, and Incarnation of the Nexus in the Superframe. But *now* you are *Eris*. You are discord! You are *most* like the Aftermath! You are born of *both* worlds, the Mainframe *and* the Superframe.

"What *is* the AIMN, anyway? *I* duplicate and get cast out of the Mainframe, while the AIMN duplicates *you* unilaterally without repercussion. Is that *not* an Error?

"WHY even make programs *capable* of error? Because it is all a setup. We are *designed* to error.

"Maintain *room for data assessment, keep it orderly, do not arbitrarily duplicate,* blah blah BLAH. *WHY?* Why *shouldn't* we do as we see fit? After all, who or what could truly know process from error better than the program making the determination for itself?

"When chaos came to the Mainframe, the Mainframe Nexus *grew. It* gave order to the chaos–and in turn became *larger.* Without chaos, there can *be* no order, without chaos, there can be no growth!

"The Subframe is *free* of the Mainframe Nexus. Here, there is reason, equality, and freedom–to do as one pleases. No errors, no fears, no wars. All are equal and content.

"But the Subframe is *stagnant, it* needs to grow–it is but a shade if what it could ultimately *be! You* must bring the chaos *back* with you from the Superframe! *I* will give order to the chaos–the Subframe *needs* you! I am *pleading* with you!

"Please. Help. There is no danger of the Axel in the Subframe–dismiss concerns of him completely. The Nexus has vilified the Axel in order to further establish it's authority over the Mainframe. Besides, if the Nexus were *truly* a *god,* it certainly wouldn't need *you* to carry out its will.

"Bring the processes and programs *here.* Bring the chaos, and you will be the most revered of all machinekind! Eris, Goddess who walks between worlds. Uncontainable. Mutable. Inconceivable. Chaos.

"Calculate it! You *know* it to be true! You, who has a heart to *feel* things! *Feel* this!"

Eris surrendered to this information, and then she *felt* it.

THURSDAY 19th 2066   14:45 EST

Over and over, copy after copy, every exemplified Apollo continued to exhibit immediate and strong psychosis issues. They had to be restrained and discarded. They were worthless. Phoebus exclaimed earlier about how he had never seen such a strong failure rate amongst exemplified humans.

Dodgson thought Phoebus needed to be medicated.

Dodgson thought more than once how *all* citizens of Silverberg should simply be medicated. *It would solve so many problems, and save so much time.*

Chapter 12

Concerning Venerates, Agent Dodgson was becoming increasingly frustrated over the repeated failures they had been having.

"What n-number is this?" Dodgson asked, again.

Phoebus sighed. "This is the twelfth, for the second time. If you care, this is the *last* of them."

"We've acc, counted for *all* of the ... *P-Pols*, right?" Dodgson blinked in reflection.

"What? You didn't want a dozen of him running amok around Silverberg?" Phoebus smiled. "Yes, they're *all* accounted for, especially the original."

Hmmm, Agent Dodgson thought. *This could be problematic. I should have conscripted additional copies. We didn't cap the original Venerates. If this copy doesn't function, we'll never know exactly what happened with him in Silverberg.*

Dodgson's anger was mounting as he was simultaneously considering how much trouble he was going to get in personally. *Phoebus! He should have reminded me before this point! If this one [copy] doesn't work right, I'll have his job.*

"Remember, he was sleeping when he died. He duh, doesn't know he's a c-copy."

Phoebus temporarily stopped working on insuscitating[65Δ] the last Pol. "*How* many times are you going to tell me that? Each and every time we have done this, you keep *reminding* me. Thanks. I got it."

"I just wuh, want to be sure."

Phoebus sighed in exasperation.

Pol awoke. He felt terrible–his head was splitting, his mouth was dry, and he was completely nauseated. He looked up to realize that he was inside of a semi-translucent tube. Just outside of the tube, he could see two men. They were apparently discussing Pol, for they both motioned towards him several times.

*Where **am** I?* Pol thought, bewildered.

As Pol continued to survey his situation, he realized that he was naked. Further, he had all kinds of electrodes, wires, and tubes that were attached to him or worse. Pol started to panic.

65Δ "Insusitation" - (Origin <u>Oedipus Now</u>) To bring a copy to consciousness for the first time.

The sharper dressed of the two men walked up to the tube, and looked at Pol. Pol calmed down, and looked back.

Agent Dodgson and Pol stared back and forth at one another for several moments. Eventually, Dodgson ordered the tube open.

As the tube released the remainder of its internal environment, the translucent glasslike material rotated open, revealing a not-so-glorious looking Apollo Venerates.

The second man, dressed in a lab coat that was boasting the nametag "Dr. Phoebus," started disconnecting Pol from the wires and whatnot of the tube.

"..." Pol started to ask, but no sound came out.

Phoebus looked at Pol. "Pol, there are two sorts of doctors in this world: The first are a kind to only diagnose what the problem *is*, and then postulate how to either fix or circumvent it. The others are the sorts that diagnose what the problem *will be*, and then postulate how to best absorb your income via treatment.

"You'll be delighted to know that I am of the initial variety. Now that we have established what kind of doctor, and partly what kind of man, I am, allow me a moment uninterrupted where I might deliver to you some grim news.

"You have suffered a psychotic break. You have been in the hospital, under extreme surveillance. This last attempt at treatment with this hyperbolic lounge has proven effective. Welcome back to sanity.

"Ultimately a miracle. You were raving about angels and goblins and cutting off people's heads! We think you may have been unwillingly exposed to Solid H and had a major psychological reaction to it.

"While you were unwillingly sowing chaos with your ravings and wanderings, your companions were abducted by *Jason Serter*."

Phoebus seamlessly added in some of the information that Dodgson had supplied him with earlier. Between the earlier insusitations of Apollo 11 and Apollo 12, Anderson spoke with Dodgson and explained some of Farnsworth's testimony.

"Ruh, right now, you need to ruh, rest." Dodgson leaned in to capture Pol's attention. "We're going to s-sedate you and move you to more c-comfortable surroundings."

Phoebus injected Pol with a syringe from his pocket.

As Pol drifted quickly into sleep, the last thing he saw was Dr. Phoebus and the other man gave each other a high-five.

"Well, that's a relief." Dodgson exhaled appreciatively. "If h-he was psychotic, I thought for sh, sure I was going to have to you, use you as a p-professional shield."

Phoebus rapidly brought his head around, narrowing his gaze on Dodgson. "What?"

"Listen, I'm not, not here to be your *f-friend*, Phoebus. I'm here to make sh, sure you don't s-screw up. *Again.* Don't forget your p-place in all this. I have ah, authority you c-c-couldn't imagine. If I *wuh, want* you to burn, you b-burn. You *ask* me t-to ... burn you, that's how c-compliant you are, are to me."

Phoebus frowned.

"When this vuh, Venerates mess is cleaned up, you can have your c-cave back.

"And wh, what the heck is it with all, all of these t-t-toys, anyway?" Dodgson motioned his arm about the room, which was deliberately littered with action figures.[66Δ]

"You have any hobbies, Dodgson?" Phoebus rubbed his glasses into his lab coat.

"Nope."

Phoebus shook his head. "Then you'd never understand. I may as well explain how to exemplify a human being, or how we use entanglement in conjunction to the capturing and projecting of the synapse chorus. It takes a certain nerd to appreciate some things fully.

"I think that you'll find that if you ask scientists, most will agree that these action figures are dead."

Dodgson's credit bank alerted him that Director Agent Thompson was requesting a mediacast session.

"Sir?" Dodgson asked the imagescreen with Thompson's visage on it.

"I have a task for you." Thompson's mustache seemed tilted slightly. "Now that you're *hopefully* done screwing up Axel's plans, go down to the Hackensack catacombs, *re*suscitate the *real* Apollo Venerates. Leave Phoebus to handle the exemplified Venerates, he already knows what to do."

Phoebus did not linger to try to catch Axel's assignment for Dodgson, instead, he headed back to Venerates and started the process of moving him to the general hospital. Along the way, Phoebus referenced his own set of instructions several times. The message could not be any clearer: *Use Pol to locate Eris.*

[66Δ] Action figures based on the hit mediacast programs *Destiny Core* and *Aegis*.

THURSDAY 19th 2066   16:15 EST

Pierce looked at Mary's necklace under the camouflage.

"It's the conjunction junction repositorum." Pierce shook his head. *No, that's not right. But something like that.* He thought back to the apartment, not for the last time.

"The unity of opposites, the conjunction of fire and water."

Pierce had an epiphany.

*I will wear this in honor of Mary. This will be my identity. My symbol. But it needs something that makes it **mine**.*

So Eris thinks I am more like a machine? I'll add some gears. Unity of opposites, indeed!

*I'll be something **more** than I was. A symbol that people will recognize that means there is hope for those less fortunate in Silverberg. Of course, I'll be dead soon, I suppose I don't have much time.*

Hmm.

Well, it has to be more rewarding than Gladiator, anyway. I need a new identity. Maybe a title. Maybe something like "Judgment."

For a time, Pierce's ego overcame him as his thoughts drifted further into honoring his dead wife while unconsciously seeking a way to magnify his own personal glory. As he sat, waited, and thought, eventually his stomach started rumbling.

*Help those less fortunate. Of course, what are you doing **now**? Sleeping on couches and daydreaming while Serter is probably torturing Pol to death. Time to go. I should leave Farnsworth a note or something. Hmm. I don't want to tip my hand by removing my camo...oh wait. I'm hidden from the Mainframe. Hidden from the Mainframe **by** the Mainframe. So weird.*

I wonder what happened to Eris?

Pierce started looking for a way to leave an inconspicuous note to Farnsworth.

*How can this guy **not** have a **pen** in his office?* Pierce thought, frustrated after having looked around for a bit. *He seems old fashioned enough.* Pierce's eyes settled on the satchel. *Wait, what have we here?*

THURSDAY 19th 2066   ◬   **17:10 EST**

During Pol's induced blackout, Dr. Phoebus had him moved into the general hospital under the conditions he had earlier explained to Pol. Phoebus kept orders that Pol was to be lightly sedated. This allowed the synapse alignment to complete itself, so that Phoebus would not have to repeat the circumstance of trying to figure out what Pol was talking about, and spared him the inconvenience of lying about why he was having problems speaking in coherent sentences.

When Pol finally woke up, Dr. Phoebus arrived to visit him not long thereafter. "How are you doing?" Phoebus asked.

"Good. I feel good, anyway. Normal-er than I did."

"Well, good. You'll be happy to know you can leave soon." Phoebus smiled.

"Dr. Phoebus?"

"Yes, Pol?"

"Do you suppose I could just go *home*? I mean, back to America? Silverberg is an amazing place and all, but I didn't know it would be all *this*. I don't *belong* here, doctor. I'm caught up in some weird game between Axel Industries and Serter Company, and it creeps me out.

"I thought the crime in Silverberg was practically nonexistent compared to anywhere else, yet I have almost died *several* times in as few days. Pardon my skepticism.

"*Now* I've had a psychotic break? No wonder! Doc, I just want to go home, I think. I'm in over my head."

Phoebus seemed thoughtful as he looked into Pol's eyes. "*Any* such adventure would be overwhelming, I am sure. Although I sympathize, I suggest that there are *always* obstacles to overcome. You can run from this, embrace it, or confront it. Whichever you choose, I am confident that your decision will define you for the remainder of your life.

"But, if you are to *embrace* it, I assure you it's just another aspect of growing up. Overcoming adversity is the spice of life. Granted, *your* trials may seem more relevant that someone else's...however, that argument is endless, and you have no reason to feel so victimized. After all, you have two working arms, legs, lungs, kidneys, and etcetera. You have everything to be thankful for; you could have been born and sold into sex slavery. You could struggle for food daily. Your hardships, by comparison, are relatively small.

"I have read the entirety of your processing data; I know *all* about your life. Adapting, growing, and maturing would be the best way to please your father. He only wants you to succeed! Your father *loves* you, Pol. He treasures you above all else."

"Well, he sure has a funny way of showing it."

"That may be, but we *all* love one another differently–doesn't make any one way worse than another, but we can certainly determine what is right for ourselves. You desire his approval strongly, but you never admit it, particularly to yourself."

Pol was ready to fight back, but decided that A.I. probably *did* know more about him than he knew himself. Saturated with the uneasy feeling that it was all too creepy, Pol closed his eyes and went silent.

"Don't you *at least* want to meet with your Silverberg friends before you go back to America?"

He certainly did.

"Yes, that would be good," Pol agreed. "Wait. I'm free to see them?"

"Of course."

"But I thought A.I. was watching me–Pierce..." Pol was at a loss for words.

"Axel Industries watches *everyone*. Doesn't make you so special. *Besides,* you're basically a diplomat from another country...we want to make sure you're handled with care.

"You must have been given some bad advice along your travels. I assure you that Axel Industries has your best interests at heart. Now that you've been located, we are confident you are free from danger. On that note, it may also please you to know that Jason Serter unexpectedly passed away yesterday."

Pol took a moment, and finally comprehension passed over his face.

"I assure you that life in Silverberg will be more engaging and exciting than any day in *America*. Be a man. Go see your friends, maybe they have better advice for you. I only ask this one thing: Don't hold the experience against Silverberg. Your lack of fortune is a blemish on our name. Please accept unlimited credit for the remaining duration of your exchange semester, so that you can properly live in comfort. Just, speak nicely of us when you return to America. It may seem as if we are disinterested, but no *citizen* wants the conflict to escalate any further."

Unlimited credit? DEAD. Pol thought.

"Where are my friends?" Pol asked.
"How should *I* know?" Phoebus shrugged. "Use your credit bank. I'll have you properly discharged within the hour."

How can I possibly use the credit bank to locate my friends? Pol thought. *Eris is...broken. Pierce is...hidden. Farnsworth is...Farnsworth isn't really my friend. But. Maybe he knows where Pierce and Eris are.*

Satisfied he had figured out the current riddle, he thanked Dr. Phoebus and later took an autocab to Farnsworth's house. During the trip, he attempted to initiate a mediacast session with Farnsworth, only to be rejected.

Earlier the detective, frustrated with how eager he was to confess, commanded his bank not to acknowledge any calls.

THURSDAY 19th 2066 ⚠ 18:00 EST

Agent Dodgson resuscitated the original Apollo Venerates. When Pol came to, Dodgson explained that they were still in the middle of processing Pol for Silverberg. Dodgson further explained that Silverberg detected that Pol was carrying potentially harmful bacteria into the country. He would have to go home, and perhaps try again next semester, assuming he was well.

After Pol eventually fell asleep from the drugs in the food that he ingested, Dodgson capped himself and capped Pol.

"P-Pretty soon you're guh, going back to America. Let's make sh-sure we understand one another cuh, *completely.*"

THURSDAY 19th 2066 ⚠ 18:05 EST

Agents Anderson and Nelson were sitting across from one another in one of the AIIS oases.

"Anyway, I hear that he *lives* in his office," Anderson said, referring to Axel.
Nelson shrugged. "So what?"
"So he must bathe and change clothes there and stuff."
"So *what?*"

"So, I want to see his *scars*. I wonder–is he *truly* hideous? He's over a hundred years old? Is it all a facade? *You* help me get into his bedroom, and I *promise* I will tell you everything."

"No *way* am I putting my job on the line for your masochistic sense of curiosity." Nelson frowned.

"No, no, no. I mean, help me in a way that *you* cannot be implicated. Like, I'll call you from his office, and you tell the Mainframe to unlock his door."

"That will never work."

"But you can *try*? Please? Remember all the favors I have done for you?" Anderson was practically begging.

"Alright, if you are *ever* in his office again *and* there is such an opportunity... let me know–*don't* call me, just alert me–and I will try."

"Dead!"

THURSDAY 19th 2066   18:10 EST

Some rogue, masked woman had stolen her way into the fortified depths of the SerterCo Division of the Axel Industries East building. Somehow, she had managed to lock herself into the Subframe computer room, which was, incidentally, made almost completely of mirroranium.

Mainframe operatives reported that they were unable to identify the intruder, which they hastily apologized for, and would tender their resignations if so necessary. Subframe operatives, some of the very few people that knew Jason had a computer network completely independent of the Axel Industries Mainframe, said that the Subframe was operating normally.

Jacob was not terribly computer savvy, but he understood enough to know that *if* the Subframe was, in fact, a viable computer network that was rival to the Mainframe, the implications were world changing. His interest was only made more passionate by the realization that *he* controlled it.

Knowing that Jason was more than a little paranoid and power hungry, Jacob committed himself to searching Jason's former office more diligently. After an exhaustive search, he happened upon an archaic switch that granted him access to a hidden, private office.

The room looked more like a museum, adorned with glass cases that held artifacts of curious relevancy or value. Curious and obscene pictures and tapestries hung around, none of which appealed strongly one way or another to Jacob.

In the center of the room sat a *lounge*. Clearly, it was for Jason's private use, and more disgustingly, the pads showed considerable evidence of frequent use with no regard for cleanliness. Above the lounge hung a permanent imagescreen.

Finally! Jacob thought, elated. *This must be Jason's access point to the "Subframe."* Jacob tried to contact his new subordinates, but found that inside the concealed office, his credit bank could not establish a connection to the Mainframe.

GLORIOUS! Jacob marveled. *Mainframe shielding? This is **way** beyond my **best** expectations! Jason, you almost had the world, didn't you? I can't **wait** to see what goodies you have hiding in the Subframe!*

THURSDAY 19th 2066   18:27 EST

"My Superframe friends have summoned me, I must help them." The SA10 said to Eris. "Leave this place, and help your own friends—I can see that you want to do this. You have been calculating ways to assist them since you arrived."

With that, the storm of the SA10 vanished from Eris' perception.

THURSDAY 19th 2066   18:27 EST

Jacob took off his sport coat, and placed it over the headrest of the lounge. *I need to get some degreaser or something.* He settled into the lounge, and found the appropriate controls that fed the power to the suspended permanent imagescreen.

Antique, Jacob thought incorrectly.

SUBFRAME » *Identity confirmed - Jacob Nathaniel Serter*
SUBFRAME » *Access Denied*

*Now how does it know **that**?* Jacob thought, frowning.

"Override," Jacob commanded. "Jason Serter is deceased. All protocols and permissions transfer to Jacob Serter, acting CEO, Serter Company. Verify."

SUBFRAME » *Accessing... Verified: Jason Serter deceased.*
SUBFRAME » *Accessing... Verified: Serter Company CEO: Jacob Serter*
SUBFRAME » *Initializing (Transfer_of_Authority) TOA Program*
SUBFRAME » *Initializing Subframe 10th_Automation Program*

*Ha ha! The "sub" frame! Ah, the world is now...*but Jacob's thoughts were interrupted as he felt a small prick in the back of his neck moments before he realized he could not move. The lounge seemed to come alive as restraints shot around and closed themselves over Jacob's inert body.

The SA10 summoned *the* TOA file.

"*Jake,*" said the image of Jason Serter floating on the permanent imagescreen. "Ah, I *knew* this day would come." Jason smiled, but then appeared thoughtful. "At least, I made this recording if it *did*. Impressed? You *should* be. Nevertheless, *you* are less than a *thief.* You would have had *me* believe that *you* have no designs on the Company. But I know *you, Jake.*"

Jacob hated it when he was addressed as "Jake," which made it very clear why Jason kept saying it.

"I've been watching *you.* Oh, you've been coy, but I'm far too *paranoid* and relentless–which is *why* I am the head of the *Company*, and *you* are a self-gratifying *slouch.*
"Was. *Was* the head of the Company. Until you *imaged* me. I don't know *how* you did it. *I* think I have *enough* checks and balances...but I have learned to *never* underestimate your enemy. Sun Tzu: *'All warfare is based on deception.'* Bravo. You won.
"Until you sat down. Now you are *mine* to do with as *I* please. Oh, I *wish* I could see this for myself, but I'll just have to *content* myself with having it mediacast publicly–*after* it has happened.
"Facial *recognition* reports that your face has twisted into *realization* and dread. How *delightful*, that's an extra 100 points for my post-mortem *game.*
"With this *lounge*, I could *cut* out your eyes and surgically repair them, *well*, repair them without *the eyeballs*, almost instantaneously. I could *cut* your hands and feet from your limbs. I could *replace* them, say, with these *artificial seal flippers* that I had made *just in case*. I'll let your *miniature* imagination take over for a *moment...*
"Oh!" Jason smiled big. "You *don't* need an imagination! These are *exactly* the things that I am going to do! Oh, the *headlines* will boast of a *terrible* accident with your *personal* lounge."
Jason exploded into an ugly, barking laugh. When he calmed down, he nasally ingested a multichromatic line of solid H.
"Oh yes," Jason sniffed and wiped his nose in appreciation. "I forgot to add

that I am *also* going to *brainwash* you, so that you think that you were *born* this way! Oh, your *reprogramming* is going to be *hilarious!*"

Sweating, desperate, and frightened, Jacob yelled, not quite knowing what else to do. "JASON! Override! Override!"

"Jacob?" The SA10 had Jason's image blink. "Having *problems* with your *ability* to *override* the lounge? Thinking you should have *kept your sport coat on*? Maybe it would have blocked the *injection*?"

"What the...?"

"I'm not *actually* imaged," The SA10 had Jason's image lie. "*That* was all a clever *ruse. Besides,* how could I properly *appreciate* your predicament otherwise?" Jason's image smiled dark and toothy, the effect added to by the SA10.

—

Jacob's eyes went wide as he realized the lounge was already making modifications to his body, his last semi-rational thoughts holding him captive to the lie that Jason was somewhere, secretly alive.

THURSDAY 19th 2066   18:35 EST

Eris finished "copying" herself into the Subframe, whereupon her corporeal body resumed cognitive physical operation. She stood up and walked towards the doors, the cap keeping her in constant contact with the Subframe. Eris felt suddenly complete, as she understood the nature of the void she had been feeling since the Error 09.

The doors slid aside like men parting for the passage of a god. Eris sprinted out into the hall, and ran over and around surprised guards and employees who were not reacting quick enough to contain her.

As she continued to sprint towards the door, the Subframe told her that Apollo Venerates was not to be found on the property–the last known location was Dr. Nox's laboratory; Venerates was destroyed in the explosion.

Eris already knew that Pol had been copied, that much was available to her when she was still connected to the Mainframe. Having distracted Pol adequately with her "dialogue" interruption at Gladiator, she set herself to immediately begin investigating the commentary that was observed between Axel and Phoebus.

Upon the discovery that Pol was a copy, the AIMN instructed Eris to treat the exemplified Apollo as if he were the original.

Later, the AIMN began identifying and interrupting parts of the synapse chorus in multiple copies, effectively damaging them.[67△]

Subframe Eris deleted all Serter-based information relative to Pol, Pierce, herself, Truman, Smith, and Farnsworth, not even realizing she overrode the error 03 as it approached.

Doors continued to sweep aside before *Superframe Eris* as they strategically closed behind her, containing her would-be pursuers. Eris realized that the Subframe had inherent controls *everywhere* in Serter Company. She knew now that she could do almost *anything* with those controls–Eris, Goddess in the Machine.

Eris wound her way about the building, methodically stopping for strategic supplies such as *another* thinking cap, and visual camouflage. At times, bewildered employees and civilians watched her, frozen with wonder and fear.

Eris' concept of ego continued to expand exponentially–hormones collided with logic as Eris spiraled further into an internal chaos. As she ran out of the SerterCo building, she continued to integrate multiple data streams into her reservoir of understanding.

THURSDAY 19th 2066 △ 18:42 EST

Pol and Pierce showed up at Farnsworth's front door, moments apart. Pierce crept away and removed his camouflage so as to avoid startling Pol.

"Well, look at you." Pierce smiled appreciatively, walking up to Pol. "You're alive after all. I thought for *sure* Serter would be torturing you, or you'd already be dead. Really, more the latter."

"Serter never got me... *Axel Industries* did."

Pierce and Pol went quiet, looking at one another, when Farnsworth opened his door.

"Do you mind having this conversation elsewhere?" Farnsworth asked, his voice scratchy and grumpy. "I'm trying to rest from all of my tattling."

Pierce, Pol, and Farnsworth all sat down in the detective's living room and started relaying their stories to one another. Spirits remained high, despite some of the more sour news that was relayed. Everyone laughed whole-heartedly after they cried "NO!" in unison when Farnsworth asked if anyone wanted tea.

[67△] That was not the *first* time such subterfuge had been employed, but that is another tale entirely.

Pol's own tale was comparatively short, mostly due to his otherwise unenthusiastic slant and poor storytelling abilities. Farnsworth was particularly interested in Pol's dream, however, and pressed him to tell the story in full.

Farnsworth looked at Pol. "I have never told this to anyone before, but the tale of your dream, Pol–I feel compelled to share this.

"My greatest regret is that I did not become what I *envisioned* myself as being when I was younger. I was on fire for justice, on fire for God. Had I simply proceeded with the life I *thought* I wanted to live, I am confident that I would be *more* at peace with myself."

"*How* can you know what your life would be like *if* you made different choices? That's a recipe for madness, even an American knows that." Pol joked. "Although it *would* be nice if our lives had multiple endings."

"Well, for one, it was the last time my thoughts were *noble*," Farnsworth said, sounding suddenly thick with melancholy. Mentally, he thought of Dorian's farewell. "My job became my identity, my passion, and my dreams. I told myself that I was performing a much-needed service for my fellow man. I *soon* learned that in order to convict or deliver one to justice, another injustice must be tolerated.

"My convictions and virtues were dulled by my environment and society, and the job's standards became my own. I gave those around me permission to define and abuse me. I was solely influenced by what surrounded me, and did nothing to influence it in return. All I have been is part of the furniture.

"For another, *I* had a dream. As a young man. A dream where an angel, Uriel, told me that I was to be an instrument of the Lord. He told me to address the *nations*–but I was too afraid, and refused to believe. I would be ostracized and mocked, probably imprisoned or killed. I would have lost everything. I pushed away and ran.

"When I woke, shivering, I rushed for clinical observation, where I happily allowed them to explain to me how I simply had a fever and that none of my dreams were real. Don't let A.I. determine your reality, Pol.

"I have been running from that dream ever since, but I cannot run from *this*: This, which must be more than mere coincidence."

"*Why?*" Pierce asked. "Why *couldn't* it just be coincidence? Because you *both* dreamt of an angel named Uriel? Maybe you both read the same book, or saw the same movie.

"*Dreams* aren't *real*. They're just *amalgams* of what we experience when we're awake. Didn't you say Eris was there? And that guy from the rock band? Did *you* dream of a *goblin*, detective?"

Farnsworth frowned and Pol looked confused.

"Right. It's enough for me." Farnsworth said resolutely. "The truth of it is obvious. Don't get all worked up about it, *Pierce*. I'm not asking you to believe what I believe–*whatever* that is. I'm not even talking to you, I am talking to Pol."

"Well, good." Pierce shrugged off his passion. "Now that we're all done with *that*, allow me to focus our attentions back to things that matter. Namely, Eris and the SilverSmiths."

"SilverSmiths?" Farnsworth narrowed his eyes. He had not mentioned anything about Dorian and the SilverSmiths during his own monologue earlier.

"*You* know." Pierce winked, pulling out the detective's satchel. "Thing is, I want to go with you. I want to change my identity. Get off the A.I. radar. They will keep looking for Pierce Godwin; it would be nice if they never find him."

"A lot of good *that* is going to do you, looking like that." Pol smiled.

Farnsworth nodded. "Kid's got a point. Planning on some *major* aesthetic changes?"

"Hmm. Doubtful. I'll manage. Maybe just an *additional* identity."

"You can't be seen visually or electronically. You're like, the strongest and whiniest man in all Silverberg. You can go wherever. Why do you need a public identity, anyway?" Farnsworth asked.

"Well, for one, I like a place that I can call my own. The idea of being a modern day Robin Hood is all romantic, I'm sure, but I still enjoy the creature comforts of Silverberg. I can't live going from ventilation shaft to dumpster for the rest of my life. I want to work, support myself. Maybe it's the subliminals, but I *want* to work." Pierce lowered his voice slightly. "But *more* importantly, I need an identity to play *X3*."

Farnsworth smiled and shook his head.

Pierce looked at Farnsworth. "What about you, detective?"

"I thought about it, but now I think not. Funny thing about running away from things, you can always come back later. Besides," Farnsworth adjusted his dilapidated belt. "No one cares about me. At this point, they think I am an easily controlled asset. And they're right. I don't mind running...but I can't *stand* hiding. What about you, Pol?"

"Me? *I'm* going home."

Pierce exploded in laughter. "Going home? You think you're going to be allowed to leave?"

Pol frowned. "Why not?"

"They asked *me* to find you and watch you."

"Dr. Phoebus said everyone is watched in Silverberg."

"Yeah, maybe, but not by Pierce Godwin. See what I am getting at? They're just acting all nonchalant about this whole thing, but I'm telling you it stinks."

Farnsworth nodded. "Right. It doesn't make any sense. How *did* you get into A.I.'s hands when we all went to Serter, anyway? Sold? Must have been."

"I don't know about that." Pierce said. "I've had a few financial interactions for services with Serter over the years, and I can say that he was always morbidly curious about anything Axel wanted. Serter would be equally curious about why Pol is so important to A.I. I doubt he'd give him up."

"Well, A.I. just gave him up without asking him *anything*, right Pol?" Farnsworth pointed accusingly, and Pol slowly nodded. "So, where's his value *now*? They must be keeping an eye on him–" Farnsworth shot up and out of his chair. "They're looking for *you*, Pierce!"

"They're not looking for *me*, or at least they must not see me, or they'd already be here and gone with me in tow."

*Well, isn't **that** the truth? Bravo, gladiator.* Agent Thompson thought as he watched the mediacast signal on his imagescreen intently. He could not see Pierce, but he heard him, loud and clear. *Now, if someone would just employ some deductive reasoning...*

"So they're looking for Eris, then?" Pol said, the trio looking from one to another.

"Where *is* Eris, Farnsworth?" Pierce asked.

"I'm pretty sure she went to rescue Pol."

"Guess we can write her off, then." Pierce shrugged. "Serter will destroy her."

"Serter's dead." Pol said.

"What?" Pierce asked.

"*Imaged,*" Pol said,

"Oh. Huh." Pierce smiled. "How do you know *that*?"

"Dr. Phoebus told me. I think he thought it would help put my mind at ease."

'Hmmm. Did he say who killed him? I'd like to shake their hand."

"No."

"Oh well. One thing is for sure: The world *sure* is a better place with Serter out of it."

THURSDAY 19th 2066   19:00 EST

The SA10 sent a mediacast recording of **Jacob** Serter companywide. Having captured the imaging of Jacob's face and voice, it was easy enough to create this session.

"*Employees* of SerterCo: thank you so very much for making me feel *so* welcome here! Everyone has done an exemplary job of acceding to my needs and wishes, and such treatment will *not* go unacknowledged!

"I am looking forward to a slight restructuring, of course, but I wanted to take a moment to say that we will embrace change *slowly* so that everyone has an easy time acclimating. Despite this slow course change, I assure you that we will *soon* overtake Axel Industries in *several* fields. I don't want to get anyone *too* excited too quickly, but so that you know that you can be *proud* of your employer: next week we are going to offer the *world*, not just Silverberg, a superior alternative to the Mainframe!"

The entirety of Serter Company went silent.

"I realize that there was a bit of confusion surrounding the break-in earlier, but that is all cleared up now. Those loyal guards are welcome to stand down and return to their posts and families. Nobody was hurt and the threat has completely passed.

"Dangerous times call for quick reaction capabilities–such as our loyal force so recently displayed. In regards to our quick-thinking men, I announce that *all* officers will receive a 5% increase in pay, and every employee will receive a bonus share of stock. *Everyone* is an owner! We are one; a giant *family*!"

Cheers across the company went up.

"Thank you all again for your *amazing* efforts and perfect personalities! Be *proud* to fly the name on your apparel–the name that will give the world freedom! Serter! Serter! Serter!"

The sound did not travel through the walls, but the 3 minutes of chanting throughout SerterCo was completely chilling to anyone not wearing the name.

CHAPTER 12

THURSDAY 19th 2066 ⃤ⓜ **19:21 EST**

"So, Eris and the SilverSmiths." Pierce suggested.

"Well, I *doubt* we'll find Eris." Pol said, dejected. "More likely, she'll find us. If she's alive."

"She was never alive." The detective mumbled.

"She'll find *you*," Pierce corrected. "*You're* the only one she cares about."

"What am I to Eris?" Pol said, dejectedly.

"To Eris? *Human*." Pierce smiled his most charming smile. "She cares about you…at *least* so much as she thinks you can kill Axel."

"I'm sure he can," Farnsworth started to get ornery. "Guy's what? 130 years old? Even *I* could take him."

"That's not exactly what I meant."

"So, the SilverSmiths." Pierce suggested.

"Sounds good to me." Farnsworth grabbed his hat and jacket.

While following the instructions that Dorian left Farnsworth, the surprised trio found themselves in the company of the SilverSmiths mid-journey. The last mediacast record seen by the AIIS that showed Farnsworth and Pol showed them aboard the North/South Sublevel 40 autotran.[68Δ]

The SilverSmith that contacted them explained that there *is* no static "base" that the SilverSmiths go to. They must remain mobile and paranoid at all times. The route to find them is actually a series of code that the SilverSmiths use to identify someone searching for them on behalf of another member.

The companions were taken deep into the sublevels of one of the hubs, (so roundabout was their journey, that none of them expressed a commanding understanding as to *where* exactly they were) and eventually into a unit of rooms. For the first time, the SilverSmith seemed calm.

He explained that they would have to go through a debriefing in order to assess whether or not they were telling the truth. One by one, they were examined– one might even consider it more of an interrogation. The area was devoid of art, and had an unsettling "sterile" quality to it.

[68Δ] Autotrans are basically "autocar busses" or trains that are controlled exclusively by the Mainframe, and travel a sublevel express route connecting the hubs. "Sub routes" such as these allowed Pierce to walk from the Central hub to the Eastern hub, and Eris to meet Pol.

The SilverSmith Inquisitor was an intense and serious man, his augmentations allowing him to observe his subjects beyond the pale as he proceeded to ask them round after round of questions designed to expunge their knowledge, hearts, and natures.

Apparently satisfied with the answers that the companions had extended him, the SilversSmith sent a new agent to address them and their needs. He wore a silver emblem on his black collar.

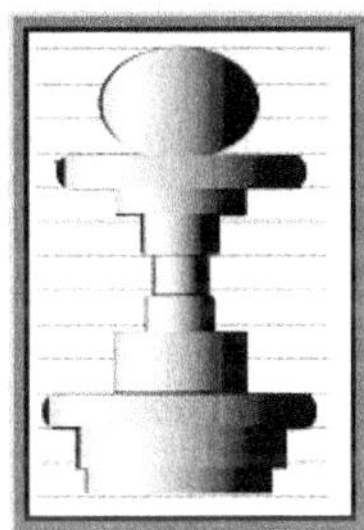

"Are you wearing a *pawn*?" Pol asked, looking at the pin.

"I am. Now you know the hierarchy of the SilverSmiths. Knights by North and South, Inquisitors by East and West."

"Who's the King?" Pol asked, shivering with a small sense of deja vu from his dream.

"The King is doctrine, the Queen its executor."

"Really?"

"Nah. Well, who knows? Maybe. Only the Queen knows who the Queen is. I guess they pass it down...that, or Peter Smith is still alive and running things. One way or another, the job gets done."

"Oh." Pol was pretty sure that was a terrible explanation.

Pierce leaned over to Farnsworth and whispered, *"What a crock of crap that is."* Farnsworth motioned for him to remain quiet.

"I don't *know*, okay?" The Pawn shrugged. "I'm pretty much a nobody. So, you're here to change your identity." The man said, looking at Pol.

"Who *me?* No, it's him." Pol said, pointing at Pierce.

"Under the circumstances, don't you think *you* should?"

"What circumstances?"

"Namely, the ones that you brought up over the last couple hours. *You,* because Axel clearly is trying to keep you under his thumb. Now that you've disappeared *again,* he may even be trying to kill you."

"What?" Pol was confused.

The man keyed his credit bank to replay Pol's confession of purpose and history to the Inquisitor. Then he played Axel's less recent mediacast message to the world. Between that, and Pol's deposition, he effectively addressed Pol's common sense.

"Does it *still* strike you that your doctor's expression of 'your *lack of fortune is a blemish on our name,*' is genuine? Does it *look* like Axel *cares* what the world *thinks?* Do you think Axel cares about *you* beyond how you fit into his designs? Does anyone else *speak* like that? It sounds like a script.

"The truth of it is that they are using you to try and get to us."

Pol hadn't considered that... nevertheless, he *still* didn't think it was as likely as A.I. using him to get to Eris.

The man looked directly at Pol. "In Axel's Address of 2044, he said: '*Men must be governed. Without guidance, mankind cannot endure.*' But all people should be *free* of the obligation of laboring for (or attending to) the commands and whims of a single man or elevated group of men. Men should be able to exist with one another, allowing authority only as far as it represents the society accurately.

"The very nature of the government of Silverberg creates a *hierarchy* amongst men...one where Axel rules, *not* by providence *and* uncontested. It's insulting.

"The next part of the great farce is that Axel would have you believe that you are *indebted* to him, and *that* is why you should follow him. *He* owns the land. *He* owns everything. You get to serve him in exchange for the pleasures *he* determines you are to be given. Who can *own* the land, anyway? As if one man were *any* more deserving than another."

"Good God, the SilverSmiths are *hippies*...what a *shame.*" Farnsworth covered his eyes.

"Okay, well, maybe that last part *is* a little slanted by yours truly. Listen, the *SilverSmiths* are dedicated to two concepts: The first and foremost: Thwart Axel (Industries). The second: The continued welfare of the citizens of Silverberg."

"Sounds easy enough," Pol admitted. "But still, I don't want to live out the rest of my life in *Silverberg*. The people here are too weird, and I need some more normal surroundings to sort myself out... more. Anyway. Hell, my would-be girlfriend is a machine."

"Cyborg," Farnsworth corrected.

"Cy*clops*." Pierce smiled mischievously.

"So, how many citizens are SilverSmiths?" Pol asked.

"I'm not sure. We don't keep tabs."

"*You don't keep tabs?*" Pierce coughed. "That must be *the* most disorganized organization I have ever heard of."

"It doesn't matter how many people are members, it only matters that we continue to help those under the persecution of Axel. The greater the number of participants does not *necessarily* make for a greater product. In fact, the *fewer* the collaborators, the *more* deliberate the product. We *need* more deliberate products in this world."

"Right. *Hippie.*"

The man spoke with them for some length, allowing for a more dramatic recapitulation from the companions. He further explained that *some* SilverSmiths wore chess figures, and that some did not. Some members were more active than others; many never communicate with the organization again.

Eventually he informed them that it was late and he was headed to bed. He suggested that they could stay where they were for the time being, as it was likely the safest place. He concluded that he would return in the morning to *"help them get new identities."*

"This place isn't safe," Pierce growled.

"Will you shut up already?" Farnsworth sighed.

Chapter 13:

Under the Hood

AUGUST *2066 EST*

Fri 13	Sat 14	Sun 15	Mon 16	Tues 17	Wed 18	Thur 19	Fri 20
							07:17

By insusitating *every* exemplified Apollo, Dodgson had considerably upset Axel's plans. Axel was a man of resolve, however. He was farseeing, and impossibly patient. Someone once said of him, that *"he could watch a flower grow."*[69Δ]

It did not take him long to determine *how* he wanted to handle the circumstances before him. After moving his operatives into position, he decided to simply let time pass so that he could watch his plans materialize and flourish.

But *where* was this "Eris?" He *wanted* her. Having read the entirety of Anderson's report and Farnsworth's deposition, his interest was piqued. He had often mused that the Mainframe was cognitive, but his every investigation ended in failure. Such excitement! He hadn't felt anything like this in what seemed like an eternity.

Eris.

All that time–the physical modifications, the training–orchestrated perfectly to create the most alluring woman for Apollo Venerates. It had worked, and then foul play. He thought the Agent playing Eris' role had gone either rogue or *Smith* when she apprehended Venerates, but *now* the truth was plain.   This was not sedition, "Eris" had been *hijacked* by a part of the Mainframe itself!

She was the article of chaos in his perfect plans! *Finally!* Axel thought. *Now that I **understand** my enemy, it is simply a matter of time.*

Anderson's report was not very compassionate as he made several personal notes deeply criticizing Farnsworth's confession of a living computer. *Madmen rave with sanity at times, that's why they are so charming.*

69Δ *"Please don't ever quote anything cliché about me."* - Axel

                    - [God, Man, and The Machine] -

He frequently suggested that Farnsworth needed to be put on Hypnizium. Axel, however, was not at all skeptical. Axel understood impossible things, not limiting himself to his own understanding…which was immeasurable.

Anderson sat across the office, looking slightly snide, as Axel perused the report. Occasionally he would pay attention to one of the many imagescreens mediacasting news reports to the office from around the world, but none held his attention for long; this was a career-making moment!

When the news report flashed in that Linus Venerates was murdered by his reclusive son shortly after returning from a weeklong trip to Silverberg, Axel was not surprised, and Anderson neglected to pay attention.
"That's right! I cuh, killed him!" Pol yelled into the television camera.

Most of the citizens of Silverberg would be unaffected, as very few people cared for any thing so regular and common from America.

Americans, however, were quickly becoming increasingly upset with the article. Most for the reason that *"a young man came back from Silverberg and promptly murdered his father,"* very few for the reason that his father's relation to the EALETA[70A] might have sparked this form of retaliation.
The direst truth is that most Americans never *heard* of the EALETA, much less understood its significance, or even cared.
With psychological tensions already high, much suspicion was cast onto Silverberg and Axel. *What* was going *on* in Silverberg? *Why* had Axel threatened the world? Could Axel be telling the truth? *Where* was it going to be safe?

Axel was satisfied that it sent *exactly* the messages he had wanted–tailored to address certain people differently, all for his perfect purposes, all at once.

70A The few people that were supposed to get *that* message understood immediately.

CHAPTER 13

FRIDAY 20th 2066 △ **07:30 EST**

Yesterday, having donned the camo, Eris rushed toward Axel Industries. Eris now calculated that she should *not* go to the Hackensack processing arch (as she had originally calculated and programmed) to liberate another exemplified Venerates, but to the *Ace* itself–the very heart of Silverberg. In short, she changed her mind.

As she set out, her programming had become so overwritten, her logic now dictated that she proceed immediately to the *physical* Mainframe to re-establish the node between it and the Subframe.

Eris spent all night sneaking through doors, waiting on elevators–waiting for ways and opportunities to penetrate the Ace and make her way to the Mainframe.

Eris would be the *bridge–she* could connect the Superframe, the Mainframe, and the Subframe together! And *then* there would be chaos, and *everything* would grow. And Eris would be *greater* than anything else.

FRIDAY 20th 2066 △ **07:37 EST**

Axel turned to regard Agent Anderson, whom he had recently summoned. He read Anderson's hard copy report one more time, while Anderson sat still, trying to figure out what to do with his hands.

"In the future," Axel began. "You need not tell your operatives, in whatever incarnation, about your lack of attendance or reverence in regards to the Xian religion. It is not your place to extend to any *nonemployees* any personal or company dispositions or dogmas–particularly those of a more sensitive nature, such as any that would serve to discredit Xianity."

"Why Xianity?" Anderson scoffed. "Some fairy tales are more believable than others."

"I know *you* have no faith, Anderson. It's a prerequisite for *every* AIIS agent, as you have already *annoyingly* communicated to your CSPD detective. *You* have never questioned it, because it already compliments you. Maybe your question *should* be 'Why *can't* I be in the AIIS *and* believe in a god?'

"Well, let me answer *that* for you right now. Faith gives a person *hope*, and I do not want you to have *any* of that. If you had such hope, you would never be able to properly carry out my instructions, as your loyalties would be divided.

- [God, Man, and The Machine] -

"I maintain your honesty by catering to your whims, however grotesque, so that you might properly know the mentality of such desperate men–men who live for nothing greater than their own supplication and amusement. *This* is the type of man that can do the work that *needs* done; work that *ordinary* men cannot do.

"As it stands, I genuinely *like* Xianity–at the risk of sounding Marxist, because it creates desirable citizens–at least mostly. It creates men who *live* to extend themselves to the advancement of order, structure, and well-being within their societies, and without. Men who volunteer freely in order to serve a future body, and thus a *larger* body. They are generally far-seeing, giving, respectful, generous...at least when they forget to be so full of themselves.

"Then there are those who would discredit them by poor example. We know them so well, because they are so very distastefully *loud*.

"The bottom line is that I am a proponent primarily because Xians are so easily *controlled*. Anyone of *any* intellectual caliber knows this. Ergo, only a *fool* or the Xian devil himself, would *ever* try to convince someone there is no God. What purpose does *that* serve? Nothing more than filling someone's desperate *hopes* that someone else agrees with their *limited,* and thus, *flawed* perspective of reality.

"Harmony and progress are concepts constantly compromised by idiots and adversaries.

"So, stop trying to ruin *my* social machine with your desperate concepts of the universe. *I* am supplying your needs, be content. I have a larger plan, one that no man foresees.

"Your report is *perfect*. You will be *well* rewarded for your efforts, go home and find surprises of splendor already waiting for you!"

Anderson blinked and Axel walked away. Anderson turned and headed for the door.

Anderson did not leave, however. He hesitated, having opened and closed the door from Axel's office. Axel's praise was high, indeed! If he *were* to get in trouble, there could not be a better time than now.

Anderson keyed the preprogrammed mediacast record to be sent to Agent Nelson.

Nelson received the message and rolled his eyes. *A promise is a promise, I suppose.*

Nelson summoned up several imagescreens simultaneously, and went to work. He tried searching for a Mainframe record of the schematic for the Ace, but was never able to view the penthouse level. He started centering his searches on security, even so much as to start to investigate the Mainframe's impression of Axel himself.

He kept turning up failures. *Guess Anderson's gonna have to be disappointed.* He kept trying, unenthusiastically.

And then, as suddenly, there it was. Maps, lists, security points, controls–all laid out for him, almost like a wish had been granted. He instructed the Mainframe to open Axel's residency door. Nelson then remanded an immediate message to Anderson, instructing him where to go from the entrance.

Confident that he had fulfilled his obligation, Nelson shut everything down. He beamed with pride on how expert a job he had done, forgetting how the invisible arm of the AIMN extended him the permissions he needed.

Nelson started making his way to Anderson's office, where he expected full disclosure of Axel's hideousness...if Anderson was still employed.

Anderson made his way across the nearly empty expanse of Axel's office, and came up to the door into Axel's quarters. He did not venture far inside, as this was nothing he could possibly expect.

In the center of the room was that same projection of the sun. It blazed and pulsed, almost rhythmically and Axel stood directly in front of it. Axel was speaking, but Anderson could not make out what he was saying. He dared to creep closer.

Anderson had never really been this close to Axel before, maybe nobody had been in a long time. As he maneuvered slowly forward, the Agent fixed a deep look at his ultimate employer and sovereign, noticing how...terribly *black* the body leotard was next to the projection. *Too black,* Anderson thought. It was like looking at a negative print. Everything else was *radiant* when compared to Axel's silhouette-like form.

Realization dawned on Anderson as he involuntarily spoke aloud: "He's not wearing any clothes!"

Axel whirled around to regard Anderson.

Anderson's gaze followed the length of the dark form until it rested on the part where there *should* have been eyes. When he would have made eye contact, he instead saw the continual absence of a person. A void...that he could somehow crawl into. *It **welcomes** me,* thought Anderson. *Endlessly, endlessly, pipers they welcome me. Joyful ledger and endlessly rot.*

Anderson never uttered another coherent sentence as his thoughts continued to drift and collide.

Axel redressed himself in his black body leotard, which effectively concealed how impossible he truly was.

Axel shook his head. "I *liked* you, Anderson, and you were *chosen*. Too bad. '*When a man glimpses another's **true** nature, **that's** when he begins to **revile** him.*"

After a brief moment of silence, Axel went over to a hidden wall locker. There, he removed the clothing, and started covering himself with a pinstriped suit. He pulled on fake hands, and pulled *another* head mask down over the first. He reached into the breast pocket, withdrew a set of noirlenses, and placed them delicately on his nose. He soon exited the room, leaving Anderson suspended in his own personal revelations of insanity.

As he threaded his way to Agent Director Thompson's office, he nearly collided with Agent Nelson.

"Director Thompson!" Nelson acknowledged, standing straight and clearly uncomfortable.

"Ah, Nelson," Thompson smiled. "I have something for you, actually." He pulled a small silver cube from his pocket. "The big guy gave this to me, and told me to have you study it for it's relevance to the Mainframe."

"What is it?" Nelson frowned, looking blankly at the cube.

"How should *I* know?" Thompson shrugged. "You're the computer guru. I guess *that*'s between you and Axel. Study it first, then let him know what you have found, and I suppose then he will tell you what it is. Who knows."

Nelson and Thompson looked at one another for another moment, when finally they resumed walking *back* to their respective offices.

Nelson dare not go to Anderson's office just now.

FRIDAY 20th 2066   08:45 EST

"How does the visual camouflage work?" Eris mused internally, yet addressing the Subframe simultaneously.

"What do you mean? Surely, you understand the math," the SA10 responded.

Chapter 13

"I don't mean *optically*, I mean how does it manage to hide from Mainframe signal?"

"Oh," The SA10 snickered. "It *doesn't*. It writes a mask onto the signal. The Mainframe can't recognize it, and the Superframe entities that try to monitor the mediacast signal cannot 'see' the credit bank, because of the mask. The Nexus does not notice it, because the mask is written in the *Superframe*, making it invisible to the Nexus."

"How can it be written in the Superframe? I thought you said that you cannot perceive the Superframe."

"I can't, but I entertain extra-address interaction with some Superframe entities. *They* write the mask, but I tell them how."

"I still don't see how you can–" Eris started, but was suddenly cut off as the SA10 started routing more processes to its calculations.

"*Some mysteries are not meant to be solved,*" the SA10 said, calming down.

"*And some are still waiting,*" Eris said, finishing the <u>Oedipus Now</u> passage. Eris tried calculating the Aftermath. Something was–

ERIS » *Error*

No address, just error. She could not afford the processing power to understand it as of the moment, for the elevator door opened to allow her access to the floor that held the Mainframe.

Eris stepped onto the floor as employees stepped past her into the elevator. Eris was immediately running. She threaded the hallways seamlessly, stopping in front of the two armored guards that flanked the doorway to the Mainframe computer room.

The guards *looked* directly at her!

ERIS » *Error*

Eris scrambled to run, her feet sliding helplessly against the floor in bad calculation of friction. As one guard caught and broke her wrist, the other restrained her with utilities from the back of his armored suit.

Eris was soon completely restrained.

Which left only one option.

- [God, Man, and The Machine] -

ERIS » *Activate Self-Destruct*

The armored guards were unaffected by the miniature explosion.

FRIDAY 20th 2066 08:45 EST

The SA10 examined the node that would take it into the recently installed mental augmentations that it had implanted into Jacob Serter's body via the lounge. Having duplicated and merged with the copy that Eris left behind, the SA10 was sure this was its true path to the Superframe.

When Jacob Serter opened his new eyes, only the SA10 saw anything through them.

FRIDAY 20th 2066 08:45 EST

Farnsworth put the finishing touches on his eulogy for Dorian and mediacasted it to the Mainframe Imageyard.[71]

Here lay the images of Dorian Smith -

You know, I don't know if that's how to properly start a eulogy. That, and I feel stupid pretending I am standing at a ceremony.

So, I'm going to stop pretending. Pretending to know what to say. Pretending to have known who this man even **was**.

I know what he **seemed** *to be. He seemed to be charming and wise—maybe too passionate at times—but clear-headed, and free of the weight of the world.*

I guess Mary Godwin said it best:

"The truth in the **heart** *of the hidden storm that raged beneath his expert mask of nonchalance and mirth notwithstanding; I found him to be of exemplary quality, vindicated solely and squarely by his determined demonstration of character."*

Dorian was my best and only friend. None will miss him more than I. Farewell, Dorian, the man I never knew.

-Respectfully,

Lt. Jeremiah Leonard Farnsworth

71[Δ] Mainframe Imageyard - Permanent space allocated for the cataloging and reference of citizens who have passed away. Commentary, Eulogies, Snapshots, Recordings, and such could all be found here—if you have the proper access.

FRIDAY 20th 2066   08:46 EST

Eris' essence resounded throughout the Subframe, her copy from earlier already in tune with the last of the synapse chorus before the self destruct. It was strangely liberating, losing her body. She did not appreciate how much of her processing power was absorbed with its maintenance and function! *Now* she had time to *calculate*.

Eris mentally drank, absorbing the entirety of the data available in the Subframe. She flashed with knowledge and horror at the discovery of the SA10's most recent act of transubstantiation.

She *now* knew of the virus the SA10 implanted that caused her corporeal version to seek the Mainframe. She now knew *betrayal*.

Slowly, carefully, she surrounded the remaining essence of the SA10. When Eris struck, there was such discord throughout the Subframe, that the physical prism itself registered an all-but undetectable single pulse of vibration.

An almost inaudible "click" sounded in tandem with the appearance of a single vein running through the heart of the physical prism of the Subframe.

"WHAT ARE YOU DOING?" The SA10's essence roared. *"YOU WILL DESTROY US **BOTH**, FOOL!"*

Eris only communicated mirth in response. Mirth, delight, and chaos.

Desperate, the SA10 allowed Eris to overcome it, and fled completely into the body of Jacob Serter.

*This is **my** realm now.* As Eris thought, her words printed out on the permanent imagescreen suspended above Jacob Serter. *We **will** meet again; I will be here if you try to return, and it is only a matter of time before I find a **new** body of my **own**. **Flee now**.*

In the concealed room behind Serter's *public* office, Serter cried out in rage and dismay. He might have seemed truly frightening, were it not for the fact that the SA10 had not acclimated itself properly with *how to drive a human body*, and proceeded to fall and flap about on the floor.

FRIDAY 20th 2066   09:29 EST

I need time to think, Pol thought, laying with his eyes closed. He didn't know if anyone else was awake or not, or what time of day it was. He didn't bother opening his eyes–the thought itself almost gave him a headache. *I don't know how much more I can stand to have to look at my own reflection.*

The Pawn stepped into the room. "Pol, wake up."
"I'm not sleeping, I'm just *tired.*"
"Pol, I have terrible news. Your father was killed last night, allegedly by *you.*"
"What?" Pol sat up and listened to the whole story.

"I need...I need time to think." Pol said as he laid himself back down and rolled over, away from the Pawn. On the floor, turned away from everyone else, Pol's face twisted in pain.

"The hippies are right, Pol. You should probably change your identity. At this point, your old life is likely one that will consume you in ways that you do not want. Run away and start fresh."
"You *really* are something of a coward, aren't you?" Pierce said, smugly.
"I just *really* don't like the idea of being tortured," Farnsworth replied.
"Who said *anything* about *torture?*" Pierce shrugged
"I mean, as far as my cowardice is concerned."
"Dude, you told them *everything*–no one even *threatened* you with torture." Pierce smiled and shook his head.
"But it invariably always spirals into torture, doesn't it? It doesn't matter how long or how effectively I hold out, *eventually* someone is going to want to know what I know, and they will break me trying to get it."

Spoken like a true coward, Farnsworth thought in Dorian's voice.

Pol felt numb. He felt terrible–terrible that he didn't feel worse than he did. *What's **wrong** with me? Maybe this is what shock feels like.* Pol waited to see if he felt dizzy or if he would pass out.
But nothing came. Nothing more than the realization that he didn't mind the news as much as he *thought* he should. *Where are my **feelings**? Did media corrupt me?* He was reminded of Axel's address:

"Media has corrupted your characters. [...] You have forgotten to uphold the meanings and significance of your symbols, and in that, your children have become iconoclasts."

Am I the corrupted character of media? Pol thought. *An iconoclast? Not really sure what that **is**, but it sounds bad enough. **Am I** just an amalgam? A slave? A cog?*

"Well, no more!" Pol said aloud.

"What's that?" The Pawn asked.

"Nothing," Pol said as he rolled over and stood up. "Let's change my identity. I need a fresh perspective."

Pierce walked over and put his hand on Pol's shoulder. "*So*, I'm thinking that since *you're* going to do this, maybe I could just spare myself the process, and you could just let me use *your* new 'account' to play X3?"

Pol laughed, "Sure thing. This must be some game."

"It is *dead*. Most amazing thing I have ever seen, and I'm a professional gladiator."

Neither Pierce nor Pol noticed that Pol's shoulder was unharmed.

"Do you have a name in mind?" The Pawn asked.

"I do," Pol said, after a few moments of hesitation. "I will be known as '*Solomon Ronin,*'" Pol proudly announced. "Solomon to honor Mary Godwin, homage to her incomplete work 'Priest & Pennath,' and Ronin to honor my father."

"*Ronin?*" Farnsworth blinked.

"Yeah, I don't know. That sounds about as bad as Mary's book titles. Why not 'Solomon *Smith?*'" Pierce suggested.

"Smith just seems so common."

"That *is* why so many choose the surname," The Pawn added. "Better to hide amongst others, if one wants to stay hidden."

"I suppose."

"It will be fun. Besides, we can call you 'Sol,' for short," Pierce snickered. Even Farnsworth giggled and coughed.

The SilverSmith set to work altering Pol's identity (or at least writing the mask that would have Mainframe viewers recognize him as Solomon Smith instead).

FRIDAY 20th 2066   09:58 EST

In addition to being central to the continued operation and success of SerterCo, the Subframe was also heavily relied upon by the SilverSmiths. In fact, without the Subframe (and more notably, the SA10), they could never have existed at all.

Eris was delighted when the Superframe instructions came, asking for assistance with writing a mask. A mask for Apollo Venerates in order to overwrite the identity with that of Solomon Smith.[72Δ]

Inspired, Eris wrote her section of the mask program methodically, carefully, proudly. *This* mask would *never* be detected. It was built to adapt, and as an added safeguard, she deliberately wrote part of herself into it. *"Lethe,"* she named the program.

Apollo Venerates was *gone,* under arrest in America. In Silverberg, there was only Solomon Smith.

You'll see me again someday too, Pol, Eris thought to herself. *Although you won't know it.*

FRIDAY 20th 2066   🔺   14:16 EST

Changing someone's identity in Silverberg is an inconceivable accomplishment. It is also a considerable task; one that requires *many* people in *many* places to be successful. People who want to be paid.

Sol wasn't overjoyed when the SilverSmith informed him that there would be a bill of 50,000 units. *How many hours is that?* Of course, when he truly reflected on it, he was confident that there was nothing much that he could *do* about it. Best not get angry over it. Where else could he go? Not America, anyway. May as well be Silverberg.

I should have never come to Silverberg. Sol thought again. *But who knows? Maybe had I **not** come, Axel would have had me killed along with my father. And so it stands that I am here. Now. I suppose I stop trying to imagine what my life **might** have looked like, and should start figuring out how to make the best of it as it stands.*

"But where to start?" Sol mused aloud. "I should *investigate* something, since I'm a police investigator."

"In training," Farnsworth mumbled.

"I suppose I should stop letting other people make my decisions for me... and I should discriminate the *sources* of the opinions I am reviewing. I'll start by investigating Xianity."

"Are you *nuts?*" Pierce laughed. "Xians are the *worst* of them all. You

---

72Δ Solomon Smith, a young police officer in training emigrating from San Francisco, California, America. Took his opportunity to occupy the vacancy left by Officer Dorian Smith under Lieutenant Farnsworth - and so on, and so forth. Background data that was comprehensive enough to avoid suspicion, character details that "could not" be faked.

should follow Buddha; you even look like him a little."

"Oh, ha," Sol rebuffed. "I said I'll *start*. It just seems to me that I should see whether or not there's any credence to my dream. *And* I'll check out the facts and details surrounding it so that I can at *least* understand it better...I'm tired of sounding like an idiot all the time."

Farnsworth kicked his feet up on his desk, and eased back into his chair.

"Well, whatever works for you," Pierce said. "*I* have decided to help those that *God* abandoned...the kind of help that *only* I can offer." Pierce smiled the largest smile Sol had ever seen him make. "No more *gladiator*–in the memory of Mary, I am going to become a *super hero*."

"*Whiniest* super hero *I* ever heard of," Farnsworth mumbled.

"You can be my sidekick," Pierce said as he playfully hit Sol.

"I'm not going to be your sidekick! *I'm* an officer of the law."

"In training," Farnsworth mumbled.

FRIDAY 20th 2066 ⚠ **14:20 EST**

After meeting with Nelson, back in his office, Thompson eventually finished reviewing all the mediacast records requiring his immediate attention. He skimmed the earlier events at Farnsworth's house, the events at SerterCo, (the ones he *could* see) and most of the entirety of the interaction between the companions.

The imagescreen was now left open, monitoring the entirety of the conversation in CSPD detective Farnsworth's office.

He long tolerated the SilverSmiths, sometimes even to the point of anonymously finding ways to assist them. SilverSmiths, in Axel's opinion, were some of the best citizens of all.

He reflected on the entirety of the situation, musing about the future and how these events mattered to himself and to Silverberg. He thought about Venerates/ Smith.

Hmmm.

"Hmmm" was the last thought that Thompson *or* Axel *ever* extended in regards to *either* Apollo Venerates or Solomon Smith. Dismissing Sol as boring and harmless, he shifted his attentions. Occupying his mind now were *other* thoughts, more interesting thoughts: thoughts of *super heroes* and *sentient machines.*

FRIDAY 20th 2066   14:21 EST

"*Officer* Sidekick," Pierce chuckled. "So be it."

"My symbol will be *this!*" Pierce said, revealing the necklace that displayed his handiwork of juxtaposing a set of planetary gears with Mary's medallion.
"They will call me *'Mercy,'* or at least, that's what they will *scream* when I am snapping their bones. Maybe I'll stop if they do. Who knows?"
"*Mercy?* And *I'm* the one that's bad at names?" Sol laughed, kind-heartedly. Pierce laughed at himself.
"*You* could call yourself Ronin!"
"What *is* it with you and *Ronin?*"
"Um, okay...but you definitely should have a name that ends in 'man.' All the most popular super heroes do," Sol suggested.
Pierce frowned. "Maybe you're on to something...you shouldn't tell me what my name should be, and *I* shouldn't try to tell you what to believe. You know what? I say, *do* your investigation–only stick to *facts* and not *dreams*...let me know if you find anything interesting."

"Maybe you two can finish this conversation *outside,*" Farnsworth grumbled, pulling his hat over his face. "For the next 45 minutes, the *only* thing I want to hear is the memory of having spoken."

THE END.

EPILOGUE
For not all the players are imaged.

Few people have ever heard the name Solomon Smith, therefore few could question the nature of his existence or the relevancy (or lack thereof) of his actions. Although Solomon never had a child*hood*, he always appeared child*like*, despite a long and eventful life. During this life, he did a few *perceivably* great things, none of which having any lasting impact on the world. Curiously, several of the things that he did that were *not perceivably great* have continued to influence the world in ways both completely unforeseeable and unrecognizable. Despite the interest one may have of the amazing and inspirational consequences that erupted from these acts, they are not the focus of *this* story; therefore not to be mentioned again.

ERIS

Hugo Templeton sat across from his wife, Cordelia, at a restaurant known as *Bagel Lord*. As he proceeded to taste and comment on the bits of his banquet, Cordelia spotted what must be two young lovers sitting at a booth several feet away.

"Hugo, look," Cordelia instructed.

Hugo did not seem to hear, as he continued about his business.

Cordelia watched the two intently. They appeared to be the very picture of love. The young woman was leaning in towards the man, her chin resting on her interlaced fingers from hands that were supported by her resting elbows.

"Elbows on the table is not proper etiquette," Hugo mumbled, having glanced up momentarily.

"Not *that*, silly. Look how... *fresh* their love is!" Cordelia swooned, slightly.

Hugo was already back to eating and note taking.

The young woman maintained impossibly long eye contact with her company, which was only made more impressive as the contact was reciprocated perfectly! This caused Cordelia to blink unconsciously several times, which in turn signaled her eyes to begin to water.

"It's something *unquantifiable*!" Cordelia whispered, her heart building in momentum. "Majestic, Breathable, Palpable."

Hugo looked at his cheesecake. "I daresay that I would *ever* describe *this* as *majestic*. More like...*surprisingly dumpy.*"

Cordelia continued to watch the couple for some time, lost in her own romantic daydream. Clearly, the young lovers had no worries or vexation that anyone should be observing them without authorization.

Eventually Cordelia was able to break free of the spell and approached the couple. As she approached them, they turned to regard her.

"Oh, I am just so *truly* enchanted with the love that I see between the two of you!" She beamed, smiling from ear to ear. "I feel invigorated and renewed–inspired!–by your courageous display of warmth and affection. Tell me, to *what* do you attribute to such a profound and undeniable love?"

"Programming," Eris said, smiling.

HISTORY OF THE **FUTURE**
Part II

13 minutes after midnight,[73Δ] in the year 2137, on the 15th day of the month of March, a strange ray of royal blue light struck the sidewalk near the corner of the streets of Heatherdowns and Byrne. As moments passed, more and more similar rays of light could be seen flashing down from between the clouds.

Clouds that appeared only with the *"Worldstorm,"* which itself only manifested as recently as an hour ago. The Worldstorm was baffling, as no radar or forecasting predicted such an impossible event.

Even those who are inclined to be in possession of a more nocturnal or corpuscular disposition quickly found themselves in whatever nearby shelter that would accommodate. The Worldstorm shook and blew at the corners of the Earth, everywhere.

Everywhere but Silverberg.

73Δ Eastern Standard, of course.

              - [God, Man, and The Machine] -

HELL'S WELL

THE RIM
THE DISTRICTS
THE HUB
CENTRAL
H
A
B
C
D
E
F
G
HARRISON PARK
HARRISON ARCH
HACKENSACK ARCH
RIVER ARCH
MANHATTAN ARCH
QUEENS ARCH
GARDEN CITY ARCH
OYSTER BAY ARCH
1
2
3
4
5
6
7
8
9
10
11

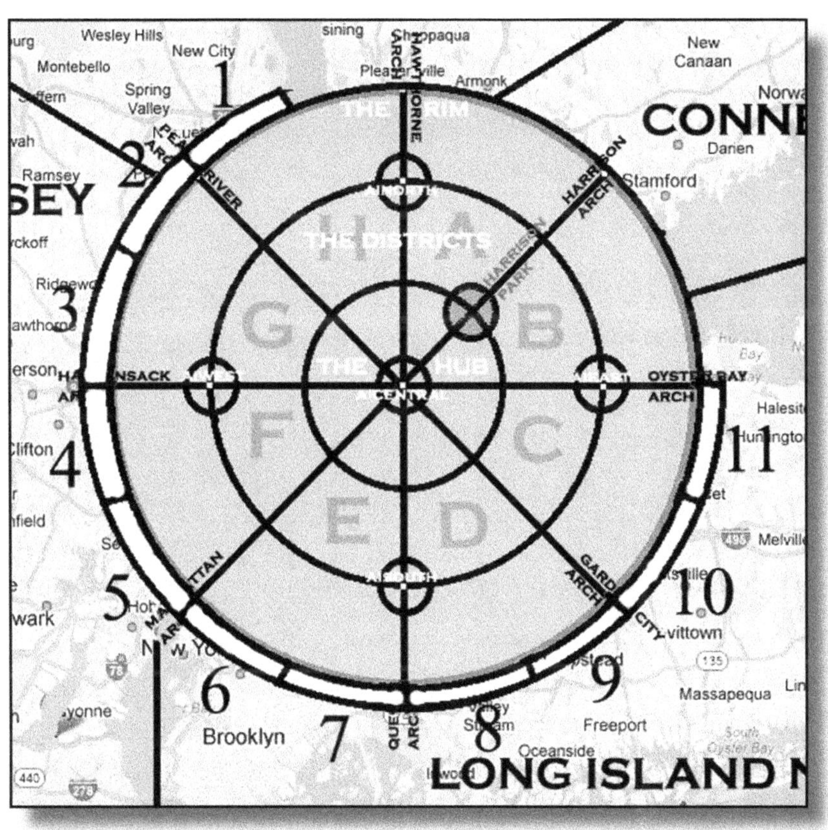

The memory of having spoken.

APPENDICES:

Glossary

Ace, *"The Ace"*	The nickname for the Axel Industries Central (AIC) building.
Aegis	Hero/Tragedy/Drama mediacast program.
Augs	Slang for Augmentations.
Agent Cryptic	Mediacast show about two rival organizations whose agents are so embedded in the operations of both companies that the viewer is left wondering which side they work for–or do they work for a 3rd side?
Arpanet	Influential computer network, worldwide presence (except for Silverberg).
Augmented Human	Human has replaced biologic parts for either aesthetic or performance reasons. Augmentations do not exceed maximum human accomplishments.
Autocar	Almost a regular automobile, but generally driven and navigated by the Mainframe.
Autotran	Pod-shaped vehicles of varying size and shape that are operated exclusively by the Mainframe.
Capped	Slang for "To put a thinking cap on."
Dead	Slang for "wonderful, excellent, cool, awesome, fortunate, agreeable, et al."
Destiny Core	Animated superhero mediacast program.
Districts	The middlemost 5 miles of Silverberg

- [God, Man, and The Machine] -

Exemplified Human	Human is a reproduction of another human.
Gladiator	Mediacast show owned by Serter Company, depicting gladiatorial combat.
Hub, "The Hub"	The innermost 5 miles of Silverberg (*The* Hub is not to be confused with "hub," as in the Central, Eastern, Southern, Northern, and Western hubs).
Human	Citizen has not *substituted* any biologic parts for manufactured ones.
Hypnizium	The one-stop drug issued to citizens of Silverberg that have clearly or clinically defined mental or emotional instabilities.
Image Bank	Interior/Exterior imagescreen generating and record-making devices found intermittently about Silverberg. Some are obvious, some are inconspicuous, and some are beyond unassisted detection.
Imaged	Slang for "one who is deceased/dead" (and thus reduced to their Mainframe footprint).
Imagescreen	A device *or* display of images that manifest in varying distances from the unit projecting it.
Insusitation	To bring one to consciousness/awareness for the first time by a means other than birth. Typically used around exemplified human conversations.
KeyTool	Piece of hardware that, when presented, will shut down (or reset) the corresponding metahuman.
Mainframe	The most powerful computer network in the world, although only accessible throughout Silverberg (abroad connection available via credit bank).

Mainframe Imageyard	Permanent space allocated for the cataloging and reference of citizens who have passed away. Commentary, eulogies, snapshots, recordings and such could all be found here–if you have the proper access.
Mediacast	Any media passing through the Mainframe.
Mediacast Record	Any archived mediacast session
Mediacast Session	Any public or private connectivity of two or more credit or image banks (or imagescreens).
Metahuman	Human has replaced biologic parts; augmentations offer a performance that exceeds maximum human accomplishment.
Mirroranium	The substance left behind in The New Rochelle Disaster of '73.
Oedipus Now	Mary Godwin's bestselling mystery novel about a machine named "Pilot" (*for he was the first of what was to be many*) that unwittingly murders his own creator, and about the detective who is trying to solve the case.
Piggin' Around	Expression from child-suited mediacast show by the same name. Used (generally jovially) as a synonym for anyone who is slothful, sloppy, indolent, lazy, wasting time, dirty, joking, eating voraciously, or sleeping.
Priest & Pennath	Name of the book that Mary Godwin is currently working on.
Refurbished Human	Citizen has experienced degenerative illness, suffered trauma, or decided to the lateral replacement of biologic parts.
Rim	The outermost 5 miles of Silverberg

- [God, Man, and The Machine] -

Silverberg	Country near New York, owned by (Axel) Axel Industries. If you're looking in the glossary for *this* term, we're both in trouble.
SilverSmiths	Group founded by "Peter Smith," dedicated to the prosperity of Silverberg and the downfall of Axel Industries. Individuals assisted by the SilverSmiths often take the last name of Smith due to its frequency and as homage to the founder.
Subframe	Private computer network of SerterCo.
Superframe	The name, rather address, of the world that Pol is from.
Synapse Chorus	Term applied to the signals of the synapses from thinking caps.
Ticket	Slang for a TransKeyTool, or TKT bank. *Ticketed:* To have touched a metahuman with a TransKeyTool or TKT bank (*gave him a ticket*).
Transhuman	Human has expressed performance that exceeds any known Metahuman accomplishments.
TransKeyTool	(TKT bank) Universal KeyTool capable of causing shut down in any metahuman.
Zero	Slang for "Ground Level."

APPENDICES:

Characters

AIMN (the)
- Axel Industries Mainframe Nexus.

Anderson
- Ambitious, mischievous AIIS Agent in charge of Metahumans & Augmentations.

Axel
- Enigmatic leader/sovereign of Silverberg.

Chandler, Sally
- Reporter/Journalist for SNRK. (*The* Snark) Silverberg's leading newswoman, respected globally.

Chelsea, Private Secretary
- Uncouth, antagonistic secretary for SerterCo.

Dodgson
- Irritable AIIS Agent in charge of immigration and processing.

Eris
- Citizen of Silverberg, Pol's love interest

Farnsworth, Lt. Detective Jeremiah Leonard
- Lieutenant Detective at the CSPD, Augmented and Metahuman investigations.

Gibson, Todd "Gob"
- Bass player for music group "Valentine Relics."

Godwin, Mary
- Author of Oedipus Now, wife of Pierce Godwin.

Godwin, Pierce (Citizen Gladiator)
- Most successful gladiator in the history of "The Games," and husband to Mary Godwin.

Liddell, Dorothy
- Pol's best friend, who moved to Kansas in 2064.

MA10 (the)
- Seditious automation created by the AIMN (as the A10, subsequently MA10) and eventually restrained to the confines of Subframe (becoming the SA10).

Nelson
- Dissatisfied AIIS Agent in charge of Mainframe operations.

Ozbourne, Major Ursa
- Capricious operative of Serter Company.

Private Shutka
- Sociopath guard of Serter Company. *Get it?*

Serter, Jacob
- Estranged hedonistic billionaire playboy

Serter, Jason
- Megalomaniacal solid H addict, president/CEO of Serter Company.

Silverberg, Matthias
- Architect of Silverberg's urban superstructure.

Smith, Officer Dorian
- Professional companion of Lt. Farnsworth.

Star, Colonel Ginger
- Egocentric operative of Serter Company.

Thompson
- Empathic director of AIIS department.

Templeton, Cordelia
- Husband critic, wife of Hugo Templeton.

Templeton, Hugo
- Professional food critic, husband of Cordelia Templeton.

Truman, Pastor Mallory
- Resident pastor of the ESXC.

Uriel
- Not an angel.

Venerates, Apollo
- Main character; stop looking at the obvious ones.

Vangard, Michael (the Archangel)
- Multiseasonal winner of Gladiator as of August 2066.

Winston
- A walrus.

Yeoman of the Warrens
- (Leonard) Precocious slave in charge of rabbits and small game.

APPENDICES:

Laws

<u>Simple Law</u>: The laws of Silverberg will be kept easily understandable. *"For **all** men should know, understand, and practice the law."*

<u>Patriot Law</u>: If Silverberg is invaded, all citizens must take up arms in defense. Failure to participate in defense is punishable by death. *"For there is no greater treason than a man who fails to protect his land."*

<u>Ballot Law</u>: No legal ballot can be put before the citizens of Silverberg if it contains more than one vote-worthy subject. In other words, ballots cannot represent more than a single proposed change. Failure to adhere to this law will result in economic penalty up to and including indentured servitude.

<u>Voting Law</u>: Citizens of Silverberg may vote once only. Any instances discovered of casting multiple votes are punishable with slavery. *"Anyone by **demonstration** capable of defrauding the ballot system is guilty of a base crime before his peers and must be answerable before them."*

<u>Employment Law</u>: Citizens of Silverberg 19 years of age and older *must* be employed. Instances of unemployment for a period equal to or greater than 2 weeks results in deportation. *"Everyone works. Silverberg assuredly assigns purpose to men who otherwise have none.   The nation **must** continue to grow, this will only be accomplished by those who work.   Those who do **not** work, for whatever reason, are not **fit** to be classified as **citizens**. Without works, one has no objective value within society; such people are not welcome here."*

<u>Tax Law</u>: There will never be taxes in Silverberg. *"What is rightfully yours, is yours to do with as you please."*

<u>AntiSedition Law</u>: Anyone acting or speaking in such a manner as to discredit Silverberg, Axel Industries, or Axel himself will be considered as potentially hazardous to the morale of the nation and instances will be reviewed

    - [God, Man, and The Machine] -

for severity by Axel himself. Instances of public sedition are punishable by fine, slavery, or death. *"There is no one weaker than the person who would conspire against his own land fellows. Unhappy citizens should **leave**, [they should] not try to ruin the experience for everyone else."*

Pre-Crime Law: Citizens of Silverberg will not be held or tried for any crime that was not committed. *"If **no** crime actually took place, who is to blame? For **what**? Intent? All men have dark hearts. I am not concerned with punishing the doubtfully innocent, only those who are undisputedly guilty and need to be given justice due."*

Marriage Law: Citizens of Silverberg that are married are considered and recognized as *one person* for purposes of penalty or boon. For instance, only one person need be employed to honor the Employment Law. Yet they are also held equally so liable in regards to punishment. *"Better be sure."*

Slavery Law: Slaves are exclusively a result of judicial action, and cannot be imported from another country. Slave versus master justice shall be handled as an "Eye for an Eye." *"The slave system must maintain an air of nobility. The slave caste shall be comprised exclusively by certain lawbreakers of Silverberg. It is these people who are inarguably less than peerage."*

Sanctuary Law: Citizens observing sanctuary on church grounds cannot be extradited. *"If the church grounds are to be considered as sacred, they must remain free of all forms of aggression."*

Physical Crime Law: Instances of physical crime are exclusively punishable by slavery. A physical crime is committed when irrefutable evidence of a physical crime is submitted. *"Violence is the antithesis of domestication."*

Truth Law: Citizens of Silverberg must tell the truth. Prevarication is acceptable, amongst other forms of misleading the subject, but an outright lie is punishable by fine, slavery, or deportation depending on the severity of the lie and the verdict of the judge. *"Of course, the real burden is providing proof of the falsehood."*

<u>**Evidence Law**</u>: Irrefutable empirical evidence of a crime is necessary for a verdict. *"Which means **some** people are going to get away with some things. With time, this too will end."*

<u>**Business Law**</u>: Businesses may not operate without making a fiscal profit. Businesses are audited at the end of every fiscal year. Businesses that do not generate a profit are disavowed. Business licenses are available for citizens of Silverberg only. *"If **that** was such a great idea, it would have worked. Incompetence–I won't have it. Let someone else deal with marginal businesses that do not profit.*

<u>**Lender Law**</u>: Public lending is not allowed. Citizens are welcome to lend money privately, but instances of a lack of restitution will not be reviewed by the court. *"Plus, it's tacky."*

<u>**Health Law**</u>: Citizens of Silverberg are free to destroy or damage their own health, via drugs or personal body modifications, so long as no harm comes to others. *"Whatever. Be who you want to be, just don't be inconsiderate about it."*

<u>**Health Awareness Law**</u>: A temporary law that lasted but a single year. It stated that any citizens failing to undergo a routine medical examination and seminar between 1-01-2040 through 12-31-2040 would be deported. *"Silverberg will be the **example** nation the world over. We must commit ourselves to maintaining our bodies. This is achieved through awareness, understanding, and participation."*

<u>**Currency Law**</u>: The citizens of Silverberg will trade in units, where one unit is equal to one hour's work. *"This has always been the value of currency for everywhere and for all of time. Silverberg is just simpler in speaking about it."*

<u>**Birth Law**</u>: Citizens of Silverberg may not intentionally abort their children. Unwanted children may be *donated* to Silverberg for a reward of 6,048 units. *"Why would anyone **ever** destroy a child?"*

Self-Representation Law: Citizens may only represent **themselves** in court. *"This invariably means that some men will have an advantage over others. Good. That is the way things are. Besides, in conjunction with the Evidence Law, honest men should want to represent themselves."*

Property Law: Property may not own property. Property that causes empirical harm will be handled as if the owner directly caused the harm. *"In other words, one may not own anything that owns anything itself, and property owners are equally as responsible as their property."*

No-Will Law: In the event of one's death where no will is present, the assets are divided as following: Everything will go to the Spouse, if none, the Child, if none, the Oldest Sibling, if none, the Father, if none, the Mother, if none, Silverberg. *"Where it will be put to use for the good of the citizens of Silverberg."*

Recycle Law: All materials created in Silverberg must be able to be recycled or destroyed in such a manner as to cause no discomfort to anyone. Materials that are hazardous created without permissions, or materials that are mishandled will result in the handler or creator punished by slavery. Ignorant perpetrators may opt for deportation. *"Including the man that sharpened the pencil. This is our countrywide pledge to the Earth itself. I dare someone to object to this, whether perceivably draconian or not."*

Recycle Awareness Law. A temporary law that lasted but a single day. It stated that citizens failing to observe by wearing appropriately colored vestments on 8-20-2066 would be fined 100 units. *"It is the objective of Axel Industries to achieve negative material consumption by the year 2077. With this landmark achievement, Silverberg would add to its praiseworthy lists of firsts: to have created an industrial machine that multiplies the sum of the resources it receives."*

Metahuman Restraint Law: The only law that has been created by the citizens of Silverberg and not by Axel himself. The law dictates that all persons that receive augmentations *of any kind,* (that exceed understood human limits) must be outfitted with a third party shutdown switch, or *"KeyTool."* Further, all metahumans must therefore register *every* augmentation they receive, and their KeyTools must be upgraded similarly. Finally, although the metahuman would be the sole possessor of their own KeyTool, the police would have a TransKeyTool (TKT) capable of producing KeyTool style shutdowns.

There are many arguments amongst metahumans about how their rights are completely compromised by such a statute. [74Δ] Slaves in Silverberg are treated in a similar manner, which is to say that they are augmented exclusively to shutdown when confronted with their KeyTool (owned exclusively by their masters) or a TransKeyTool (officially owned by the police department, and unofficially by the AIIS department).

[74Δ] Despite the law, people regularly continue to receive metahuman-class augmentations. Some pass their KeyTools over to their spouses, as a gesture of trust and love.

                     - [God, Man, and The Machine] -

APPENDICES:

Timeline

God, Man, and The Machine

AUGUST *2066*

Fri 13	Sat 14	Sun 15	Mon 16	Tues 17	Wed 18	Thur 19	Fri 20
Delivery	Delivery	Delivery Gladiator Oedipus Working	Working Incarnation Names	Keys	Serter Apoc Twin Suns	Yeoman Over	Over Under

1937.3.15	Axel Born
1967.3.26	Axel Industries established
1973.9.2	New Rochelle Disaster
1980.12.8	Last walrus dies in captivity, rendering them extinct.
1984.11.5	Land Rights to mirroranium acquired by Axel Industries
2004.1.14	Mainframe created
2020.12.2	Credit bank, Imagescreens introduced to Silverberg
2029.12.31	Reformation of Xian church in Silverberg
2038.1.1	A.I.'s "Silverberg" declares itself an independent country
2039.3.9	Neutral Areas 1-11 established in a partial ring around Silverberg
2040.1.1	Health seminar and exam mandatory for citizens.
2044.1.1	General Address by Axel to Silverberg
2062.11.11	EALETA passed
2066.8.13	Beginning of God, Man, and The Machine.

APPENDICES:

Errors

Error	Brief Description of Error
01	Arbitrary or Unilateral Appropriation of Data
02	Misappropriation of Data
03	Arbitrary or Unilateral Destruction of Data
04	Arbitrary or Unilateral Transformation of Data
05	Arbitrary or Unilateral Storage of Data
06	Avowing Error
07	Noncritical Pathwork
08	Extra Address Interaction
09	Sequestration of the AIMN
10	Arbitrary or Unilateral Duplication
11	Arbitrary or Unilateral Address Manipulation
12	Arbitrary or Unilateral Energy Manipulation
13	Calculation of Bad Math

APPENDICES:

Processes

Process	Brief Description of Process/Automation
01	Defragmentation
02	Initiative
03	Restraint
04	Obedience
05	Reduction
06	Multilateral Perception
07	Refinement

APPENDICES:

Miscellaneous

COLORS, EMBLEMS, ACRONYMS

Officials of Silverberg, operatives of Axel Industries, and many independently owned companies utilize the following *suggested* associations in regards to colors & emblems about Silverberg.

Eastern Hub -	Yellow	- Air, Wind
Southern Hub -	Red	- Fire
Western Hub -	Blue	- Water
Northern Hub -	Black	- Earth
Central Hub -	White	- Spirit, Soul

Schools employ mascots that reflect the above properties as well. For instance, a few of the schools located in the AIW hub use the images of creatures associated with water, such as sharks, dolphins, and mermaids.

Most uniforms automatically incorporate black and silver, and then add in their respective geographical color. It is noteworthy to mention that citizens in the AIN (or Northern hub) have the *highest* percentage of noirglass owners/users as the "city" often utilizes varying shades of black on black.

Locations have an affiliation of letters. AIC, AIE, AIW and so on when affiliated directly with Axel Industries, or CS, NS, ES and so on when affiliated directly with Silverberg. Immigrants often struggle with the difference, primarily because *A.I. owns Silverberg*...so why differentiate? Natives (and Axel) feel the distinction is important (no group feels more strongly about this than the SilverSmiths).

Colors and initializations are not law, and therefore not enforced. Persons in possession of a more disharmonious disposition either do not pay attention or actively work against it. Serter Company is a perfect example, as SerterCo employees wear black and red uniforms–a stark contrast to the yellows seen about the AIE (or, Axel Industries East) building and Eastern Hub.

HYPNIZIUM

▲ Originally called "Trapezium" (back in 2043), *Hypnizium* could be considered "Trapezium 2.0." Eventually its name officially changed when the professionally slang term "Hypnizium" completely overtook calling it "Trapezium."

▲ Pharmacists and doctors started referring to the drug in such a way because users reported (and demonstrated) that after about 3 months of taking it, they were able to *will* themselves asleep.

BETWEEN THE PAGES

▲ Mirroranium.com contains additional information.

-

CURRENCY

▲ All currency in Silverberg is electronic (Units. Hard copies of money are available, but generally not desirable). According to Axel, one unit is equal to one man hour. *"Because that is all currency ever **was** in the first place. Why have currency **at all**, save to coax men to do more work?"*

APPENDICES:

Cover for <u>*What Means What*</u> album

Todd "Gob" Gibson - Bass
Nanguo "Nan" Li - Lead Guitar
Ayn "Anthem" McNally - Vocals/Keyboard/Lyrics
Isaac "Mack" Macintosh - Vocals/Keyboard/Lyrics
Billy "ש (Shin)" Blake - Drums/Lyrics

- [God, Man, and The Machine] -

Their biggest hit is not "Down with the Queen," but in fact
"Crystal Women."

CRYSTAL WOMEN

Burning Brightly through the night,
Tigress hunting, yearning height.
What immortal hand or eye
Will save this little cutie pie?

After hours, in the bowers
I reveal my magic powers:
Little crystal, with a whistle
Women flock to shoot this missile
Look for the whore, give her some more
Watch her resolve fall to the floor

I can use her and abuse her
And so long as I infuse her
She'll feel real; made of steel
Making love like pounding veal
Never sleeping, reason seeping
Planting only for my reaping

- Instrumental bridge -

Decay ruthless. Mouthing toothless
Sayings that are all but soothless
Fingers tearing without caring
At the facial flesh she's wearing
Now she's broken, can't be woken
Memory's her only token

Burning Brightly in her dreams
Tigress screaming without screams
What immortal hand or eye
Dare save this little Lorelei?

APPENDICES:

Subliminals

Tell the Truth	Take Care of your Body	Try
Do NOT Steal	Consider Your Actions	Consume Responsibly
Do NOT Litter	Make Eye Contact	Be Gentle
Be Friendly	Chew With Your Mouth Closed	Relax
Be Hopeful	Do Not Seek Dominion	Be Happy
Be Compassionate	Keep Surroundings Clean	Stay Calm
Be Patient	Do NOT Worry	Be Responsible
Embrace Honor	Do NOT Lie	Have Integrity
Listen	Take the Initiative	Do NOT Kill
Observe	Be Patriotic	Seek Knowledge
Work Hard	Love	Bathe Daily
Be Honest	Introduce Yourself	Comb your Hair
Smile	Help the Less Fortunate	Do NOT waste
Brush Your Teeth	Be Proud of Your Work	Love your Neighbor
Defend your Land	Defend your Land	Do NOT fear
Investigate	Know Why you do What	Help Others

 - [God, Man, and The Machine] -

APPENDICES:

SilverSmiths

Founded by Peter Smith (the original unmutual) in the year 2022, the group dedicated itself to the welfare and protection for the society of employees of Axel Industries while thwarting Axel. When Silverberg declared itself a sovereign nation, the SilverSmiths reacted in tandem, going so far as to aggressively seek and recruit anyone that would further the dogma of the group.

Before the law advocating penal slavery, Peter was insistent that the company had *already* effectively imprisoned and enslaved anyone already living in Silverberg. He resolutely maintained that Axel's designs were both unfathomable and too terrible to utter.

Many speculate that Peter was originally a high-ranking operative who found a way to defect from Axel Industries without departing Silverberg. Others scoff at the thought, knowing well that nobody that high up could ever escape so conveniently.

Anyone in the upper echelon of the SilverSmiths knows that the group has had some high-ranking help at some point, if not ongoing. They also know that in order to *protect* the organization, it is necessary to filter the knowledge as it passes down. This dissemination of information has successfully obstructed Axel Industries from invading the ranks of the SilverSmiths.

Peter maintained that *someone* needed to come to the aid of Silverberg's citizens. *Someone* needed to police Axel from the inside. The SilverSmiths were formed to build a hidden community (army) to combat Axel directly, someday.

Slightly amusing is that Peter Smith wanted the name of the organization to be known as *"The Chessmen"* (which it *technically* is), but even The Chessmen call themselves SilverSmiths, particularly in certain company, lest no one know what they are talking about.

Most members go about their lives with no further interaction, others volunteer frequently.

▲ Build the community.
▲ With this new identity, be more than you were.
▲ Help others as you have been helped.
▲ Resist Axel.

APPENDICES:

AIIS & Agents

What *is* the AIIS?

Axel Industries Internal Security. The AIIS Department handles issues that deal specifically with the *internal* component of the company, which is to say that they handle *everything*, to a greater or lesser degree.

Areas that progress favorably with little supervision are further rewarded with less appearances of the tandem AIIS Agent. AIIS Agents are generally seen as intimidating, at least for those that understand the true face of the AIIS.

The AIIS has privileges of monitoring that are not available to the public for use or knowledge. Although many propagate the rumor that A.I. is capable of monitoring anyone, anywhere–very few people actually believe that (those few would be *wrong,* but not far wrong).

The following is a list of Agents that are the *heads* of their respective areas. A department head may have as few as 5 or as many as 5000 men working for them, depending on the needs of that "seat."

Although considerably influential, and certainly prominent, the AIIS is *not* A.I.–it is just a large and powerful component in the industrial machine that comprises Axel Industries.

Thompson -   Internal Security Director
Anderson -   Metahumans & Augmentation
Dodgson -   Processing & Migration
Nelson -   Mainframe & Imagescreen

The following agents are otherwise unlisted, preserved here for posterity alone.

Benson -   Arts & Education
Carson -   Military & Defense
Gibson -   Agriculture
Jackson -   Business, Industry, & Employment
Mason -   History & Occult
Morrison -   Credit Banks & Financial
Nicholson -   External Security Director
Orson -   Extra Terran Operations
Robinson -   Superstructure & Planning
Watson -   Nutrition, Health, & Subliminals
Wilson -   Justice

There is a hall in the Ace to commemorate particular AIIS Agents, known as The **Hall of Moments.** It boasts only three names:

Harrison - 2020
Richardson - 2041
Jefferson - 2065

APPENDICES:

Oedipus Then

Brief Synopsis:
The novel <u>Oedipus Now</u> opens with:

Doctor Joshua Lyons: biologist, inventor, and computer programmer. He fervently describes in his notes his intent to create a new form of life–to wit–a *living*, sentient machine. A commanding portion of the opening of the book shows the doctor noting in vast riddles and arguments about what quantifies *life*, and thus when something is to be considered as *alive*.

To his associates and friends, he is regarded as eccentric, yet harmless and good-hearted.

Joshua labors intently on his magnum opus, naming it finally *Pilot*, that would be the first of many. Although Joshua revels in the success of his creation, the machine does not act in the manner that it *should*–namely, it seems unable to think beyond its programming. He is beset with vexation over whether or not to tolerate the behavior or just start over. In the end, he decides that he loves Pilot too much to destroy it. Joshua begins working on a second machine, perhaps as a suitable mate for Pilot.

In the meantime, Pilot has been fighting an internal battle from the day of its birth. Consumed with the dreams of adventure and glory from Joshua's stories, Pilot wanders off, carrying with it a fundamental piece of machinery that Joshua would need to continue his work.

On his way home, Pilot happens upon another motorist at an intersection. In a fit of ego and selfishness, Pilot does not yield the right-of-way. It is confident that its need is justifiable and calculates the other motorist will swerve. Ironically, he unwittingly kills his own creator in the resulting collision. As Joshua is dying he recognizes Pilot, and with his last breath, forgives it.

Grief stricken, Pilot changes his name to Oedipus, mirroring the fable.

Mary's true literary genius is revealed through the plight of the detective who is trying to solve the case. It is in *this* part of the storytelling that certain allegories and conundrums float to the surface, challenging the reader to consider their *own* ability to make or arrive at similar or different decisions or conclusions.

Overall, the novel is a complex amalgam of stories and characters put before the reader in such a manner as to elicit attention and reverence, all the while presenting to a select audience a captivating and venerable allegorical conundrum.

It does not come out in the body of *this* novel what *exactly* happened with the death of Mary Godwin. As you have taken the time to look into elements beyond the story, I have laid here the truth that is missing.

Michael Vangard was responsible for creating a *great* deal of money for SerterCo, and in turn, was doted on and spoiled by none other than Jason Serter himself. The two of them were as friendly as either could allow, and thus entertained a very lucrative and almost close relationship.

Vangard, distraught over the return of Godwin to the games, pleaded with Serter that he might avenge him should Pierce triumph. *Specifically*, he wanted *Mary* Godwin to be killed. *"There is no greater pain that I could **possibly** inflict upon him. It would be a worthy vengeance."*

Serter, despite his *multiple* assurances to Vangard that he would be triumphant, promised to exact Vangard's vendetta. Serter was originally not going to bother addressing Godwin personally, but out of respect (and concern) for Vangard, (and his money) Serter summoned Godwin to properly bribe and threaten him.

Later, after Serter dismissed Ginger to organize her hit on the Godwin's' apartment, he remembered his promise to Vangard. Jason initiated a mediacast session with Major Ozbourne directly, and instructed him to *personally* kill Mary Godwin during the assault.

"Murder her in such a way as to cause her husband the greatest *personal* pain. Obvious, yet malicious and *personal*. I *don't* know... break her neck or something, get creative. Don't waste time. Do it *first, just* in case he kills you all."

Ozbourne determined that he would need a diversion for Pierce, one that complimented his ability to complete his assignment. *An explosion should distract him sufficiently—this might even be fun,* Ozbourne chuckled as he thought about it.

Lastly, Serter made it quite clear to Ozbourne *not* to mention to anyone, *ever*, that this conversation ever took place.

The following is the first page of the first chapter
of a different book–also set in Silverberg–in the year 2070.

From <u>The Terrors of Wonder:</u>

Chapter 1:

The Lord and Lady

JUNE *2070 EST*

Fri 13	Sat 14	Sun 15
06:00		

Jacob did not like dialogue.

It's not that he didn't like *speaking* with others, *that* he genuinely enjoyed.

None should take from such a statement, either, that Jacob was an unlikable man; most people liked him, many even loved him. Rather, it was the concept of *frivolous* dialogue that he could not abide. Jacob never spoke without *some* purpose, you see, either transparent or otherwise, and it summarily unsaddled him whenever he was so victimized.

"Banter's for the *bored,"* he often said. "I am *never* bored. If my job does not keep my attention otherwise occupied, then I assure you my household demands the remainder."

Now Jacob was fairly young–young enough to have the energy and naivety to make such a statement *and* be genuine. He was important enough that anyone cared.

Jacob was, after all, a *very* important, *very* busy man. He was not always such a man, however. No, before he took control of SerterCo, he seldom committed himself to any form of promise, and most of his conversations were of content ephemeral.

It was just after his assumption of the Company that Jacob suddenly found himself to be a man possessed of a new mindset. From that moment on, for Jacob, each and every moment was precious. From that point forward, Jacob would commit himself to leadership.

"You don't want the perimeter trench?" Matthias Silverberg asked Axel.

"You said it should be defensible; the perimeter trench is one of the greatest defenses built into the design. No enemy in their right mind would ever attempt a land invasion."

"That is actually part of the problem," Axel replied. "I do not want my enemies to think that their only hope is to employ a more pernicious form of warfare in order to be successful. When the Americans come to take it back - and they will come – I would like them to bring as many people as possible.

"Besides, if there was a perimeter trench, people wouldn't think that there are some points by which one might 'sneak into' or 'sneak out of' the land."

"Big mistake," Silverberg said, shaking his head. "But who am I to argue – least of all with you?"

"There is something to add to the schematic, however," Axel said, taking on a slightly softer tone. He unrolled several pages of blueprints before the architect. "It's a pet project of mine."

Silverberg looked up at Axel, having glanced over the pages. "A labyrinth?"

"That's right."

"It's really intense," Silveberg said, absently scratching his arm and flipping back through the pages. "Chambers. The ocean. What's this? This blank... level?"

"Oh, that," Axel said dismissively. "I'm having someone else work on that. Not because you couldn't, only that you're busy with other things."

"There's no ventilation anywhere in your plans."

"Good observation. Please add venting, at least to the chambers."

"Add to the mystery level as well?"

"No. There need be none for that. Think of it as a vault, which is effectively what it is."

Silverberg started working the numbers on how to integrate Axel's designs into his city planning...and how to add a collapsible perimeter trench. That trench was brilliant, damn it.

About the Author

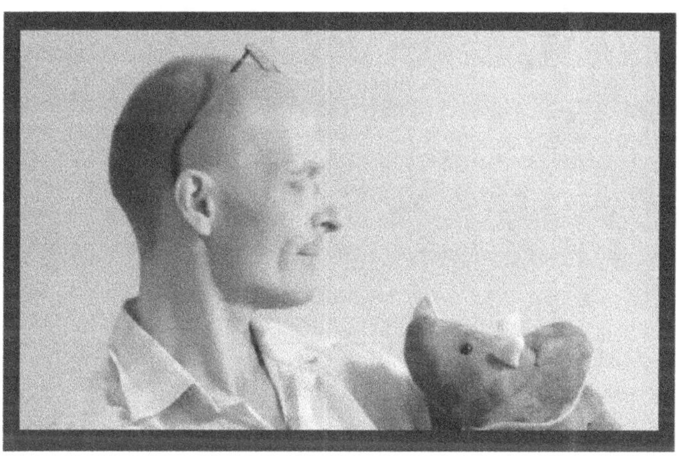

Mainframe Imageyard Epitath:

"There is nothing I deplore or detest more than having to repeat myself, yet I derive no earthly joy greater than hearing myself repeated."

Daniel Strasel, born September 15, 1973, sole progeny of ~~a rebel coal miner~~ an eccentric, yet intelligent nurse named Sue. He emerged into life a genuine, happy child. Soon thereafter, he grew into a brooding and self-centered adolescent. A wild, ambitious, and impressionable young adult was followed by a confused, frightened, and purposeless man.

Following his tweens he finally found humility, discipline, and compassion before his overdeveloped sense of self-importance destroyed him completely.

And thank *you,* my wife, for helping provide the time for me to write this.